The Atlantis Code

Charles Brokaw is a well-known figure in the literary community, with many awards and books to his credit. He's been a university professor, a teacher, a little league coach and a rodeo cowboy. He's a frequent speaker, who has given lectures at such widely divergent places as the CIA, West Point and science-fiction conventions. He's travelled widely, and has more interests than he can possibly keep up with, even if he lives to be a hundred. Among his other many passions, he's an expert on aviation, international politics, advanced weaponry and pulp fiction. He collects both scholarly military non-fiction and comic books. He lives in the Midwest with his family.

The Atlantis Code

CHARLES BROKAW

PENGUIN BOOKS

PENGUIN BOOKS

Published by the Penguin Group
Penguin Books Ltd, 80 Strand, London WC2R ORL, England
Penguin Group (USA) Inc., 375 Hudson Street, New York, New York 10014, USA
Penguin Group (Canada), 90 Eglinton Avenue East, Suite 700, Toronto, Ontario, Canada M4P 2Y3
(a division of Pearson Penguin Canada Inc.)
Penguin Ireland, 25 St Stephen's Green, Dublin 2, Ireland
(a division of Penguin Books Ltd)
Penguin Group (Australia), 250 Camberwell Road, Camberwell, Victoria 3124, Australia
(a division of Pearson Australia Group Pty Ltd)
Penguin Books India Pvt Ltd, 11 Community Centre, Panchsheel Park, New Delhi – 110 017, India
Penguin Group (NZ), 67 Apollo Drive, Rosedale, North Shore 0632, New Zealand
(a division of Pearson New Zealand Ltd)
Penguin Books (South Africa) (Pty) Ltd, 24 Sturdee Avenue,
Rosebank, Johannesburg 2196, South Africa

Penguin Books Ltd, Registered Offices: 80 Strand, London WC2R ORL, England

www.penguin.com

First published 2009
3

Copyright © Trident Media Corporation, 2009
All rights reserved

The moral right of the author has been asserted

Set in 11.75/13.75 pt Monotype Garamond
Typeset by Rowland Phototypesetting Ltd, Bury St Edmunds, Suffolk
Printed in England by Clays Ltd, St Ives plc

ISBN: 978-0-141-04080-6

www.greenpenguin.co.uk

Penguin Books is committed to a sustainable future
for our business, our readers and our planet.
The book in your hands is made from paper
certified by the Forest Stewardship Council.

This book is dedicated to my family,
especially to my wife, who endured
a great deal as I wrote it.
I love you, and I thank you from
the bottom of my heart.

Acknowledgements

Thanks to Robert Gottlieb at Trident Media Group, LLC and all the terrific agents who work there with him. Thanks also to all the librarians who helped me find obscure material on ancient artefacts, the travel agents who verified that transit was possible in the far corners of the globe, and to my friends in law enforcement who took me out to the shooting range and demonstrated the many weapons I describe in this book. I'd also like to thank my editor Bob Gleason and Linda Quintin from Tor, for their terrific input on and help with this book.

Moscow,
Russia
August 21

London, England
August 21 & September 14

Leipzig, Germany
August 28–September 3

Odessa,
Ukraine
August 23

Paris,
France
September 5

Venice, Italy
August 28

Chamber of Chords
Cadiz, Spain
September 14

Alexandria, Egypt
August 16

THOMAS LOURDS'S
JOURNEY IN

The Atlantis Code

Dakar, Senegal
September 6

Lagos, Nigeria
September 11

Ile-Ife, Nigeria
September 11

I

Kom Al-Dikka
Alexandria, Egypt
16 August 2009

Thomas Lourds abandoned the comfort of the stretch limousine with reluctance and an unaccustomed sense of foreboding. He usually enjoyed opportunities to talk about his work, not to mention the chance to solicit funding for archaeological programmes he believed in and consulted for.

But not today.

Under the sweltering heat of the Egyptian sun in full midday bloom, he dropped his scarred leather backpack at his feet and gazed at the huge Roman theatre that Napoleon Bonaparte's legions had discovered while digging to build a new fortification.

Although the Kom Al-Dikka dig site had been explored for the last two hundred years, first by treasure hunters, then by learned men seeking knowledge of ancient times, the Polish-Egyptian mission that had been established there over forty years ago continued to make new and astonishing finds.

Burrowed into the ground, Kom Al-Dikka stood as a semi-circular amphitheatre not far from the train station in Alexandria. Passengers stepping off the platform only had to cross a short distance to peer out into the ancient stage. Cars passed nearby on Nabi Daniel and Hurriya Streets. The ancient and modern worlds lay side-by-side here.

Constructed of thirteen tiers of marble that provided seating for up to 800 spectators, with each seat carefully numbered, the theatre's history reached deep into the past and throughout the ancient world. Its white marble stones had been quarried in Europe and brought to Africa. Asia Minor had provided the green marble. The red granite had been mined in Aswan. Geometric mosaic designs covered the wings. Roman houses and baths stretched out behind it. The whole complex was a symbol of the global reach of the great empire that had built it.

Lourds studied the vast stone structure. When Ptolemy was still a young man and his greatest works were ahead of him, Kom Al-Dikka had been here hosting plays and musicals and – if some of the inscriptions on the marble columns had been translated correctly, which Lourds believed they had – wrestling. He smiled to think that Ptolemy might have sat in those marble seats and worked on his books. Or thought about them, at least. It would have been incongruous, like a Harvard professor of linguistics attending a world wrestling event. Lourds was such a professor and he did not follow wrestling. But he loved to think that Ptolemy had.

Although Lourds had seen the place a number of times, the sight of it never failed to stir within him a desire to know more about the people who had lived here during those years when it was new and filled with crowds. The stories they'd told barely survived these days. So much had been lost when the Royal Library of Alexandria had been destroyed.

For a moment, Lourds imagined what it must have been like to walk through the halls of the great library. Its collections were reputed to include at least half a million scrolls. They had supposedly contained the entire known world's knowledge of the day. Treatises on mathematics, astronomy, ancient maps, animal husbandry and agriculture, all those subjects had been represented. So had the works of great writers – including the lost plays of Aeschylus, Sophocles, Euripides, Aristophanes and Menander, artists of such power that their surviving works were still performed. And more. Men – knowledgeable and clever men – had come from all over to make their contributions to the ancient library and to learn from it.

Yet all of that was gone, shattered and burned.

Depending on the latest round of politically correct scholarship, the destruction was either ordered by the Roman emperor Julius Caesar or Theophilus of Alexandria or Caliph Umar. Or maybe all of them, over the course of time. Whoever had been ultimately responsible, all of those wonderful writings had burned or crumbled or vanished along with the secrets and wisdom held within them. At least for now. Lourds still hoped that some day, somewhere, a treasure trove of those works – or at least copies of them – might still exist. It was possible that someone during those perilous years had cared enough to protect the scrolls by hiding them, or by making copies that they hid once the library was destroyed.

The vast desert surrounding this city still held secrets, and the dry hot sands were wonderful for preserving papyrus scrolls. Such treasures still turned up, often in the hands of rogues, but sometimes under the supervision of archaeologists. Scholars could read only the scrolls that again saw the light of day. Who knew how many more caches were still out there, waiting to be found?

'Professor Lourds.'

He picked up his backpack and turned to see who had spoken his name. He knew what the speaker saw. He was a tall man, slender from years of soccer. A short-cropped black goatee framed his strong chin and softened the hard planes of his face. His wavy black hair was long enough to hang in his eyes and fall over the tips of his ears. Trips to the barber took too much time out of his day, so he only went when he could no longer stand to go unshorn. That time was getting close, he realized, brushing hair out of his eyes. He wore khaki shorts, a grey shirt, Gore-Tex hiking books, an Australian outback hat and sun-glasses. All well broken in and a bit worn around the edges. He looked, he thought, like a working Egyptologist, much different from the tourists and hawkers in the amphitheatre.

'Ms Crane,' Lourds greeted the woman who had called out to him.

Leslie Crane strode toward him. Men's heads turned in appreciation. Lourds didn't blame them.

Leslie Crane was beautiful, golden-haired and green-eyed, dressed in shorts and a sleeveless white linen shirt that emphasized her tanned and trim figure. Lourds thought she was perhaps twenty-four, fifteen years younger than he was.

She took his hand and shook it. 'It's so good to finally meet you in person.' She had a crisp English accent, and in her lush contralto voice the effect was soothing.

'I've been looking forward to this as well. Email and phone calls aren't a replacement for actually spending time with another person.' Although either of those forms of communication were rapid and kept people in touch, Lourds preferred speaking in person or on paper. He was something of an anachronism in that he still took time to write long letters to friends who did the same in return. He believed that letters, especially when someone wanted to get a point and a line of thinking across without interruption, were important. 'Handshakes do have their advantages.'

'Oh,' she said. As if just realizing she still held his hand, she released it. 'Sorry.'

'No problem.'

'Did you find the hotel suitable?'

'Of course. It's wonderful.' The television company had put him in the Montazah Sheraton, a five-star hotel. With the Mediterranean shoreline to the north and King Farouk's summer palace and gardens to the south, staying there was an incredible experience. 'But it's close enough that I could have walked

5

here. Though the limo was lovely. A university professor isn't quite the same as a rock star.'

'Nonsense,' Leslie said. 'Enjoy it. We wanted you to know how much we look forward to working with you on this project. Have you stayed there before?'

'No.' Lourds shook his head. 'I'm just a humble linguistics professor.'

'Don't discount your training or your expertise. We're not.' Leslie hit him with a dazzling kilowatt smile. 'You're not just a linguistics professor. You teach at Harvard and were trained at Oxford. And your background is hardly humble. You're the world's foremost expert on ancient languages.'

'Trust me,' Lourds said, 'no few scholars contest that assertion.'

'Not at *Ancient Worlds, Ancient People*,' Leslie assured him. 'When we complete this series, the world will view you as exactly that.'

Ancient Worlds, Ancient People was the name of the show produced by Janus World View Productions, a United Kingdoms affiliate of the British Broadcasting Corporation. It featured interesting histories and people, presented by lively commentators like Leslie Crane, who interviewed recognized scholars in various fields.

'You smile.' Leslie grinned, and it made her look even younger. 'Do you doubt me, Professor Lourds?'

'Not you,' Lourds replied. 'Perhaps I doubt the largesse of the viewing public. And please call me Thomas. Do you mind if we walk?' He thrust his chin toward a shady area. 'At least to get out of this damnable sun?'

'Sure.' Leslie fell into step beside him.

'You said you had a challenge to put before me this morning,' Lourds reminded her.

'Nervous?'

'Not so much. I like a challenge. But conundrums do leave me somewhat . . . curious.'

'Isn't curiosity a linguistics professor's best tool?' she asked.

'Patience, I think, is the best tool. Though it's one we often struggle for. Records of a nation's or empire's intellectual life – be it history, mathematics, the arts, or sciences – took time for the scribes to write. Unfortunately, it takes even longer for today's scholars to decipher those ancient works, especially when we no longer have access to the languages in which they were written. For more than a thousand years, for example, no one left on the planet could read Egyptian hieroglyphics. It took patience to find the right key, and then more patience to decipher the code of their meaning.'

'How long did it take you to crack *Bedroom Pursuits*?'

Out of the direct glare of the sun and in the shade now, Lourds smiled ruefully and rubbed the back of his neck. The translation of those documents had earned him a lot of attention, as much negative as positive. He still didn't know if the time spent on them was a career milestone or a misstep.

'Actually,' he said, 'those documents weren't called *Bedroom Pursuits*. That was the unfortunate nickname given to them by the members of the mass media who covered the story.'

'My apologies. I didn't mean to offend.'

'You didn't.'

'But those documents were the histories of the author's sexual conquests, correct?'

'Possibly. Perhaps they were only his fantasies. Walter Mitty by way of Hugh Hefner. They were rather vivid.'

'And surprisingly explicit.'

'You've read them?'

'I have.' Leslie's tanned cheeks flamed. 'I have to say that they are quite . . . compelling.'

'Then you also know that some critics called my translation pornography of the poorest sort. An ancient version of *Penthouse*.'

Delight shone in Leslie's green eyes. 'Oh, now you're just being salacious.'

'How so?' Lourds raised his eyebrows innocently.

'A university professor with knowledge of *Penthouse* magazine?'

'Before I was a professor,' Lourds said, 'I was also a college student. In my experience, most male college students have at least a passing acquaintance with it.'

'Even though that translation got you lambasted among the pedagogue crowd, I know several top professors who say it was an important piece of work on a difficult document.'

'It was a challenge.' Lourds warmed to the topic, hardly noticing the passers-by. Voices out in the street offered bargains in Arabic, English, French and local

8

dialects, but he paid them no attention. 'The original document was written in Coptic, which was taken from the Greek alphabet. The man who created it also added in a number of letters, some used only for words that were originally Greek. The document, written by a man who called himself Anthony, doubtless after the saint, though the man was more of a satyr, or at least he imagined himself so, at first looked like gibberish.'

'Other linguistic experts had tried to translate it, but none of it made any sense. You figured out that it was written in code. I didn't know codes existed that far back.'

'The first known codes are attributed to the Romans. Julius Caesar used a simple letter substitution, or shift, to mask messages to his military commanders. His traditional shift traded three spaces.'

'A becomes D.'

'Yes.'

'We used to do those when I was a girl.'

'At the time, the shift was a clever scheme, but even then Caesar's enemies quickly caught on. So it is today. Substitution codes are no longer used by anyone interested in keeping things truly secret. They're too easy to crack. In the English language, the most often used letter is E, and the second most used is T. Once you can ascertain those values in a block of text, the rest of the letters fall into place.'

'But the *Bed*—, that is to say, the piece that you deciphered, was unusual.'

'Against what we've uncovered so far from that time period, yes. Given the content, the writer had every reason to code his words.'

'The thing that made it even more interesting to me as I read your translation was that the Copts were an extremely religious sect. Even by today's standards, that document is a bit shocking. So something like that would have been quite ...' Leslie faltered for words, evidently unsure of how risqué to be.

'Exotic,' Lourds supplied. 'Or inflammatory, depending on your point of view. Of course, today's standards are a lot more confined than they were back in the ancient world – a legacy left over from Saint Augustine, the Victorians and the Puritans, among others. But even by ancient standards, those documents were inflammatory. Possibly even dangerous to the life of the writer. I agree. So he was careful. In addition to the coding, the document was also written in the Sahidic dialect.'

'What's the distinction? Isn't it still a Coptic language?'

'Not exactly. The Sahidic dialect was an offshoot of the original Copt language.'

'Which began as Greek.'

Lourds nodded. He liked the young woman. She was quick and knowledgeable, and she seemed genuinely interested in what he had to say. Some of the doubts he'd felt about agreeing to this meeting started to fade. The university was always looking for ways in which to increase its exposure to the public, but that didn't always turn out favourably for the professors put on the firing line. Most journalists and reporters only listened long enough to hear a sound bite they could use – even taken out of context – to make whatever points they wanted to make. Lourds had seen his share of what could happen when a professor was chewed up by the media. It wasn't pretty. So far, he had held his own, but his work with *Bedroom Pursuits* had come closer to the edge than he'd liked.

'Sahidic was originally called Thebaic, and was used in literary form beginning around 300 AD. Much of the Bible was translated into this language. Coptic became the standard dialect for the Coptic Orthodox Church. Later, in the eleventh century, Hakem b'Amr Allah pretty much abolished the Christian faith, chasing it into hiding.'

'So much turmoil,' Leslie commented.

'Here as well as around the world. Conquerors often try to destroy the language of a civilization they overpower. Look at what happened to Gaelic when the English conquered the Scots. The clans were forbidden from speaking it, from wearing their hereditary dress, even from playing the bagpipes. Killing their language breaks a conquered people's connection with their history.'

'Takes away their knowledge, you mean?'

'More than that,' Lourds said. 'Language is ingrained in people. I believe it gives them a sense of who they are and where they're headed in their lives. It shapes them.'

'By that definition, even rap singers create a language.'

'No. They don't exactly create it. They're lifting it from their people, then turning it into a unique art form much as Shakespeare did the English language.'

'Comparing rap singers to Shakespeare? That would be considered scandalous in some academic circles. Even dangerous.'

Lourds grinned ruefully. 'Maybe. Probably more a flagrant violation of scholarship than a killing matter. But it's true. If a section of people divide from the larger majority, they tend to develop their own language. Just as university professors and reporters – each with a defined field – develop specialized words that provide a shorthand method of commentary within that group. Or a culture may develop an entirely new language to avoid being understood by a larger population they exist within. A major case in point is the Gypsies.'

'I knew they had their own language.'

'Do you know how Gypsies came about?'

'Mother and Father Gypsy?' she guessed.

Lourds laughed. 'At some point, yes. But in the beginning, they were probably low-caste Hindus recruited into a mercenary army to fight against the Islamic conquerors. Or they may have been slaves taken by the Muslim conquerors. Either way, or even if neither of those two answers are right, the Gypsies became their own people and created their own language.'

'Subjugation leads to the creation of a language?'

'It can. Or the destruction of one. Language is one of the most highly evolved tools and skill sets humanity has fashioned. Language can unite or divide people as quickly and easily as skin colour, politics, religious beliefs, or wealth.' Lourds peered at her, surprised at himself for talking so much. And at the fact that the young woman's eyes hadn't glazed over as yet. 'Sorry. Caught me in a lecturing moment. Am I boring you?'

'On the contrary. I find myself more fascinated than ever. And I can't wait to show you our *mysterious* challenge. Have you had lunch?'

'No.'

'Good. Then I'm inviting you to lunch.'

'I'm honoured,' he said. 'And hungry.' And hopeful of getting an interesting meal here, though he didn't say that to his hostess.

Lourds lifted the backpack he carried and heaved it over his shoulder. It contained his notebook computer and several texts that he felt he couldn't travel without. Much of the information in them was duplicated in his computer's hard drive, but he loved the feel and smell of books when he had his choice between virtual and actual text. Some of the texts had travelled with him for twenty years and more.

He walked beside Leslie as they made their way through the foot traffic and vendors, listening to the sing-song voices of hawkers calling out their wares. Alexandria was in full swing, hustling for a living one more day between tourists and thieves.

An uncomfortable sensation of being watched grew in the middle of Lourds' back. Over the years of travelling in foreign countries, including many troubled nations in far parts of the globe, he'd learned to heed such warnings. A time or two, those feelings had saved his life. He paused a moment, looking back, trying to see if anyone in the crowd was showing any undue interest in him. But all he saw was a sea of faces, all of them moving and jostling as they skirted the traffic.

'What is it?' Leslie asked.

Lourds shook his head. He was imagining things. *Serves me right for reading that spy novel on the plane*, he chided himself.

'Nothing,' he said. He fell into step beside Leslie once more as they crossed Hurriya Street. No one seemed to be following them. But the feeling didn't go away.

'Did he see you?'

Standing across the busy expanse of Hurriya Street, Patrizio Gallardo watched the tall university professor striding away. Gallardo let out a tense breath. He still didn't know everything that was going on. His contact, Stefano Murani – Cardinal Murani, these days – was close-mouthed with his secrets. That was how their employers had taught them to be.

Both of them had been recruited by the Society of Quirinus for their respective strengths. Murani had come from an aristocratic family that lived on old money. With that as his stepping stone, he'd gone into the Catholic Church, quickly rising through the ranks to become a cardinal. In his position at Vatican City, Murani had access to secret documents and papers that had never been in the public eye.

Gallardo came to the Society's attention another way. His father, Saverio Gallardo, was part of an organized crime family in Italy that harvested money from the unwary. Patrizio Gallardo tried the organized crime route, but hadn't been very happy with working under his father's thumb, despite his talent for the trade. He liked the work, and – working for the right person – it paid really well. Anybody could shove a gun in someone's face and demand their money but not everybody had the guts to pull the trigger and wipe the blood from their face afterward. Patrizio Gallardo did. And that was what he did for the Society. It was what he was prepared to do today. All the Society had to do was point.

Today they had pointed at university professor Thomas Lourds.

'Did he see you?' Cimino asked again.

Gallardo glanced at their quarry. This time he didn't stare at the man, just took in the whole street scene. Lourds continued on his way, chatting amiably with the woman.

'No,' Gallardo replied into his small headset mostly hidden by his shirt collar. He was almost six feet tall, a blunt fireplug of a man in his early forties. Browned by the desert sun, scarred from battles against people who had tried to take from him and from people he'd taken from, he was a round-faced man with thick black hair, unshaven jaw, and a heavy mono-brow arranged in a scowl over close-set eyes. Anyone who met his direct gaze usually crossed the street to avoid his path.

'We could ambush this man,' Cimino said. 'Killing him would be easy. Then we could take what we came for.'

'If we kill Lourds now,' Gallardo pointed out, 'there's a chance that we won't find the artefact we're looking for. He doesn't have the artefact. We have to wait until the woman leads us to it.'

Stepping out to the curb, Gallardo waved a hand.

Three blocks down the busy thoroughfare, a ten-year-old cargo truck surged away from a side street and motored along Hurriya Street. It pulled in at the curb and Gallardo climbed into the passenger seat. The dirty windshield blunted some of the sun's stare. The air-conditioning wheezed asthmatically and only brought slight relief from the unrelenting heat.

Gallardo mopped his face with a handkerchief and cursed. He looked at the driver. 'How's our guest?'

DiBenedetto shook his head and took a hit off his Turkish cigarette. He was young and hard-edged, maintaining a steady morphine addiction that would one day be the end of him. He was a ruthless killer by choice, even worse than Cimino because the drug robbed him of most of his feelings. He only stayed loyal to Gallardo because Gallardo provided enough of the drug to keep the addict happy.

'He still hasn't talked?' Gallardo asked.

DiBenedetto turned and smiled at Gallardo. His

face was young despite the drug-taking. He was twenty-two, but his ice-blue eyes were ancient and alien. If humanity and compassion had ever dwelt there, they were long gone.

'He screams,' the young killer said. 'He cries. He pleads. Sometimes he even tries to guess at what we want to know. But he doesn't know.' He shrugged. 'It's pathetic. Still, Farok has enjoyed the struggle to get him to talk.'

Gallardo opened the panel that connected the truck's cab to the cargo area.

Their guest lay in the back. His name was James Kale. He was a television producer on the show *Ancient Worlds, Ancient People*. In his late thirties, he'd been a handsome man before Gallardo's butchers had got to him. Now his ginger-coloured hair was matted with his blood, his face torn by brass knuckles, one eye was gouged out. They'd also amputated the fingers of his right hand and castrated him.

The last had been Farok's touch. The Arab was cruel, taking pleasure in the torture he inflicted.

Kale lay curled in a foetal ball, his maimed hand held tightly against his chest. His pants were dark with blood. More blood covered the interior of the cargo space, streaking the floor and the walls, even sprayed onto the ceiling. The producer was balanced precipitously on the ragged edge of living, about to take a last plunge into the abyss.

Farok sat with his back against the side of the van and smoked a cigarette. He was in his fifties, a dark, hard man dressed in a blood-stained burnoose. Grey flecked his beard, but there was blood mixed in there, too. He looked up at Gallardo and smiled.

'He still insists,' the Arab said in his guttural accent, 'that he knows nothing of the artefacts the woman is going to show to the professor.' He dropped a hand to Kale's thigh.

Kale yelped and drew his trembling leg away.

Farok moved, caressed the producer's leg. 'I have to admit, after I claimed his eggs, I began to believe him.'

The bloody sight disgusted Gallardo. He'd seen such things before. In fact, he'd even done them, and would again if he had no one to do them for him. But he didn't care for it. He looked at Farok, then drew a line under his chin with his forefinger.

Smiling, the Arab pulled a straight razor from inside his burnoose. Dropping ash from his cigarette, he leaned forward and smoothed Kale's hair, causing the man to flinch and cry out in fear. Gripping a fistful of hair, Farok yanked his victim's head back and slashed his exposed throat with the knife.

Gallardo turned away and closed the panel. He concentrated on watching the professor and the television woman.

2

'Hi. This is James Kale. If you've reached this message, I'm obviously not answering the phone. Either I'm busy or I've dropped signal. Leave a message and I'll get back to you as soon as I'm able. And, Mum, if this is you, I love you.'

Listening to the familiar message, Leslie Crane frowned. James was reliable. He prided himself on staying available to the people he worked with. He should be answering his phone. Unless he'd let the darned thing run out of juice – again. It wouldn't be the first time he'd done it. Leslie was going to tie the man to his recharger one of these days.

'Is something wrong?' Lourds asked. He sat across from her at the small table in the outdoor café where she'd taken him for lunch.

Traffic passed by slowly accompanied by men on camels and horses. Donkeys pulled carts with rubber bicycle tyres heading for the suqs. The open-air markets drew many of the locals as well as the tourists. The locals bought fresh vegetables while the tourists bought keepsakes and gifts for relatives. Even though she'd been here for a few days, Leslie still marvelled at the way the modern city seemed somehow jammed into a way of life that had existed for thousands of years.

The waiter had cleared away their plates after an array of dishes that included *molokhiyya* soup with rabbit, *torly* casserole made with lamb, grilled pigeon breasts stuffed with seasoned rice, melon slices and grapes, followed by raisin cake soaked in milk and served hot and cups of Turkish coffee.

'I was trying to call my producer,' Leslie explained.

'Is he staying nearby?' Lourds asked. 'We could wander over that way and check on him.'

'There's no need. I'm sure he's fine. James is a big boy, and I'm certainly not his mother. He should be at the set. I'll check in with him when we get there.'

'So what got you into show business?' he asked.

'Do I detect disapproval?'

He grinned. 'Perhaps wariness is a better word choice.'

'You don't like television?'

'I do. But I often find it self-serving.'

Challenged a little, Leslie said, 'I love being on camera. I love seeing myself on television. More than that, my dad and mum like seeing me there, too. So I try to do as much of it as I can.' She grinned. 'Is that self-serving enough for you?'

'Yes. And more honest than I'd expected.'

'What about you?' she asked. 'Why are you willing to be part of this series? Does it play to some dark part of your vanity?'

'Not at all,' Lourds assured her. 'If it hadn't been for the dean and the board of directors prodding me to go, I would have graciously declined. I'm here at the university's insistence and because it offered me a chance to return to Alexandria once more. I love this place.'

Intrigued, Leslie rested her chin on her crossed hands, elbows resting on the table. She stared into his warm grey eyes. 'But if you hadn't agreed, you wouldn't have been able to enjoy this lovely place.'

'And the lovely woman who brought me here.' Lourds' eyes met hers evenly, holding them for a moment.

Warmth spread throughout Leslie that had nothing to do with the afternoon sun. *Oh, you are good, Professor Lourds. I'm going to have to be careful around you.*

DiBenedetto pulled the truck into an alley only a few blocks from the open-air café where Lourds now sat with Leslie Crane. Before they'd come to a full stop, a five-year-old German Mercedes slid into the alley after them. Gallardo caught sight of the car in the side mirror.

He reached under the lightweight jacket he wore and gripped the 9mm pistol in the shoulder holster. 'Pietro,' he called over the headset.

'Yes,' Pietro's gravelly voice responded. 'It's me. Don't shoot.'

Relaxing a little, Gallardo kept his hand on the pistol as the Mercedes slid to a stop behind the truck. He peered through the smoky glass and saw Pietro's impressive bulk seated behind the wheel of the luxury car.

Gallardo slid out of the vehicle. DiBenedetto fell

into step with him. They swung open doors of the sedan and dropped into seats.

Farok climbed out of the truck in a clean burnoose. He'd left the bloody one inside the rear compartment. For a moment, he occupied himself with carefully closing the door behind himself. Even after the back of the truck was sealed, the smell of petrol whipped through the alley. Satisfied with his handiwork, Farok joined them in the car. He stank of petrol as well.

'Everything set?' Gallardo asked.

Farok nodded and passed James Kale's identification, passport and personal effects to him. The corpse had been stripped clean.

'Yes. Everything is set,' Farok said. 'I doused the interior with the petrol and detergent, and I rigged a road flare to the door. When anyone opens the cargo area, the interior of the truck will become an inferno.'

Gallardo nodded. The petrol and detergent mixture was a poor man's substitute for napalm. It would burn hot and concentrated, making immediate identification of the body very difficult – even more difficult than the loss of all his identity papers now in their possession. The truck had been stolen last night in preparation for its use this morning. There was nothing in it that would tie it back to them.

Pietro drove through the other end of the alley and pulled out onto the street, drawing angry honks from the other drivers and startling a camel.

'Cimino,' Gallardo called over the radio.

'I'm here,' Cimino said. 'They're moving again.'

'Are they still on foot?'

'Yes.'

'Drop out of the loop. Get someone else in there.'

'All right.'

Gallardo's stomach tightened. They'd followed the trail of the artefact that Stefano Murani had charged them with finding for eight months. The trail had finally led them from Cairo, where the artefact had only been a whisper, to Alexandria, where Gallardo should have known it probably was anyway.

The problem with illegal artefacts was that they left no trail, or a spotty trail at best. And if some of them hadn't moved much, as this one had not – the shopkeeper who had sold it had reported that it had languished on a shelf in a back room for seventeen years – then the trail was masked by the passage of time as well.

Even before they'd killed the producer, three dead men lay along the bloody trail they'd followed from Cairo. All of them had been dealers in rare – and stolen – antiquities.

'They're headed back to the studio,' Cimino said.

A hollow *boom* sounded from the left, in the direction of the place they'd left the truck. Turning, Gallardo saw a cloud of smoke mushroom into the air above the buildings. Sirens sounded soon after.

'Well, now,' DiBenedetto mused from the back seat, 'that didn't take long, did it? This city is filled with thieving bastards.'

'A few less of them at the moment, perhaps,' Farok chimed in.

They exchanged a high five.

Gallardo ignored the bloodthirstiness of his hire-lings. It was normal for them, and it was why he employed them. He turned his thoughts to the studio room. He and his men had already been there once in preparation. They knew the layout. Going inside today would be easy.

'Put them there,' Leslie directed. 'While we're setting up, has anybody heard from James?'

'No, but he approved the set and the camera layout last night,' one of the young men, the one running the camera, said. 'He was going to check out some new locations today.'

'Thanks, Gary,' Leslie said. 'Tell me if he calls in.' She turned her attention to the arrangement of the objects she wanted Lourds to look at.

Seated at a small desk at the back of the large room, Lourds watched the young woman's prep-arations with mounting interest. She'd obviously gone to the effort of making the presentation of the arte-facts she'd promised to show him elaborate. They were even recording the event.

A slim man of Egyptian ancestry crossed the room pulling a wheeled aluminium pilot's case behind him. With an air for the theatrical which would have fitted him perfectly for life on the stage at Kom Al-Dikka, the man produced a key and slid it into the locks holding the case shut. He snapped open the locks and put the key away.

Lourds was only partially distracted by the sound of emergency vehicles attending to a nearby problem.

One of Leslie's crew had reported that there was a vehicle fire of some kind only a few streets over. Official vehicles were, according to the kid, swarming like flies.

Moving slowly, the man reached into the case and removed six objects, placing them reverently on the desk in front of Lourds. When the man was finished, he bowed to Leslie, who thanked him, then he went to stand nearby.

Lourds looked around the room, unable to keep from smiling. Six young men and women stood with Leslie, waiting to see what he would do. He felt like a kid playing his favourite game.

'What do you find so humorous?' Leslie asked.

'This.' Lourds waved his hand at the six objects. 'Every year at the university, students bring me things to read. Usually replicas, though. Not the real thing.'

'My resources run somewhat deeper than the average university student's.' Leslie's voice held a note of determination. She was evidently not prepared to have her investment of time and research casually tossed off.

'That they do.' And Lourds meant that as a compliment. 'Still, this is rather like a stage magician at a dinner party. He hasn't gone there to entertain, yet once other people find out what he does, they want him to do magic tricks so they can "ooh" and "ahh" over them.'

'Or maybe they want to catch him in a pratfall, landing him flat on his arse,' one of the young men volunteered. His head was shaved and he sported tattoos all over his arms.

'Is that what Ms Crane is hoping for?' Lourds asked him. 'A pratfall?'

The young man shrugged. 'Dunno. I bet her a few pounds you couldn't read 'em all. But I think she hopes you get 'em all right.'

'I don't mind having a few extra pounds, Neil,' Leslie responded. 'I'm confident Professor Lourds is exactly what Harvard claims him to be: proficient in all known ancient languages.'

'Proficient,' Lourds corrected, 'in several.' *Though I can find my way through all*, he amended to himself. It wasn't bragging. He could.

'Sounds like he's laying out his excuses, he does,' Neil said, grinning.

The building was one of the older ones in the city. Air-conditioning here was an afterthought. As a result, the room was comfortable, but not hermetically sealed like the hotel environment Lourds had left. They were in a corner office. One set of windows overlooked the grey-green Mediterranean and the other had a fine view of downtown Alexandria. Lourds was willing to bet he could probably see Kom Al-Dikka from the window.

Leslie had told him the office had been stripped and set up to handle the television show's production needs. A small set, lit and ready to go, occupied one side of the room, which was blocked off from the windows so they could control the light. It was decorated to look like someone's study, with bookcases full of fake books behind the desk where Lourds had been told he'd sit. The desk was larger and better than the one he had in his office at Harvard. Covered with computer equipment that looked capable of launching spacecraft, it looked like it fit the rock-star status the programme aspired to lend him.

The other side of the room, and the majority of the space, was filled with cameras, boom microphones and sound and audio equipment that lined shelves. Bundled wires snaked in all directions and looked as though they were barely being kept under control. The whole room was, Lourds found, somewhat intimidating.

Lourds picked up the first item, a wooden box about six inches long by four inches wide by two inches deep. Colourful hieroglyphics were traced on the top and sides. Lifting the lid, he found a small figurine of a mummy.

'Do you know what this is?' Lourds turned the small box around to display the contents to the group of television personnel.

'A *shabti*,' Leslie said.

'Very good. Do you know what a *shabti* is?'

'A good-luck piece that was left in an Egyptian tomb.'

'Not exactly.' Lourds tapped the figure. 'A *shabti* figurine was supposed to represent the deceased's major domo, someone who would work in the afterlife for him.'

'It's one thing to know what it is,' Neil suggested, 'but it's another to read the writing.'

'It's from chapter six of the *Book of the Dead*.' Lourds studied the inscription, not wanting to assume in case someone had altered the writing that should have been there. But everything was as it was supposed to be. He read the hieroglyphics easily. 'If N is called up to do any work that is done there in the underworld, then the checkmarks (on the work list) are struck for him there as for a man for his (work service) duty be counted yourself at any time that might be done to cultivate the marsh, to irrigate the riverbank fields, to ferry sand west or east. "I am doing it – see, I am here," you are to say.'

Leslie glanced down at her notebook, then handed it over to Neil.

'So he got one right,' Neil said, handing the notebook back. 'For all you know, he memorized that passage.'

Lourds moved on to the next item: a replicated papyrus written in Coptic which looked entirely too familiar. He glanced up at Leslie. 'This is from the coded document I translated.'

'It is,' she agreed. 'Since they didn't have a books on tape version, I thought I'd like to hear an audio presentation.'

Neil looked at her. 'Is this the kinky thing you told me about?'

'Yes.' Her brilliant green eyes never left Lourds'.

A challenge, then? Lourds was amused and interested to see how far she'd let him go. After all, he'd had to present the piece a fair number of times at different committees, including the dean's house for a celebration on the translation's acceptance. The reading, rendered with an orator's skill that had developed naturally from Lourds' years as a teacher, had been a major hit and had set academic tongues to wagging scandalously. She didn't know his world at all if she thought mere words could embarrass or frighten him here.

He read the first section of the document aloud, then translated it. Leslie stopped Lourds before the first session of foreplay got serious. 'All right,' she said, blushing. 'You know the text. Move on to the next one.'

'Are you sure?' Lourds said. 'I'm quite familiar with this.' He purposefully didn't clarify whether he was familiar with the text ... or the technique presented. His words were every bit as much a challenge as hers were.

'I'm sure,' she said. 'I don't want the network bigwigs twitching.'

'Wow, man,' Neil said, grinning from ear to ear. 'That's brill. Didn't know porn could sound so ... so ... bitching.'

Lourds didn't bother to correct the misrepresentation of the piece. It wasn't intended to be porn – not exactly. It was more a diary of the writer's experiences – a reminder of his past. But read aloud now, its use had changed. Once a listener heard words, the words as well as the meaning became subjective, applied to what that individual's view was on life and the moment. For Neil, it probably was porn.

The third piece was Ethiopian, written in Ge'ez, which was *abugida*. As a grapheme form, transcribed in signs, it denoted consonants with inherent trailing vowels. Besides Ethiopia, the form was also used by certain Canadian Native American tribes – the Algonquian, Athabaskan and Inuit – as well as the Brahmic family of languages – south Asia, south-east Asia, Tibet, Mongolia. It had penetrated east as far as Korea. The piece was a length of elephant tusk used by a trader to record his journey into what was then called the Horn of Africa. From what Lourds gathered from the record, it had been intended as a gift to the man's eldest son, a marker and a challenge to go further and dare more than his father had.

Evidently Lourds' translation matched what Leslie had in her notes, because she kept nodding as he read.

The fourth piece seized Lourds' attention completely. It was a ceramic bell, probably once used by a priest or shaman to call a community to prayer or announcement. It was divided into two sections: there was a clapper at the top and a reservoir for holding herbs at the bottom. A ring at the top invited speculation that it had hung from a shepherd's crook or a similarly shaped staff. The piece had the burnished look of an object that had been handled and cared for continuously over many centuries, perhaps even over millennia. The reservoir might even have held oil at one time to provide an ancient lantern for the bearer.

The inscription on the bell truly set it apart from

the other pieces Lourds had sitting before him. In fact, the most fascinating aspect about the bell was the writing that went around it.

He couldn't read it. Not only that, he'd never seen anything like it in his life.

In the alley behind the building where the television people had their rented rooms, Gallardo got out of the car. He stepped quickly to the back of the vehicle, followed by Farok and DiBenedetto.

Pietro released the trunk latch from inside. The lid rose slowly, revealing the duffels stashed within. Unzipping the top duffel, Gallardo took out a Heckler & Koch MP5. He added a specially modified silencer to the weapon as Cimino joined them.

Cimino was a thick, squat man who spent all his time in gyms. His drug of choice was steroids, and he kept himself painfully close to overuse, staying just this side of healthy and sane. His square head was shaved. Aviator sunglasses bisected his face.

'They're inside?' Gallardo asked.

'Yes.' Cimino picked up a machine pistol as well.

'Security?'

'Building only. Not much of that.' Cimino threaded a silencer into place on his weapon with practised ease.

'Sounds good to me.' Farok armed one of the machine pistols, then dropped it into a canvas bag and slung it over his shoulder.

'All right,' Gallardo said, feeling a thrill sizzle through his stomach in anticipation of the action and the success he knew was soon going to be his. He tapped the bag, then entered the building's side entrance.

Feeling as though someone was pulling a fast one on him, Lourds examined the writing more closely, thinking perhaps it had been inscribed recently upon an ancient bell – which would have been foolish under the circumstances because such an act would have destroyed the bell's huge intrinsic value – to fool him. If it was a forgery, it was a masterpiece. The inscription felt smooth to the touch. In places it was even worn to the point that it was almost faded.

Yep. If it was a fake, it was a damned good one.

Operating by instinct, Lourds reached into his backpack, which was beside his chair, and took out a soft graphite pencil and a tablet containing sheets of onion-skin tracing paper. Placing a sheet of paper on the bell, he rubbed the pencil against the surface, creating a negative image of the inscription.

'What are you doing?' Neil asked.

Lourds ignored the question, consumed by the puzzle that was before him. He took a small digital camera from his backpack and took pictures of the bell from all sides. The camera's flash, especially when used on smooth ceramic, didn't always allow the image to pick up shallow markings. That's why he'd done the rubbings.

He was engrossed. He didn't even notice when Leslie approached and stood on the other side of the desk.

'What's going on?' Leslie asked.

'Where did you get this?' Lourds asked, turning the bell in his hands. The clapper *pinged* softly against the side.

'From a shop.'

'What shop?'

'An antiquities shop. His father's shop.' Leslie nodded toward the man standing against the wall. The man looked a little worried.

Lourds pinned the man with his gaze, not wishing to be trifled with. If that's what this was, of course. He was halfway convinced that this wasn't a joke. It felt far too elaborate. The bell felt real.

'Where did this come from?' Lourds asked in Arabic.

'From my father, sir,' the man said politely. 'The young lady requested that we put something old in with the other items. To better test you, she said. My father and I told her we could not read what was written on the bell either, so we didn't know what it said.' He hesitated. 'The young woman said this was all right.'

'Where did your father get this bell?'

The man shook his head. 'I don't know. It's been in his shop for years. He tells me that no one seems to be able to tell him what it is.'

Lourds switched back to English and looked at Leslie. 'I want to talk to his father. See the shop where this bell came from.'

Leslie looked surprised. 'All right. I'm sure we can arrange that. What's wrong?'

'I can't read this.' Lourds looked at the bell again, still not believing what he knew to be true.

'It's okay,' Leslie told him. 'I don't think anyone's really going to believe that you can read all those languages. You knew a lot of others. The people who watch our show will still be impressed. *I'm* impressed.'

Lourds told himself to be patient. Leslie truly didn't understand the problem.

'I'm an authority in the languages spoken here,' he told her. 'Civilization as we know it began not far from here. The languages used here, living and dead, are as familiar to me as my own hand. Given that, this writing should be in one of the Altaic languages. Turkic, Mongolic or Tungusic.'

'I'm afraid I don't know what you're talking about.'

'It's a family of languages,' Lourds explained, 'that encompassed this area. It's where all language here sprang from although the subject is hotly contested by linguists. Some linguists believe the Altaic language resulted from a genetically inherited language, words and ideas – and perhaps even symbols – that are written somewhere in our genetic code.'

'Genes predispose language?' Leslie arched a narrow eyebrow in surprise. 'I've never heard of anything like that.'

'Nor should you. I don't believe it's true. There's another, more simplistic reason why so many languages at the time shared common traits.' Lourds calmed himself. 'All those people, with all their different languages, lived in close proximity. They traded with one another, all of them in pursuit of the same things. They had to have common words in order to do that.'

'Sort of like the computer explosion and the internet,' Leslie said. 'Most of the computer terms are in English since the United States developed much of the technology. Other countries simply used the English words because they had no words in their own language to describe the computer parts and terminology.'

Lourds smiled. 'Exactly. A very good analogy, by the way.'

'Thank you.'

'That theory is called the *Sprachbund*.'

'What is the *Sprachbund*?'

'It's the convergence area for a group of people who ultimately end up partially sharing a language. When the Crusades took place, during the battles between the Christians and the Muslims, language and ideas were traded back and forth as much as arrows and sword blows. Those wars were as much about expanding trade as they were about securing the Holy Land.'

'You're telling me that they ended up speaking each other's language.'

'The people who fought or traded, yes. Bits of it. We still carry the history of that conflict in modern English. Words like assassin, azimuth, cotton, even the words cipher and decipher. They come from the Arabic word *sifi*, which is the number zero. The symbol for zero was central to many codes. But this artefact shares nothing with the native languages of this area – or with any language I've ever heard or seen.' Lourds held up the bell. 'In those early years, craftsmen – especially craftsmen who wrote and kept records – would be part of that *Sprachbund*. That's a logical assumption. But this bell . . . ?' He shook his head. 'It's an anomaly. I don't know where it came from. If it's not a forgery, and it doesn't feel like one, what we're looking at is an artefact from some place other than the Middle East.'

'What other place?'

Lourds sighed. 'That's the problem. I don't know. And I should know that as well.'

'You think we have a real find here, don't you?' Excitement gleamed in Leslie's eyes.

'A find,' Lourds agreed tentatively, 'or an aberration.'

'What do you mean?'

'The inscription on that bell could be . . . humbug, for lack of a better term. Simply nonsense made up to decorate the bell.'

'Wouldn't you know, if that were the case? Wouldn't it be easy to spot?'

Lourds frowned. She had him there. Even an artificial language would require a basis in logic. As such, he should be able to spot that as well.

'Well?' she pressed.

'I should be able to tell. This looks authentic to me.'

Leslie smiled again and leaned toward the bell, regarding it with intensity. 'If that's truly written in a heretofore undiscovered language, then we've made an astonishing find.'

Before Lourds could respond, the door was suddenly ripped from its hinges. Armed men burst into the room, aiming their weapons at the people inside.

'Everybody freeze!' a man yelled in accented English.

Everybody froze.

Lourds thought he recognized an Italian accent in the man's words.

The four armed men pressed into the room. They used their fists and their weapons to drive the whole television crew to the floor. All of Leslie's people cowered there and remained still.

One of the men, the one who had spoken, crossed the room in long strides and grabbed Leslie by the arm.

Lourds stood instinctively, not able to calmly sit by and watch the young woman get hurt. But he wasn't trained for this kind of thing. Sure, he'd spent time in rough parts of the world. But he'd been lucky. The worst violence he'd ever experienced personally was a dust-up in soccer.

The man put the machine pistol's barrel to Leslie's head. 'Sit back down, Professor Lourds, or this pretty young woman dies.'

Lourds sat, but the fact that the man knew his name unnerved him.

'Very good,' the man said. 'Put your hands on your head.'

Lourds complied. His stomach turned sour. Even as wild as it had sometimes been while he'd been in unsettled lands studying languages, he'd never had a gun pointed at him.

'Down,' the man ordered, dragging Leslie to the ground. When she was down, the man looked at the items on the desk. Without hesitation, he took the bell.

And that's when he made his first mistake. He and his men took their eyes off Leslie.

Before Lourds fully realized what was happening, she pushed herself to her feet and flung herself at one of the men. She knocked him over and took his gun, then dived beneath the heavy desk at the back of the set in a single fluid motion.

Her move took the thieves by surprise. Clearly they weren't expecting a mere woman to put up much of a fight. They had underestimated her, but they were clearly professional because it didn't take long for them to catch up.

The sounds of gunfire filled the room as the desk took punishment it was never intended for. Bullets filled the air with wooden splinters.

Leslie fired back. Her shots were much louder than their attackers, and she clearly knew what she was doing. Bullet holes tracked the walls behind the four men, coughing out puffs of plaster dust that looked surreal to Lourds.

Meanwhile, the crew scrambled for cover.

So did the thieves.

No! Lourds thought. *No artefact is worth the deaths of all these people.*

Then he heard the familiar ping of Leslie's satphone.

He could call for help.

In the middle of the chaos, Lourds rolled across the floor and dived behind the desk with Leslie.

'I'll talk. You shoot. Or we'll both die.'

'Good point,' she said.

She handed over the phone, already keyed to an emergency number. More gunfire. And then a scream. Lourds hoped that it was one of the robbers, not one of the crew, who had been hit.

When a burst of startled Arabic came across the line of the phone in his hand, Lourds started talking. Before he'd finished his second sentence, the sound of sirens outside intensified.

Help was on the way.

And the robbers could hear it, too.

They took off, one of them leaving a blood trail.

Leslie took off after them, holding her fire until she could get a clear shot.

Lourds followed, just in time to pull her out of the way as a final volley from the thieves splintered the office door.

On the floor, terrified but still whole, Lourds wrapped his arms around Leslie. He felt the sweet press of female flesh against his body and decided if he had to die in that instant that there were worse ways to go.

He held onto the woman, trapping her body under his.

'What do you think you were doing?' Lourds demanded of Leslie. 'Do you want to get killed?'

'They're getting away!' Leslie tried to pull free from his grasp.

'Yes, and they should. They should get far away. They have automatic weapons, they outnumber us, and the police are coming – most of the force if the sound is any indication. You've already saved our necks. It's enough. Put that gun down and let the professionals take over.'

Leslie relaxed in his arms. For a moment he thought this was the point she was going to remonstrate with him and call him a coward. He'd discovered that good sense was often confused with cowardice in the heat of the moment by people watching from the sidelines.

Two of the young men from the production crew poked their heads up from where they were hiding. When they weren't shot on the spot, Lourds deemed it safe enough to stand. He did so, helping Leslie to her feet.

Walking out to the hall, Lourds stared at the bullet holes that marred the hallway's end as well as the walls, ceiling and floor. The bad guys hadn't been sharpshooters, but they'd certainly sprayed enough bullets into the general vicinity to make a statement.

'Call the police,' Lourds told one of the young Arabic men. 'Tell them that the thieves have gone, and the only ones left here are us. We want them aware of that when they get here or things could get exciting again.'

One of the crew, already pale, turned white and dived for the phone.

Leslie pulled away from Lourds and ran to a window. She looked out over the city.

Lourds joined her, but he saw nothing.

'We lost the bell,' she said, 'before we even knew what it was.'

'That's not entirely true,' Lourds told her. 'I took copies of the inscription with a rubbing as well as taking a full set of photos of the bell with the digital camera. We may have lost the bell itself, but not the secrets it contains. Whatever they are, they aren't totally beyond our grasp.'

But he had to wonder if pursuing the puzzle wasn't going to put them back in front of someone's guns. Somebody had wanted that bell enough to kill him and the entire crew for it. Would they kill to squash research about it as well? That wasn't what being a professor of linguistics was about.

Nor was talking to a hundred revved up Egyptian cops.

But, judging from the sounds of the footsteps in the hall, it looked like he was about to learn all sorts of new things today.

3

Less than a thousand people lived inside the walls of Vatican City, but millions of tourists and faithful visited from all around the world every year. Consequently, the smallest nation in Europe also had the highest per capita crime rate on the planet. Every year, along with the tourists and faithful, the purse snatchers and pickpockets turned out in droves.

Cardinal Stefano Murani was one of the year-round dwellers in the Holy City, and – for the most part – he loved living there. He was treated well, and given immediate respect whether he wore his robe of office or an Armani suit, which was what he often donned when he wasn't in his vestments. He wasn't in them today because he was on personal business and didn't care to be remembered afterward as an agent of the Roman Catholic Church.

At six feet two inches tall, he was a good-looking man. He knew that, and he always took care to make certain that he looked his best. His dark brown hair, cut once a week by his personal stylist who came to his private suite to groom him, lay smooth. A thin line of beard traced his jaw line and flared briefly at his chin to join the razored moustache. Black eyes dominated his face, and those were the things that most people remembered when they met Murani. He'd been told by some that they were cold and pitiless. Others, who were not so experienced in the worst that the world could offer, thought that his eyes were merely direct and unwavering, a sure sign of his faith in God.

His faith in God, like his faith in himself, was perfect. He knew that.

His work was God's work, too.

At the moment, the ten-year-old boy struggling in Murani's grip was convinced that the devil himself had hold of him. Or so the boy had said, before Murani had silenced him. Now terror widened the boy's eyes and drew plaintive mewling sounds from him. He was a thin whisper of a boy, no more than bones and rags.

Murani felt the boy should not have been allowed entrance to Vatican City. He should have been stopped and turned away at once. Anyone could see that he was a thief, a pickpocket only now beginning to learn his trade. But there were those who believed that it only took a visit to Vatican City to for ever alter the lives of men. So even the vermin from the street, like this specimen, were allowed in. Perhaps, those believers in mercy and access said, they would find God here.

Murani didn't count himself among the fools who thought that.

'Do you know who I am?' he demanded.

'No,' the boy said.

'You should learn the name of a man whose pocket you're about to pick,' Murani went on. 'It might inform you of your choice of target. Since I don't know you, your punishment will be swift and light. I'll only break one of your fingers.'

Frantic, the boy tried to kick Murani.

The cardinal dodged to one side so the ragged tennis shoe missed him by inches. He snapped the boy's forefinger like a breadstick.

The boy dropped to the ground and started howling.

'Don't ever let me see you again,' Murani told him. It wasn't a threat. It was fact, and they both knew it. 'If I do, I'll break more than a finger next time. Do you understand me?'

'Yes.'

'Now get up and get out of here.'

Without a word, the boy struggled to his feet and lurched through the crowd, cradling his injured hand.

Murani gazed around at Vatican City, ignoring the stares of the tourists. Those people were nothing, not much more worthy than the young thief he'd released. Gawkers and sheep, they lived in awe and fear of true power. And he was part of that power.

One day, he believed, he would be all of that power.

He walked across St Peter's Piazza, his physical presence dwarfed by the massive bulk of the Sistine Chapel to the left and the Palace of the Governorship

44

behind him. The Excavations Office, the Sacristy and Treasury stood ahead on the right, flanked by the Vatican Post Office and the information booth at the entrance. Michelangelo's *Pietà* stood before him.

Gian Lorenzo Bernini had created the overall effect of the plaza in the 1660s, laying the area out in a trapezoid. The fountain designed by Carlo Maderno became a primary focus as people walked through the area, but the huge Doric colonnades stacked four deep seized everyone's attention immediately. The colonnades created an imperial look, laying out areas for everything, especially the Barberini Gardens. At the very centre of the open area, an Egyptian obelisk stood nearly 135 feet tall. The obelisk had been crafted 1,300 years before the Blessed Birth, had spent time in the Circus of Nero, and then Domenico Fontana had moved it to the square in 1586.

Over the centuries, the square had been added to and changed. The cobblestone pathway had been moved. Lines of travertine broke up the look. Circular stones added in 1817 were scattered on the pavement around the obelisk, creating a towering sundial. Even Benito Mussolini had been impressed with the piazza and had torn down buildings to provide a new entrance to the area, the Via della Conciliazione.

Murani had first come to Vatican City as a small boy with his mother and father. He'd been filled with a wonderment that had never left him. When he'd told his father that he was going to live in the palace some day, his father had only laughed.

As his father's son, Murani could have had his pick

of mansions and villas scattered around the world. His father was a wealthy man several times over. As a boy, Murani had been impressed with his father's millions. People treated his father well and with respect wherever he went, and many of them even feared him. But his father had his own fears as well. Those fears included other men as ruthless as he was and policemen.

Only one man walked through Vatican City fearless, and Murani hoped to one day be that man. He wanted to be pope. The Pope had money. Vatican City yielded over a quarter of a billion dollars annually through its various tithes, collections and commercial enterprises. The money wasn't what Murani wanted, though. He wanted the Pope's power. Even when the position of pope had been filled by men bent by age, illness and infirmity, the respect for the office had been there. They were mighty.

The people – the believers and the world at large – thought that the Pope's word was law. That was without a show of force, without any attempt to demonstrate the power the Pope wielded.

Cardinal Stefano Murani was one of the few that truly knew the amount of power the Pope could raise if he so chose. Unfortunately, the current Pope, Innocent XIV, didn't believe in flexing the power of the office. He was trying to preach about peace despite the constant terrorist attacks and economic devastation that troubled the world.

The old fool.

At an early age, Murani had been drawn to the

Catholic Church. He'd served as an altar boy in the church he'd grown up near in Naples and loved the organized way the priests performed. He wasn't supposed to become a priest. His father had other ideas for Murani. But when he became a young man and had explored his father's business interests and found them lacking, he'd turned to the cloth.

His father had become angry at that announcement, and had even tried to beat such a notion from his son's head. For the first time in all his twenty-five years, Murani discovered that his willpower was stronger than his father's: he could take all the abuse his father handed out and still not waver. But he did find his father's training of some use in his new career. When he was ordained, he continued his studies in the field of computers and excelled. He was fast-tracked to Vatican City and soon made his way to the top of the computer division where he now served. He'd eventually been made a cardinal, one of the men capable of electing a pope. He'd barely missed out on the last papal convocation, but he'd been part of the gathering of cardinals that placed Innocent XIV in power.

During the last three years, just days before his forty-first birthday, he'd been brought into the Society of Quirinus, the clandestine group of the Church's most powerful men who held the most closely guarded secrets within it. Most of those secrets were minor matters – instances of papal mistakes or children born out of wedlock to cardinals and archbishops, or high-ranking priests who paid too much attention to the altar boys. Those were things that could be quietly dealt with, although even that was getting harder to do in this day of instant media attention. Tales of sexual misconduct dogged the Church these days, bringing her down into the gutter and making her appear weak. In 2006, a priest had even been convicted of a particularly abhorrent murder.

The scars to his beloved Church troubled Murani.

For the last three years, he had become convinced that the Popes before him – and he thought of himself as papal, for he knew that he would one day be among them, without a doubt – had squandered their power, constantly backing away from securing what was rightfully theirs. People needed faith. Without faith, they couldn't understand all the confusing things that were a part of simply being alive. The great masses had an animalistic panic about them today. But being truly faithful meant being truly penitent, truly fearful.

Perfect fear was a beautiful thing.

He loved to inflict it.

Murani intended to bring that fear of the papacy back into the world.

As a child, he'd sat on his mother's knee and listened to the old stories of the Church. In those days, the Pope's blessing could make kings more powerful, wars last longer or end abruptly, and trigger conquests and shatter empires. The world had been better organized and operated during those years when the papacy had ruled supreme.

Murani craved that kind of power. His father had turned from him, but his mother was wealthy in her own right, having inherited from her father. What Murani's father would not give him, his mother would.

One day, when he was Pope – and Murani was certain that day would not be long in coming – he would break his father and make him acknowledge the fact that his chosen course – no, his *destiny* – had delivered more power than all his father's ill-gotten gains.

Concentrating on his goal, Murani stepped from Vatican City and spotted Gallardo's dark blue Hummer waiting at the curb. Gallardo reached across the passenger seat and opened the door. Murani stepped onto the running board and slid into the passenger seat.

'Did you have any further trouble in Alexandria?' Murani asked.

Gallardo checked back over his shoulder, found a lull in the traffic and pulled smoothly out into it. He shook his head and frowned. 'No. We got away clean. We left nothing behind that connects to us. The TV personnel will move on to the next big story. They always do. And Lourds is a university professor. A mere flea in the grand scale of things that matter. How much trouble could he possibly be?'

'He's also one of the most erudite men on the face of the planet when it comes to languages.'

'So he knows how to say, "Please don't shoot me!" in several languages.' Gallardo smiled. 'I can't say that

I'm impressed. The woman with him is worth ten professors. She alone prevented us from killing the witnesses. But she is merely a woman. Admittedly, she found something that you want.'

'Where is it?'

'There's a hidden compartment.' Gallardo pointed a beefy finger toward the passenger-side floorboard.

'In the car?' Murani peered hard at the carpet.

'Yes. Just push down. Hard. And twist to the right.'

Murani did and a section of floor popped up almost imperceptibly. If he hadn't been looking for it, with precise instructions to locate it, he didn't think he would have found it.

The cardinal's hands shook a little as he reached inside the hiding space for the box. The trembling in his fingers surprised him. He wasn't given to physical weakness of any sort. Growing up with a hard task-master like his father, he didn't let his emotions show unless he wanted them to.

Gallardo gave him the code to the locked box.

Murani punched in the sequence of numbers and heard the lock whir within. Only days ago, he'd found the bell while searching through websites dedicated to archaeological discussions. He'd been searching for the musical instruments since he'd heard of them from the other members of the Society of Quirinus. No one among them had thought to search the inter-net, believing the instruments to be either myth or destroyed. They were content merely to protect their secret. Most of them were old men without many years left to them. Ambition and desire had been milked away from their ancient bones by the security and the crumbs of recognition given to them by the Church.

Murani had ambition enough for all of them.

He moved his fingers covetously over the bell's surface. The inscription on both sides was worn, feeling smooth beneath his fingertips instead of edged. He supposed that, after 5,000 or more years, its continued survival was a miracle.

An act of God? he thought. If so, it was the God of the Old Testament, not the God of the New Testament. The God who had allowed the bell to come into existence was vengeful and jealous enough to have drowned the world in floods not once but *twice*. The secrets of the bell were many. Murani knew some of its history, but he didn't know all of it – and he certainly did not know enough about its usage.

'Can you read it?' Gallardo asked.

Murani shook his head. He had studied several languages, oral and written, in addition to his work on languages in the computer field. According to legend, only those special few born every generation could read what was written on any of the instruments. 'I can't.'

'Then why do you want it so badly?'

Tenderly, Murani replaced the bell in the case, reseating it carefully once more into the foam cut-out. 'Because this bell is one of five keys that will open the greatest treasure in the history of mankind.' He gazed at the bell. 'With this, we will be closer to knowing God's will than we have ever been.'

The cardinal's cellphone vibrated in his pocket. He answered it smoothly, hiding the excitement that coursed through him.

'Your Eminence,' Murani's secretary, an enterprising young man, said.

'What is it?' Murani asked. 'I gave express orders that I wasn't to be disturbed this afternoon.'

'I understand that, Your Eminence. However, the Pope has requested that everyone from his offices give a written statement of support for a dig site in Cadiz. He wants the statement now.'

'Why?'

'Because the archaeological excavation is drawing fire from some of the media.'

'Surely the Pope can issue a statement on behalf of the Church.'

'The Pope feels that he is so new to his office that statements should also be issued by senior members among his staff. You were one of those named.'

Murani agreed, said he would attend to that upon his return, and closed the phone.

'Problem?' Gallardo asked.

'The Pope's worried about Father Emil Sebastian's efforts in Cadiz.'

'Talk Radio is filled with speculation about why the Vatican would take such an interest in those ruins down in Cadiz.'

At a red traffic light near the Piazza del Popolo, Gallardo reached back between the seats for a copy of *La Repubblica*. He opened the national newspaper for Murani to see. The banner headline proclaimed:

VATICAN SEARCHING
FOR LOST TREASURES
OF ATLANTIS?

Murani scowled.

'The paper is poking fun at the Church's interest,' Gallardo said.

Unfolding the paper, Murani quickly read the accounts of how the concentric rings in the swamps near Cadiz had been located through satellite imagery. The site was located not far from the nature parks near the basin of the River Guadalquivir north of Cadiz.

Cadiz was the oldest city in Spain. In 1100 BC, the city started out as a trading post. The Phoenicians named it Gadir, and most of the goods exported from there were silver and amber. The Carthaginians followed, building the seaport up and increasing the trade still more. The Moors followed them, but Cadiz had come into its own by then and was accepted as the main trading port to carry on business with the New World. Two of Christopher Columbus's voyages had been launched from the city's docks. Later, the city was invaded by Sir Francis Drake. Napoleon Bonaparte was nearly taken there by his enemies.

And now, perhaps, Atlantis had been found there. For millennia, since Plato had first written of the fabled city that had experienced some kind of environmental disruption and sunk into the sea, all mankind had talked of the glories that might be found in the lost civilization. Claims that Atlantis was a city of super scientists, of magicians, even of aliens from another star system, constantly circulated through the conspiracy websites on the internet.

No one knew the truth.

No one except the Society of Quirinus and Cardinal Stefano Murani.

And he didn't plan to share his knowledge.

'Truthfully, I wondered at the Church's interests there,' Gallardo said.

Murani said nothing as he read the story. Happily, it was tissue-thin, mere speculation. There were no concrete facts, only guesswork on the part of the reporter. Father Emil Sebastian, the director of the dig, was quoted as saying the Vatican was interested in recovering any artefacts that might once have belonged to the Church. A sidebar, much more factual, documented Father Sebastian's previous involvement with various archaeological efforts. He was listed as an archivist in Vatican City.

'The Church works in mysterious ways,' Murani said, but he was thinking that the newspaper reporter would have been more interested, even more dogged in his pursuit of the truth if he'd known what Father Sebastian's true field of study was. The title of archaeologist barely scratched the surface of what he did. The man had hidden away far more secrets than he'd ever revealed.

'What are you supposed to do for Father Sebastian?' Gallardo asked.

Murani folded the paper and put it onto the back seat once more. 'Write a letter praising his efforts.'

'His efforts to do what?'

'Restore the Church's past.'

'The Church had a presence in that area?' Gallardo shook his head doubtfully. 'From what I've read and seen on CNN, that section of Spanish swampland has been underwater or close to it for thousands of years.'

'Probably.'

'The Church was there?'

'Possibly. The Church has been all over Europe since its earliest days. We often attend notable new excavations.'

Gallardo drove in silence for a time.

Murani thought about things. He hadn't counted on the dig in Cadiz generating so much attention. That could be a problem. The Society's business should be conducted in absolute secrecy.

'I could go over to Cadiz,' Gallardo suggested. 'Take a look around and let you know what I find out.'

'Not yet. I have something else for you to do.'

'What?'

'I've located another object that I want you to acquire for me.'

'What?'

Murani took a DVD and a sheet of paper from inside his jacket. 'A cymbal.'

'A symbol of what?'

Unfolding the paper, Murani showed Gallardo the clay cymbal, a greyish-green disk against a black background. 'I've got more information regarding the cymbal's location on the DVD.'

Gallardo took the DVD and shoved it into his pocket. 'Can just anyone find it?'

'If they know where to look.'

'So how much competition should I expect?'

'No more than you had in Alexandria.'

'One of my men is still puking up pap after that bullet hit his stomach.'

'Do you care?' Murani asked.

'No.' Gallardo regarded him.

'Then keep looking.' Murani cradled the box containing the bell.

'This is going to be expensive.'

Murani shrugged. 'If you need more money, let me know.'

Gallardo nodded. 'Where's the cymbal?'

'Ryazan, Russia. Have you been there?'

'Yes.'

Murani wasn't surprised. Gallardo was well travelled. 'I've got an address for Dr Yuliya Hapaev. She has the cymbal.'

Gallardo nodded. 'What's she a doctor of?'

'Archaeology.'

'You seem to be focusing on linguists and archaeologists.'

'That's where these items turned up. I have no control over such things.'

'Do Hapaev and Lourds know each other?'

'Yes. As colleagues and as friends.' Murani's background research had revealed that tie. 'Dr Hapaev has often consulted with Professor Lourds.'

'It's a problem, then. That connection could start

people looking,' Gallardo pointed out. 'First Lourds loses an artefact, then Hapaev – assuming I'm successful.'

'I have the utmost faith in you.'

Gallardo grinned. 'I'm flattered. But we still have the problem of the connection. Has Hapaev been in contact with Lourds concerning the bell?'

'No.'

'She has no reason to suspect that anyone might come looking for her?'

Murani shook his head.

'When do I leave?' Gallardo asked.

'The sooner,' the cardinal told him, 'the better.'

4

Montazah Sheraton
Alexandria, Egypt
19 August 2009

The knock on the hotel door jarred Lourds' senses back to the real world and out of the quiet place he habitually went into when he was unravelling a particularly knotty problem. His heart rate immediately accelerated. Glancing through the balcony windows, he saw that full night had descended upon the city. It was late. Especially for someone unannounced.

Although the attack on the television studio had taken place three days ago and Lourds trusted the hotel security, a wave of panic still ran through him. He pushed it back into the dark corner of his mind it came from. Then he straightened up, feeling the familiar ache in his back and shoulders from staying hunched over the desk too long.

With the help of Leslie Crane's studio team, he'd blown up the pictures of the bell. In the hotel room, he'd taped them to the wall over the desk, then taken them down to study and try – in vain, so far – to crack the mysterious language. He didn't doubt that he would eventually get it, but success, it seemed, was going to take time.

Crossing to the door on his bare feet, clad in a T-shirt and walking shorts, Lourds halted before his hand hit the doorknob, then thought better of where he was standing, considering recent events. He stepped into the closet beside the door. His hand curled around the iron mounted on the wall. It wasn't much of a weapon perhaps, but at least with it in his hand he didn't feel as vulnerable.

Ah, Lourds, you're a Neanderthal at heart, aren't you? He knew he wasn't, though. Otherwise nearly getting killed three days ago wouldn't have bothered him so much. He just wasn't civilized enough – or foolish enough – to believe the Alexandrian police had everything in hand, no matter what they said. They still had no clue who had invaded the television studio. Or who had killed poor James Kale. The sight of the man's burned body in the hospital morgue, with the fingers cut off one hand, still gnawed at Lourds' dreams. He'd gone with Leslie and the crew that day to identify the man's remains.

The knock sounded again.

Lourds realized he'd hidden but forgotten to speak. 'Who is it?' He was embarrassed at how his voice cracked, like he was going through puberty all over again.

'Leslie.'

Now that he knew the young woman was outside his door, Lourds wasn't quite as concerned as he'd been about getting a bullet through his head as he checked the peephole. He peered through the fish-eye lens, saw only Leslie standing there, and opened the door.

She was dressed for the heat, clad in sandals, bronze capris, and a lime-green sleeveless crop top that showed a delicate diamond stud in her belly button. The gem winked up at Lourds in a fascinating manner. During the last three days he'd spent with her, he wouldn't have guessed she would wear such a thing.

Something quite primitive and very interested stirred inside him, displacing all thoughts of the dead producer for the moment.

'Did I catch you ironing?' Leslie asked.

Perplexed, Lourds looked at her and wondered what she was talking about. Then he realized he was still holding his weapon du jour, the iron.

'Sorry. I was just feeling a little insecure. I don't normally greet guests with an iron in my hand.' Lourds turned and replaced it on the mount in the closet.

'Personally, I prefer a golf club,' Leslie said.

'Do you golf?'

Leslie smiled. 'Not as well as I'd like, but my dad gave me a pitching wedge for home protection. I asked for a Glock. He gave me a golf club.' She shrugged, clearly shorthand for: *What are you supposed to do?*

'Where did you learn to shoot?'

'Dad gave in to my love of firepower eventually. He taught me to do both – golfing and handling weapons. He spent time in Special Forces, then served as a trainer before he retired. He's a great teacher. Good thing, huh?'

'After the incident the other day, I'd have to agree,' Lourds said. 'Won't you come in?'

Leslie entered and looked around. Lourds was curious. In the three days that he'd been there, she'd never come calling before.

'I'm impressed,' she said.

'At what?'

'The room's clean. I figured since you're a professor *and* a bachelor, things wouldn't be so tidy.'

'Looking for a stereotype? The absent-minded professor?'

'Expecting one, I suppose.'

'I don't exactly fill the bill as curmudgeonly either.' Lourds waved her toward the chairs out on the balcony. The room was well-appointed with a work area and an entertainment area. 'If you don't mind, maybe we could sit outside. The view is incredible, and your company's paying for it.'

Night draped Alexandria, and the city glistened like a jewel box in the darkness. The full moon hung high above, silver among the shadowed clouds scattered across the sable heavens. To the north, moonlight kissed the white curlers running in from the Mediterranean. Far below, the discordant noise of the evening traffic and the joyous cries of tourists who had indulged too much filled the streets.

Lourds pulled out a chair and sat her at the small circular table. 'Egyptian nights are full of exotic mystery. While we're here, you should get out and see as much of the city and the outlying areas as you can. It's incredible. Do you know who C. S. Forester is?'

'A novelist. He wrote the Horatio Hornblower books.'

Flabbergasted, Lourds dropped into the wicker chair across the table from Leslie. Over the past three days he'd grown quite enchanted with her wit, personality, and charm. He could easily see why the television producers had chosen her to be the show's moderator. 'You've read the books?'

Leslie shook her head and looked a trifle embarrassed. 'I watched the movies. I'm not much of a reader. No time.'

'You're a fan of old movies?' At least that was something. 'I thought Gregory Peck was particularly good in that film.'

'I didn't see the classic version, just the remakes with Ioan Gruffudd. I purchased them all on DVD.'

'They can't be as good as the novels.' Lourds waved that idea away as pure folly. 'Anyway, C. S. Forester wrote: "The best way of seeing Alexandria is to wander aimlessly."'

Leslie leaned over the table and tucked her chin onto her interlaced fingers. 'Surely seeing the city would be better if I had a guide.' Her green eyes glittered.

Lourds placed his elbows on the table and leaned towards her. 'If you find yourself in need of a guide here, just ask me.'

Leslie smiled a bit impishly, and said, 'I will.'

'So what brings you here?'

'Curiosity.'

'About?'

'Every night after dinner, you just disappear. I was beginning to think that I'd somehow offended you.' Leslie hesitated. 'Or that maybe you were spending time with a loved one on the phone. Or even sending pictures over the internet.'

'No. On all counts. No offence taken. I have no significant other. I'm not avoiding you. I've been consumed by the puzzle of the bell.'

'When I walked in and saw all the pictures in your room I gathered that. The bell is one of the reasons I decided to drop by. I thought perhaps you needed a diversion.'

'A diversion?'

'When I get stymied on a project, I usually try to get out of my work environment and talk it over with my friends. Sometimes that will lift something from my subconscious mind that's been waiting for the chance to get out.'

'Are you suggesting a walk? Me and you?'

'I am.' Leslie met Lourds' gaze directly.

Lourds looked at the wall covered with photos of the bell. He didn't worry about leaving them here. The bell looked like what it was: a curious antique.

The question was, did he want to leave the puzzle of the bell alone long enough to spend time with an interesting and beautiful woman in one of the most romantic cities on earth?

It seemed he did.

'I can get dressed and meet you downstairs,' he said.

'Nonsense. You look fine.'

Lourds grinned at her. 'Well, I need shoes, at least.' He was ready in less than a minute.

Frustration and excitement chafed at Professor Yuliya Hapaev as she sat at the tiny desk in the basement office she'd borrowed at Ryazan University while she worked on a pet project. The underground room held a chill that she hadn't been able to shake, even with a sweater under her lab coat.

Without any real hope of finding an answer, Yuliya checked her email. Again. She stared at the industrial grey walls, and waited for her mail client to pump out the latest messages.

She checked the time, discovering that it was almost eleven p.m. She groaned. She'd promised herself that she would get back early tonight to the dorm she'd been assigned while she was working. The feeling that she'd forgotten something else nagged at her, though she couldn't imagine what that something was. Her family was in Kazan. She had no meals to prepare, no laundry to do, nothing outside of her work to distract her here.

Working fourteen and fifteen hours a day in her chosen field was almost like being on vacation. Her husband didn't like that so much, but he understood because he felt that way about some of the construction projects he worked on.

Fortune had smiled on her when her grant had been approved to study the recently uncovered arte-facts found in the archaeological dig on the hill between the Oka and Pronya rivers. Although the area had been sealed off in 2005 and further digging banned, a number of things hadn't been properly catalogued from the original excavations.

And a few items had wandered in after the fact despite the ban.

The area between the Oka and Pronya rivers had been a meeting place or melting pot of a myriad of cultures from the Upper Palaeolithic times to the early Middle Ages. A wooden structure that had resembled Great Britain's Stonehenge had been uncovered in 2003 by Ilya Akhmedov, an archaeologist and contemporary of Yuliya's. Scientists believed that the structure had been used for mapping the stars as well.

The thing that had interested Yuliya most – and infuriated her beyond all measure – was the cymbal made of clay that currently lay on one of the tables out in the lab. It was definitely celadon pottery, reminding her of delicate Chinese and Japanese musical instruments. But the cymbal had writing on it that she couldn't decipher. Nor could any of the Russian linguists that Yuliya had access to.

In the end, she'd shot some pictures of the cymbal and sent them to Thomas Lourds, hoping that his expertise in ancient languages would churn out an answer to the puzzle that faced her.

When the cymbal had been discovered at the site, it had been locked away in a protective bone case. Remnants of that bone lay around it now. The case had either been shattered or had simply decomposed with the passage of years – Yuliya wasn't sure which. She'd sent fragments of the bone off for carbon dating, and was waiting for the answer. The artefact was old. Maybe even impossibly old.

Her mail client dinged, letting her know the contents had come through. This time Yuliya had received a response from Lourds' graduate assistant, Tina Metcalf.

Her hands trembled as she moved to open the file.

DEAR YULIYA,
SORRY. THE PROF'S NOT IN. AND YOU KNOW HOW HE IS
ABOUT CHECKING HIS EMAIL.

Yuliya did know how Lourds was about email. She'd never met anyone who detested electronic communications more. She often exchanged long letters with Lourds, snail mail, of course, discussing various finds they'd both taken part in, as well as the ramifications of those studies. Over the years, she'd saved all of those letters, had, in fact, used some of the material in the graduate-level archaeology classes she taught at Kazan State University.

She loved his letters, and she loved Lourds' mind. That was something Yuliya's husband, a mason, was sometimes jealous of. But Yuliya also knew that no woman was ever going to completely claim Lourds' heart. The professor's true love was knowledge, and he would spend his life looking for what had been lost at the Royal Library of Alexandria. No mere woman could compete with a passion like that. Still, a few of the young ones seemed to catch his eye occasionally, and some even caught more than his attention for a time.

If he'd had the inclination, she thought, Lourds could have given Don Juan a run for the money.

Tina's email message went on:

HOWEVER, I'M HAPPY TO SUPPLY YOU WITH THE EMAIL
CONTACT I HAVE FOR HIM IN ALEXANDRIA.

Alexandria, eh? Yuliya laughed. Lourds must have been drawn back into the arms of his true mistress – the search for remnants of the great library. She wondered how that mistress was treating him.

HE'S OVER THERE SHOOTING A PROGRAMME FOR THE
BBC. A DOCUMENTARY ON LANGUAGES OR
SOMETHING. THE DEAN WAS EXCITED ABOUT THE
WHOLE THING, TRIED TO FORCE HIM INTO THE DEAL,
BUT THE BBC DIDN'T GET THE PROF UNTIL THE FILM
COMPANY AGREED TO SHOOT IN ALEXANDRIA. IT WAS
SOMEWHERE ON THEIR LIST OF POSSIBLE LOCATIONS.
YOU KNOW HOW *HE* GETS ABOUT ALEXANDRIA! THE
LIBRARY AND SO FORTH. AFTER A WHILE, ALL YOU CAN
HEAR WHEN HE OPENS HIS MOUTH IS BLAH, BLAH, BLAH.

Yuliya suspected that maybe young Miss Metcalf had also been smitten by the professor, and was somewhat irritated that he hadn't yet noticed she was female or available. Yuliya had seen women nearly swoon whenever Lourds entered the room. Not that he noticed.

I THINK HE'S SUPPOSED TO BE OVER THERE FOR A FEW
WEEKS. I DON'T HAVE A PHONE NUMBER FOR HIM YET,
AND YOU KNOW HE REFUSES TO CARRY A CELLPHONE.
THAT MAN!
IF YOU NEED ANYTHING (OR IF YOU FIND OUT HOW I
CAN REACH HIM!), PLEASE LET ME KNOW.

YOURS,
TINA METCALF

GRADUATE ASSISTANT TO
THOMAS LOURDS, PhD
PROFESSOR OF LINGUISTICS
DEPARTMENT OF LINGUISTICS
BOYLSTON HALL
HARVARD UNIVERSITY
CAMBRIDGE, MA 02138

So. No Thomas. Maybe for weeks.

Irritated, Yuliya abandoned the computer and walked back out into her borrowed lab. The clay cymbal still occupied the centre of one of the tables.

It was almost like it was taunting her.

'Understand me!' it said.

She only wished she could.

The low ceiling of the basement felt oppressive, as though the weight of the building was slowly sinking on top of her.

After a moment, Yuliya got the distinct feeling that someone was watching her.

Strange. No one should be at the university at this time of night. And she wasn't the type to have ridiculous fancies.

Then another thought hit her. Security, even when there was a lot of it, tended to be abysmal here by most standards.

Fear trampled through her body, filling her nervous system with a huge hit of adrenaline. Rape and murder occurred on university campuses with appalling regularity. Acting casually, Yuliya reached out for the small knife she'd used to clean the mysterious and maddening inscription she'd found. Her hand curled around the wooden handle.

'If I'd truly wanted to hurt you, you'd be too late. In fact, you'd probably already be dead.'

Anger exploded inside Yuliya as she recognized the taunting voice. She spun to face her tormentor.

Natashya Safarov leaned against the wall in the mouth of the stairwell.

At least she didn't creep up on me and touch the back of my neck! Yuliya absolutely hated it when her younger sister did that.

'Are you spying on me?' Yuliya demanded.

Natashya shrugged and showed Yuliya a disinterested moue. 'Perhaps.'

At twenty-eight, ten years Yuliya's junior, Natashya

was an Amazon. She stood five feet ten inches tall, six inches taller than her sister. Her dark red hair fell to her shoulders and framed a model's face. Sparkling brown eyes revealed her amusement. She wore slacks and a blouse under a long black duster. She looked as though she was draped in Dior.

It was infuriating.

But she loved her sister anyway.

'Natashya, what are you doing here?' Yuliya put the knife down on the table and walked over to her sister. They hugged, fiercely, because they had always been close, even though they seldom saw each other these days.

'I called Ivan and found out you were here,' Natashya said. Ivan was Yuliya's husband. 'Since I was in the neighbourhood, I thought I'd drop by.'

'I've got some coffee on. And rolls that are almost fresh. Would you care for some?'

Natashya nodded and followed her sister into the office. She took one of the straight-backed chairs at one of the desks. To Yuliya, she looked like royalty sitting there, despite the wretched decor.

After microwaving the coffee and the rolls, Yuliya placed the plate and the cups on the desk and sat.

'This reminds me of what it was like when we were girls,' Natashya said as she took a roll. 'You making breakfast for us before we went to school. Do you remember?'

'I do.' Sadness touched Yuliya's heart. Their mother had been taken from them too young by a respiratory illness. Sometimes, late at night, Yuliya thought she could still hear her mother's agonized wheezing. And she remembered the night that the sound suddenly went away for ever.

Yuliya had been fourteen. Natashya had been four. Although she tried, Natashya could never remember their mother – a big woman who loved to bake – except from photographs and from the stories Yuliya told. Their father had worked in a warehouse.

'As I recall,' Yuliya went on, 'you almost made me late every morning.'

'As I recall, you were always primping for some boy.'

'I primped for Ivan. And it worked for me. We are married and have two beautiful children.'

'They get their looks from their aunt.' Natashya grinned.

'No,' Yuliya declared, going along with the old joke. 'You'll not take that from me. I am their mother. *I* made them beautiful.'

They nibbled on their rolls and sipped coffee in silence for a moment.

'I miss you making breakfast for me,' Natashya said quietly after a bit.

From her sister's words, Yuliya knew that Natashya had been off in some corner of the world that had briefly flamed into a private hell for her. Yuliya knew better than to ask where or how, though. Natashya would never talk about it.

'Well, then,' Yuliya stated matter-of-factly, 'as I see it, you only have two choices.'

'Two?' Natashya arched her eyebrows.

Yuliya nodded. 'You can hire a maid, whom I can train to take care of you.'

'Train her?'

'Of course. It's the only way. But to do it properly, she'll have to spend a few years with me.'

'A few years.'

'If you want her trained to my satisfaction.'

'I see.'

Yuliya almost giggled and spoiled the moment. Natashya was always so in control of herself, always able to keep a straight face. 'Or . . .'

'Good,' Natashya said. 'There's an "or", because I didn't care for the other suggestion.'

'Or,' Yuliya went on unperturbed, 'you can move in with Ivan and me.'

Natashya went quiet and still.

Yuliya knew that she'd dared too much, but she couldn't stop herself. 'The children would love it. They love you, Natashya. You're their favourite aunt.'

'They have good taste,' Natashya said.

'You're also their only aunt.' Yuliya couldn't resist the dig. They were sisters and they'd never allowed each other to posture too much. Ivan had three brothers and no sisters. As yet, none of the brothers were married. She missed her little sister something fierce, and not just because of the lack of female relations currently in her life.

Natashya smiled. 'Thank you. But I would only be intruding.' She took another roll and broke it. 'Tell me what you're doing here, Ivan said you'd found someone's unwashed plate.'

Sadly, Yuliya dropped the subject of her sister sharing her home, knowing that Natashya would speak of it no more. Yuliya leaned back in her chair. 'It's not a dirty plate. It's a cymbal. Several thousand years old from the looks of it. Maybe more. I'm waiting for confirmation.'

Natashya shook her head in mock sadness. 'My big sister, who went to university to learn to prowl through someone's garbage.'

They bickered for a moment as they always did, then Yuliya told the story of the cymbal as she knew it. As always, Natashya was more interested than she thought she'd be.

And in this case, that interest was much deserved.

Alexandria, Egypt
19 August 2009

'You believe there's more than one language on the bell?' Leslie walked arm-in-arm with Lourds down one of the side streets not far from the hotel.

'Yes. At least two,' Lourds agreed.

'But you don't know either one of them?'

'No. At least, not yet.' Lourds looked at her and smiled. 'Does that shake your confidence in me?'

Leslie looked into his clear grey eyes. They were beautiful eyes, warm and honest and . . . sexy. Definitely sexy. Just looking into them made her tingle.

'No,' she answered. 'That doesn't shake my confidence at all.'

'I'll break those languages,' he told her.

'It's what you do.'

'Yes. It is.' Lourds munched on a piece of the baklava they'd bought from an outdoor café serving the late-night crowd.

'Have you heard of the Rosetta Stone?'

'Of course.'

'What do you know about it?'

'It was . . .' Leslie thought about her answer, 'important.'

Lourds chuckled. 'Yes, it was.'

'And it's kept in the British Museum in London.'

'That's true as well.' Lourds took another bite of baklava. 'The important thing about the Rosetta Stone was it was written in two languages, Egyptian and Greek.'

'I thought it was three.'

'Two languages, but there were three scripts used. Hieroglyphic, Demotic Egyptian and Greek. Napoleon's army found that stone. The artefact gave us, eventually, a path to understanding the ancient Egyptian language. We knew what the Greek inscription said. By assuming all the passages said the same thing, scholars eventually worked out the meaning of the hieroglyphs. All they had to do to crack the hieroglyphic code was to match the hieroglyphics to the meanings we had from the other two sections. Finding that stone allowed the decryption and translation of all the writings from ancient Egypt that we'd stared at, for hundreds of years, on tomb and temple walls, without having a clue what they said. Of course, it took over twenty years and a number of brilliant minds to get there, even with the existence of the Stone.'

'Do you think the bell is like the Rosetta Stone?' The ramifications of that cascaded through Leslie. 'A missive from antiquity in two languages waiting to be translated?'

'I don't know,' Lourds replied. 'I don't know, for example, if the two languages say the same thing. That was one of the reasons the Rosetta Stone was so important. It repeated. And I can't read either language. That's another reason the Rosetta Stone was such a breakthrough – we could translate the Greek. But I've got no frame of reference. All I know is that two languages are written on it that I can't understand. And I don't like it. I'm not accustomed to drawing a blank with ancient languages.'

'It would be so brill if the bell were some kind of Rosetta Stone.'

'The Rosetta Stone only had *one* language on it that we didn't understand. And it was a single message repeated three times. I don't believe that's the case here.'

'You believe there are two different messages?'

'I don't know yet. But the length of the passages and the structural differences in the text indicate to me that might be the case. All of which means that it's going to take longer to work out than I like. I'll apologize in advance for my distraction. This is a puzzle that calls to me.'

'Not a problem. I totally understand.' Leslie finished her baklava. 'You aren't alone, you know.

When I put pictures of the bell on the internet on some appropriate academic boards and sent it to all the scholars I knew, no one could tell me what language was on it. Or languages, I suppose.'

Lourds stopped walking and looked at her. 'You put pictures of the bell on the internet?'

'Yes.'

'Did anyone respond to your internet postings?' Lourds asked.

'A few people did.'

Excited, Lourds gripped Leslie's elbow and turned her. He glanced around, got his bearings – only then did Leslie realize that he'd been following C. S. Forester's advice of wandering aimlessly through the city – and headed back to the hotel.

'Where are we going?' Leslie asked.

'Back to the hotel,' Lourds answered. 'I think we may have just discovered how the thieves targeted us.'

Ryazan City, Ryazan
Russia
19 August 2009

Gallardo waited in the Russian-made GAZ-2705 cargo van outside Ryazan State Medical University where Professor Yuliya Hapaev was working. Magnetic signs on the van's sides advertised a local cleaning company that had contracts with the university.

Shifting in the seat, Gallardo forced himself to

remain detached and not take the long wait personally. He'd expected the woman to step out of the building before now and return to the dorm where she was staying.

So where was she? Even a workaholic wouldn't work this late.

'Someone's coming out,' Farok called over the radio.

Gallardo picked up the night-vision binoculars from the glove compartment.

'It's her,' Farok said.

Training the binoculars on the lone figure that walked out of the building, Gallardo studied her. The night-vision capability washed out the woman's colour, turning everything into soft greens. He couldn't tell if she was a brunette or not, but the size and shape looked right.

Gallardo knew that Farok and DiBenedetto's team would close in and prepare to take her. 'Is she carrying anything?'

'No,' Farok answered.

Gallardo thought about that. 'The object must still be inside the building.'

'Yes.'

Gallardo opened the van door and got out. The light didn't come on because he'd removed it as a precaution. He caught a brief glimpse of the woman, striding purposefully back to the parking lot, then she was gone.

'Take her,' Gallardo instructed. 'I'll get the prize.'

After Farok responded that they would take her

alive if possible, Gallardo transferred his pistol from its shoulder holster to the right pocket of his coat. Then he trotted towards the building, staying in the shadows as much as he could.

Natashya Safarov knew the men were following her. She'd been followed before, so she knew what to look for and what to listen for. Her heart rate increased slightly as her body readied itself for fight or flight. She kept her breathing slow and even. In the cold anyone watching her could tell if it changed because the grey puffs of her breath would give her away.

Her mind flew, taking in her options and laying out her odds. Everywhere she went was a potential battlefield. She'd been trained to take advantage of whatever was there. She always saw terrain, not scenery. It might not help her here, though. On the university grounds at this time of night, there wasn't much in the way of useful cover.

She wondered who the men might be, wondered if they were part of that bad business that had taken place in Beslan: a faction of militant Ossetians, rioting again for the return of their ancestral lands, had taken hostages. Natashya had gone in and retrieved them. There had been considerable bloodshed. She didn't doubt that some of their number would want revenge. Nor that she would be a likely target.

And if it isn't the Ossetians, Natashya reflected, *it could be many others*. She'd left a long line of enemies behind her. The job demanded it. Anger seeped into her because these men had brought violence so close to her family.

She focused, listening to the rhythm of her pursuers, picking out the sound of their feet from all the other noises that trickled through the quiet night. She had them now, all tracked on her personal defence systems, each one indelibly marked.

Sliding her hands into the pockets of her coat, she fisted the two Yarygin PYa/MP-443 Grach pistols she carried there. Both pistols held seventeen-round magazines. She had extra magazines tucked into an inside pocket. She hoped she wouldn't need them.

The men were patient though, closing gradually from three sides.

Without warning, Natashya turned and sprinted up the steps of a nearby building. Shadows filled the breezeway and she felt fairly confident that she would become invisible to her pursuers almost at once. They were determined not to lose her. The sound of their footsteps, hesitating for just a moment, came hard after her.

Natashya ran, light on her feet and silent in her crêpe-soled shoes. At the end of the breezeway, she leaped from the steps to her left and took cover against the building's side behind a line of bushes. Taking out both pistols, flipping off the safeties with her thumbs, she waited.

Two men ran through, stopped and peered out at the open expanse before them. *It's too bad that there isn't another nearby building*, Natashya thought, *otherwise they would be confused longer.*

Both men drew weapons, obviously sensing that they were in danger. Their presence decided Natashya's course of action. There were more of them. That number gave them the advantage. But she could make the odds stack more in her favour, right here, right now.

She levelled her pistols.

One of the men turned towards her. His gun was raised, his arms bent to keep it close to his body as he held it in a shooter's triangle before him. He looked at her just over the open sights.

Natashya squeezed the trigger of the pistol in her right hand just as he saw her. The 9 mm round blasted through the space between the man's widening eyes. She fired again, shifting to the other pistol, and put two rounds through the second man's neck. From the way he tumbled, she suspected that one of the rounds had severed his spinal cord. Moving quickly, she walked over to the two dead men. The flat, harsh cracks of her pistol shots echoed in the breezeway behind her.

Kneeling, replacing her left-hand pistol in her duster pocket just for the moment, Natashya frisked the men. They had no ID. That wasn't unusual. On an assassination assignment, the handler usually took all of a hitter's identification so he – or she – couldn't be traced back to the people who initiated the hit. The band on one of the dead men's wrists caught Natashya's attention as she heard voices over the radio headsets. They'd been alerted now. Who-ever her attackers were, they knew she was armed.

She studied the wristband, recognizing it as a tactic used by Special Forces around the world. She flipped open the protective cover, expecting to see her own face.

But the face in the picture wasn't hers. It was Yuliya's.

Rising, Natashya plucked her other pistol from her duster, turned, and ran back toward the building where she'd left her sister.

5

Alexandria, Egypt
19 August 2009

Leaning closer to the computer screen, Lourds
studied the pictures of the mysterious bell. The
images Leslie Crane had posted to various archaeological and history sites had been professionally done.
But they didn't show the entire surface area of the
bell. They'd been taken from either side, leaving out
a lot of the inscription. Thankfully, he had those.

Leslie stood beside him and Lourds was more
conscious of the heat of her body than he wanted
to be. He didn't like distractions while he was
working.

The text that accompanied the images of the bell
was simple and direct, merely asking if anyone had
any knowledge of the history of the thing. A few
responses had accumulated over the two weeks the
images had been on the internet sites, but nothing of
them seemed out of the ordinary.

'Did you ever receive any email regarding the bell?'
Lourds inquired.

'Nothing that revealed its history,' Leslie answered.
'There were a few questions about it.'

'What kind of questions?' Lourds leaned back.

'Where we got it? What we were going to do with it? That kind of thing.'

'Did you reply?'

'No. I was looking for information, not wishing to give it away.' Leslie was silent for a moment. 'Do you truly think the men who burst in on us came because of these postings?'

'I think that had to be the case. How else would they have known where the bell would be?'

'I used a blind drop. It was supposed to be secure.'

Lourds nodded. 'According to my assistant, the problem with internet security is that as soon as someone writes a supposedly "secure" program to protect traffic, someone else is busy finding ways around it.'

'I know. I did a piece on encryption before I was hired by the present programme.' Her voice broke a little. 'I just can't believe this has happened. I emailed scholars. I posted on university sites. Why would an obscure artefact like the bell draw the attention of killers?'

Noting the young woman's troubled expression in the depths of the computer screen, Lourds turned to her. 'What happened that day wasn't your fault, Leslie.'

She crossed her arms over her stomach. 'If I hadn't posted the images of the bell on the internet, none of this would have happened. James wouldn't have –' She took a ragged breath. 'No one would have been hurt.'

'What you did,' Lourds insisted, 'was to unwittingly

step into a particularly nasty situation.' He took one of her hands in his for a brief squeeze. 'What you've managed to uncover –'

'Inadvertently,' Leslie put in.

Nodding, Lourds said, 'Inadvertently though it may be, you've still managed to find an incredible thing.'

'The trouble is we've lost it.'

Lourds returned his attention to the bell images. 'Sometimes you don't have to actually have possession of a thing to learn from it. Sometimes it's enough to simply know that it exists.' He gestured at the screen. 'That's what put whoever stole the bell from us onto our track. They knew it existed. All we have to do is figure out how they knew that.'

'I thought they were just thieves hired by someone who wanted the bell.'

'Exactly. That is just what they were. But judging from the violent way the men acted, and by the look of them, I would say they were skilled mercenaries. Perhaps even hired thieves. After all, they hardly looked like collectors. They looked more like some kind of rent-a-thug convention product – although one of the more expensive options on that menu.'

'But if someone knew about the bell, wouldn't that person have bought it from the shop years ago?'

'Knowing about an object and knowing where that object is are two very different things.' Lourds brought up his email client.

'You're saying that as though it's a good thing?'

'Because it means that there's a trail out there. One

84

that led those men to the bell and to us, and one that we can hope to find ourselves. A trail goes in two directions. We might be able to find whoever was searching for the bell. And we might be able to find out what they know about it.' Lourds waited as the mail server clicked through the mail. He hadn't checked it in days.

Many familiar names popped up onto the screen.

'What are you doing?' Leslie asked.

'I'm going to contact a few people I know. Generate a few enquiries of my own. Perhaps we'll get as fortunate as the men who came looking for the bell.'

The mail continued to cycle.

'Wow,' Leslie said. 'Don't you ever answer your email?'

'Occasionally. People who know me know it's often best to call. You can lose entirely too much time responding to every piece of email that comes your way.' A name caught Lourds' attention.

Yuliya Hapaev. It had popped up more than once.

Lourds knew Yuliya personally. Whenever he travelled to Russia, he tried to make sure he visited her. He clicked on the mail sorter, bringing up all the email from Yuliya.

There were a half-dozen messages. Three of them had attachments.

'Ardent fan?' Leslie asked.

'An archaeologist I know.'

'The name looks Russian.'

'It is.' Lourds clicked on the earliest email. It was dated eleven days ago.

'Do you know her well?'

On the surface, the question sounded innocuous. But Lourds knew what Leslie implied. 'I know Yuliya, her husband, and her children quite well.'

'Oh.'

Lourds read the first message.

DEAR THOMAS,

I HOPE THIS MESSAGE FINDS YOU DOING WELL AND ON THE BRINK OF AN EXCITING DISCOVERY. I'VE FOUND SOMETHING INTERESTING MYSELF. SHOULD YOU GET TIME, I'D APPRECIATE A CONSULTATION. I WOULD HAVE CALLED, BUT I JUST DON'T KNOW IF IT'S WORTH THE BOTHER YET.

SINCERELY,

YULIYA

Three other messages contained similar enquiries, offered more as a backup in case his email client had dropped mail. The university's server had been known to do that.

The fourth message contained the first of the attached images. Lourds clicked to open it, then waited for a moment for it to download. It instantly seized his attention. He tapped the keys, enlarging the image so he could see the writing on the surface.

'It looks like some kind of ancient Frisbee,' Leslie said. 'Or a plate.'

'It's neither,' Lourds said. 'It's a cymbal.'

'A symbol? Of what?'

'A musical instrument.' Excited, Lourds used the

mouse and keyboard to bring up one of the digital images he'd shot of the bell.

'What are you doing?' Leslie leaned closer, peering over his shoulder. Her hair lightly brushed his cheek.

'Did you notice the writing on the cymbal?' Lourds knew his voice was tight with excitement. He could feel it and hear it.

Leslie hesitated. 'You think it looks like that on the bell?'

'It *does* resemble that on the bell.'

'I'll have to take your word for it. You're the expert.'

'I am,' Lourds agreed. He stared at the inscription on the cymbal. Like the writings on the bell, he couldn't decipher it.

He got up from the desk and retreated to his backpack sitting on a chair by the bed. Rummaging through it, he took out his cellphone and a small address book. He looked up Yuliya Hapaev's number. He had two for her. One for home and one – a satellite phone – for work.

Lourds guessed that with the recent find Yuliya would be at work even though it was late. He called that number.

Looking back at the computer screen, Lourds studied the two images. There was no doubt about the similarity of the two inscriptions. Whatever language they were written in, they shared a history.

The phone rang again and again.

Yuliya stretched, listening to her vertebrae snap and crack. Many people thought the hardest part of an archaeologist's job was the actual dig. But unearthing artefacts from a site was pleasant compared to staying seated at a desk poring over those things for hours at a time.

You need a break so you can look at this with fresh eyes. Yuliya knew it was true. She'd stayed with the research as long as she could, but she was well and truly stuck. She couldn't remember ever being this stymied.

She decided to make a call home, then retire for the night. Lifting the cymbal from the lab table, she started back across the room to lock it away in the vault.

That was when she saw the man standing at the doorway.

Yuliya stopped and stared at him, frightened immediately because of his size and the roughness in his face.

'Do you speak English?' the man asked in Russian.

'Who are you?' Yuliya demanded. 'How did you get down here?'

The man smiled, but the expression didn't look disarming. Instead, he had the cold smile of a predatory shark. 'I speak a little Russian, but not enough to talk about what we need to discuss.' The man came closer.

Yuliya took a step back.

'You are Professor Hapaev, right?' the man asked. 'You were making internet enquiries about that?' He nodded at the cymbal in her hands.

'Get out before I call security.' Yuliya tried to make her voice firm.

The man ignored her. He reached for the cymbal.

Yuliya stepped back, remaining out of reach. She didn't have much room to manoeuvre.

As if by magic, a pistol appeared in the man's hand.

Gunshots, muffled by the walls, sounded outside. Yuliya knew what the flat cracks were. She'd been around weapons before. Natashya had tried to teach her to shoot, but Yuliya had proven miserable at the skill. She'd finally protested that even if she learned how she didn't intend to have a gun in the house with her children.

More gunshots sounded.

The man spoke in Italian but the weapon in his hand never wavered.

Yuliya knew enough to identify the language, but not enough to understand it. At first she thought he was talking to her, then she saw that he was speaking into a pencil-thin microphone along his cheek.

'Who is the woman who left this building?' the man demanded.

Natashya! Cold fear ran through Yuliya's veins and her heartbeat sped up.

'Who is she?' The man stepped forward and grabbed Yuliya by the arm.

The cymbal almost slipped from her hands. She caught it at the last minute.

Gunshots cracked again.

'Who is she?' The man pointed his weapon at Yuliya's left eye.

'My sister,' Yuliya croaked. She felt horrible revealing that, but she desperately wanted to see her children again. She didn't want them to grow up without her. 'Natashya Hapaev. She's a police inspector.' She pulled her courage together. 'Doubtless she has already notified the police.'

The man cursed, then snatched the cymbal from Yuliya's grasp.

Yuliya thought that she might live, that her words and Natashya's gun might have scared him off. Even when the bright light from the muzzle-flash blinded her and her head rocketed back against the wall behind her, she thought she was going to get through the encounter alive.

Then emptiness sucked her away as blackness clouded her vision.

Heart thudding like a sledgehammer in her chest, Natashya Safarov ran through the darkness. The men were after Yuliya. That thought crescendoed inside her head.

Bullets chased through the night, striking the ground and trees around her as she sped back toward the building where she'd left Yuliya. She recharged her weapons on the run, then tucked the left one back in the duster so she could reach her sat-phone.

She punched up the emergency police number.

'Ryazan Police Department,' a laconic male voice announced.

'This is Inspector Safarov of the Moscow Department,' Natashya said quickly. The flat cracks of gunshots punctuated her words. She added her identification number. 'I'm under attack at Ryazan University.'

'By whom, Inspector?'

'I don't know.' A bullet tore bark from a tree only inches from her head. 'Get someone here. *Now!*'

'Yes, Inspector.'

Natashya folded the phone. She felt heartened that the dispatch officer hadn't tried to verify her identity. Of course, Moscow was only three hours away by rail and there weren't many female inspectors even in the Moscow division.

Shadows danced out across the space between the buildings behind her. Natashya lifted her pistols and fired at them.

A man cried out in pain as one of the shadows stumbled and fell. The other stepped back into hiding.

Abandoning her position, Natashya ran, looping back behind the building next to the one where she'd left Yuliya.

Inside the lab, Gallardo peered down at the dead woman. The bullet had ruined her face. He compared what was left of it to the image inside the plastic pocket on his sleeve. He had no doubt that the woman was the professor he'd been sent to terminate if necessary.

Kneeling down, he called out to one of the men who'd followed him inside the room. He held the cymbal out. The man gingerly took it and packed it into the protective case they'd brought to transport the artefact. Gallardo quickly went through the dead woman's pockets and dropped everything into a large plastic bag. When he had the lot, he sealed the bag. He doubted there would be anything worthwhile in the clutter, but there was a zip drive that looked promising.

Standing, Gallardo waved to the room. 'Burn it,' he ordered.

Two of the men ran through the lab and poured flammable liquids onto the floor. The burning stink of alcohol filled the still air.

A third man stood near the door with an assault rifle.

Gallardo walked back to the small office in the back, drawn by the blue glare of the computer monitor. Inside the office, he looked at the screen. The email client showed a list of messages. Some were in Cyrillic, but others were in English.

A name caught Gallardo's eye: Thomas Lourds. Gallardo cursed, remembering the uncanny luck the professor had back in Alexandria. Now his name had turned up here.

Gallardo wasn't a man who believed in luck, good

or bad, but he hated the insistence of fate. Lourds' constant turning up in the chase for the artefacts the Society of Quirinus wanted wasn't something he was prepared to tolerate.

He listened to the gunshots, then spoke into the microphone. 'What the hell is going on out there, Farok?'

'It's the woman,' Farok replied. 'The archaeologist.'

'The archaeologist is down here,' Gallardo corrected him. 'She's not going anywhere.'

'Then who is this one?'

'Her sister. She's a police inspector.'

'She's deadly as anything with her pistols,' Farok said. 'She's killed two of our men and injured three others.'

Gallardo couldn't believe it. The mercenaries he'd hired for the assault on the college were good. 'Is she dead?'

'No. In fact, she's headed back toward your position.'

Cursing again, Gallardo said, 'Get the bodies and the wounded loaded up. I've got what we've come for. We need to get out of here.'

Farok hesitated.

Gallardo knew that Farok hated to walk away from a fight. 'If she's a police inspector, then there's every chance she's called in reinforcements. It's time to clean house and get out of here.'

'All right,' Farok said, his reluctance clear in each word.

At the doorway, Gallardo took an emergency flare from his combat harness, armed it, then tossed it onto the floor. The flare sparked only a moment later, then lit the spilled alcohol and chemicals. The wavering blue haze quickly spread across the liquid pooled across the floor.

Natashya saw that the men were pulling out as she reached the back of the medical building. She was torn for just a moment over the thought of pursuing them. But there was no choice. Even if it meant they escaped, she had to find Yuliya.

The back door was locked.

Stepping away from the door, Natashya took deliberate aim at the lock and fired three times. The bullets ripped through the metal in a flash of sparks. She was aware that the muzzle flashes clearly marked her position, so she kept low to the ground.

A warning klaxon roared to life.

She tried the door again, and this time it opened. Yanking it wide, she dashed inside just as a brief flurry of bullets struck the door and the alcove.

Staying low, Natashya sprinted down the hallway, looking for a stairwell that led to the basement level. She told herself to slow down, that the men might still be inside the building. But all she could think of was Yuliya.

When she found the stairwell, she hurled herself down it, crashing against the back wall of the landing. The impact hurt her shoulder, but she forced herself to keep moving. At the bottom of the stairwell, she stepped through a door with her pistols crossed over her wrists. Her breathing rasped in the emptiness of the hallway.

No one moved.

For a moment Natashya stood frozen, not certain which way to go. Then she spotted the grey column of smoke pouring from a room to her left.

Yuliya!

She ran, unable to control the fear that thrummed through her. Shoving her left pistol into her duster pocket, she grabbed the knob and pulled the door open.

Smoke roiled from the room, pressing towards Natashya and clinging to her. The acrid smell of burning chemicals pinched her nose. Holding her duster sleeve over her mouth, she breathed through the fabric and ran into the room, desperately searching for her sister.

Flames danced across the floor, licking at the liquid spilled across the tiles. Fire covered the back wall. Several glass containers along the shelves to the left exploded.

A quick inspection of the office revealed that Yuliya wasn't there. Looking at the blazing inferno continuing to gain strength, Natashya thought that it was possible the men had taken Yuliya prisoner. She hoped so.

Then that hope died as she moved around the room and spotted her sister lying on the floor. The blood that had seeped from her head held back a line of flames.

No!

Natashya ran to her sister. One look at the grievous injury done to her told Natashya that there was no hope for her. Tears, from the burning chemicals as well as the emotional pain, blurred Natashya's vision as she dropped beside her sister's body. Firelight danced across the smooth pool of blood. The heat blackened it at the edges. Natashya put her pistol down on the floor and cradled Yuliya's head. Crying, she thought of all those mornings when there had only been her sister and her after their father had gone to work. If not for Yuliya . . .

The door rasped open behind her.

Whirling, Natashya plucked her pistol from the floor and pointed it at the dark figures that entered the room. The men were dressed in uniforms that identified them as campus security.

'I'm Inspector Safarov of the Moscow Police,' Natashya said loudly.

'Inspector,' one of the men said, 'I'm Pytor Patrushev. I work security here at the college.'

'Keep your hands up.'

The man complied. 'You need to get out of here. I've called the fire department, but these chemicals –'

'Come closer. Let me see your identification. Only use one hand.' A coughing fit tore at Natashya's words.

Patrushev approached her and proffered the clip-on ID attached to his coat lapel.

Blinded by tears from the chemicals, denying the

pain, physical as well as emotional, that raked at her, Natashya could barely see the rectangle. She felt that the man offered no threat and trusted her instincts.

'We've got to get her out of here,' Natashya said.

Together, Natashya and the man carried Yuliya's body from the room before the fire or the smoke could take them.

Firemen carried Yuliya's body to a waiting ambulance. Natashya steeled herself, pulling herself from the abyss of despair. The scene was like too many she'd gone through in Moscow. Shootouts with mafia members, confrontations with drug dealers, and hunts for murderers all span into a surreal confection that bloated her skull.

The Ryazan police had arrived with the fire department. The police, however, stayed back from the area the firemen had roped off. But a few of them were starting to ask questions of the spectators.

Natashya sat with Yuliya. She felt certain the men who had killed her sister were gone.

The fire lit up the first floor, but the powerful streams of water gradually beat it back.

A cellphone rang.

Automatically, Natashya reached for hers, but when she brought it from her hip holster, she saw that it wasn't her phone ringing. She turned to Yuliya and tracked the shrill tone to the pocket of her sister's lab coat. She pulled the sat-phone to her face and shielded the mouthpiece with her body. She spoke in Russian. 'Hello?'

'Yuliya?' The voice was distinguished, speaking Russian with a slight American accent.

'Who is this?' Natashya continued in Russian.

'Thomas Lourds,' the man replied. 'Look, I'm sorry to call at such a late hour, but it's important. I just saw the cymbal you've been working on. It ties in with an artefact I recently came into contact with . . .' The man hesitated.

Natashya forced herself to be calm. The man didn't sound like he would be one of the men who had killed Yuliya and hunted her. There was something familiar about the man's name. She felt certain Yuliya had mentioned him to her.

'What I wanted to tell you,' Lourds went on, 'is that there could be some danger attached to your artefact.'

'Excuse me,' Natashya said. 'What did you say your name is?'

Lourds didn't answer immediately. 'You're not Yuliya,' he said accusingly.

'My name is Natashya Safarov. I'm –'

'Yuliya's sister,' Lourds replied, 'she's often talked of you.'

For a moment the pang of hurt that lanced Natashya's heart stilled her tongue. She struggled to speak.

'I'm a colleague of Yuliya's,' Lourds said. 'May I speak to her?'

'She can't come to the phone.'

'It's important that I speak to her.'

'I will give her a message.'

Lourds didn't say anything for a moment. 'Tell her

that I think her life may be in danger. I'm in Alexandria, Egypt. I was – briefly – in possession of an artefact that might tie in with the cymbal that she's contacted me about. A few days ago, men attacked us and took it. They killed two people during the theft. These are dangerous men.'

'I'll let her know.' Natashya forced herself not to look at Yuliya's body. 'Do you have a number where she can call you back?' She pocketed her pistol and took out a pen, quickly jotting the number down on her notepad while she balanced the sat-phone on her shoulder.

'Ask her to call me at her earliest convenience. And let her know that I apologize about being remiss in not responding to her emails.'

Natashya promised that she would, then hung up. She made a note to check Yuliya's email as well.

Looking through the crowd, Natashya spotted a young police officer in uniform. She called him over and showed him her identification, asked the name of the inspector in charge and where she could find him, then ordered the officer to watch over Yuliya's body.

'You're sure you wounded some of the men, Inspector?' Captain Yuri Golev asked politely. He was a blunt, squared-off man in his late fifties. His hair was silver, but his moustache and eyebrows remained black. He put a cigarette to his lips and took a deep pull. The flashing lights of the fire trucks and police cars carved deep hollows under his sad eyes.

99

'I killed at least two of those men,' Natashya said.

Golev gestured with his cigarette, waving at the college grounds where uniformed policemen searched the dark landscape with flashlights. 'Then where are their bodies?'

'Obviously they took them with them,' Natashya replied.

'Obviously,' Golev echoed, but he didn't sound sincere. 'Why did those men come here looking for your sister?'

'I don't know.'

Golev looked at her. 'Or perhaps they were looking for you.'

'No one knew I was going to be here. Yuliya had been here for days.'

'Did anyone wish your sister ill will?' Golev asked.

'Not that I'm aware of.'

Golev smoked in silence for a moment while staring at the medical building. The fire department had finally put the chemical fires out. 'Your sister was an archaeologist?'

'Yes.'

'Sometimes those people find interesting things.'

The statement was deliberately leading. Natashya knew what Golev was thinking, and she knew he was aware that she did.

'She was working on a state assignment,' Natashya said. 'She wasn't working with anything valuable.'

'Something this highly organized, especially if they took their dead with them – an unusual occurrence in the sort of bottom-feeding criminal I generally come in contact with – wouldn't be initiated on a whim.'

Natashya agreed but didn't say anything.

'She gave no indication that she feared for her life?' Golev asked.

'If she had,' Natashya said as evenly as she could, 'I would never have left her.'

'Of course.' Golev sighed and his breath plumed grey in the night. 'This is a very bad business, Inspector.'

Natashya didn't reply.

Golev looked at her then, and his gaze was softer. 'Are you sure you want to be the one who tells her family?'

'Yes.'

'If there's anything you find you need, Inspector, please let me know.'

'I will.' Natashya said goodbye and trudged back to the parking lot where she'd left her car. Thomas Lourds was uppermost in her mind. Even if the man wasn't involved in Yuliya's murder, he might know something that would lead to those who were. Natashya intended to find out everything he knew.

6

'Wake up. It's on the news.'

Lourds woke slowly. A fog enveloped his mind. He knew from the uncomfortable way he was sleeping that he wasn't at home. He slitted his eyes and saw blurry movement in front of him. Before he could sort things out, bright light stabbed into his eyes. He growled a curse and covered his eyes with a forearm.

'Sorry. You have to see the news. They're talking about Yuliya Hapaev. She's dead.'

Dead? That got Lourds' attention and burned away the fog in his mind.

Across the room, Leslie folded herself back onto his bed and pointed the remote control at the television. The volume increased.

Blinking away the pain as his pupils adjusted, Lourds looked at the television screen. The headline, MOSCOW ARCHEOLOGIST SLAIN, screamed in large letters behind the male news anchor.

'– as yet Ryazan police officials say they don't know why Dr Hapaev was murdered,' the anchor said.

The television cut away to a blazing fire in a building. The dateline tagged the scene as: Ryazan State Medical University, Ryazan, Russia

'There's still no explanation for the fire that broke out in one of the lab buildings at Ryazan State Medical University, destroying everything within it,' the anchor said. 'The blaze claimed the life of Professor Yuliya Hapaev.'

A small picture appeared inset in the footage of the fire. Lourds saw that it was a recent photograph of Yuliya working at a dig. She looked happy.

'Professor Hapaev has been involved in a number of notable studies,' the anchor went on. 'She's survived by her husband and two children.'

The camera cut away to one of the constantly developing stories in the Middle East.

'That's all there is?' Lourds asked.

'So far.' Leslie looked at him. 'I'm sorry about your friend.'

'So am I.' Lourds forced himself up from the couch where he'd spent the night after Leslie had fallen asleep on his bed. He retreated to his computer and quickly linked to the internet. 'Was there any mention of the cymbal?'

'No.'

Lourds brought up the news sites in quick order, sorting through them for more information. He even read through the Russian news services, but there was precious little more information than FOX News had just presented.

'Do you think the cymbal had something to do with her death?' Leslie slid from the bed and walked over to join him. She still wore her clothes from yesterday and was barefoot.

'Of course. You don't?' Lourds countered.

'It would be a stretch.'

'Not much of one.' Lourds clicked through the news stories, saving them as documents that he could review later. 'You posted images of the bell and it was only a short time before we had armed men beating the door down, ready to kill us to get it. Yuliya sent out photos of the cymbal and she's dead in a suspicious fire, one that destroyed her lab. It connects.'

'But she sent the pictures to you.'

'Yes. Still, I wasn't her only resource,' Lourds said. 'No archaeologist or researcher exists in a vacuum. Each of us is only as good as the network we can assemble. Yuliya's network was extensive. I'm sure she sent the pictures to other people beside me.'

'But if she didn't post the cymbal publicly –'

'Then logic would dictate that someone close to her, someone she sent the pictures to, would be the guilty party for her murder. Which is why I'm going to track everything I can about that cymbal.' Lourds bent to the task.

Within a few minutes, Lourds had ascertained that Yuliya had posted enquiries about the cymbal on at least five different archaeological boards. All of the pictures were identical to the ones she'd sent him. All of them showed the inscription that was so disturbingly like the inscription on the bell.

Part of him – the part that wasn't consumed with

the mystery of what it all meant – felt the loss of his friend.

Yuliya had been bright and witty. He'd met her and her family on a dozen different trips into Moscow. Twice Yuliya and her husband, Ivan, had put Lourds up in their home while he was there doing research.

'Is there any way to see everybody who viewed these images?' Leslie asked.

'Not everyone,' Lourds said. 'These pages are open to the public.' His worst fears confirmed, he leaned back in the chair and crossed his arms over his chest. 'I'm afraid we're going to have to put the rest of your series on hold for a little while.'

'What do you mean?' Leslie looked troubled.

'I've got to go to Moscow.'

'To visit the family? I understand that, but –'

'Not just to visit the family,' Lourds said. 'To track down more information about the cymbal. Yuliya was a brilliant archaeologist. Even though the lab burned, she never kept all of her research in one spot.'

Leslie was intelligent. She read between the lines immediately. 'You think she might have left information about the cymbal somewhere besides her lab?'

Lourds nodded. There was no reason to lie. Leslie didn't know what he did about Yuliya.

'She would have kept a second set of information about the artefact,' Lourds said. 'She was very careful about things like that. Sometimes it can be hard to protect research. Scholars take every precaution.' He frowned. 'I'm sorry about the show, Leslie.'

'That's no problem,' Leslie assured him. 'We have a tight deadline, but I'm sure we can sweat a couple days out of production.'

'It may be more than a couple days,' Lourds said.

Leslie looked at him.

'Something ties the cymbal and the bell together,' he told her. 'If I can find the trail, I'm going to try to find out who killed Yuliya, as well as James Kale.'

'That could be dangerous.'

'Oh, I don't intend to be foolish about this,' Lourds told her. 'Once I have enough to go to the police with, I fully intend to do that. I'm a linguistics professor. If Yuliya hadn't been a friend, if I wasn't certain that I might be able to do more at this juncture than the police can to track her killers, I wouldn't try.'

Later, after Leslie had gone, Lourds turned his attention to scheduling an immediate flight to Moscow. Unfortunately he didn't meet with any great success. Russia, even these days, wasn't the hottest of destinations, the kind that had flights leaving every thirty minutes.

After dealing with three airlines and not getting much in the way of satisfaction, he turned his attention to getting packed. One way or the other, he was going. He also knew he was going to need to buy clothes because he had hardly packed for the current Moscow temperatures.

As he stowed his gear, he grieved for Yuliya and her family. He didn't know what Ivan and the children were going to do, and he couldn't imagine the pain they were going through. Thinking about their loss sparked Lourds' own determination. He couldn't allow the killers to go free. With renewed deliberation, he turned his attention back to the travel agencies.

Standing in the hotel lobby, Leslie felt uncomfortable, feeling she stood out like the Sunday morning date still in her Saturday night clothes. She wanted a shower and a change of attire, but her reporter's instincts were firing on all cylinders.

So was her paranoia.

While waiting for the connection to be made over her sat-phone, she tried to organize her thoughts. When the switchboard operator answered, Leslie asked to be connected to Philip Wynn-Jones, her supervisor.

'Wynn-Jones,' he answered in that quietly controlled voice he had.

'Philip,' Leslie greeted him, 'it's Leslie Crane.'

Wynn-Jones's smile sounded in his voice. 'Ah, Leslie. So good to hear from you. I was so sorry to hear about Kale. Thanks for your work down there in keeping our crew alive. Your heroics have generated a lot of publicity for the coming programme. Speaking of which, I've been looking at the dailies of your footage. Cracking good job. I think it's going to be absolutely brill. Your Professor Lourds is quite cinematic. The camera seems to love him.'

'Thanks,' Leslie said. 'I think so, too.' She hesitated, unsure of what to say next or how to get there.

'What's on your mind?' Wynn-Jones asked. 'I can

always tell when you're trying to work out an approach. It'll save us both some time if you just spit it out.'

'There's a new wrinkle. The show may be on hold for a few days,' Leslie said.

Wynn-Jones became quiet. He didn't like going over budget or past due dates. 'What's going on?'

Quickly, Leslie outlined the events of the latest tragedy in Russia.

'Are you sure these two artefacts are related?' Wynn-Jones asked when Leslie had finished.

'Lourds thinks so.'

'And he's going to Moscow to follow up on this?' Wynn-Jones asked.

'Yes.'

'Hmmmm.' Papers shuffled at the other end of the connection. 'This affair seems to be getting interesting. We do have some leeway in our schedule, I suppose. You're actually ahead of production. Do you know how long the professor's trip will take?'

'I want to go with him.'

That seemed to have shocked Wynn-Jones for a moment. 'You?'

'Yes. Me.'

'Whatever for?'

Leslie took a deep breath. 'Think about it, Philip. I found a mysterious artefact and armed hooligans showed up to steal it as soon as I brought it to the one man who could decipher it.'

'You're putting an awful lot of stock in this professor of yours.'

'Yes, and you know why. You liked his credentials even before the chance to cover a big story was presented to us.'

'"A big story?" Aren't you being a little premature?'

'Think of it. Two unusual ancient artefacts surface, half a world apart, maybe related somehow. Two murders occur in less than a week, along with armed break-ins and the thefts of those very same artefacts. If it's the same person responsible, or even two groups that were sent by the same person, they've killed professionals connected to the artefacts on two different continents.' Leslie stared at the hotel desk and mentally crossed her fingers. 'It's a HUGE story. So far, nobody but us has connected it. Philip, we've got the inside track on this so far.'

Wynn-Jones sighed heavily. 'We're not a news agency.'

'I realize that.' Leslie scarcely contained the excitement that clawed at her. *He hasn't said no!* 'What we do have here is a chance to seize the spotlight for a moment. If Professor Lourds is able to ferret out the secret of the bell and the cymbal, wouldn't that be a fabulous piece of luck? Plus if we have a criminal conspiracy surrounding these artefacts, it would certainly bring more attention to the series we're doing, wouldn't it?'

'Possibly. But I don't like the sound of criminal conspiracy – especially with you in the middle of it.'

Leslie couldn't hold back. Nervous energy cascaded over inside her. She paced in a small oval, aware that she was drawing attention from hotel guests in the lobby. 'Please don't be obtuse, Philip. You know this could potentially garner a lot of attention.'

'Does the headline, "Esteemed American Linguistics Professor And Desperate British Television Personality Meet Their Doom" do anything for you?' he said.

'I want this, Philip. I have a good feeling about it.'

Wynn-Jones remained silent.

'Furthermore, I think Professor Lourds is holding something back,' Leslie said.

'If he's holding secrets, what makes you think he's going to tell you?'

'I can be very convincing, Philip.'

'Are you sleeping with him?'

'That was cheeky. And for your information, no, I'm not.'

'I've seen your dear professor. I wouldn't blame you. Unfortunately, he doesn't appear to be the type to look my way.' Philip was gay, though not many people at the studio knew that.

'He's definitely not.'

'Pity.'

'One more thing. I would like for the studio to pick up the airfare and travel expenses for the Moscow trip,' Leslie said.

'That's expensive.'

'Yes, but the professor is bankable and the story is big. If we're bankrolling, he won't try to lose me or hold out on me if he finds something out. And I want to take one cameraman.'

'You're going to be the death of me, you know that, don't you?' Philip complained.

'Thank you, Philip, you're a dear.' Leslie headed back to the bank of elevators. Her heart sang in her chest. 'Could you ask Jeremy to arrange the plane and hotel? That would be absolutely brill.'

'I'm sorry, Mr Lourds,' the airfare specialist said. 'I don't have any seats open headed north out of Alexandria until tomorrow.'

Lourds stood at the balcony and stared out over the city. Blazing heat shimmered out on the streets. Frustration chafed at him. He politely thanked the young man he'd been talking to, then hung up.

Someone knocked on the door as he looked up the next number on the web page he'd pulled up on his computer. A wave of trepidation filled him. He looked around and once again found the iron, this time sitting on the bathroom cabinet.

'Who is it?' he asked.

'Leslie.'

He gave a relieved sigh. This was getting to be a habit. Lourds checked the peephole and saw Leslie standing in the hallway. She looked agitated. Just as she was about to knock again, he opened the door.

'Is anything wrong?' he asked.

She smiled. 'Actually, many things are very right. May I come in?'

Lourds stepped back.

Leslie cocked an eyebrow at his iron. 'You've really got to get an upgrade.'

'A bigger iron?'

'I was thinking you might need a cricket bat, actually.' Leslie entered the room. 'Have you had any luck securing passage to Russia?'

'Not yet.'

'I've just finished talking with my supervisor. He's agreed to pick up the tab for your trip to Moscow.'

'You'll forgive my impudence, but I've been too long in university surroundings to think that "free" things or "help" come without price tags.'

'The price tag on this one is simple,' Leslie responded. 'I think you'd enjoy the company.'

Lourds liked that she didn't bother to deny the charge. 'You want to accompany me to Moscow. Why?'

Leslie folded her arms across her breasts. 'I suspect that you're not telling me everything about your friend.'

'I'm not,' Lourds admitted.

'You mentioned that she often duplicated her research.'

'Not "often". Always. Yuliya was fastidious about it.'

'So you're going after that research.'

'Yes. And I'm hoping that she has better digital images of the cymbal than the ones she put on the websites. The more material I have to work from, the better my chances of translating the language.'

'If I don't get in your way, do you mind if I go?' Leslie asked.

'No. I've got nothing to hide.'

'You weren't exactly forthcoming with information earlier.'

Lourds smiled. 'I told you enough to get you interested enough to call your boss.'

Pouting, Leslie said, 'I do believe I've been . . . how is it you Americans put it . . . "played"?'

'Perhaps a little,' Lourds admitted.

'What would you have done if I hadn't made the call to my supervisor? Or been able to convince him to make this trip happen?'

'Gone anyway,' Lourds replied. 'By any means possible. But I had to assume that your studio's ability to arrange for immediate travel visas, not to mention plane tickets, is vastly superior to mine. I've been banging my head against a wall talking to travel agents today.'

Leslie frowned. 'You think you're very clever.'

Lourds put his iron away. 'I do try.'

British Airways Flight BA0880
In-Flight From Heathrow
21 August 2009

Hours later, and once more back in Europe, Lourds sat in the quiet darkness that filled the large passenger jet's interior. He'd had a few hours' layover at Heathrow before he'd had to climb aboard this jet after his flight landed from Egypt. Lourds had used his downtime to read the information he'd downloaded from the internet. He had a small satellite link for his notebook computer, a top-of-the-line gadget that he'd been persuaded to invest in. It had come in handy several times.

'You should get some rest,' Leslie said. She was in the seat beside him.

'I thought you were asleep.'

'I was. Did you have any luck with your search?'

'No.' Lourds sipped the water. 'I've looked in any number of places, hoping for more information about the bell and the cymbal, but it doesn't appear to exist.'

'Is that unusual?'

'You're dealing with thousands of years of existence. A great number of things have gone missing during that time.'

'Surely not important things'

'How about the classical Egyptian language? That vanished for over a thousand years. It was a fluke that we could recreate it.' Lourds smiled at her, loving her naivety. 'And would you consider a nuclear weapon important?'

'I don't understand.'

'The United States has lost at least seven of them since World War Two. That's only counting what's been confirmed. There may have been more. Not to mention all those nuclear weapons that *disappeared* when the Soviet Union collapsed.'

'Those were secret things,' Leslie said. 'No one was supposed to know about them.'

'Perhaps the bell and cymbal were secret things, too.'

Leslie stared at him with more interest. 'Is that what you think?'

'I've contacted several friends in museums and private collections as well as insurance companies. When that bell went missing, I figured that our unfortunate adversaries might have stolen other related artefacts. That I turned up absolutely nothing except the cymbal indicates to me there were very few things like them made.'

'You think the bell and the cymbal were unique?'

'I'm not yet ready to make that assumption, but yes.'

'You know, the bell and the cymbal were so far apart . . . and relatively unknown. Neither item was in the care of a collector or an institution. But when they turned up, it appears that someone very ruthless was searching for them. I'm betting my reputation that you will figure out why.'

'There's something here,' Lourds said. 'Otherwise nobody would be killing for these pieces.'

Domodedovo International Airport
Moscow, Russia
21 August 2009

After gathering their carry-on luggage, which was all they'd brought with them from Alexandria, Lourds and Leslie walked through the tunnel to the security checkpoints inside the terminal.

Lourds glanced at his watch and discovered that

the local time was barely after five a.m. He was tired because he hadn't rested well on the flight. Normally he could sleep like the proverbial baby on aeroplanes, but his mind had remained too busy this time. Leslie, on the other hand, had slept quite well.

They stood in line with the other passengers. Lourds gazed at a knot of uniformed East Line Group security guards.

One guard in his fifties fixed Lourds with dead grey eyes. He glanced at a photograph in his hand. 'Mr Lourds?'

'That's *Professor* Lourds, actually,' Lourds said. He didn't try to deny his identity. If the security men had his picture he felt certain they knew he was on the passenger manifest.

'You'll come with me, please.'

'What's this about?'

'No questions,' the man said. 'Come with me.'

When Lourds didn't move fast enough to suit him, the man closed an iron grip on the professor's arm and pulled him from the line.

'What's going on?' Leslie asked. She tried to follow.

A young male security guard intercepted her and held her back. 'No,' the guard said.

'You can't do this,' Leslie protested.

'It is done,' the young man said. 'Please stay in line. Otherwise we will have you detained or deported.'

Leslie stared after Lourds.

'Perhaps you might contact the embassy,' Lourds said, trying to sound calm, as if this sort of thing happened to him every day. It didn't, though, and he was surprised to discover that he was actually quite frightened. It was one thing to be a guest inside a foreign country. It was quite another to be treated as an enemy of the state.

7

Lourds tried to keep calm as he sat in the detention room, even though the windowless, featureless walls felt like they were closing in on him. The grey paint was a dismal addition; it felt to Lourds as though it sucked all the life and colour from the room and everything in it, including him. A scarred wooden table and three chairs occupied the centre of the space. Lourds' chair sat on one side of the table by itself. The walls seemed to exude memories of harsh interrogations held here. Perhaps the new Russia didn't indulge in strong-arm tactics with the same abandon that the old Soviet Union had, and the Tsar's special police before that, but Lourds knew his captors wanted him to remember that ruthless past.

They'd taken his computer, his baggage, and his cellphone.

He knew they were watching him. Since the blank grey walls held no mirror or one-way glass, he assumed they spied on him through hidden cameras embedded in the walls or ceiling. Every time he'd stood up to stretch his legs, a guard stepped into the room to tell him to sit down again.

The woman who walked into the room was beautiful. Rich red hair rippled to her shoulders. Her warm brown eyes regarded him. She wore a grey business suit that complemented her hair and fair complexion.

Without thinking, Lourds got to his feet. His parents had taught him manners so well, that even now, the lessons held.

The woman stopped him immediately, though. 'Sit,' she ordered in English. Her hand slid to her hip.

Lourds sat. The move she'd made, he decided, meant she had a weapon.

'I meant no offence,' Lourds said. 'When a beautiful woman enters a room, I was trained to stand. Out of respect. I suppose I have my mother to thank for nearly getting shot.'

The woman remained standing. Her eyes were flat and hard.

'Look,' Lourds said, 'whatever you think I've done –'

'Quiet,' the woman ordered. 'You are Professor Thomas Lourds?'

'Yes.'

'What are you doing here?'

'I'm an American citizen with a visa to travel in this country.'

'One word from me,' the woman interrupted, 'and your visa is cancelled and you're on the next plane out of here. Do you understand?'

Lourds knew she wasn't bluffing. 'Yes.'

'You're here, at this moment, at my sufferance. Why are you here?'

'To see a friend. Ivan Hapaev.'

'How do you know Ivan Hapaev?'

'Through his wife.'

'Yuliya Hapaev.'

Lourds nodded. 'Yes. Yuliya and I often consulted each other. I teach' –

'Languages,' the woman said. 'Yes, I'm aware of that. However, Yuliya Hapaev is dead.'

'I know. I came here to offer my condolences.'

'Are you a good friend of Ivan's?'

'Actually, I knew his wife better. As I said, Dr Hapaev and I were –'

'Colleagues.'

'Yes.'

'If you were such close friends,' the woman said. 'I should have known you.'

'You couldn't know everyone who saw Dr Hapaev.'

'I knew many of them.' The woman reached inside her jacket and flipped out an identification case. 'My name is Natashya Safarov. Dr Hapaev was my sister.'

Sister! Lourds looked carefully at the woman and could see the family resemblance then. It had been there the whole time.

'I'm investigating my sister's murder, Professor Lourds.' Natashya closed her police identification case. She studied his face. He was a handsome man, and he appeared to honestly care about Yuliya.

'Why was I detained?' Lourds asked.

'The night of my sister's death, you called her on her cellphone. Why?'

'To warn her. The writing on that cymbal she was researching looked similar to writing on a bell that was recently stolen from me and my television team in a studio shoot in Alexandria. We were nearly killed.'

'Tell me about that,' Natashya prompted.

He told her, leaving nothing out. He added, after he finished the tale, 'I'm sorry about your sister, Inspector Safarov. She was a truly magnificent woman. And she loved you very much. She talked about you a great deal. She said your mother died young and the two of you were very close. I know losing her must be extremely hard.'

Natashya remained silent.

'I don't know who killed Yuliya,' Lourds continued. 'If I did, I would tell you.'

'Do you know why she was killed?'

'My only guess would involve the cymbal.'

'Do you know what it was? Or who might want it?'

Lourds shook his head. 'I'm afraid not. If I did, I'd tell you that, too. I would like to recover the bell they took.'

Reaching into her jacket, Natashya took Lourds' visa and passport from her pocket. She deliberately didn't offer them to him.

'I was there the night my sister was murdered,' Natashya said.

Sadness pulled at the professor's handsome features.

Natashya felt that the emotion was an honest one. 'I'm sorry. That must have been horrible.'

Natashya didn't respond to that. 'The men who killed her and stole the cymbal were professional killers.' She intended her words to frighten him.

Lourds didn't look surprised. 'The men in Alexandria were very good, too.'

'Enjoy your stay in Moscow, Professor Lourds. I hope you find what you're looking for.' Natashya handed him his passport and visa, and a card with her name and a number where she could be reached. 'If you should discover anything that pertains to my sister's murder, I want to know about it.'

Lourds put the papers into his jacket pocket. 'Of course. It would be my pleasure to tell you.'

One thing Natashya decided in that moment was that the American professor lied guilelessly. She appreciated that skill in another.

Tired and frustrated, feeling certain that Yuliya's sister didn't quite believe everything he'd told her, Lourds stepped into the small office outside the detention room. Leslie was waiting for him.

Nearly two hours had passed. She sat on one of the hard chairs beside all their carry-on bags. The protective case containing Lourds' computer sat on top of the heap.

Getting to her feet, Leslie inspected Lourds. Worry showed in her eyes. 'You're all right?' she asked.

'I am,' Lourds answered. 'You've been here all this time?'

'Yes. I called the American Embassy. They sent a man over, but Inspector Safarov sent word that he wouldn't be needed. She said she was going to release you once she questioned you, so he left.'

'She did release me.'

'Why did she detain you?'

'It's complicated. Perhaps we could talk some-where else,' Lourds suggested. He didn't want to talk about anything inside the terminal. The Russian federal security service, the Federalnaya Sluzhba Bezopasnosti, better known as the FSB, loved their little electronic surveillance toys. He picked up his luggage, neatly adding Leslie's to the stack. His case had wheels that made it easy to pull.

He was ready to be outside and moving. After all the hours in the plane, then in the detention room, he was feeling slightly claustrophobic.

Leslie led the way to the door and he followed.

Standing outside the security office, Natashya watched the professor and the young woman moving along with the current of human bodies heading for the car rental agencies. Confusion roiled within her. Emotions twisted inside her. She hated letting Lourds go before she had the whole truth from him. He had a plan. He'd protected it during the interrogation, had spoken all around it. Perhaps someone less skilled wouldn't have noticed it, but to Natashya the void had been immediately detectable.

'Are you just going to let him go, Inspector?' a calm male voice asked.

Glancing over her shoulder, Natashya saw that Anton Karaganov had stepped in beside her. The younger man was her partner. She was his field-training officer.

Karaganov was quiet and intense, a good Russian. He drank, but not too much, and he was respectful of his girlfriend. Natashya liked him for both those things. Such traits weren't always found in Russian policemen.

'I let him go,' Natashya said, 'but I don't want him to go far unwatched. Let's keep an eye on him.'

'Airport security has released the professor.'

Outside the terminal, Gallardo sat in a ten-year-old Lada four-door sedan. Sun had bleached the vehicle's black exterior, leaving it looking like most of the other similar cars. He held the sat-phone to his ear.

'Where is he?' Gallardo asked.

'He and the woman are picking up a rental car.' The man on the other end of the phone connection had been keeping watch over the detention centre. He'd also been the one who reported that the security guards had taken Lourds into custody.

'Stay with him,' Gallardo instructed. 'I don't want to lose him.' He ended the phone call and laid the handset on his thigh.

Three other men sat in the Lada with Gallardo. DiBenedetto sat behind the wheel. Two of the men they'd picked up for the Russian operations sat in the back. All of them were armed. Heavily armed, in fact.

Gallardo wanted to be out of Moscow. Although

the news didn't seem to indicate the Moscow FSB had any leads to the persons who had killed Yuliya Hapaev, he felt like a sitting duck here. The FSB had many intelligent police officers these days. Not all of them could be bought off.

A few minutes later, Gallardo watched as Lourds and the young woman emerged from the terminal and headed for the rental car park. They got into a newish model Lada and pulled out into the road.

'All right,' Gallardo said to DiBenedetto. 'Let's see where they go.'

Almost effortlessly, DiBenedetto slid into the traffic, cutting off a Russian taxi cab. The driver blared his horn in protest. In character, DiBenedetto returned the horn salute and kept driving.

Gallardo called the three other cars he was using to cover the professor's arrival at the airport to relay his position and get them in motion. Keeping a close tail on a target was always easier with multiple vehicles. DiBenedetto was familiar with Moscow's streets. So were the other drivers. Gallardo felt certain that they wouldn't lose Lourds.

They followed Lourds in stages, switching off the following car often so the professor wouldn't become suspicious. Gallardo didn't think there was much chance of that. Despite all his travelling, Lourds had to be new to this cloak-and-dagger kind of thing. The professor never gave any indication that he knew he was being followed. It became apparent soon enough that Lourds had a definite destination in mind.

Gallardo placed another call, this one to Murani.

Murani sat at his desk with copies of the ancient maps and old books he'd been studying for years spread out before him. Father Emil Sebastian's excavations in Cadiz had supplied a new frame of reference for all the old stories and the few facts that the Society of Quirinus had. Frustration chafed at him as he surveyed the familiar tools again, trying to find new ways to ferret out the secrets he felt certain were hidden there.

Not secrets, he told himself. *Just the one.*

He gazed at the pictures of the bell and resented the fact that the Society leaders had taken it away. They were afraid of it, terrified of the power that it represented. The bell was the first physical proof they had of the truth of the legends about Atlantis and all that had gone on before. Despite the fact that all of the archbishops involved in the Society of Quirinus had been handed down the stories by those who had preceded them, each man picking his successor from within the Church with approval of the other archbishops, none of them had ever seen any proof of the secret's existence.

When he had first been brought into the Society, Murani hadn't been a believer in the secret. There were many other secrets that the Church harboured, and some of them were only legend.

But not this one, Murani thought. *This one is the truth.*

The existence of the bell had thrown the Society into a quandary. It was one thing to protect a secret out of habit, but quite another to accept that it was real and potentially had the power to destroy the world.

Or to remake it, Murani told himself. That was the idea that he clung to so fiercely.

Looking up from the books and maps spread out around him, he stared at the television. CNN was recycling the footage they'd shot of the DESTINATION: ATLANTIS? piece they'd aired the previous night. Lifting the remote control, he turned up the volume.

The reporter was a young American man named David Silver. Murani idly wondered if the name had been shortened from Silverman and if he was a Jew. In their own way, he thought, the Jews were almost as bad as the Muslims. Both detracted from the Church and the truth. Over the years, they'd leeched power from the Church.

'– the excavation is well under way here in Cadiz,' Silver said. 'They're going slowly, though. From what I'm told, several cities have existed in this area over the last few thousand years. Each one has added to the stratification of the dig site. Normally, one city was built on top of another as they fell. Father Sebastian seems quite excited by everything they're finding.'

'Can you tell us about some of the things that have been unearthed?' the woman anchor manning the desk had asked.

'Most of it appears to be the usual artefacts that archaeologists expect to find on digs like this. Tools. Pottery. Coins.'

'Have you had the chance to speak with Father Sebastian?'

'I have.'

'Has he confirmed that he's there looking for Atlantis?'

Silver laughed and shook his head. 'Father Sebastian, as I've learned, is a very serious man when it comes to his work. He doesn't indulge in speculation about what he and his team are going to find. In fact, during the times I have heard him speak, he's gone to great lengths to point out that the idle speculation surrounding this dig site was not triggered by anything he said or suggested.'

'Then where did the Atlantis angle come from?' the desk anchor asked.

'From one of the local historians,' Silver said. 'The Greek historian/philosopher Plato first described the fabled city of Atlantis in his dialogues, *Timaeus* and *Critias*. That description, according to Professor Francisco Bolivar, fits the features of the surrounding topography of the area.'

The television screen blanked for a moment, then resumed with an overlay showing concentric rings.

'According to Plato's description,' Silver went on, 'the island that became known as Atlantis was given to Poseidon, the god of the sea. A lot of the island was supposed to be underwater. As luck would have it, and to the great delight of storytellers, if I'm to be any judge, Poseidon met a woman who lived there. Nothing's said about how she got there. But there she was.'

Murani didn't care for the reporter's cavalier tone.

'Poseidon met the woman and fell in love with her,' Silver continued. 'Together, they had five pairs of twins. All boys. Poseidon built a palace on a low mountain on the island. The story goes on to describe three moats he created to surround the city.'

The image on the television reflected Silver's description of the mountain and the three rings that represented the moats.

'Poseidon named the eldest of the first twins Atlas and made him king of the island,' Silver said. 'The Atlantic Ocean is actually named after him. The people who lived on the island became known as Atlanteans. They built bridges across the moats to get to the rest of the island. They also, supposedly at least, chopped holes through the moat walls so ships could pass, and even sail into the city.'

An artist's rendering of the fabled city appeared on the screen. Ships with full canvas stretched tight sailed elegantly through the canals and tunnels near the beautiful city at the centre of the moats.

'Walls were supposed to reinforce each of the city's rings,' Silver said. 'According to Plato, the walls were made of red, black and white rock that was dug up from the moats. Then they were covered with orichalcum, brass and tin.'

The computer-generated image gleamed with the glint of sunlight on metal.

'Sounds like a scenic getaway,' the desk anchor replied.

The camera picked up Silver again for just a moment. On the screen, Silver smiled and nodded. 'In its day, it probably was. But then – one day – Atlantis disappeared.'

'How?'

'Plato doesn't know for certain. His best guess was that the Atlanteans got into a fight with the Athenians. The Athenians were able to gather enough of the locals to put up staunch resistance against the Atlanteans because the Atlanteans were reputedly slavers of the worst sort.'

'I didn't know about the slavery issue.'

'History is fascinating stuff,' Silver said, sounding as if history was a new invention. 'At any rate, the island got racked by earthquakes and floods. The island is supposed to have submerged beneath the Atlantic Ocean in a single day.'

'But if Atlantis was an island, why is Father Sebastian working near Cadiz?' the desk anchor asked. 'The site isn't an island.'

'You have to remember, Father Sebastian hasn't claimed to be searching for Atlantis. He merely claims to be researching ancient ruins. Those Atlantis tales are rumours that have sprung up around the dig.'

'Deciding that the area might be Atlantis seems like a big jump. Why would anybody think that?'

'Because, when viewed from space, this part of Cadiz looks a lot like the description of Atlantis.'

A new image formed on the television screen.

An overlay of the simple diagram of the proposed Atlantean moats in concentric circles around the city appeared. As Murani watched, the image overlaid the topography of the area where Father Sebastian laboured. It was a close fit. However, as Murani knew from his work with the Society, a lot of other pieces had been close as well.

'The island could have become part of the mainland,' Silver said. 'Plato made it plain that the island was connected – though underwater – to the mainland.'

'All these years that treasure hunters have sought out Atlantis,' the desk anchor said, 'they thought they were looking for a sunken city.'

'For a time, this chunk of land was sunken,' Silver said. 'So was most of Europe – palaeontologists dug up a prehistoric whale buried in an Italian mountain not that long ago. But high sea levels, continental drift, tsunamis – anything could have exposed it from the sea bed, raised it, or nudged it into the mainland so that it became part of the coastline.'

Murani stared at the way the template fitted over Cadiz's topographical features. Of course an artist had put those images together. The original drawing of Atlantis was based on Plato's millennia-old second-hand description, and he knew that its ratios and proximities were matters open to discussion. But, even to Murani, it seemed to be an amazingly close fit.

'If you look,' Silver was saying, 'you can see where Atlantis once stood. Maybe. Father Sebastian's excavation has uncovered what might be one of the three moats and a series of tunnels that pass through it. Looking at this, you can see why the rumours started.'

Murani's phone rang. He muted the television and answered.

'He was picked up by the FSB,' Gallardo said. There was no need to use names. Both of them knew whom Gallardo was talking about.

'Why?'

'The archaeologist's sister turned out to be a police inspector.'

Murani leaned back in his comfortable chair to examine the implications. 'That's unfortunate.'

'It might have helped to know that before I went after the cymbal,' Gallardo said. 'We could have taken care of our current problem last night.'

Murani silently agreed. 'He couldn't have told her anything. He can't know anything.'

'He knows more than I like. He's tied the two artefacts together somehow. You already knew that because you sent me here.'

'Upon further reflection,' Murani said, 'it seems that I might have been remiss in my decision to call you off him.'

'I think he knows something we don't. We're following him closely. From the way he's moving, he's got an agenda.'

Murani turned to his computer and pulled up the file on Professor Thomas Lourds. The man was acknowledged by many scholars as the world's foremost linguist.

'The film crew took pictures of the Egyptian

artefact,' Murani said, putting it together in his mind. 'The professor had pictures of the artefact in his hotel room. With the digital images in hand, the writing on the bell could be legible.'

'Do you think he's translated the inscription?'

Murani did *not* want to think that was true. All of the scholars in the Society of Quirinus had studied the bell and the images of the cymbal – the cymbal hadn't yet arrived at Vatican City – but none of them had been able to manage a translation.

But Lourds . . .

Unease spun through Murani like a spider's web, anchoring to all the doubts in his mind. He didn't like taking chances. Everything he'd done so far, all the subterfuge he'd masterminded behind the backs of the other members of the Society, had been carefully weighed for risk. As he had planned this caper, Murani had discounted the possibility of trouble.

Lourds was a wild card.

'Find out if Lourds managed to translate either of the inscriptions,' Murani said. 'If he has, I want to talk to him. Somewhere private. But if he doesn't know, make certain he doesn't involve himself in this any further.'

8

'You haven't said where we're going.'

Lourds looked at the young woman and tried to comprehend what she'd said. 'What?'

'I said, you haven't said where we're going,' Leslie repeated. 'I've tried to remain quiet, be the good little soldier, but that's not working for me.'

'Me, neither,' Gary said from the back seat. He was the camcorder operator Leslie had enlisted for the jaunt into Moscow. Gary Connolly was in his mid-twenties. Long, curly hair hung to his narrow shoulders. He wore round-lensed glasses and a black U2 SHAKE, RATTLE AND HUM concert T-shirt that showed its age.

As a rule, Lourds didn't like revealing everything about his agenda or his thinking until he was ready. He wanted to give Leslie something, though. He felt he owed her that. 'We're going to M. V. Lomonosov Moscow State University.'

'What's there?'

'As I said, Yuliya Hapaev and I consulted on various work projects we introduced over the years.' Lourds' voice tightened. 'Yuliya sometimes worked on documents that contained state secrets. Some of her finds revealed things powerful people in Russia didn't want known by other countries. In Russia, even modern Russia, that can be a death sentence.'

'I'm with you so far, but that doesn't explain why we're going to the college.'

'Yuliya was a devoted craftsman in her chosen field,' Lourds said. 'She hated to think that whatever great story she was working on would never see the light of day. She always wanted someone to be able to finish her projects in case something happened to her. So we –'

'Set up a drop at the Moscow State University,' Leslie finished. She grinned with both excitement at what lay before them and her own prowess at figuring out the reason for their trip.

'Exactly.'

'The trick is going to be being able to get out of the country with whatever she left you.'

Lourds didn't say anything, but he felt certain escaping the country would only be one of the tricks involved.

M. V. Lomonosov Moscow State University
Moscow, Russia
21 August 2009

'I didn't know it would be this big,' Leslie admitted.

Lourds craned his neck and stared up at the imposing structure. Moscow State University's main building's central tower stood thirty-six stories tall. The university had been founded in 1755, but Joseph Stalin had ordered the construction of the main building. It had been one of seven projects the General Secretary of the Soviet Party had initiated during his term. In the 1950s the university's main building, as well as her sisters, were the tallest structures in Europe. Giant clocks, barometers and thermometers, statues and reliefs decorated the building's exterior. Inside, the building contained its own police station, post office, administrative offices, bank offices, a library, a swimming pool and several shops.

It was, Lourds had to admit, extremely impressive to someone seeing it for the first time. 'I know,' he told Leslie. 'I felt the same way the first time I saw it. I don't think you ever truly get used to it.'

They left the car near the street rather than parking inside the university area. Leslie asked why they were walking so far, and Lourds told her that he didn't want to call any attention to themselves.

Reluctantly, Leslie agreed to the long walk. Gary, the cameraman, was less enthusiastic.

The grounds, despite the economic hardship the country faced, were well-appointed and clean. Flowering shrubs and bushes, though modest, made their presence known. Several students and teachers paraded across the pavements and gathered in front of the buildings. A pang passed through Lourds when he saw the groups. He thought of his classes. His graduate assistants were capable and passionate about their studies, but Lourds enjoyed the first few days of class because he got to meet the students before they immersed themselves in their studies.

A few professors greeted him as he strode on purposefully. He returned the greetings without thought, in the speaker's language and accent. Once, though, he noticed how pensive Leslie looked. Then he remembered she didn't speak Russian, much less any of its dialects. Lourds could barely remember how that felt because it had been a long time since he'd been anywhere he couldn't communicate. But he could remember how awkward and vulnerable he felt whenever he was out of place – like that time a girlfriend had taken him to a baby shower. Lourds imagined Leslie felt something like that – didn't know the rules, the vocabulary, or the point of the exercise.

He led the way up a flight of stairs and took advantage of the fact that they were alone for a moment. 'Just smile and nod,' he told Leslie and Gary. 'I'll handle the conversations.'

'I know,' Leslie said. 'But this is strange. It's not like going shopping in Chinatown. I can get by there, even though I don't speak Chinese. I know I can talk to people because most of them know at least rudimentary English.'

'The people here,' Lourds cautioned, 'know a lot more English than that. Most Americans don't speak a foreign language. English school children are exposed to more languages than American children, so I'd imagine you can speak another language. Here in Russia, they've taken pains to learn our language. In many cases, very well.'

'Okay.'

'So you could probably converse with anyone we meet here. But I'd rather not be mentioned to anyone just now as the bunch of foreigners trooping through the halls.'

'Point taken,' she said.

Lourds flashed the library identification Yuliya had arranged for him and any of his graduate students that accompanied him. He exchanged pleasantries with the older man who shepherded the collections contained within the large library. The man remembered Lourds from previous visits with Yuliya.

'Ah, Professor Lourds,' the man said, 'back with us again?'

'For a short time,' Lourds agreed as he handed his card over to be scanned.

'Is there anything I can help you with?' The man handed Lourds' card back.

'No, thank you. I know the way.'

Lourds walked to the back of the large space filled with bookshelves. Out of sight of the librarian, he strode through the stacks, taking a meandering route to his ultimate goal. The library was wired with surveillance cameras. He didn't want to look too purposeful.

Only a few students and teachers were in the stacks. None of them appeared more than casually interested.

Lourds went deeper and found the section that held books on linguistics. He noted with satisfaction that books bearing his name had increased in quantity on the shelf. Of course, many of them were his translation of *Bedroom Pursuits*. The worn bindings indicated they'd seen serious circulation.

'I see that the reading tastes of college students don't really change from nation to nation,' Leslie commented dryly.

'Not hardly. Still, whatever brings them to quest for knowledge is fine by me. Sex, or at least the promise of sex, garners more attention than anything else in the world, especially if you are a healthy nineteen-year-old.' Lourds glanced at Leslie. 'And it isn't just teens who like it. As I recall, it was that book that brought me to *your* attention. And doubtless it was that book that you used to win over your producers.'

Leslie's cheeks flamed a bit. 'Marketing loved the idea, of course.'

'Of course. And I expect that it will be touted on the advertisements for the television series.'

'Will that bother you?'

'Not at all. I get royalties from sales.' Lourds grinned. 'As you can see, it's been something of an international bestseller. It's afforded me quite a different lifestyle than that of a simple academic.'

Lourds knelt in front of the books. He moved four of them out of the way. Reaching up, he ran his hand across the bottom of the next shelf up. He felt nothing.

Disappointment coursed through him. He hadn't really expected to turn away empty-handed. He drew back.

'What's wrong?' Leslie asked.

'Nothing's there.'

Leslie knelt beside him and crouched to look under the shelf.

'Maybe she didn't have time to leave anything. Has it always been this shelf?'

'Yes.'

Glancing up, Leslie pointed at the books above the shelf they were investigating. 'Some of your books are shelved here.'

Lourds looked and found that it was true. 'Apparently the library has seen fit to acquire more copies of my works.' He ran his hand under the upper shelf and felt the straight edges of a micro-flash drive secured there. He pulled on it, but it didn't come loose.

'What's wrong?' Leslie asked.

'It's stuck.' Lourds took a pen light from his pocket and looked up at the small protective plastic case. Light glistened on the dollops of dried liquid that showed around the edges.

'That looks like an adhesive,' Leslie said.

'I hadn't expected that.' The shelf shivered under his attack. On a second attempt, the case tore away with a loud rip. Lourds pulled his hand away. He held the case between his fingers.

'Man,' Gary said, 'I hope you didn't break that micro-flash drive.'

Lourds peered through the pale blue patina of the protective case but couldn't clearly see the contents. He hoped he hadn't damaged it either.

At that moment a figure moved into view at the end of the row.

'Professor Lourds?'

Looking up, Lourds saw the librarian standing there.

'Is something wrong?' the little man asked. 'I thought I heard a noise.'

Lourds didn't know what to say. There was no time to hide the micro-flash drive. The librarian had to have seen it.

Gallardo felt exposed as he walked through the library at the university. He wore street clothes – khakis, an Oxford shirt and sweater – all covered by a long woollen coat. He had forged ID that had passed muster with the security guards.

But his wardrobe couldn't do anything about the look in his eyes. One glance, and anyone would know that he was no student.

DiBenedetto and Cimino covered his flank. The younger man made small talk with passing women. He smiled often and looked as if he were a student himself off to work on a paper.

Miroshnikov, one of the men Gallardo had retained to help him inside Moscow, waited at the door to the library. He had been the one to follow Lourds and the television team into the building

'He's still inside?' Gallardo asked. He spoke in English because that was the only language he and Miroshnikov had in common.

'Yes.'

Gallardo nodded and dropped a hand into his coat pocket to touch the silencer-equipped pistol he carried there. 'Where?'

'At the back.'

'Let's go.'

Miroshnikov took the lead. Gallardo followed at his heels. A ripping noise sounded off to the left. The old man behind the library counter went on point immediately. He slipped from behind the counter and went in the direction of the noise.

Gallardo fell in behind the old librarian but motioned for DiBenedetto and Cimino to spread out. They disappeared into the stacks of books almost at once.

Miroshnikov stayed just ahead of Gallardo and to the left. Gallardo had a clear field of fire. His hand formed a fist around the pistol.

The librarian stopped so suddenly Miroshnikov nearly ran up his back.

'Professor Lourds,' the librarian exclaimed quietly. There was a note of accusation in the address.

Gallardo stopped just out of sight and listened. Miroshnikov crossed the aisle and fell into position at the next stack.

When Lourds spoke, Gallardo recognized the professor's voice but not what was said. Lourds evidently spoke fluent Russian.

Peering around the corner, Gallardo saw Lourds and the television crew standing like guilty children in front of the old librarian. The wizened man stepped into their midst. He was obviously concerned over what had happened.

Gallardo's attention was riveted on the small plastic case in Lourds' hands. As upset as the librarian was, Gallardo feared that security would be called. He knew he couldn't allow that to happen.

He freed the pistol from his pocket, pulled his ski mask down to cover his face, and stepped around the stack. Miroshnikov mirrored his movements. The silencers screwed onto the barrels of the pistols made them look huge and menacing. Gallardo hoped their appearance would be enough to keep anyone from being foolish.

'I'll take that,' Gallardo barked in English.

Showing obvious irritation, the librarian turned around. Gallardo guessed the man intended to deliver a scathing retort, but the initiative died on the man's withered lips when he saw the pistol.

'Down on your knees,' Gallardo ordered. 'Cross your ankles.'

The librarian dropped and barely managed the feat.

Lourds maintained enough presence of mind to start backing away. He caught the young woman with one hand and pulled her behind him.

'If I have to shoot you, Professor Lourds, I will.' Gallardo held the pistol level. 'I'm beginning to think you'd be far less trouble to me dead.'

DiBenedetto stepped out from cover at the other end of the aisle.

With his escape route closed off, Lourds froze.

Gallardo grinned. He knew the expression would show through the ski mask – menacingly, of course. He advanced slowly. Miroshnikov trailed him.

'I say we just kill them here,' DiBenedetto said. 'We don't need them alive.'

A meaty smack sounded behind Gallardo before he could make a reply. Ahead, DiBenedetto stepped to the side and levelled his pistol with both hands, taking deliberate aim at Gallardo.

'Look out,' DiBenedetto warned.

Gallardo tried to turn. He heard the movement behind him. His head swivelled and he saw Miroshnikov lying unconscious on the library floor. At the same moment a pistol barrel screwed into the side of his neck.

'If you move,' a cold female voice warned, 'I'm going to shoot you.'

Standing behind him, Natashya Safarov kept her pistol barrel tight against his neck. If she squeezed the trigger, the round would tear his throat out. Adrenaline surged through her as she tried to figure out where the fourth man was. She'd arrived at the university after Lourds and the men trailing him. They hadn't noticed her because she'd parked further up then doubled back to the library only a short distance behind them.

'Tell your friends to put their weapons down,' Natashya advised him. 'Otherwise I'll kill you and take my chances with them. Personally, I like my chances. How do you feel?'

Before he could answer, Lourds charged into action. Natashya wanted to scream in frustration. The professor was going to get himself killed.

Lourds caught DiBenedetto's hand and shoved it into the air. The pistol made a slight coughing noise and a bullet thudded into the ceiling high overhead. A thin stream of plaster dust trickled down. Before the younger man could recover, Lourds took a thick book from the shelf and slammed the gunman in the face with it. Blood spattered from his broken nose and he sagged backward. Lourds took a moment to kick the pistol from the injured man's hand. Turning, Lourds seized Leslie's wrist and pulled her into motion.

Incredibly, Gallardo started to surge after them. She reached forward and grabbed his chin, pushing the gun barrel hard into his flesh.

'Bad idea,' she said.

He froze.

They watched helplessly as Lourds and his two companions disappeared into the stacks. Natashya cursed silently.

She looked up and spotted the security camera mounted on the ceiling. She ordered Gallardo forward to the end of the aisle. DiBenedetto attempted to crawl to his weapon. Natashya kicked him in the temple and he rolled over unconscious. Then she ripped the ski mask from Gallardo's face. She threw it away and turned him to the camera.

'Tell your friend to come out of hiding,' Natashya ordered. 'Do it *now*!'

'Cimino,' the big man called, 'step out where she can see you.'

A moment later, the fourth man moved into the open. He carried a silenced pistol hanging from its trigger guard by one finger.

'Throw the pistol over here,' Natashya ordered.

The man obeyed.

'Lie down,' Natashya told him, 'on your stomach. Hands clasped behind your head. I'm sure you know the drill.'

The man hesitated, but Gallardo growled at him and he got down on the floor.

Natashya was torn. She wanted to radio for back-up and take the men into custody, but she knew Lourds might well manage to escape Russia if she lost him now. Then she spotted the wireless earwig in Gallardo's ear.

'How many men do you have outside?' Natashya asked.

He didn't answer.

Natashya decided it didn't matter. There were certain to kill or capture Lourds. 'Stick your hand out.' When the big man didn't comply, she slapped her pistol against his jaw.

He shoved his hand out.

With practised ease, Natashya closed a handcuff around his wrist. 'On your face.'

The big man sank slowly. Natashya knew he was merely waiting for an opening to present itself so that he could reverse the roles of captor and captive. He was in for a surprise. When he was on the ground, she cuffed him to the unconscious man on the floor.

Natashya whirled and ran. She hoped she could help Lourds keep from getting killed or captured by the big man's waiting goons. She had questions she wanted answered.

*

Lourds' heart beat like a trip hammer. He pressed a hand against his jacket to feel the hard edges of the protective case inside his pocket. *Still there. Thank God.* He just hoped it was worth risking his life for.

He held onto Leslie's hand as he ran. He didn't want the young woman to freeze up. He doubted that the men in the library had come alone.

Outside, Lourds streaked across the grounds. His breath burned the back of his throat. He glanced over his shoulder and saw Gary only a couple of steps back. The young man lugged the camera easily and moved at a surprisingly fast gait.

Lourds got his bearings and altered his course toward the parked rental car. He didn't bother trying to stay on the pavement. College students and personnel glanced at them in concern and puzzlement. But all of them got out of their way.

'Hey,' Gary called out. 'Hey, move it, guys. We've got company.'

Anxiety soured Lourds' stomach. He glanced around and spotted the three men speeding down the street to intercept them. Not students, not even Russian, by the looks of them. Hard men with hard eyes. He should have known that the big man would have had other compatriots lurking nearby.

Overuse of force seemed to be his trademark.

So far they didn't have guns out – but they were far enough away and moving fast enough through the crowds of students to make a clean shot almost impossible. That situation wouldn't last long.

They were gaining on Lourds and his crew.

Lourds cursed. He was so frenzied he didn't even note what language he used. He veered from the street where they'd left the rental car parked. Things definitely didn't look good, and he doubted if things could get any –

'Professor Lourds!'

Worse. He was wrong.

That demanding shout caught Lourds' attention and he recognized the voice. When he glanced over his shoulder, he saw Natashya Safarov swiftly gaining on him. The woman was evidently a runner, among her other talents. Her arms and legs worked in tandem as she sprinted. She caught up to them as if the feat was child's play. Her pistol was naked in her fist and caused immediate consternation in all who saw the weapon.

Lourds counted himself among the concerned.

'You're under arrest,' Natashya said as she pursued him. She took aim at him with her pistol.

He kept running. 'If we stop,' Lourds protested, pointing back at the running hit men, 'those men will kill us.'

Natashya darted a look at the men he indicated. Behind her, the men she'd left inside the library were just emerging through the entrance; the two who were conscious carried the unconscious man handcuffed to one of them. They did not look happy. But it was unlikely that group of thugs could catch them.

'I have a car,' she told him. 'Follow me.' Almost effortlessly, she sprinted past Lourds, Leslie and Gary. 'If you stop following me, I will shoot you.'

'*What?*' Leslie's breath came in ragged gasps. She stumbled and nearly fell. 'Stop following her? With those men behind us? She's mad.'

Lourds held onto Leslie's hand to help her keep her balance. 'Save your breath,' he advised. 'Run.' Mad or not, Natashya Safarov was their only chance.

Following their armed leader, they sprinted across the side street to a mid-sized sedan in the car park.

Natashya used her electronic keypad to unlock the doors.

'Get in.'

She skidded to a halt on the driver's side and opened the door. Instead of sliding inside the car, she put her arms across the bonnet and took aim at the three men closing on them. They scattered with practised efficiency. Weapons appeared in their hands.

The conviction that he was about to be blasted to smithereens filled Lourds. He froze for an instant.

'Get in!' Natashya ordered. 'Keep down. The mass of the car's engine should absorb any bullets.'

Lourds fumbled with the passenger-side back door and got it opened. Panic hammered him. He forced himself to concentrate on the task at hand and not to look back at their pursuers.

'Be careful! If you shoot in their direction, you could hit a college student,' Lourds cautioned in Russian so there would be no misunderstanding. Natashya spoke English well, but that didn't mean she would have that skill in the heat of combat. He pushed Leslie into the opened door, then sheltered her with his body.

'I know,' Natashya replied, also in Russian. 'I'm not going to do that, but they don't know it. Get in before they work it out.'

Leslie crawled inside the vehicle. Gary threw himself in after her before Lourds could get in. The two sprawled across the seat and left Lourds no room. He slammed the back door shut and opened the front passenger door. He dropped inside and shut the door behind him. He kept his head low, below the dashboard.

Back across the street, the three men had dropped to the ground. One of them aimed a pistol and fired. The bullet smashed through the passenger-side window. So much for the engine block stopping the bullets. Glass splinters spilled across Lourds' back. He twitched and covered his head with his arms.

Natashya flung her door open and dropped into the seat. She keyed the ignition and the motor rumbled smoothly to life.

Lourds looked over at her.

She shifted the pistol into her right hand and pointed it at Lourds. 'Stay down.'

He was convinced that she wasn't offering advice regarding enemy fire. She shot over his head at their pursuers. More bullets struck the car. The impacts sounded excruciatingly loud inside the vehicle.

'Damn!' Gary howled from the back seat. 'Move, woman! Are you waiting on a sign from God or something?'

Natashya hit the accelerator. The engine snarled like a cornered beast as the tyres gripped the pavement and hurled them forward.

Lourds kept his hands on the dash but he couldn't resist looking up. Natashya pulled into the lane of oncoming traffic. For a moment he thought they were going to get hit by a cargo truck. The driver's eyes widened on the other side of the windshield. He hit the brakes and slewed the truck around. The bumper missed striking them by inches.

'Oh, crap,' Gary screamed.

Natashya pulled hard on the wheel and steered them up onto the pavement. The car bucked in protest. A moment later, she swung the wheel again to put them back on the road. Rubber burned and shrieked as the tyres protested, then shot them forward.

Lourds had the distinct impression that his life was just as much at risk now as it had been back at the college with the four armed killers trapping him in the stacks. He pressed his hands hard against the dash and wished he'd taken the time to put a seatbelt on.

'All right, Professor Lourds,' Natashya said calmly, 'we're going to talk now.'

'Talk about what?' he asked, his words rough as he panted from the run and the adrenaline overload.

'What you were doing at the library. What you took from there.' They flew around a slower-moving sedan. She barely pulled over in time to keep from crossing bumpers with an on-coming car. 'And what you know about my sister's death.' She floored the accelerator, and the car shot forward into the traffic.

'This might not be the best time,' Lourds spat, eyes closed and body braced against the certain crash. It didn't come. Natashya swerved out of danger like a Grand Prix driver on a mountain curve.

'We may not have a better one. Talk now.' The Russian risked taking her eyes off the road long enough to shoot him a hard look.

'Uh, guys,' Gary called from the back. 'We're being followed.'

Lourds twisted in the seat and looked back over his shoulder. Two cars threaded through the traffic after them. He reached for the seatbelt and managed to snap it around himself as Natashya started taking evasive action again. The forces of the evasion slammed his chest into the belt. He took a deep breath in preparation for his next words.

The lady had a point. Space to talk was starting to look like a luxury.

9

'What did you go to the library to get?' Natashya demanded as she steered the car through traffic. She cut her eyes to the rear-view mirror. The two cars following them stood out among the other vehicles. Despite the calm demeanour she showed to her 'guests', nervous energy raked claws through her.

'What?' Lourds gazed at her as though she'd just sprouted a second head.

Natashya ignored him for a moment as she went out left wide around the car ahead of her. As soon as she was past the front of the car, she cut back to the right and took the first side street there. Tyres shrilled in protest. Horns blared behind her.

'You went to the library to retrieve something.' Natashya looked again in the rear-view mirror. The two cars made the turn and kept after her.

'Something your sister left for me.'

'What did she leave you?' Natashya demanded.

'A micro-flash drive.'

'What's on it?'

'I don't know.'

Natashya shot him a look.

'It's the truth,' Lourds said. 'You were there. I didn't have time to examine it.'

'What do you think is on it?' Natashya took another side street. Moscow University was in the Sparrow Hills region. There were a number of small, narrow roads in the area. She planned to take advantage of that shortly.

'Yuliya was working on something,' Lourds said, 'she wanted me to look at.'

'The cymbal?' Natashya interrupted.

'Did she talk to you about it?'

Irritation shattered the sadness and pain that gripped Natashya. The American professor's questions came faster than her own. Of course, she was distracted by the driving.

'A little.'

'What did she say?'

'I'm asking the questions, Professor Lourds.' Natashya swerved again. This time she headed down a narrow alley filled with garbage cans. Two of them went down under the car streaking headlong through the alley. 'What do you know about the cymbal?'

'Not enough,' he admitted.

'Then why did she contact you? Why would she have left information for you about it?'

'I don't know that she did. The flash drive's contents might concern another matter entirely.' Lourds braced himself against the dash again as Natashya swung out wide from the alley's mouth. The tyres skidded across the street.

Natashya laid on the horn, tapped the brakes then

accelerated again for a moment. As she navigated the traffic and headed into the next alley across the street, she saw Lourds flinch involuntarily as they closed on a small bus. For a moment Natashya didn't think she was going to make it.

'Ohmigod,' the woman in the back gasped.

Then the car shot down the alley. More trash cans crumpled or rebounded away.

'Was Yuliya killed because of the cymbal?' Natashya asked.

'Maybe. Was the cymbal recovered last night?' Lourds countered.

Natashya checked the rear-view mirror in time to see the lead car smash into the corner of the building and spin out of control. The second car zipped past and continued the chase.

'No,' Natashya answered. 'The artefact wasn't recovered. But the fire destroyed many things inside that room.' She glanced at Lourds. 'So you believe these men killed my sister.'

'Watch the road.' Lourds braced himself again.

The bumper struck a stack of trash cans and sent them flying. One of them came back over the front of the car and smashed against the windshield. Several cracks ran the length of the glass in a spider-web pattern.

'If it wasn't these men,' Lourds said in answer to her question, 'then it was men associated with them. Or their employer.'

'Why do you think that?' Natashya watched the pursuit car closing the distance behind them.

Lourds hesitated. He looked at her. 'Because there was another artefact with similar markings,' he said. 'We had it in Alexandria five days ago. Briefly. These men – or others like them – broke into our studio, killed people there, and took it. They'd have killed us all, but Leslie here fought back.'

Gunshots rang out behind them. At least one bullet ricocheted from the car's body. Another bullet cored through the back glass and punched through the shattered front windshield.

'I'm sorry about Yuliya,' Lourds said. 'She was smart and charming. I'm going to miss her quite a lot.'

Natashya felt certain that Lourds was telling the truth. But he did know more than she did.

More gunshots echoed inside the alley.

Once she'd driven out of the alley, Natashya dropped her pistol into her lap, took the wheel in both hands, and downshifted as she pulled hard to the left. The car shivered as she brought it around in a sharp 180-degree turn. She ended up facing the oncoming vehicle.

'What are you doing?' Lourds asked nervously.

'She's lost it, dude,' Gary yelled. 'She's going to get us all killed.'

Ignoring the anxiety that rattled through her, Natashya scooped the pistol up in her left hand, took aim through the open front windshield, and clicked off the safety. The pistol chugged in her hand as she fired. Brass spun against the broken windshield as she squeezed off rounds as quickly as she could. The bullets slammed into the driver's side of the oncoming car's window. Natashya watched him jerk under the impact. Then the car slewed out of control. The vehicle caught the front corner of Natashya's car, crumpled the fender, and slid past them to crash into the side of a clothing store.

Natashya shoved the gears into reverse and backed out into the street. She ground the gears, burned rubber, and shot through the traffic.

She glanced at Lourds. 'We're going to talk, you and I. Then I'm going to figure out what I'm going to do with you.'

The sounds of sirens filled the air, closing in on the wreckage behind them.

The crowd that gathered at the crash site choked traffic. Gallardo gazed in frustration as the car he drove became mired in the vehicles. Giving up, he flung the door open and strode forward. Snarling curses, he roughly pushed through the crowd. A few men cursed him back, but none of them tried to stop him.

Four men still remained inside the wrecked vehicle. The driver lay slumped over the steering wheel. Taking care not to touch the car and leave finger-prints, Gallardo grabbed the man by the hair and pulled him back.

Bullets had almost destroyed his face.

Cursing again, Gallardo released the dead man. The body teetered over to the side onto the man in the passenger seat. He roughly shoved the dead man from him and cursed.

'Move it!' Gallardo ordered. 'Out of the car!'

Police sirens split the air as the authorities got closer.

'Follow me!' Gallardo turned and retraced his steps through the crowd. All of the gawkers remained at a distance. They backed up even further as the three men still alive got out of the vehicle with weapons in their hands. They ran after Gallardo, weapons up and ready.

Returning to his car, Gallardo climbed inside, motioned for the others to pile in, and looked at DiBenedetto. 'Get us out of here.'

As the doors slammed shut behind them, DiBenedetto backed rapidly through the alley.

Seething with rage, Gallardo fished his phone from his pocket. He remembered the ease with which the woman had come up behind him and taken him. As if he'd been a child. It was embarrassing and unforgivable. He promised himself that he would see her again. When he did, he was going to kill her. Slowly.

He dialled Murani's phone number.

Moscow, Russia
21 August 2009

Lourds sat braced in the passenger seat of the car as Natashya Safarov sped through the traffic. She spoke quickly on her cellphone. Though he was fluent in Russian, she spoke so quickly and cryptically that he wasn't certain exactly what the conversation was about.

Leslie and Gary sat quietly in the back. They'd had enough. Leslie had demanded to know what was going on and then asked to be taken to the British Consulate. Natashya had addressed the young woman only once. She'd told her that if she couldn't keep her mouth shut she would be taken to the nearest police station.

Leslie hadn't said anything since.

After travelling for nearly an hour, passing through historic parts of Moscow that Lourds had often visited before as well as old residential areas that he doubted a tourist had ever seen, Natashya pulled up in a small parking area behind a nondescript building.

She switched off the engine and pocketed the keys then opened the door and got out. Leaning down to the window, eyeball-to-eyeball with Lourds, she ordered, 'Get out. All of you.'

With some concern, Lourds got out. His legs shook – aftershocks from the enforced stillness of the ride and the emotional letdown from the escape and the gun battle.

The building was six-storeys tall and looked like it had been constructed back in the 1950s. Its grim and forbidding appearance tied a knot in Lourds' stomach.

'What are we doing here?' Leslie asked.

Natashya's immediate irritation tightened her face. Lourds saw it and felt certain that the woman wasn't going to answer.

But she gained control of herself.

Her expression once again emotionless, Natashya said, 'It's a hideout. You'll be safe here. We need to talk. I want to see if we can sort this out before anyone else has to die. I'm sure you want the same thing.'

When Natashya gestured to the fire escape clinging to the building's side, Lourds nodded and took the lead. The front entrance wasn't an option. He put his foot on the first rung and started climbing. He knew that Leslie and Gary would follow.

Natashya stopped them on the fourth-floor landing. She used a key to let them inside the building, then directed Lourds to the third door on the left. Another key allowed them entrance into a small apartment, which consisted of a living room/dining room, a kitchen, two bedrooms and a bathroom. There was a shower but no bath. It wasn't spacious and it didn't look comfortable for the number of people in their group, but it felt safe.

Still, Lourds knew that was probably an illusion.

'Sit,' Natashya told them.

'Are we under arrest?' Leslie challenged her. She made no move to sit down.

Lourds folded himself into a wingback chair. He'd suspected Leslie would show some resistance and didn't intend to add to the confusion. Unless he had to. Deciding which side to support would be tricky. He felt loyalty to Leslie, but Natashya might offer the best opportunity to decipher the puzzle of the cymbal and the bell. She was clearly a cool head in a crisis.

The hard edges of the plastic case under his jacket

pressed against his side. He was surprised that Natashya hadn't already demanded possession of it.

'Would you like to be under arrest?' Natashya responded. 'I can arrange it.'

Bulldog fierceness swelled onto Leslie's face. 'I'm a British citizen. You can't frivolously cast aside my rights.'

'And you can't just walk into my country, drag carnage behind you and take something produced by a government employee – my sister,' Natashya retorted. 'I'm quite certain your government wouldn't condone your actions.'

Leslie wrapped her arms under her breasts and stuck her chin out. No signs of surrender there.

'Perhaps,' Lourds interjected as smoothly as he could, 'we could all keep in mind the fact that no one wants us incarcerated at the moment.' He shot Natashya a glance to underscore what he meant by *no one*.

Natashya shrugged slightly. It was an unconscious body movement that many people might not have noticed. Lourds had trained himself to watch for physical communications as well as verbal ones – it was a part of being a linguist. Often the most important parts of human communication weren't spoken. Those little gestures – and the meta-messages they conveyed – were generally the ones that crossed cultural barriers first, long before words.

'This is a safe house,' Natashya said. 'We use this place and others like it to keep important prisoners safe. The Russian mob has a long reach.'

Leslie bridled at the word *prisoners*. Thankfully she didn't voice her objections.

'The men who are pursuing you should not be able to find us here. We'll have some time to work through things,' Natashya went on.

'That depends,' Gary said. 'I mean, if your cop buddies know about this place and they see you've gone missing, they could come round here looking for you. And if they think we've kidnapped you, which might explain why you haven't been in touch with them, they might come in guns blazing, mightn't they? Makes sense, dude, doesn't it?'

It was, Lourds had to admit despite the way it was phrased, an astute observation. Gary obviously had a fertile mind when it came to projecting scenarios.

'They won't come here,' Natashya said. 'Even they don't know about this place.'

'Why not?' Leslie asked.

'Because I haven't told them about it. I am a high-ranking officer. I pursue the most dangerous cases. I'm given a certain amount of . . . latitude . . . in my investigations.'

'I don't suppose the police will come round later,' Leslie said. 'When it's more *convenient*?'

'Nothing about spiriting you people off the street is convenient,' Natashya said. 'I killed a man back there. I don't know what kind of impression you have about my country, but killing is frowned upon here as well as in your country. In fact, judging from the leniency in your court systems versus ours, I'd say America is much more lenient than Russian judges.' Her voice grew sharper.

'I'm not American,' Leslie said, 'I'm British. It's a civilized society compared to either Russia or America.'

'If we're through with all the posturing,' Natashya said, 'maybe we could get on to figuring out what we're going to do next?'

'If I may,' Lourds stated quietly, 'I'd like to suggest that we cooperate. For the moment, I think we can all agree that we have something to gain by learning more about our present predicament, and quite a lot to lose if we're caught.'

The two women stared at each other. Leslie acquiesced first, with a short nod that Natashya finally echoed.

'Good.' Lourds took the plastic case from his jacket and popped it open to survey the micro-flash drive inside. 'Then first let's have a look at what Yuliya left.'

Lourds sat at the dinette table with his notebook computer open before him. The flash drive Yuliya had left was connected through a USB port.

'Copy the information from the flash drive to your computer.' Natashya stood behind him. He felt the heat of her body radiating against his back.

'Why?' Leslie sat on Lourds' left so that she could see the screen.

'In case something happens to the flash drive.'

Although he was certain he knew what Natashya planned to do, Lourds did as the Russian suggested. As soon as the task bar showed complete, Natashya took the flash drive from the notebook computer and pocketed it.

'So much for trust,' Leslie commented bitterly.

'Trust only goes so far,' Natashya said without animosity. 'It's also not mutually exclusive of good sense. You have been robbed, yes? And followed? Having two copies is smart. Having them kept separate is smarter.'

Lourds declined to comment. He agreed with Natashya, but didn't think saying so would improve matters between the two women. He fingered the mouse pad and brought up the directory he'd created for the flash drive's contents.

One of the folders was marked OPEN FIRST in English. Lourds did so, knowing that the action would forestall any further argument on the part of the women. They were both too curious about what Yuliya had left to waste time arguing.

Gary had more important matters on his mind than the contents of the flash drive. After ascertaining the presence of a well-stocked pantry – small but effective – he had declared himself the cook of the group and set to the task. Judging from the aroma coming from the kitchen, the young man had a flair for his chosen contribution.

A video window opened on the notebook computer. Yuliya Hapaev's image blurred for a moment, then took centre stage. She sat at her desk with the camera obviously propped before her. She wore a lab coat over a pink sweatshirt.

Natashya's breath drew in sharply, but she didn't say anything.

Lourds felt bad for the young woman, but at the moment it was all he could do to keep his own emotions in check. Yuliya had been a vibrant person and a good mother. Knowing she was gone hurt him deeply. His eyes misted and he blinked them clear.

'Hello, Thomas.' Yuliya smiled.

Hello, Yuliya, Lourds thought to himself.

'If you have this little parcel, then I have to assume something has happened to me.' Yuliya shook her head and grinned again. 'It sounds so silly saying that, but you and I both know I don't mean something as outlandish as in a spy novel. I have to assume that something happened to me in a traffic accident.' She frowned. 'Or perhaps I was mugged. Or my bosses shut me down.'

Lourds forced himself to watch her trying to muddle along, knowing she'd felt foolish trying to find the words. A lump formed in the back of his throat.

'This is only the third time I've made one of these little presentations,' Yuliya admitted. 'We agreed to do this all those years ago over cognac while at the archaeology retreat in France.' She smiled. 'We were so serious about it when we were drunk.'

In spite of himself, in spite of the loss, Lourds smiled. They had met a handful of times before that encounter in France. But the friendship they'd shared had seemed to cement there.

'You probably considered the deal we made to be merely a lark,' Yuliya said. 'A joke summoned up by too much to drink, good companionship and the fact that we both love the same tawdry spy novels. But I hope you find this.' Seriousness hardened her face. She picked up the cymbal and held it out for display. 'My enquiry into the nature of this artefact has turned out to be quite interesting. I think it would be a shame if no one found out the truth about it.'

Especially since it led to your murder, Lourds thought.

Yuliya put the cymbal aside. 'I've been trying to reach you for a couple of days.' She smiled ruefully. 'I have to assume you're out on some junket the university has insisted on. Or perhaps you're chasing some big find. A book from the Alexandrian library, hopefully. I know you'd like that. And I know nothing else would take you away from your students.' The image on the computer screen paused. 'At any rate, I've arranged the files on here to show you what I've learned from the cymbal. Where it was found. How it was found. And what my conclusions are.'

Though he didn't want to, Lourds checked the meter at the bottom of the video screen and saw that the presentation was almost finished. He wasn't ready to see Yuliya just fade away. He had to restrain himself from pausing the video.

'I hope what I've put together helps,' the image of Yuliya said. 'I hope you figure out the significance of the cymbal.' She smiled and shrugged. 'Who knows? Perhaps someone from my department will have all the answers before you find this. But most of all, I hope that I'm simply discussing this with you in a few days. Over a cognac. In front of the fireplace. And with my husband and children watching us and thinking we're the most boring people on the planet.'

Lourds' throat grew impossibly tight. He felt a tear at the corner of his eye. Unashamed, he wiped it away with his fingers.

The screen blanked.

No one spoke after the video finished. There was too much pain and regret in the room. Leslie left Lourds and Natashya alone with their tears, but she didn't leave the table.

Lourds shook away the ghosts of his friend and colleague.

He had a murderer to track and a mystery to solve. Moping did Yuliya no good.

Taking out a yellow legal tablet, his favourite tool for associating his thoughts free-form, Lourds wrote down the architecture of Yuliya's documents. He made note of the dates of their creation, then of their updates as Yuliya had discovered more information.

In that way he was able to retrace her thinking and her chain of logic.

'Is there anything you need?' Natashya asked after a while.

'No.' Lourds flipped through screens of text Yuliya had prepared on the cymbal. 'I just need to get through this material.'

'All right.' Natashya fell silent again, but she never left his side, watching every keystroke.

*

Within the hour, Gary laid a feast upon the table around Lourds' computer and tablet.

The young man hadn't had any fresh vegetables to work with, but he'd still cobbled together a thick hearty stew from canned potatoes, carrots, beans and corn. He'd put it together with some kind of beef stock. Pan-fried bread slathered in olive oil accompanied the big bowls of stew.

Drawn by the heavenly scent of food when he hadn't eaten in nearly a day, Lourds pushed back from the computer. As soon as he did, though, he was hit by questions.

'Did Yuliya know who killed her?' Natashya asked.

'I don't think so,' Lourds replied. 'I found no mention of anyone stalking her in the text. She didn't seem to be worried about anyone – just political issues over the artefact. The usual fears of any academic.'

'No collectors or antiques traffickers were mentioned in the papers?'

'Not that I've seen so far.'

'But it has to be someone from that world who took it,' Natashya insisted.

'Why?' Leslie asked.

'Because of the way they located the cymbal,' Natashya answered. She had made notes in Cyrillic on her PDA. Lourds had read enough of them to realize that they were shorthand notes for herself and that he couldn't really make head nor tail of them.

'I still don't see how you inferred that,' Leslie pressed her.

Gary broke off a piece of the bread and dunked it into the stew. 'Because the killers learned about the cymbal from the website, man. Either they were looking for that piece or they were watching Professor Lourds' email. Otherwise they would have taken it when it was first found at the dig site.'

Everyone looked at him.

'Hey,' Gary said, looking slightly unsettled, 'I'm just saying is all. It's what I'd do if I wanted something bad enough to kill for it. Grab it before it gets around. Doesn't take much of a brainy bloke to figure out how the murderers happened to turn up at Professor Hapaev's lab.' He paused. 'Besides, they were looking for that bell Leslie found down in Alexandria, too. That was also listed on a website. The bad guys have a pattern.'

'Professional collectors, then?' Leslie said.

'Or professional thieves,' Natashya replied.

'Either way,' Gary said, 'you're looking for someone who knows a lot about what's going on in the antiquities area. They swooped down on the goodies long before you professional blokes knew what you had.'

'The bell and cymbal don't offer much of a draw for collectors. They're clay, not precious metal, they have inscriptions that haven't been translated and maybe won't be, and they come from a culture that seems to be unknown. Collectors love ancient objects, but they gravitate to the familiar and the coveted – Shang and Tang Chinese bronzes, Ming vases, Egyptian royal funerary items, Greek marble statues, Mayan turquoise and gold, Roman bronzes and inlays. Things like that. Collectors love objects associated with powerful or famous rulers. I know people who would happily kill for a life-sized bronze charioteer from the tomb of Emperor Chin, for example.

'These objects are different; they're ancient and mysterious, so they appeal to scholars and historians. But it's not like they're the kinds of items that would attract the interest of rich or obsessed collectors. They have no provenance. They have no certificate of authenticity. We don't even know what culture they come from. They're old, and they're interesting, but they're not some kind of Holy Grail.'

'If they aren't after the muscial instruments,' Leslie asked, 'then what *are* they after?'

'I think they *are* after them,' Lourds said. 'I believe Gary is right: I believe they have been looking for those instruments. But I don't think it was for the things themselves. Rather, it was for what they represented.'

'So we're looking for a specialized interest,' Natashya said. 'And for the people that have it?'

'Yes. I believe so.' Lourdes noted the cold glint in the woman's eye. He had no doubt that she could be a cold-blooded killer if she so chose. But he had no pity for the men who had killed Yuliya. He wished Natashya a clear shot, in fact.

'Did Professor Hapaev have any clues as to the origins of the cymbal?' Leslie asked.

'She did,' Lourds said. 'Yuliya believed that the

cymbal came out of West Africa. More than that, she was certain it was made by the Yoruba people. Or their ancestors.'

'Why?'

'The Yoruba people were noted for trade,' Lourds said. 'They still are.'

'They were also captured and sold by slavers by the boatload,' Gary put in.

Everyone looked at him again.

'Hey, I watch a lot of Discovery Channel and History Channel. Since we were going to do this special with Professor Lourds, I boned up on some of the material we might touch on. Cool stuff. It didn't turn out like I expected it to, though. I figured on more digging, fewer bad guys, man.'

'Sorry to disappoint,' Lourds said. 'According to Yuliya, the language of the Yoruba people is wide-spread as a result of the slave trade,' Lourds went on. 'The language follows the AVO pattern.'

'Now that one I don't know,' Gary said, then stuffed more stew in his mouth.

'Trade shorthand,' Lourds said. 'AVO means agent-verb-object. It's the pattern – the order, if you will – in which words appear in the spoken and written sentence of a culture. It's also known as SVO. Subject-verb-object. The English language, as well as seventy-five per cent of all the languages in the world, follow the SVO pattern. An example sentence would be: Jill ran home. Do you understand?'

Everyone nodded.

'The Yoruban language is also tonal,' Lourds

continued. 'Most languages in the world aren't tonal. Generally, the older the language, the more likely it is to be tonal. Chinese, for example, is a tonal language. Fewer than a fourth of the world's languages exhibit that feature. Yoruban's fairly unique in that regard.'

'Why did Yuliya think the cymbal came from West Africa?' Leslie asked. 'It was found here, wasn't it?'

'Yes, but she was sure it was a trade item, and that it wasn't made here. The pottery doesn't relate to the local types at all. Also, some of the inscriptions on the cymbal were done at a later date,' Lourds replied, 'to denote ownership. Yuliya made note of that in her files. You can see those inscriptions in some of the pictures.'

'They were in the Yoruban language?' Natashya asked.

Lourds nodded. 'I read enough of that language to recognize it. But the original language on the cymbal, what Yuliya believed was the original language, isn't Yoruban. It's something else.'

'Must have been maddening for her,' Leslie said. 'And it's why she was trying to contact you.'

'Yes.'

'Can you decipher the language on the bell and the cymbal?' Leslie asked.

Lourds scooped up a spoonful of stew. He chewed carefully and swallowed. 'There are two distinct languages.' He shrugged. 'Given time, I feel confident that I could decipher those inscriptions. It would help if I had more text to work with. The smaller the sampling a linguist works with, the more difficult the process.'

'How much time would you need?' Natashya asked.

Lourds looked at her and decided to answer honestly. 'Anywhere from days to weeks to years.'

Natashya cursed in Russian. Then she let out a long breath. 'We don't have that kind of time.'

'A project like this,' he said finally, 'can be daunting.'

Natashya's eyes blazed. 'Those men killed my sister to get that cymbal. I believe they're facing some sort of timetable. That's why they've gone to such desperate measures. If they're on a schedule, it's going to make them vulnerable.'

'If you're right about them knowing about the bell and the cymbal before they turned up,' Gary said, 'then whoever did this could have been looking for them for years. Maybe they were just desperate because they'd been looking for so long.'

'I can't hide you out here in the city while you look for information,' Natashya said. 'In addition to my own agency, there's the matter of the men who have tried to kill you.'

'I don't think we'll find any more information here,' Lourds said. 'If it was here to be had, I feel confident Yuliya would have turned it up.' He pulled the computer over to him and brought up another file. 'She has left us something of a lead to follow.'

'What lead?' Natashya leaned in.

'She mentioned a man in Halle, near Leipzig in

Germany, who is an authority on the Yoruba people. A Professor Joachim Fleinhardt at the Max Planck Institute for Social Anthropology.'

'Germany?' Natashya frowned.

'According to Yuliya's notes, Professor Fleinhardt is something of an authority on the West African slave trade. She'd intended to contact him after she'd talked to me.'

Natashya straightened and walked over to the window. She moved the curtain aside and peered out.

Lourds ate the stew and bread. He watched her think. He couldn't guess at everything that went through the woman's mind, but he knew her desire to apprehend her sister's killers had to be uppermost in her thoughts.

Finally, Natashya turned back to face them. 'I will make some calls. Stay here till I return.'

Leslie bridled at once. 'You can't just order us about.'

'And I can't protect you from those men if you go rushing through the streets of this city.' Natashya's voice was hard. 'They may want the information my sister left Professor Lourds. They do know you have it, you know. If you think you can do better without me, then leave. Perhaps I can figure out who they are when I investigate your murders.'

'Inspector Safarov does have a point, Leslie,' Lourds stated gently. 'Getting out of the country could be problematic. At least, in the conventional ways.'

Leslie folded her arms and didn't look happy.

'I will go,' Natashya said. 'With luck, perhaps I can find a way to get us to Halle.'

'"Us"?' Leslie repeated.

'"Us",' Natashya said. 'None of you are trained to combat men like these.' Without another word, she left the apartment. The door banged shut behind her.

10

Moscow, Russia
21 August 2009

Lourds sat on the windowsill in the apartment and watched the corner drug store that Natashya Safarov had entered. He could barely see her through the dusty window as she talked on the phone.

'Who do you think she's calling?' Leslie asked.

'I don't know.'

'Maybe she's calling the police. If she is, they're going to take us into custody.'

'If that was what she wanted, she would have already done that,' Lourds pointed out.

'She has a gun,' Gary added. 'She's already proven she's willing to use it.'

Leslie frowned at the cameraman.

'I'm just saying, is all,' Gary said. 'It's not like it was a bloody news flash.'

'My guess is that she's trying to find out who she killed,' Lourds said. 'The police might have had time to discover the man's identity by now. Hopefully all of them were taken into custody.'

'That still leaves us trapped here.'

'Not necessarily,' Lourds said. 'There are always circumspect ways into and out of countries.' He retreated to his backpack and took out his sat-phone. He dialled a number from memory.

Natashya stood at the phone. The window beside it looked out over the building where she'd left Lourds and his friends. She peered up at the apartment and thought she could see the outline of someone sitting in the window.

She scowled in disgust. *Amateurs.*

A thin woman with three hollow-eyed children walked through the front door as Natashya's superior answered his phone.

'Chernovsky,' he said brusquely.

'It is Natashya Safarov. I needed to talk to you.'

A thick and repellent silence hung for a moment. Natashya disliked making Chernovsky angry. She hated disappointing him even more.

Ivan Chernovsky had a lot of experience with the Moscow police. He'd been one of those people who had survived the fall of Communism and still remained on the job. That said a lot. Many policemen had hooked up with the criminals they'd chased and battled on the street. Chernovsky had remained loyal to his goals.

He'd also vouched for Natashya, and – when the occasion warranted it – he'd helped cover for her. She didn't always play according to the letter or the spirit of the law. Power and privilege still held sway in Moscow, perhaps more so now than ever. Natashya didn't allow either of those to stand in her way.

'What do you need to talk about?' Chernovsky

asked coldly. 'The man you killed in the street several hours ago? Or something else?'

Natashya didn't respond to the questions. She bucked authority when she could. They both knew that. But when the day was all done, she also delivered whatever the department needed.

'I've got a lead on my sister's murderers.'

'What lead?'

'I don't want to say at this point.' Natashya watched the pedestrian traffic passing by.

'You are with the professor?' Papers rustled. 'Thomas Lourds? The American, yes?'

Natashya hesitated only a moment. 'Yes.'

'He is in good health?'

'Yes.'

The chair creaked again. 'Tell me what is going on.'

'I don't know. Not all of it. Professor Lourds is connected to my sister's death.'

Chernovsky sighed. 'He was obviously not responsible or he'd be dead.'

'The same people who killed Yuliya are after him.'

'To kill him?'

'I don't think so. At least, they don't appear ready to kill him at once. I don't think they're so choosey about the British people with them.'

'Ah.' More papers rustled. 'The British television team.'

'Yes.'

'Why did you call me, Natashya?'

'My sister left Professor Lourds information about the project she was working on.'

'The cymbal?'

'Yes.'

'Why did she leave it for him?' Chernovsky asked.

'Because she believed he could decipher the language that was written in.'

'No one else can do this? There are many professors in Moscow.'

'Yuliya believed in him,' Natashya said.

'Do you?'

Natashya hesitated. 'I don't know. But there was something else that was stolen from Lourds and the Britishers.'

'What?'

'A bell.'

The thin woman guided her children through the store. One small boy remained behind in the bread aisle. He couldn't have been six years old. He looked like a bundle of sticks. He gazed at the assortment of sweet cakes out on display.

'What kind of bell?' Chernovsky asked.

'It's equally as mysterious as the cymbal Yuliya was working on,' Natashya told him.

Chernovsky was silent for a moment. 'These musical instruments aren't so mysterious to someone.'

'That's what Lourds believes as well.'

'What do you plan to do?'

'Go with Lourds. Yuliya was in contact with a professor of anthropology near Leipzig. Lourds intends to go there.'

'Disappearing out of the country with someone wanted for questioning involving a murder would be a magician's trick,' Chernovsky said. 'Even if you weren't a police officer equally as wanted.'

'I know.'

'I can't help you with that, Natashya.'

'I'm not asking you to.' But if she'd thought he could have helped, she would have.

'Then why did you call?'

'Because it was the respectful thing to do. And because I need information now and may need it again later.' If it hadn't been for the possibility of the assistance Chernovsky might be able to provide, she'd have left straightaway.

Both of them knew that as well.

'Thank you,' Chernovsky said. 'What do you need?'

'Have you identified the man I shot?'

'Not yet. But we think we'll have an ID soon. The men tried to take the corpse with them when they fled the scene. They were successful in getting away, but they had to leave the body. The forensics department has it now.'

Natashya sighed. She'd been hoping for fingerprint identification. That would have been best. Forensics was a much weaker possibility. Not even the Americans boasted the glittering array of scientific hardware of the *CSI* television shows.

'Do you have your cellphone?' Chernovsky asked.

'No.' Natashya knew he was reminding her that she could be found through the GPS technology. 'I will contact you as I can.'

'From Leipzig?'

'If I'm able.'

'Be very careful, Natashya,' Chernovsky advised her. 'These men who killed Yuliya are professionals.'

'I know that. But I'm used to dealing with professionals. The criminals in Moscow these days are very dangerous.'

'You can understand the criminals in Moscow, though. You know what they're willing to risk. In this case, you don't know what the stakes are. With these men . . .' Chernovsky took a deep breath. 'They should not have still been here today, Natashya. They should have fled Russia.'

'But they didn't,' Natashya said, 'and that will be their mistake.'

'Don't let it be yours,' Chernovsky chided.

'I won't.'

'Stay in touch as you can, Natashya. I'll do what I can to help. Your sister was a good person. So are you. Take care of yourself.'

Natashya told him thank you and goodbye. She cradled the receiver.

The mother walked through the store and made a few meagre selections. Natashya dug in her pockets and found a little money. She crossed over to the boy with the hungry eyes. She could remember the times she and Yuliya had done without so many things. It wasn't until she'd been fully grown that Natashya realized all the sacrifices her older sister had made for her.

'Give this to your mother.' Natashya pressed the money into the little boy's hands. 'Do you understand?'

The boy nodded.

The mother saw Natashya talking to her son and became agitated. Sometimes children disappeared off Moscow's streets and were never heard from again. Rumours and half-truths persisted of black market organ harvesters who took children and young adults to parcel them off to buyers.

Natashya left immediately. Showing her police identification would only have frightened the mother more. Russia was a hard and sad place to live these days.

And it was going to be even worse without Yuliya in it.

'Danilovic's Fabulous Antiquities,' a smooth male voice answered in English, then repeated the greeting in Russian and French. 'How may I be of service?'

'Josef,' Lourds greeted him.

'Thomas!' Josef Danilovic's voice slipped from professional to near-ecstatic. He spoke in English because he treasured his knowledge of the language. 'How are you, my old friend? It has been far too long since I last saw you.'

While sorting out languages on various illuminated manuscripts coming out of Russia, Lourds had come upon several volumes that were of questionable authenticity. None of them were radically outside canon as linguists recognized it, but knowing what was real and what was artifice was often helpful.

Lourds had chanced upon Danilovic while researching some of the illuminated manuscripts in Odessa, where some of them had been acquired. As it turned out, Danilovic had actually sold three of the manuscripts Lourds had been researching to American and British universities.

Over long dinners filled with much storytelling and a few lies thrown in for good measure, Danilovic and Lourds had become friends. Danilovic had also owned up to brokering the forged manuscripts. After all, he'd explained, an antiquity dealer's main task in life was to make sure a buyer felt happy about his or her acquisition. Those acquisitions didn't necessarily have to be authentic.

Danilovic was a genteel rogue. He never robbed anyone at gunpoint, though he dealt with several unsavoury types that did. Only out of necessity, he was careful to point out, but Lourds also knew the man never failed to make a profit.

'I'm doing well,' Lourds said. He watched through the window as Natashya continued her phone conversation. He and Danilovic exchanged pleasantries and a few stories, then Lourds got down to business. 'I'm in a bit of a situation, Josef.'

'Oh?' Danilovic was immediately attentive. 'I've never known you to be in trouble, Thomas.'

'It's not trouble of my own making, I assure you. But it's trouble nonetheless.'

'If there is anything I can do to help, you have but to ask.'

'I'm presently in Moscow,' Lourds said. 'And I need to get out of the country without being found out.'

There was the briefest pause. 'The police are looking for you?'

'Yes. But it's the other people looking for me that I'm more concerned about. I don't know if they've given up trying to find us.'

'Give me an hour or so. Will you be all right till then? Is there anything you need?'

Lourds was touched by the little man's concern. Over the years they had been in and out of each other's lives, but the friendship had been sporadic. Still, they shared a love and knowledge of history that few could equal.

'No. We're fine,' Lourds said.

'Good. Let me have your number and I will call you when everything is ready.'

Lourds gave his number, then added, 'I'm also going to email you some images.'

'Of what?'

'Some things I'd like you to quietly ask around about.' After everything Danilovic was doing for them, Lourds knew he had to include him in the information. He was suddenly aware of how much he was being forced to trust the man, but he was also surprised by how much he was willing to.

'What things?'

Lourds watched as Natashya hung up the phone and left the drug store. She checked the street and crossed back toward the apartment building. 'I'll explain when I see you. Until then, if you can find out any information about these things, I'd be grateful.'

'Take care, my friend. I look forward to seeing you.'

Lourds said goodbye and hung up the phone.

'You can just call someone up and get us out of Moscow, mate?' Gary asked incredulously.

Lourds looked at the younger man. Gary looked stunned. Leslie's eyebrows were arched in surprise.

'I hope so,' Lourds replied. 'But it remains to be seen.'

A knock sounded on the apartment door.

Lourds glanced up from the notebook computer. It was 10.23 p.m. He'd all but given up on Danilovic's escort service.

Gary dozed in a chair with a graphic novel spread across his chest. Leslie sat beside Lourds where she'd been nearly the whole time. She'd worked on her own notebook computer while Lourds had surfed the internet looking for the links Yuliya had mentioned in her notes.

Natashya came from the covered window that looked out over the street. Her hand slid beneath her jacket and emerged with her pistol.

Lourds' mouth went dry as he closed down the computer.

Natashya stood with her back to the wall beside the door. She held the pistol in both hands.

'Who is it?' she asked in Russian.

'I am Plehve. Josef Danilovic sent me.'

The tension wound up inside Lourds. He felt his heart hammering. Leslie laid a hand on his arm as he got to his feet.

'Are you alone?' Natashya asked.

'I am alone,' Plehve replied.

'If you are not,' Natashya told him, 'I will shoot you dead and hope to get anyone behind you.' She opened the door in one move as she levelled the pistol before her.

An old, bent man stood in the doorway. He was dressed in a weathered knee-length coat and held his battered hat in his hands.

'I would really prefer not to be shot,' Plehve said in Russian.

With one hand, Natashya pulled him into the room. He stumbled and almost fell. Natashya manoeuvred him easily. She kept her pistol close to her body so it couldn't be easily snatched away.

'Stand,' Natashya ordered. She switched to English. Lourds assumed that was to keep things orderly among the non-Russian-speaking Britishers.

'Of course.' The old man stood easily and almost carelessly. He gave the appearance that being hauled into rooms in the middle of the night at gunpoint was normal.

Natashya waited on the other side of Plehve. She kept his body between her pistol and the door. After a moment, when no one broke the door down, she lowered her weapon. But she didn't put it away. She nodded.

'May I smoke?' Plehve asked.

'Of course,' Natashya said.

The old man took a pack of cigarettes from beneath his jacket and lit one. He inhaled then released the smoke and waved it away with one hand.

'You're late,' Natashya said.

Plehve grinned. 'Your people are very good at catching individuals who try to bend the law these days. The prison systems can be awfully demanding. And perhaps Josef over-estimated my abilities.'

'Not about getting us out of Russia, I hope?' Natashya asked.

'I can do that,' Plehve answered.

Minutes later, Lourds trailed after the old man. Leslie and Gary followed in Lourds' wake. Natashya brought up the rear.

After arriving back on the street, they crossed to an alley. Plehve had a ten-year-old Russian-made Zil waiting in the shadows. With a flourish, he opened the rear door for Leslie, Gary and Lourds.

Natashya rejected the offer of sitting in the back. She rounded the Zil and got in on the passenger side. Only then did Lourds realize the interior light hadn't come on. Plehve was obviously a careful man.

After everyone was safely inside, Plehve slid behind the wheel and they got under way. Only when they were moving did Lourds release the tense breath he'd been holding. No one spoke until Plehve drove them from the Moscow city limits. The old man kept one hand on the wheel the whole time, while the other was busy with holding cigarette after cigarette. Evidently Plehve wasn't as confident that he could accomplish the transfer as he tried to act. He told them the journey would take almost twenty hours if they drove straight through and didn't stop for anything but fuel and bathroom breaks. Lourds was surprised to discover how tired he was.

But part of it was in reaction to having nothing to do.

For a while, he slept.

'Why do you think my sister contacted the Planck Institute?' Natashya asked. Her eyes burned. She hadn't rested well since Yuliya's murder. She watched Lourds closely. Only a few minutes earlier the man had roused from sleep.

'Yuliya believed the cymbal was probably carried up into Russia, then called Rus, by the Khazars.'

'Who are they?'

'Historians disagree on the actual beginnings of the Khazar people,' Lourds said. 'Some experts link them with the lost tribes of Israel who scattered after the destruction of Israel. The general thinking that's readily accepted today is that the Khazars were Turks. I know a bit about them because I've written a few monographs on the Oghuric tongue.'

Natashya didn't say anything. She knew that Yuliya had regarded Lourds highly. But Natashya also knew that she wasn't educated enough about such matters to know if Lourds was telling the truth or fabricating the story on the spot. So she watched him for signs that he was lying. That was a skill she was quite good at.

'They were part of the Hun culture,' Lourds went on. 'They formed clans and travelled the world in search of trade. Even the name has roots in that endeavour. The term "Khazar" is linked to the Turkish verb *gezer*, which translates almost literally for wandering. They were simply wanderers.'

'My sister was an archaeologist.' Natashya heard the hesitation in her voice when she spoke of Yuliya in the past tense. 'She knew about history. How can you know so much?'

Lourds sipped from his water bottle. 'Linguistics and archaeology overlap to a degree. How much they overlap depends on how deeply the linguist or the archaeologist pursues their knowledge. Yuliya and I pursued it doggedly. We learned constantly. Every day was school.'

Natashya silently agreed with that. There was never a time that she could remember her sister not having a thick book on some dusty subject near to hand.

'You're certain the Khazars didn't make the cymbal?' Natashya asked.

'Fairly certain. Yuliya felt the same way. She believed the Khazars got it from the Yoruba people.'

'Where do they live?'

'West Africa.'

'West Africa is a big place.'

'I know. That's why we're going to the Max Planck Institute. She had asked to see several of their papers.'

That surprised Natashya. 'Yuliya was planning to go to Leipzig?'

'That's what she said in her notes. If possible, she wanted me to accompany her to translate.'

'Why Leipzig? Wouldn't it be simpler to go to West Africa?'

'The documents Yuliya wanted to see are no longer in West Africa. They're being kept in Leipzig. The Max Planck Institute continues to do a lot of research and study into the history of slavery and lost African cultures.'

'Don't they have museums in West Africa? Other places to keep dry, dusty documents?'

Lourds smiled. 'Of course they do.' He took another sip of his drink. 'But they don't have the option of storing all of their history there. Many of the physical artefacts that tell such history are gone.'

From the way his eyes narrowed and he took time to scratch his beard, Natashya knew the professor was taking a moment to assemble his thoughts. Reflecting on him now, she realized that he truly was a striking-looking man. She doubted that her sister cared for Lourds only because of his mind, however fascinating that might be. Of course, Yuliya's faithfulness to her husband was beyond doubt.

'When cultures get destroyed and subjugated the way the West African peoples' were,' Lourds said, 'their history becomes scattered, lost and sometimes rewritten. The museums in West Africa – in Benin, Nigeria, Senegal and the other twelve countries recognized in that region – hold only a small fraction of the material that once existed.'

'The rest was destroyed?'

'Destroyed and lost. Sold and stolen. But mostly lost. The knowledge isn't all gone. A lot of the peoples in the region keep their culture alive orally. They tell tales that have been handed down through generations of people. Many of those, sad to say, are gone for ever. But bits and pieces of the cultural tradition of the region were bought by collectors. Much is in the hands of private collectors and museums all over the world. You never know where a piece of it might turn up. Like that cymbal.'

'You haven't said why Yuliya believed the Khazars brought the cymbal north into Russia,' Natashya pointed out.

Lourds took out his computer and opened it. He tapped the keys in quick syncopation. Immediately afterwards, a picture of old-looking coins opened up on the screen.

'What are those?' Natashya found herself growing more interested.

'Those,' Lourds said, 'were found at the same time the cymbal was. They were taken from the same site excavation. Stratigraphal comparisons indicated that they were left there at the same time.'

'"Left"?'

'That was Yuliya's guess. According to the site notes left by the archaeological team that uncovered the artefacts, the cymbal and coins were found together.'

'Why would they be left behind?'

'I can only hazard a guess, but I agree with what Yuliya surmised. Whoever left the cymbal and the coins was attempting to hide them so they wouldn't be taken.'

Natashya turned that over in her mind. The possibility that the cymbal had been sought hundreds of years ago intrigued her. Just as it was being sought now. Who would know about something that had been lost for so long? Who would remember it over the vast amounts of time since it had been hidden, and would chase it now?

'These coins are what convinced Yuliya that the Khazars carried the cymbal north into Rus,' Lourds went on. 'The coins are called *yarmaqs*. The Khazars minted them. They were so uniform and pure that they were used in trade throughout Rus, Europe and China.'

Natashya peered at the coins in the digital image. A man lying on a litter showed on one side of the coin. Yuliya had also captured images of the obverse. That showed a structure that looked like a temple or perhaps a meeting hall.

'So we're going to Leipzig to find out why the Khazars were carrying the cymbal into Rus?' Leslie asked. She'd evidently awakened some time during the discussion.

'Not exactly,' Lourds answered. 'We're going to Leipzig to search for documentation about the cymbal. Since the language on the cymbal, part of it at least, contains Yoruban writing, I hope that we can find some clue of where the cymbal came from. Discovering how and why the Khazars came by it would be a bonus.'

Cardinal Stefano Murani's Quarters
Status Civitatis Vaticanae
22 August 2009

The knock on the door woke Cardinal Murani. Fatigue held him in its thrall. He felt like he'd been drugged. He still lay abed in pyjamas. One of the heavy tomes he'd been studying lay in his lap.

'Cardinal Murani,' a young man's voice called.

'Yes, Vincent,' Murani replied in a hoarse voice. Vincent was his personal valet. 'Come in.'

Vincent opened the bedroom door and entered the room. He was little more than five feet tall and thin as a rake. As a result, his head looked too large for his body. He wore an ill-fitting dark suit and had his hair neatly parted.

'You weren't at breakfast, Cardinal,' Vincent said. He didn't look Murani in the eye. Vincent never looked anyone in the eye.

'I don't feel well this morning,' Murani said.

'I'm sorry to hear that. Would you like to have breakfast brought to you?'

'Yes. See to it.'

Vincent nodded and excused himself from the room.

Murani knew the young man didn't believe him, but he also didn't care. Vincent was the least of his concerns. The man was his vassal, totally under his control. Vincent had seen Murani call in sick several times over the last few weeks.

Sitting up, Murani reached for the phone and rang his personal secretary. He gave orders to cancel his appointments and the lunch he'd scheduled with one of the Pope's yes-men.

Clearing the day to work on the secrets hidden within the bell and cymbal felt good. He switched the television on and watched CNN. There was no mention of the dig at Cadiz, but Murani knew there would be in short order. The dig had taken over the news like the sudden death of some drug-addicted starlet.

He got up, intending to shower before breakfast, when his cellphone rang. He answered and recognized Gallardo's voice at once.

'Things haven't gone well,' Gallardo said without preamble. 'We lost the package.'

Murani easily read between the lines. 'What happened?'

'We followed the package to the state university here,' Gallardo said.

'Why did he – it – go there?'

'There was another package waiting. He got it.'

Murani's heart thudded. *Another package?* 'What was in the other package?'

'We don't know.'

'How did he know the package was there?'

'We don't know that either. But we do know we were followed. And we do know that the person who followed us is now there with the package. What we don't know is why.'

Black anger stole over Murani. On the television

CNN had started spinning the story about Father Sebastian's dig at Cadiz again. Murani knew time was working against him now. Every moment was precious.

'I don't pay you not to know things,' Murani said coldly.

'I'm aware of that. But you don't pay me well enough to take the risks I'm taking now.'

That declaration was a shot fired across Murani's bows and the cardinal knew it. This far into the search for the instruments, there wasn't anyone else he could call in on such short notice, much less anyone of Gallardo's calibre, and with his connections. He made himself breathe out and remain calm.

'Can you retrieve the packages?'

Gallardo was silent for a moment. Then he said, 'For the right price, we can try.'

'Then do so,' Murani replied.

I I

Tension gnawed at Cardinal Murani's stomach and flayed his nerves as he sat outside the Pope's study. The chair was comfortable despite the ornamentation. He occasionally flipped the pages of a book on Eastern European history, but he didn't read. His mind was too jumbled for that.

He glanced at his watch and found it was 8.13 a.m. The time was only three minutes after he'd looked at it last time. He reached to turn a page and found that his hand trembled slightly. The tremor seized his attention. He studied it with bright interest.

Fear? he wondered. *Or anticipation?* He didn't know why the Pope had called this meeting.

He flexed his fist and willed his hand to be still. It became so. He smiled at his control over himself. In the end, that was all that really mattered.

The door to the Pope's study opened. A young priest stepped from within and looked at Murani.

'Cardinal Murani?' the young priest asked.

At first Murani thought the priest was being impudent by having to ask his name. After all, he was known throughout the Vatican. Then Murani realized that he didn't know the man. Of course, that was acceptable. Murani didn't trouble himself to learn the names of priests unless they aided him or offended him.

'Yes,' Murani answered.

The young priest nodded and waved toward the study. 'His Holiness will see you now.'

Murani placed the book back into the leather bag he carried. Then he stood. 'Of course he will,' he said. But he wished he felt more confident.

'Good morning, Cardinal Murani.' Pope Innocent XIV waved a hand at one of the plush chairs before his huge desk. The polished surface reflected the opulence of the room. 'I trust I didn't keep you waiting overly long.'

'Of course not, Your Holiness.' Murani knew no other answer was permitted. He approached the Pope.

Pope Innocent XIV looked good for a man in his early seventies. His spare frame held no extra flesh and his blue eyes gazed clearly. He had a hawk's beak for a face, pulled out behind his large, long nose. Years of poring over arcane texts had left his head slightly sunken between his shoulder blades. The overall effect was that of a predatory bird. His white robes resembled a dove's plumage, but Murani knew that image was misleading. There wasn't anything gentle about the Pope.

Before he had been elected to the papacy by the Sacred College of Cardinals, Wilhelm Weierstrass had been a librarian within that body. Prior to that he had been a bishop with an undistinguished career. And, Murani felt certain, his years as pope were going to be equally undistinguished. He would change nothing, lead nothing, and – in the end – accomplish nothing toward reaffirming the Church's place in the world. Murani hadn't voted for the man.

'I've been told you're feeling better,' the Pope said.

'I am, Your Holiness.' Murani briefly knelt and kissed the Fisherman's Ring on the Pope's finger before sitting. Gazing around the room, Murani took note of the two pontifical Swiss guardsmen inside the room. They stood at attention on either side of the Pope.

The pontifical Swiss Guard had been created in 1506 by Pope Julius II, but Popes Sixtus IV and Innocent VIII had provided the groundwork for recruiting the mercenaries for protection. To date the pontifical Swiss Guard was the only such unit still in existence. They'd begun as an offshoot of the regular Swiss mercenary army that had placed soldiers throughout Europe.

Although the Swiss Guard still wore their traditional red, blue, yellow and orange uniforms during special occasions, most often they were dressed as they were now in solid blue uniforms, a white collar, brown belt and black beret. The ones in the Pope's chambers also carried SIG P75 semi-automatic pistols. The sergeant carried a Heckler & Koch submachine pistol. The weapons had been integrated into the bodyguards' armament after Pope John Paul II had nearly been assassinated.

Murani placed his elbows on the chair arms and rested his fingers under his chin. He didn't feel comfortable in the Pope's chambers, but he strove to give the appearance of being so.

'You've been sick for a few days,' the Pope said.

Murani nodded.

'I was wondering if perhaps you might think it was time to seek a physician's attention.'

For a moment Murani was puzzled. Then he realized that Innocent XIV was actually pointing out the fact that throughout his continued 'illness' he hadn't once been to a doctor. It was an oversight. Murani promised himself that he would be more careful in the future.

'I think it was just a bout of the flu, Your Holiness. It was nothing to trouble a physician with.'

The Pope nodded. 'Still, this . . . flu has claimed a number of days from your work.'

A heavy and oppressive silence rang throughout the room. Murani knew that the Pope didn't believe him.

'Yes, Your Holiness. Thankfully I have many more years to give in my service to God.'

'It also comes to my attention that you've taken an inordinate interest in Father Sebastian's work in Spain.'

'The world seems to have taken an inordinate interest in Father Sebastian's effort,' Murani countered. 'The dig at Cadiz has captured the attention of everyone.'

'That is, perhaps, unfortunate. I feel the world

would be better served if it turned its attention to other pursuits.'

Murani knew that the Pope wasn't overly concerned with the attention of the world. It was Murani's attention that the Pope was addressing.

'Surely only another two or three days will pass before an incident in the Middle East, the economy, or the death of a celebrity will seize their attention,' Murani said.

'I wouldn't wish for any of those things to happen,' the Pope said.

Anger stirred within Murani and he barely restrained it. *No,* he thought fiercely, *you wouldn't have anything happen if that was under your control. You would simply fill the office of pope and churn out more of the emptiness the Church has suffered for the last several Popes.*

He made himself breathe calmly, but his rage was a rock in his chest that threatened to break free. Innocent XIV was merely one more cancer that thrived on the Church and leeched away her strength.

'I know you have a great many things to do, Cardinal Murani.' The Pope flicked his gaze to the appointment book on the desk before him. 'You and I haven't had a chance to talk for some time. I thought it was best if we became reacquainted.'

'Of course, Your Holiness.' Murani knew he was being put on notice. The Pope was watching. The message – and the implicit threat – were clear.

'You've been remiss in your duties, Stefano.'

Murani looked at the older man seated across from

him at the small, elegant table. Murani snapped a breadstick and kept silent.

Cardinal Giuseppe Rezzonico was in his early sixties. His white hair was carefully combed and he was attractive enough to draw the attention of several women at nearby tables. Tall and thick through the middle these days, he still radiated power. He had come to service in the Church at a late age, but had risen quickly among the scholars till he achieved a position within the Sacred College of Cardinals. Like Murani, he wore a dark blue business suit.

Staring at the man, Murani shook his head. 'And what duties would those be?'

'The duties of your office, Stefano,' Rezzonico replied. 'Calling in. Cancelling the appointments you were assigned on behalf of the Church. Those things are red flags to our present Pope.'

'*Your* Pope,' Murani said sourly.

Rezzonico frowned. 'Everyone is aware that you didn't vote for His Holiness.'

'No, I didn't.' Murani placed his breadstick aside.

'I'm quite sure the Pope knows that too.'

'Do you think he's being vindictive, then?'

'No.' Rezzonico shook his head. 'His Holiness wouldn't succumb to that.'

'So you've already placed him next to godliness, have you?' Murani found that interesting. Rezzonico normally didn't get taken in quite so easily. 'He's still just a man, you know. Despite the office and vestments.'

Rezzonico's frown deepened. 'That's sacrilege.'

'It's the truth.' Murani wouldn't let it go. He'd had to be embarrassed before Innocent XIV this morning; he wasn't going to allow himself to be bribed with a good meal and a kind word. 'He's short-sighted and you know it. He continues to entertain talks with the Jews and the Muslims.'

'Of course he does,' Rezzonico said reasonably. 'The things that happen in those places affect the rest of the world. All economies are tied too closely today for it to be otherwise.'

'Would you listen to yourself?' Murani shook his head. 'The *economies*? That's what the Church is about these days? *Economies*?'

The older man leaned back and regrouped. 'You swore an allegiance to the Pope.'

'I swore an allegiance to God,' Murani said harshly. The anger and frustration were loose in him now. He was unable to stop himself. 'That supersedes any oaths of fealty I might make to *anyone* else.'

'You're treading on dangerous ground.'

A young female server brought out salads and more wine. They ceased talking till after she'd gone.

'We're all treading on dangerous ground these days.' Murani had himself under better control.

Rezzonico's eyebrows shot up. 'Because of Father Sebastian's excavation?' He shook his head. 'We don't yet know if anything will come of that.'

'And if something does? If Father Sebastian does find something? Even if it's not the book, what if it's something else that points to the secret texts?'

'Then we will deal with it.'

Murani scoffed. 'Dealing with something after it's happened is worthless.'

Rezzonico said sharply, 'Stefano, please listen to me. I'm your friend. Everything is under control.'

Murani refused to believe that. 'Everything is not under control.' He wanted to tell Rezzonico about the bell and the cymbal, and what he thought they might be. But he couldn't. Rezzonico was part of the Society of Quirinus, and Murani didn't trust them not to take everything away from him. That was something he couldn't bear.

For a moment Rezzonico just looked at him. 'We control the Swiss Guard. They've got members at the dig site. Should Father Sebastian find something – *anything* – they have orders to step in and seize it.'

Murani knew that. He'd helped arrange that negotiation. Thankfully, after all their years of service, many of the leaders within the Swiss Guard maintained the same core beliefs as the Society of Quirinus. For both those bodies, the preservation of the Church was of the utmost importance. Lives would be taken and lies would be told to get that job done.

Father Sebastian's effort endangered the Swiss Guard as much as it did the Church. Their leader, Commander Karl Pulver, recognized the threat of the secret texts as well, though he was not knowledgeable about what they contained.

'Something more should be done,' Murani said.

Wariness entered Rezzonico's eyes. 'Like what?'

'Father Sebastian is the Pope's picked man. He's not one of us.'

'But that's even better,' Rezzonico said. 'If Sebastian should find something, he won't recognize it for what it is. Only those of us know what the secret texts are.'

'The Pope thinks he knows.'

Rezzonico waved the comment away. 'The Pope only knows what we told him. Even then he lacks our understanding.'

Murani shook his head. 'That's not enough. We need to control that site. Without any interlopers involved. To do that, we need to be in charge of it.'

'The Pope chose Father Sebastian. The man was clearly a good choice. His field is archaeology. Of us all —'

'He's the least reliable.' Murani hardened his voice. 'He was out in the secular world for a long time before he came to the Church.'

Rezzonico's face darkened. 'We could take steps to correct the situation.'

Murani's voice softened, 'Other priests and cardinals could have taken charge of that dig site.'

Rezzonico smiled. 'Like you, perhaps?'

Murani didn't even try to feign modesty. 'Yes. I would have been the perfect choice.'

'Why you?'

'Because since my earliest days I have given my life to the Church. I believe in the power of the papacy. The Church needs to take her proper place in the world. The Church has become weaker and weaker, for example, the loss of the Latin Mass as well as the talks with the other religions and countries.

The papacy has conducted their office since Vatican II like they're heads of state –'

'Which they have been,' Rezzonico pointed out.

'And treated other nations and religions as if they were equals.' Murani's voice hardened. '*No one* is the equal of the Church. We were put here by God Himself to shepherd the people He has given us to care for. We're supposed to guide and shape their lives. We can't do that when we constantly give up the power and prestige that makes us God's chosen instruments.'

Rezzonico took a quick breath and let it out. He hesitated. 'All the points you make are valid.'

'I know that they are.'

'But . . .'

Murani overrode the other man. 'Don't keep saying *but*. The Church is sacrosanct. It is, and should be, the ultimate power here on earth. And any objects that control that kind of power belong to the Church. Sacred artefacts are ours by right and by the grace of God Himself.'

'The world is a different place, Stefano,' Rezzonico said softly. 'We have to move with more care and deliberation these days.'

'We're talking about books and artefacts capable of ending this world and launching a new one,' Murani said. 'They've been buried for untold years, and they're about to re-emerge.'

'Only if we're correct about the dig.'

'Do you doubt?'

'It has yet to be proven.'

Murani leaned back in his chair in disgust. 'You need to have faith.'

For the first time, Rezzonico's glance turned to ice. 'Don't forget yourself, Stefano. You've ridden roughshod over other lesser priests and cardinals, but I'm here at the behest of the Society.'

That announcement took Murani back a little. However, he'd expected as much. Despite his over-tures toward autocracy and independence, Rezzonico often served as a lapdog for the more senior members among the Society of Quirinus.

Murani counted to ten and marshalled his reserve control. 'We wouldn't be in this shape if the selection of the Pope had gone differently.'

'Spilled milk,' Rezzonico said.

The Sacred College of Cardinals had been split in their decision. Each faction had picked one from among their number. The two who *should* have become Pope, men already entrusted with the divine duty to protect the world from the secret texts, were left bereft of enough votes to win. A third faction, seeking to further their own aims, had suggested Wilhelm Weierstrass as an alternative. In the end, because of the split, the new pope to take office knew nothing of the secret texts.

In fact, Murani wasn't certain Pope Innocent XIV even believed in the secret texts after he'd been told about them. The man had listened to everyone, but kept his own counsel until he'd chosen to send Father Sebastian to take command of the dig. That had, in Murani's estimation at least, spoken volumes.

'You're right,' Murani said.

Rezzonico studied him for a moment. Then he said, 'Everything is in order, Stefano. You'll see. What the Society would like you to do is keep a low profile. The Pope's trust in us is a fragile thing. Especially now. If he'd come to power at another time, we might have been more certain of our influence over him.'

Murani quietly disagreed. Wilhelm Weierstrass had been left amid his books in the libraries far too long. The man had opinions about everything. And he didn't hesitate to use the power of his office. He'd shown that by choosing Father Sebastian over the other candidates the Society of Quirinus had put forth. And he'd shown it again by putting Murani on the carpet this morning. In fact, Murani realized, it had been more a warning to the whole Society of Quirinus not just to him. Suddenly seeing that, Murani realized as well that things were in direr straits than he'd thought.

'Fret not, Stefano,' Rezzonico said. 'You have many friends among the Society of Quirinus. I hope you continue to count me as one of them. I have only your best interests at heart. We are in this together. You must be more patient.'

'I know.' Murani sipped his wine. 'But this is the closest we have been to the secret texts.'

Rezzonico nodded. 'Everyone is aware of that. Everything is in place. Nothing can happen that we don't control.'

That might be true, Murani thought, but none of

them were prepared to use those texts. The Society of Quirinus controlled a great many secrets. Over the years, they'd quietly and brutally killed those who had stood against them or had tried to reveal the secrets they hid.

They weren't afraid to get blood on their hands. Neither was Murani.

Seventh-Kilometre Market
Outside Odessa, Ukraine
23 August 2009

'Where did this place come from?' Leslie asked.

Lourds had to smile at the young woman's naivety. For all that she was a 'worldly' television journalist – and probably well-travelled in her own right – the world remained a big, unimagined place for her. She hadn't seen as much of it as she'd believed.

The Seventh-Kilometre Market was a raging circus of black marketing slavishly devoted to capitalism. The market covered nearly two hundred acres and was filled with steel shipping containers made over into buildings. Narrow streets filled with people meandered between them. The containers came from all over the world. They ranged from twenty feet long to monster sizes coming in at fifty-three feet. Merchants warehoused their goods in the containers and often lived in them. The containers were new and old, and every colour of the rainbow. Most of them had been added to and connected. They looked like small metal buildings with advertising and side-walks, sometimes stacked to two- and three-storeys. Cars and trucks backed up to the front of them to load and off-load. Voices rang out everywhere in a multitude of languages. Mounted lights at intervals along the 'streets' made certain darkness wouldn't stop the sales.

Lourds was tired and cramped from riding in a car for something under twenty-six hours. But he couldn't help rising to the chance to be both a tour guide and an educator. The old man who had brought them had turned back toward Moscow immediately.

'Welcome to Seventh-Kilometre Market.' Lourds waved at the complex maze of shipping containers. 'The original market was located inside Odessa city limits, but when capitalism invaded the area after the fall of the Berlin Wall in 1989, more merchants set up shop.'

'This is incredible,' Leslie said.

Gary took footage with the mini-cam.

'Be careful with the camera,' Natashya ordered.

'Why?' Gary placed the camera back into the protective case hanging from one shoulder. 'Don't they allow tourist pictures?'

'They do,' Lourds said, 'but several of the merchants in the marketplace aren't legitimate.'

'Many of them are wanted by police and intelligence communities of different countries,' Natashya said. She remained watchful. Despite the day spent travelling, she still appeared rested and ready to go. 'If one of those men thinks that you've been sent here to spy on them, they could try to slit our throats.'

'Oh.' Gary definitely didn't look pleased with that possibility.

'When the market began to grow inside Odessa, it was ordered out of the city,' Lourds said. 'It simply became too successful. It relocated here: seven kilometres outside Odessa.'

'Hence the name,' Leslie said.

'Exactly.' Lourds took the lead. They passed containers offering Asian electronics and tourist goods as well as counterfeit high-end Western products. 'Over six thousand shops here rent space, paying thousands of dollars a month. Renting space alone is a huge money-maker, but the sales exceed twenty million in US dollars.'

'Twenty million a year?' Leslie asked.

Lourds smiled at her. 'Twenty million dollars a day.'

Leslie stopped at a four-way intersection and glanced in all directions. People choked the passageways and stood haggling with merchants.

'Efforts were made to shut the market down after it started growing,' Lourds said. 'By then it was too late. It had taken on a life of its own. It continues to grow. But Russia would still like to shut this place down. Merchants and buyers would take up arms to prevent that.'

'Why would anyone want to shut it down?'

'Because they can't control it.'

'Why would they want to control it?'

'For taxation purposes.'

'These are all untaxed goods?' Leslie stopped in

front of a container that advertised Italian hand-bags. 'Twenty million dollars a day, and it's all untaxed?'

'Yes. Basically what you're looking at is Europe's largest marketplace. Interestingly enough, it's also a smuggler's den. You'll find legitimate goods, counter-feit goods and illegal products – munitions and drugs – all here for sale. The businesses simply operate in the open because no one can stop them.'

Leslie examined one of the handbags sitting on a small table. Women, Lourds knew, couldn't pass up bargains although he sincerely doubted anything bought off that table would be a bargain.

'We don't have time to shop,' Natashya said.

Reluctantly, Leslie returned the handbag.

'Where are we supposed to meet your friend?' Natashya asked.

'It's not far,' Lourds replied.

An hour later, Lourds stood nursing a cup of Turkish coffee in front of a shop advertising American jeans for sale. Leslie had immediately dismissed them as knockoffs. Lourds wouldn't have known. Gary passed the time filming bits and pieces of different shops, and even had Leslie doing lead-ins and closings for a proposal they were going to do for the BBC.

'Are you certain your friend is going to be here?' Natashya asked in Russian.

'Josef said he would be here,' Lourds replied in English. He didn't want Leslie and Gary to feel shut out of the conversation.

Another uncomfortable minute passed. It slowly stretched into five more.

Natashya moved to stand in front of Lourds. For an instant he thought she was going to take umbrage with him over their situation, but her attention was focused on a young man who was approaching them. Her hand was in her coat pocket. There was no doubt about the young man's destination. He stopped a few feet away. Both his hands were in his pockets. Lourds knew what he had his hands on. The man's eyes never left Natashya's and Lourds figured that was because the man had assessed her as the most dangerous among them.

'Professor Lourds.' The young man's English was impeccable.

'Yes.'

'Josef Danilovic sent me.'

'Do you have any proof?' Natashya demanded.

The young man grinned and shrugged. 'This isn't a place for proving things. Nor is it a place for police. I come to offer you a way out of the city. It's your choice whether you follow me.'

Lourds' phone rang. He answered it. The battery charge was almost exhausted. 'Hello.'

'Thomas,' Danilovic greeted him in a jovial voice that betrayed a little tension.

'Hello, Josef. I think you've just met your intermediary.'

'His name is Viktor,' Danilovic said. 'You can trust him.'

Lourds knew the young man was expecting the

call. Viktor remained totally relaxed. Natashya hadn't let her guard down.

'Perhaps you could describe him,' Lourds suggested. 'We tend toward a little paranoia at this end these days.'

'Certainly. These are very paranoid times.' Danilovic provided a good description.

'Thank you, Josef. I hope to see you soon.' Lourds ended the call.

'Is this him?' Natashya asked.

'Yes. Josef described him. Including what he was wearing.'

Viktor grinned. 'Of course, I could have an associate who's holding a gun to your friend's head. I mean, if you want to follow your paranoid tendencies. But if you do, I doubt you'll ever leave here.'

Lourds gathered his backpack and slung it over one shoulder. 'Let's go.'

'You've outdone yourself this time, old friend.' Lourds congratulated Danilovic. He was referring to the table laden with food that sat in the large dining room of Danilovic's home. Lourds had been there on several occasions as a guest and was used to the luxury with which Danilovic furnished his home. An ornate dining room and chairs that could have graced a royal's home occupied the centre of the room. The walls were covered with paintings while vases and other collectibles filled in the gaps.

Danilovic waved the compliment away. He was a small, fastidious man with a thin moustache. He wore his expensive suit with confidence and pride.

'I figured if I were going to effect an escape from Moscow for you, then it should be one of great style, yes?' Danilovic's wide smile revealed a gap between his teeth. He held his forefinger and thumb a small distance apart. 'And, perhaps, with just a hint of danger.'

'I'll take a pass on the danger if you don't mind,' Lourds said ruefully. 'In my opinion we've had quite enough of it in the last few days.'

The table even had name cards to designate the seating arrangement. Lourds and Danilovic occupied the ends. With no real surprise, Lourds noted that Danilovic positioned the two women at his end of the table.

White-bloused servers poured wine, then the chef came out to announce the menu. Despite the tension that was on the face of everyone at the table, Lourds saw that all of them listened to the chef raptly.

'I thought perhaps French cuisine might be in order,' the chef said. 'We will begin with a nice salad then *escargots de Bourgogne* with parsley butter, *boeuf bourguignon* – beef stewed in red wine – *fondue bourguignonne, gougère* and *pochouse*, which is one of my specialties.' He clicked his heels and returned to the kitchen.

'I don't know what he said,' Gary told them, 'but it sounded great.'

'Auguste is an excellent chef,' Danilovic replied. 'I borrowed him from one of the restaurants for the evening.'

'You didn't have to go to all this trouble,' Lourds protested.

'I know,' Danilovic said. 'For you, you would have been satisfied with a sandwich and a beer. But for the ladies' – he glanced at Natashya and Leslie – 'I was most eager to impress them.'

'I'm dutifully impressed,' Leslie said.

'Thank you, my dear.' Danilovic picked up her hand and kissed it.

You old ham, Lourds thought, but he couldn't help but smile at his friend's antics. Danilovic was one of the most social men Lourds knew. He enjoyed putting on a show and being at the centre of it.

Dinner followed in short order. A zesty, crisp salad, then escargots baked in their shells. Gary baulked at the snails and wouldn't eat them. Lourds thought the parsley butter was the best he'd ever had and sent word back to the chef. The fondue had pieces of beef that rounded out the flavour and made it even more tasty. The gougère were cheese balls rolled in choux pastry. But the crowning achievement was the *pochouse*, fish stewed in red wine. Desert was a strawberry and mascarpone cream tart that melted in the mouth.

Later, they gathered in Danilovic's den in front of a fire that staved off the outside chill of the night. Lourds and Danilovic fired up cigars, and both were surprised when Natashya agreed to smoke one as well. They drank brandy from large glasses.

'You don't know these men who are pursuing you?' Danilovic asked.

Lourds shook his head. 'I think I recognized some of them from Alexandria.'

'So you think they are on the same trail as you?'

'It's the only answer.' Lourds had settled into a deep easy chair that he found entirely too comfortable. 'There's no reason for them to be interested in me.'

Danilovic leaned forward and patted Lourds on the knee. 'I've always found you interesting, my dear Professor.'

'You're drunk,' Lourds accused.

'Perhaps a little.' Danilovic looked at Leslie. 'But perhaps it was not you, my friend. Perhaps it was our television star.'

'I'm no star,' Leslie said. 'And I don't know anything about history or language or artefacts.'

'You know that they all go together,' Danilovic said. 'Most people don't know that.' He tapped ash into an ashtray as he gazed at her speculatively. 'Yet you found the bell in Alexandria.'

'That was quite by accident.'

Danilovic shrugged. 'I tend to be a man of faith, dear lady, though I am in a profession that some might feel descried that. These other men, the ones who pursue you, were already looking for this bell — or at least something similar — otherwise they wouldn't have come for it.'

'We can work out who is chasing you,' Natashya stated quietly, 'by identifying them and by knowing more about why they want the instruments. We know about the instruments themselves.'

Danilovic smiled beatifically. 'Yes. You see, my friend, whenever I sell a piece that has come into my possession, I have to know who I'm getting it from, who I'm selling it to, and enough about the item to know what makes it valuable to both. Why are you so interested in these items?'

'Because of the language,' Lourds answered immediately.

'That's your value, but few people would be interested in a dead language that might take years to unravel.'

'I don't think it will take that long,' Lourds said. 'If I can figure out what the instruments pertain to, I should be able to make an educated guess and back that up with facts.'

Danilovic patted Lourds on the shoulder. 'I'm sure that you will. However, the materials those instruments are made of are basically worthless. Not gold or silver. Not encrusted with gems. Plain things. With secrets written on them.'

'But maybe the people who swiped those instruments already know what's written on them,' Gary said. He leaned forward excitedly. 'At least, maybe they know whatever's supposed to be written on them. Like a treasure map or something.'

Lourds considered that. 'The people who took the instruments know what they're looking for. They just don't have what's written on the instruments.'

'So where did their knowledge come from?' Leslie asked.

'That's one of the questions you should be asking,' Danilovic said. 'By asking that, you've already narrowed the field of who might be chasing you.'

'And why are they still after us?' Gary asked.

'For two reasons,' Natashya announced quietly. 'One is that they're afraid Professor Lourds will crack the language and possibly expose the secrets they're protecting. And the other is that Professor Lourds has been, by luck or by design, in touch with two of the instruments they're searching for.'

'We're going to have to be off to Leipzig as quickly as we can, old friend,' Lourds said to Danilovic.

'And quit my hospitality so soon?' Danilovic looked surprised.

'If it were for any other reason . . .'

Danilovic held up a hand and smiled. 'I take no slight. I understand your pressing need. The matter has already been arranged. Viktor will take you to a ship in the morning that I've secured passage on for you.'

'Thank you,' Lourds said.

'For tonight, we should enjoy what's left of this fine brandy and talk of old times.'

I 2

'Where are you, Natashya?' Ivan Chernovsky sounded calm, but Natashya knew from long association that the man was anything but those things.

'In Illichivsk.' Natashya didn't lie. She thought perhaps he would recognize her lies as easily as she recognized his.

The port area was jammed with business and trade. Twelve miles south-west of Odessa proper and the second largest warm-water seaport in the *oblast*, Illichivsk had sprung up around the port as the home of the Black Sea Shipping Company. Ships of all sizes were anchored at the docks or moved slowly through the waters. Longshoremen moved freight onto and off the cargo ships.

'What are you doing there?' Chernovsky asked.

'I'm looking for my sister's murderer. I called hoping you could help me.'

'Forensics found an old bullet in the man's body,' Chernovsky said. 'Evidently he'd been shot at some point and hadn't had access to a medical facility. The wound eventually healed, but the bullet remained.'

'You identified the bullet the way we did when we worked the Karpov murder?' Natashya said.

'Yes. The bullet belonged to the weapon we took off a mafia enforcer,' Chernovsky continued. 'Once the bullet was identified, I went to see this man.'

Natashya kept her gaze roving. Leslie had returned to Lourds and Gary. But another man stood only a few metres away.

The man was slovenly. He wore a cap pulled low over his eyes and a checked lightweight jacket. A casual observer might have mistaken him for a dock worker. Natashya noted the good boots he wore and knew that he wasn't used to working on the dock even though he'd dressed for it. Chernovsky had taught her to watch people's shoes. They often changed their clothing before or after an illegal activity, but they seldom changed their shoes.

Standing against a container awaiting loading, the man occasionally nodded to other dock hands and sipped from a Styrofoam cup. He also spoke on a cellphone. Not many of the longshoremen could afford to carry a cellphone.

'This man identified the dead man as part of a crew that attempted to steal a load of illegal Iraqi antiques that came in during the American war. I talked with some of the street dealers that traffic in such things. I also flashed the dead man's picture. His name was Yuri Kartsev.'

'His name means nothing to me.' Natashya knew Chernovsky was waiting for a response.

'Perhaps it might to the professor.'

'I'll ask him.' She also knew that was Chernovsky's way of confirming they were still travelling together.

'This Kartsev was known to work with a man named . . .' pages rustled as Chernovsky checked his notes '. . . Gallardo. Patrizio Gallardo.'

'I don't know that name either.'

'Well, that name comes with a history.' Chernovsky took a deep breath.

The man watching Lourds and his group put his phone back into his pocket and lit a cigarette. Natashya's stomach unclenched a little at that. Whoever he was waiting for wasn't yet in the area.

Natashya watched the watcher but spoke quickly to Chernovsky. 'I know you want to keep me hanging on as long as you can, Ivan. If I were in your shoes I'd do the same thing. The problem is that we are exposed. And I think that the men chasing us are closing in even as we speak. So perhaps you could tell me what you know.'

Chernovsky hesitated. Natashya suspected their supervisor might even be listening to the phone call.

'Patrizio Gallardo is a very bad man, Natashya,' Chernovsky said. 'He's a thief and a killer. Not a man to trust.'

'Does he work for himself or someone else?'

'Both. He does piece work. He specializes in illegal antique acquisitions.'

'Who does he work for?'

'He owes no allegiance that I have discovered yet. I will keep looking.'

'Please,' Natashya said. 'I will be in touch again when I am able.'

'Where should I expect you to call from next?'

'I will let you know. We're going to be moving a lot. Thank you, Ivan.'

'Keep yourself safe, Natashya. I would like to see you home again soon.'

Natashya cradled the phone and headed across the street. It was time to do something about the watcher.

Patrizio Gallardo bulled through the port as he folded and pocketed his cellphone. He picked up the pace as he spotted the freighter *Carolina Moon* lying at anchorage about three hundred metres away.

According to his informant's report, Lourds and his party were nearby.

Four of his men walked with him. All of them had weapons tucked beneath their coats.

A police car pulled into the street beside Gallardo. Two uniformed policemen sat up front. A man in plainclothes sat in the back.

Gallardo's personal radar for policemen jangled. Instinctively, he turned towards a side street. They'd left a hell of a mess in Moscow and he had to wonder if it was coming back to haunt him.

Brakes squeaked out on the street. A motor changed pitch.

'The police car is coming after us,' one of the men said.

'Break off,' Gallardo directed. 'Cover me if they pick me up.' He kept walking but listened intently as the tyres of the approaching car crunched across loose gravel.

A voice addressed Gallardo in Russian. He ignored it. A lot of the sailors who came to the port didn't speak Russian.

'Sir,' a man called out in English this time.

Gallardo continued without pause. Some sailors didn't speak English.

Car doors opened. Footsteps ran after him.

Calmly, Gallardo reached through the opening in his coat pocket for the 9mm pistol holstered on his hip. If the police were looking for him, they weren't just going to ask him a few questions.

A hand fell onto his shoulder.

'Sir,' the policeman said.

Gallardo stopped suddenly and turned. The movement caught the policeman off guard. Gallardo had his pistol against the policeman's stomach before the man knew what was going on. Holding his left hand behind the man's head so he could use him as a shield, Gallardo fired three times in quick succession. He would have fired at least one more time, but the pistol's action jammed on the folds of the coat.

The harsh *cracks* of the pistol filled the alley.

The policeman staggered and slumped against Gallardo. The young man's features went wide with shock.

The plainclothes inspector and the policeman tried to get out of the car with their weapons drawn. DiBenedetto walked up behind the police inspector almost casually, put a pistol to the back of the man's head and blew his brains out. Realizing the danger he was in, the driver tried to turn around. DiBenedetto shot the policeman in the face twice and kicked him to the ground.

When Gallardo pushed the dead man away from him, the corpse hit the ground. A rectangle of plastic on the man's left sleeve caught Gallardo's eyes. He knelt for a closer look.

The rectangle contained a photograph of him. It was the same kind of set-up they'd used to get the Russian professor.

'Patrizio,' DiBenedetto called. He held up the plainclothes inspector's arm. Blood covered much of it, but the plastic rectangle was visible.

They knew who he was.

Cold realization twisted in Gallardo's stomach. He didn't know how they had identified him. He'd been careful most of his life, but the police had jailed him a couple of times.

He dropped the dead man's arm and stood. He opened his coat and freed the pistol. Working quickly, he slipped the magazine free and replaced the spent cartridges.

'We have to get out of here,' DiBenedetto said. 'The shots will draw more police, and they're already searching for you.'

Gallardo nodded and pushed his breath out. 'I know. Let's see if we can find the professor first.'

'Where's Natashya?' Leslie asked.

Turning his attention from the big ships out in the

harbour, Lourds looked at the small store where Natashya had been standing only moments ago. She wasn't there now.

'She was at the phone,' Gary said. He'd been filming the harbour.

'Well she's not there now.' Leslie looked at her watch. 'When are we supposed to meet the ship's captain?'

'At ten thirty,' Viktor said. He looked calm and confident.

Worry gnawed at Lourds' thoughts. If Natashya had a clue to her sister's killers, would she tell them? Or would she simply act and leave them? He was pretty sure she would act independently. Natashya obviously didn't care about the history involved.

'There she is,' Gary said. He pointed at a building just across the street.

Lourds looked and saw Natashya chatting with a middle-aged man who looked rather shabby. Lourds guessed that the man was probably a dockworker, but didn't know why he would be loitering when there was work to be done. The man gave Natashya a cigarette. She leaned in for a light from the lighter cupped in his hands. Without warning, she stiff-armed the man in the throat and sent him to his knees. A spinning sidekick dropped the man to the ground.

'Bollocks,' Leslie said. 'What the bloody hell did she do that for?'

Lourds ran over to Natashya as she crouched down and started going through the man's pockets.

'What are you doing?' Lourds demanded.

Natashya took a cellphone from the man's pocket and tossed it to Lourds. 'He's been keeping you under observation.'

The implication staggered Lourds. There was so much about the fugitive lifestyle that he didn't know. And he had precious little time to learn. He stared around. Several pedestrians crossed the street to avoid the scene.

'Maybe you could have waited for a more public area to pull your ambush,' Leslie said.

'He was talking to someone on the phone.' Natashya took out a wallet, shoved it into her coat pocket, and then found a packet of pictures in his shirt pocket. When she fanned them out like playing cards, Lourds', Leslie's and Natashya's photographs were there.

'He was definitely looking for you,' Viktor said. He waved his hands. 'Come on. We need to get out of here.'

Natashya abandoned the unconscious man. 'Do you know him?' she asked.

Viktor shook his head and took off down an alley.

Before Lourds could move, gunshots rang out only a short distance away. A short time after that, police klaxons blared to strident life. By then Lourds and the others were moving swiftly through the dockyards.

Winding Star hailed out of South America. A lot of pirate ships did, Lourds knew. Modern-day pirates flew flags of convenience, and it was mostly convenient to fly flags out of South America. It had been amusing to note how many land-locked South American countries hosted veritable navies out around the world. All the ship's owner had to do was pay a fee to the country, and they were officially recognized as a ship from that country. As a result, they were afforded international protection, privileges and rights. They couldn't be boarded by police of any other nationality without just cause without risking an international incident.

Viktor made quick introductions to the lantern-jawed first mate, a man called Yakov Oistrakh. He was in his forties and had scars to show for his years at sea.

'Welcome aboard,' Oistrakh greeted them as he made the fat envelope Viktor gave him disappear beneath his coat.

'We should get below deck quickly. I'm anticipating some trouble,' Lourds said.

'The gunshots?' Oistrakh raised an eyebrow.

'Perhaps they're on our account. Men are looking for us.'

'But of course,' the first mate said. 'That is why you are coming with us, *nyet*?'

'It is,' Natashya replied. She gave Lourds a shove and got him moving.

'You'll find no trouble here, Professor Lourds,' Oistrakh said. 'We have every right to defend our ship and all those on board it. Once you are on our deck, you are – in effect – in another country. They will have to have proper documentation to take you. The captain and I were told that the men pursuing you had no such papers.'

'That's correct,' Natashya said.

Lourds gripped the rope sides of the gangplank and walked up the steep incline. He looked back over his shoulder several times.

Further down the docks, several police cars converged on an alley between warehouses. The action drew a large group of spectators.

A couple of moments later, winded from the long, steep climb, Lourds stood in the stern and looked back at the docks. A radio in the hands of a crewman crackled only a few feet away. Russian voices talked quickly and Lourds picked up enough of the conversation to realize the man held a police scanner.

'Do you know what's happening?' Lourds asked the man in Russian.

The crewman, stocky and grey-haired, shrugged. 'Some policemen were shot.'

'Professor Lourds,' Oistrakh said, 'if you don't mind me saying so, I think you and your friends would be better off in the galley. You're too much in the open up here.'

'He's right,' Natashya said. 'A sniper on the rooftop, if Gallardo is so inclined, can put an end to your pursuit of the bell.'

'Who's Gallardo?' Leslie asked.

'The man who has chased us from Moscow.'

'How did –'

Oistrakh motioned them along like children. 'No more talking. You can talk down in the galley.'

Reluctantly, Lourds went.

*

Gallardo moved at almost a run with DiBenedetto at his side. The other men trailed only a few feet behind. Gallardo cursed the circumstances that had brought him to this. He was exposed; the police knew who he was. Thankfully over the years Gallardo had done business with the black marketeers who did business out of Odessa. There were places he could hide. He went to one of them now.

The bar was one of several that served the needs of the ships' crews. Neon signs hung in the windows. Gallardo climbed the short flight of steps and went through the door into the dark, smoke-filled interior. Only a few customers lingered at the bar and in the booths. Televisions showing a sports channel hung over the bars and in the corners.

Mikhail Richter stood at his customary spot by the bar. He was fat and shaved his head but wore a bushy beard. He had an evil-smelling cigar clamped between his teeth. An apron hung from his waist. Two beautiful women worked the bar under his watchful eye.

'Ah, Patrizio,' Mikhail greeted. 'How have you been?'

'Busy,' Gallardo answered. 'I don't have time to talk. I need to use the back door.'

Mikhail nodded at one of the men sitting near the door. The man got up and walked outside.

'A moment,' Mikhail told Gallardo. 'If no one comes this way, then I will let you go.'

If no one comes after me, I don't need your way out. Gallardo blew out an angry breath. But he bellied up to the bar and accepted the glass of beer one of the women gave him at Mikhail's instruction.

The man Mikhail sent outside came back in. He shot Mikhail a look and shook his head.

'You are in luck, Patrizio. Come this way.' Mikhail waved them behind the bar.

Gallardo and his men followed the big man into the back storeroom, then down the stairs to the basement. Mikhail switched on the naked light bulb that hung from the ceiling. Pale yellow light filled the room. Across the room, Mikhail rolled a stack of beer kegs out of the way. He pushed a section of the wall and a stone slab at his feet slid aside to reveal carved stone stairs that corkscrewed downwards.

Much of Odessa's foundations were limestone. As such, it was easily mined. Taking advantage of the local rock, many people quarried the stone for use in buildings and homes throughout the area. Later, when the need arose and smuggling became the highest-paying profession, tunnels were built to connect the mines and create catacombs to store and hide goods.

'Here.' Mikhail took a lantern from the storeroom.

Gallardo touched his lighter to the wick and pulled the hurricane glass back down. When the flame was properly adjusted and burned well, he stepped down into the bowels of the earth.

Lourds and his companions had evaded him for the moment, but he still had his means of tracking them. However, it was going to be a long time before Gallardo did business within Russia again.

Hopefully Lourds wouldn't be staying in the area. That would be a problem.

Lourds sat in the transport boat setting out from *Winding Star* and looked out over the city. The stink of the semi-stagnant water took away some of the allure, but there was nothing grander than Venice to his mind. Late morning hung purple and gold in the east, and tourists filled the streets and canals.

'You're smiling,' Leslie told him. She sat beside him on the bench seat. Every now and again the chop of the waves rolled their bodies together in a manner that was altogether too pleasing and too tempting.

'Am I?' Lourds asked. He felt his face as if to find out for himself. But he was smiling, of course. 'It must be the company.'

Leslie smiled back at him. 'I'd be flattered if that were the case, but I'd be foolish to think so.'

'It's this city,' Lourds answered honestly. 'Some of the greatest minds in the world came here to talk. They wrote books, plays and poems that are still studied today. Royal families, merchant houses and empires rose and fell here.' He stopped himself before he launched into a lecture.

'Have you ever been to a place that didn't fill you with wonder?'

Lourds shook his head. 'Never. At least not places that have history. I've been to a few places that I knew little about, but as long as I had the language of the people who lived there, I found stories and dreams I could marvel over. Societies and cultures are unique and extraordinary, but they're at their best when they're juxtaposed – when they clash or compete.'

'Do you mean fight wars? That doesn't sound good.'

'War isn't good. But war is part of the process of world civilization. If we didn't fight wars, people would seldom learn anything about other people. They wouldn't exchange ideas, passion or language. Everyone knows what an impact the Crusades had on the world at the time, in food, mathematics and science. But few people realize that the Chinese were mariners and explorers. They had huge sailing junks, some of them nearly seven and eight hundred feet long, and their sailors interacted with a number of cultures during their heyday.'

'But wouldn't those *juxtapositions* break down languages instead? Adulterate them so they weren't pure any more?'

'Possibly, but the roots of the original language would be there, and the overlap of the languages allow a better study of both. Their similarities, their differences. It could actually sharpen a linguist's appreciation of both.'

'I'll take your word for that.' Leslie looked more sombre. 'On another note, I talked to my producer this morning. He's bought us some time to pursue this story, but I'm starting to get some pressure to show them something.'

Lourds thought about that for a moment. 'Have you told him about the cymbal?'

'You asked me not to.'

'Perhaps you could tell him that.'

'And that we're on our way to the Max Planck Institute to find out about the slave trade?'

'Yes. But he has to remain quiet about that for now.'

'All right.' Leslie looked out at the city. 'How long are we going to be here?'

'We'll be headed to Leipzig immediately. Halle is less than an hour's drive from Leipzig, but booking a room there could be more problematic. Also, as Josef pointed out, in a town as small as Halle, we'd be easier to find. Josef has put everything together for us. There's supposed to be a rental car waiting on the mainland.'

'Professor Lourds?'

Lourds studied the middle-aged woman sitting at a table at the outdoor café. A lime-coloured *gelato* in the shape of a flower and garnished with a waffle biscuit sat before her.

'I recognized you from the picture Josef sent.' She opened the folder in front of her and displayed the picture Danilovic had taken at his home.

In the picture, Lourds held a brandy snifter and a cigar. He didn't look like a fugitive either in the picture or in person, but his insides had turned to ice water when she'd called his name.

'It's quite a good likeness,' the woman said. 'You're a handsome man.'

'Thank you,' Lourds said, still off balance.

Leslie slid in smoothly at his side and took his arm.

The woman looked at Lourds, then at Leslie. She smiled again, but it wasn't as friendly this time. 'Well, then, Josef wanted me to give you this package.'

Lourds took the proffered manila envelope.

'You'll find keys to the rental car and directions how to find it inside the envelope.' She stood and took her *gelato* with her. 'I hope you have a safe and productive trip.'

'Thank you,' Lourds said.

'And if you ever get to Venice when you're not babysitting, call me.' The woman gave Lourds a card. Swivelling gracefully, she turned and walked away in a manner that left both Lourds and Gary staring after her.

Lourds smelled the card. It was lilac scented.

Leslie plucked the card from Lourds' hands. 'Trust me. You won't need that.' She deposited the card into the nearest waste receptacle and guided Lourds from the outdoor café and back into the street.

Lourds didn't mind. He had a photographic memory for telephone numbers. Even international ones.

Although she hadn't driven on the autobahns in Germany before, Natashya proved quite skilled. Lourds wasn't too surprised because he'd seen her drive in Moscow. Gary and Leslie sat in the back of the rental car and cursed and cried out respectively as Natashya wove in and out of the fast and frantic traffic.

The Radisson SAS Hotel Leipzig was located downtown on Augustusplatz. They left the rental in the parking garage and entered the main lobby.

'I'm going to secure our rooms,' Leslie said. 'Why don't you forage for food?'

They'd driven the last several hours and stopped only for petrol. Lourds was ready for a real meal, but since it was so late – after eleven p.m. local time – he doubted they'd have much success finding a restaurant open to serve them. His fears were confirmed when the clerk started talking.

'I'm afraid the restaurant Orangerie is closed,' the young desk clerk said. She smiled an apology. 'But the lobby lounge and foyer bar is open. They have a limited menu.'

'Thank you,' Lourds told her. Things were looking up. At least they wouldn't starve.

'Just let me know if you need anything else, sir. Anything at all.' Her eyes gleamed with possibilities.

'Are you always this brill with the women, mate?'

Gary asked quietly as they walked away from the front desk. 'Because if you are, I just don't get it.'

'No,' Lourds said, and let it go at that.

Later, after they'd consumed appetizers, entrées and desserts, Lourds sat back on one of the big sofas and stared at the television. Only a few people were in the lounge.

Their conversation was light and mostly tired, but it cantered around the upcoming meeting with Professor Joachim Fleinhardt at the Max Planck Institute. Lourds had contacted him en route and set up the meeting for the morning.

'Okay,' Leslie said, 'I've had all the fun that I can enjoy for one day. I'm off to bed. Tomorrow seems to be something of a red-letter day for us.'

'Possibly,' Lourds said. 'It's research. You can never quite tell what you're going to get out of research.'

Leslie patted him on the shoulder. 'I have faith in you. Professor Hapaev believed she had an answer to the origins of the cymbal and she placed her trust in you to find it. I think we're in good hands.'

Lourds thanked her for the compliment, but he knew from his own work that universities and news people tended to be quite disappointed when someone didn't deliver something astounding when there had been a big build-up.

'I'm to bed as well,' Gary said.

'You? Sleep?' Lourds asked. Of them all Gary seemed to sleep the least.

'They have cable,' Gary replied with a grin. 'That means either *Adult Swim* on the Cartoon Network or porn. Either will be entertainment enough.' He left.

Lourds turned to Natashya. 'What about you?'

'What about me?' Natashya asked. She sat across from him. Even though she appeared relaxed, Lourds was aware that she was constantly on point. She saw everyone and everything in the lobby area.

'Too tired for a nightcap? I'm buying.'

'Trying to be polite, Professor?'

Lourds shrugged. 'The thought of you going up to your room and sitting there staring at walls bothers me somewhat. You didn't get to sleep in the car during the drive.'

'Sleeping isn't a necessary thing when you're being hunted. While we're in motion, I feel we're safest.'

The idea of being hunted was disconcerting to Lourds, and it must have shown on his face.

'You've got your eyes so firmly on the prize that you're forgetting others are doing the same. Only we're the prize to them. We're a threat to whatever they're doing.'

'And they can't have that?'

Natashya shook her head. 'Apparently not. Otherwise they wouldn't have sent Gallardo after us.'

'But how did they find us in Odessa?'

A mirthless smile curved Natashya's mouth. 'That is the question, isn't it? How would you think Gallardo found us?'

'If this were a spy movie, one of us would be carrying a tracking device. But we haven't had that much contact with Gallardo – or his minions – for that to happen.'

'I agree.'

'His presence in Odessa wasn't a coincidence.'

'If you thought so even for a moment, I'd consider you dangerously ignorant. For a university professor, your survival skills are impressive.'

'But not enough to keep me from getting killed.'

'Probably not.'

Lourds winced. 'That's brutally honest.'

'You live longer if you're aware.'

'That leaves only one possibility, and I refuse to entertain it.'

'Then you're more foolish than I'd hoped.' Disappointment showed on Natashya's beautiful face.

'You're insinuating that someone – either Leslie, Gary or Josef – betrayed us.'

'Gallardo and his men nearly got us,' Natashya pointed out. 'That's more than someone telling him that we were in Illichivsk.'

Lourds silently conceded the point. 'There has to be another answer.'

'There is. I could have turned us in.'

That surprised Lourds.

Natashya looked at him and shook her head. She looked both sad and amused. 'That thought never entered your head?'

'No,' Lourds said truthfully.

'Why?'

'You're Yuliya's sister. You wouldn't do that.'

'You are a man of the world, Professor Lourds.

But do you know what my sister most enjoyed about you?'

Lourds shrugged.

'Your naivety. She always maintained that you were one of the most innocent men she'd ever met.' Natashya stood. 'It's an early morning before us. I'd suggest you get some rest before then. Good night.'

'Good night.' Lourds watched her walk away. She had an admirable walk and a figure to flaunt it. He appreciated both in a manner that he considered was *not* overly naive.

13

'Are you familiar with the work the social anthropology institute does, Professor Lourds?'

Joachim Fleinhardt turned out to be an interesting man. From their phone conversations, brief and to the point, Lourds had expected the man to be a pasty and portly chap who spent far too much time in the lab.

As it turned out, Fleinhardt was six feet six inches tall at least and was a stunning example of hybrid vigour. He said that his German father had married a black American officer. The genetics of the match were clearly superior. Fleinhardt's position here at the institute and his reputation indicated that he was as bright as they came. His skin was beautiful, dark and smooth, and he was lean and handsome. He moved like a professional athlete. That was intimidating enough but he was also impeccably dressed, which made Lourds feel awkward in his jean shorts and loose shirt unbuttoned over a soccer T-shirt. Lourds had dressed weather appropriate but not scholastically appropriate.

'No, I'm not as familiar as I should be, I have to admit,' Lourds said.

Fleinhardt strode through the pristine hallways of the institute with authority. Other people quickly gave way before him.

'My group deals with integration and conflict,' the professor said.

'The study of tribal wars?'

'And of the slave trade. You don't get one without the other, I'm afraid. Africa, especially North Africa after the Europeans arrived and introduced new markets that the Yoruba people and others had never thought of, changed the face of those tribes.'

'Trade often does that, for better and worse.'

'We research and document integration and conflict because we feel those elements most designate identity and difference between cultures.'

'Because of their views on kinship, friendship, language and history.'

'Exactly.' Fleinhardt smiled in a pleased manner. 'A culture's need for rituals and beliefs give us many clues as to who they were and who they came in contact with.'

'Not only that,' Lourds said, 'but it helps build a timeline.'

Fleinhardt nodded. 'I'm impressed. You've been keeping up. Most people these days don't favour interdisciplinary training or pursuits.'

'Actually, the project caught my eye. Besides that, linguists, archaeologists and historians tend to feed at the same troughs. It's far too difficult these days to keep up with everything going on in science. But I try to supplement as much as I can.'

'I know.' Fleinhardt frowned ruefully. 'We're losing our core knowledge, I'm afraid, the basic language scientists use to speak to each other. But then language is your field, isn't it?'

'Yes. The core-knowledge problem is one every expanding civilization eventually faces,' Lourds said. 'Even two and three thousand years ago, technology advanced more rapidly than people could share it. The advent of libraries, places where knowledge could be kept and shared, helped somewhat, but until Gutenberg came along with his printing press, sharing and distribution remained a problem.'

'Sharing and distribution is *still* a problem. If it weren't for this job and the budget that comes with it, I wouldn't be able to afford most of the technical manuals and resource books I keep on hand.'

'I understand the problem. Even the internet, with all its pirate peer-to-peer sharing capabilities, can't keep up. My budget never quite covers everything I want to read. I end up with huge out-of-pocket expenses every year.'

Fleinhardt laughed. 'That's the common complaint of every working scholar who's serious about his craft.'

The room holding the Yoruba records and artefacts was smaller than Lourds had expected. Some of his disappointment must have shown on his face.

'Not everything is kept here,' Fleinhardt explained

as he booted up a computer. 'Even as large as the institute is, we simply don't have enough space. Many of the documents we've recovered, or at least made physical copies of, have been translated to digital images. Our database is quite extensive.'

Lourds placed his backpack on the floor and took the seat Fleinhardt indicated.

'I took the liberty of securing the files Professor Hapaev had enquired about.' Fleinhardt tapped keys. 'Is that what you're here to see?'

'To begin with, yes. I don't know how far my search will take me.'

'Well, if the research you're doing here benefits your efforts for this television show, I hope you see fit to mention us. The institute can always use donations.'

Lourds said he would keep that in mind, but he was already on the prowl for information. He crawled into Yoruba mentally and got to know that country, its history, and its people. In only a few moments, he was thoroughly fascinated.

Trastevere
Rome, Italy
29 August 2009

'Welcome, Father. Please come in.'

Murani ignored the slight, even though he was so much more than a simple priest. He knew that the speaker hadn't intended to ignore his position. These days the old woman couldn't remember much or keep things straight.

'Thank you, Sister.' Murani allowed her to take his coat. He wore traditional black today. His rosary hung around his neck.

'The others are in the back, Father.' The old woman put his coat on a hanger.

Murani walked through the spacious, elegant home. Not all of the members of the Society of Quirinus had remained with the Church. The society needed some autonomy and didn't exist solely under the prying eyes of the papacy. Also, some of the members weren't church officials. Sometimes the money had to come from somewhere else. Deals had been struck with believers.

Once through the narrow hallways filled with paintings and sculptures that delineated much of Rome's and the Church's history, Murani found Lorenzo Occhetto holding court in his large study. The double doors were open.

Occhetto was a wizened man with a bald, liver-spotted head. He looked like an animated cadaver, but his yellowed eyes never missed a trick. In his day, Occhetto had been a fireball for the Church, and had stood against every loss of power and prestige the Church had suffered.

In addition to Murani's host, three men occupied the room. All of them sat listening to Occhetto. A large, wide-screen monitor built into the wall showed real-time footage of the excavation in Cadiz. There was no doubt about the topic of conversation.

'Ah, Cardinal Murani. It's good to see you.' Occhetto's voice was raspy, but it carried a sense of power. 'I'm glad you could visit.'

In the end, there had been no choice. When Occhetto sent for someone, that someone had to come.

Murani shook hands.

'We have no reason to talk here. I want to walk with you a bit while I am still able.' Occhetto rose slowly from his desk.

'Over the years,' Occhetto said as he stepped into the private elevator that led to the underground section of the house, 'we've shown you many secrets.'

The elevator was hidden behind a wall and a grandfather clock that swung inward when the latches were released. Murani entered the elevator and closed the doors. Occhetto pressed the button and the light dimmed. After a moment, the cage jerked into a slow descent.

'But we haven't shown you every secret.'

That incensed Murani. When he'd been accepted into the Society of Quirinus, he'd expected to be told the whole truth.

'What haven't you told me?' He knew the demand in his voice might cause problems, but the question was out of him before he could stop it.

Occhetto waved the question away. 'We've *told* you everything, Stefano. We've just not *shown* you everything.'

The elevator bucked to a stop. Murani shoved the

doors open and they walked out into a large room cut from the limestone under the city.

The rooms under Occhetto's home had been used for smuggling operations. The family had been deeply religious, though, and had been forgiven on a regular basis. Of course, their ill-gotten gains had been properly tithed so their souls would be cared for.

'What I'm about to show you is the prize of my collection.' Occhetto slowly made his way across the cavernous space and stopped at one of the rooms. There were several. Murani hadn't even been to half of them. 'Only a few members in the Society of Quirinus know that I have this.' Occhetto took a ring of keys from his pocket and fitted one to the lock. The mechanism opened with a faint, smooth *snik*, proving that it was often used.

Occhetto took a candle from a shelf on the wall and lit it with a match from a box beside it. The candle's flame guttered for a moment, then burned strongly. He placed it in a lamp.

The first thing that caught Murani's attention was the Madonna in the niche carved into the opposite wall. It was almost three feet high. Mary, the Mother of God, stood with her hands out from her sides in silent supplication. Then he noticed the large table in the centre of the room. The candle was barely bright enough to lift enough of the shadows to reveal strange glass shapes.

Mesmerized by the sight, matching the shapes up to a pattern he still didn't quite recognize, Murani went forward.

'Wait,' Occhetto said. 'You'll need a candle.'

Murani took one and lit it from the one in the lantern Occhetto held in a shaking hand.

'Do you see the glass reservoir on the side nearest you?' Occhetto asked.

Murani looked and said that he did.

'There's a wick in that. Light it and step back.'

At the table, Murani dipped the candle to light the wick suspended in oil. As it turned out, the wick was strung throughout the glass model.

As Murani watched, the flame caught slowly but made its way throughout the tubing that ran through the structure. The glass amplified the light as it spread. Within minutes a miniature city stood ablaze in the darkness.

Atlantis!

Stunned by the beauty that lay before him, Murani advanced cautiously. Hot wax dripped down his hand but he barely noticed it.

Pale green crenulated towers rose up from the darker green and amber of the glass houses and building at the base of the model. Yellow lamps lit narrow streets that wound through the city in concentric circles. That alone marked the city as Atlantis. Beyond the city, more glass formed the surrounding sea, but this glass burned lambent blue. The colour came from the tint of the blown glass. Each piece had been carefully made and put together.

Hesitantly, Murani lifted the candle and blew it out. The gentle light of Atlantis continued to burn.

'This was made from one of the illustrations of

the city,' Murani said. The illustration had lived in his head since the time it had been shown to him.

'Yes.'

'Who did the work?'

'A priest who wasn't quite faithful in his vows,' Occhetto answered. 'His name was Sandro D'Alema. He was a third son, so his father gave him to the Church. He would have been better off as a painter or sculptor, but his journals say his father was afraid he would starve. Instead, he slipped away from the Church for weeks and months at a time and studied art.'

'How did he come to make this?' Murani said. 'Being uncommitted as he was in his faith, no one would have told him of the secret texts or Atlantis.'

'One of the cardinals wanted the drawing rendered, so he conscripted D'Alema. But he didn't tell him what it was.'

Murani stared at the city.

'The reason I'm showing you this,' Occhetto said, 'is to remind you how powerful and beautiful this city was, and how – at the end – it was so fragile. The power that was used there . . .'

'The fruit of the tree,' Murani murmured.

'Yes. But not the apple that so many painters depicted in Eve's hand as she offered temptation to Adam. It was a book. The true word of God as it was written down in the Garden of Eden.'

'The word was holy and unknowable.' Murani repeated the story by rote from the information he'd been given upon his acceptance into the Society of Quirinus. 'But they tried anyway.'

'It *was* temptation,' Occhetto said. 'So much power.' He held out a withered claw of a hand. 'Right there for the taking.'

Murani said nothing, but his thoughts were filled with the possibilities of what he could do with such a power. With an effort, he tore his eyes from the fiery city burning in the shadows.

'I'm telling you this so that you remember,' Occhetto went on, 'those people in that city lost the *world*. A far better world than we'll ever have. And the few who survived had to make their own path through the wreckage of what was left of their civilization and back to God. Not all of them did.' He paused. 'Not all of *us* will.'

As he held the older man's gaze, Murani wondered how much Occhetto knew or guessed about what he was doing. The others didn't know about the instruments. Only he had discovered that. The truth had been before them, written into the pages and drawn in the paintings of Atlantis, but no one had seen it.

If he hadn't constantly been watching archaeological sites and digging through information, he would have missed it as well.

Occhetto walked over to the glass city and leaned down. He blew on another reservoir. The flame guttered and went out.

As Murani watched, he saw how cunningly the city

had been wrought. As each tiny fire died, it pulled air from the next section and created a vacuum that sucked away the flames.

In moments, the room was once more swathed in darkness.

'Let their lesson be your lesson,' Occhetto said. 'Don't covet that which should not be yours.'

'Of course,' Murani lied. The problem with the other cardinals was that they were afraid to use power. He wasn't. Whatever it took to pull the world back into order he would do.

Less than an hour later, Murani still couldn't get the image of the flaming city out of his mind. Ever since he'd learned of Atlantis and how closely it was tied to the Church, he'd been fascinated by the idea of it. Finding out about the secret texts and the holy word that was written there in that book had made his fascination even stronger.

He sat in one of the back pews of Basilica di San Clemente, one of his favourite churches, and prayed for God to give him the strength to be patient.

The pew shifted slightly as someone sat beside him.

Murani opened his eyes and glanced to his right to find Gallardo sitting there. The man was punctual.

'I didn't want to interrupt,' Gallardo apologized. 'But I didn't want to stand about waiting.'

Murani nodded. 'That's fine.' He took a last look around the church and stood. 'We can go.'

'Lourds is in Germany,' Gallardo said as they

walked along Via San Giovanni. The street was busy with shoppers, tourists and locals.

'Do you know where?' Murani walked with his hands behind his back. His cardinal's robes drew attention, but people quickly glanced away when he threatened eye contact.

'Leipzig. At the Radisson.'

'I don't want Lourds getting too far ahead of you.'

'He won't.' Gallardo said. 'As long as he has the Englishwoman with him, Lourds *can't* get too far away.' He paused as they walked by a young mother pushing a baby carriage. 'In the meantime, maybe it's not a bad idea to let Lourds have some rope.'

Murani shook his head. 'The man is dangerous. If he's able to translate the writing . . .'

'You told me no one could, except you.'

That hadn't been quite the truth. Murani had managed to decipher some of the notes about the instrument, but not much. If there hadn't been accompanying illustrations, he wouldn't have figured out as much as he had. But he'd come closer to reading the old language than anyone he knew.

'Lourds is highly skilled,' Murani said.

They walked in silence for a short time, gradually wandering in a square back toward the garage that held Murani's car.

'Lourds is on to something,' Gallardo announced.

'How do you know?'

'Because I know what to look for when it comes to watching people. He thinks he's on to something. That's why he's in Leipzig. Otherwise he would have run for home after I caught up with him in Moscow.'

'What's there that he would be interested in?'

'I don't know yet. If everything is quiet in Germany, I'm going to get over there in a day or so.'

'He may be gone by then.'

'If he is, we'll find him. In the meantime, I want to hire people to break into his home back in Boston.'

'Why?'

'To get to know him better. I often have clients' homes burglarized to check on things. Usually to find out if they have enough money to pay me. If they don't have a good alarm system, the answer is generally no. But it would be worth checking Lourds' home to find out if he does information dumps while he's out of town.'

'Information dumps?'

'Sure. A guy out on the road with a computer might download his files to the hard drive at home. Or at an off-site place. If I have someone raid his home and copy his hard drive, we'll find out what he's seen fit to send home. Maybe we'll discover what he knows.'

Murani hadn't thought about that. 'Do it.'

In the night's darkness, Murani was glad the big man was accompanying him to his car.

'As soon as you know anything about Leipzig or Lourds' residence, let me know,' Murani said.

'I will.' Gallardo stood at the front of the car.

Just as Murani was about to get in, he spotted a familiar face in the shadows beyond the reach of the parking area's security lights. A chill of dread spilled through him.

The Pope had sent a man to spy on him.

For a moment Murani couldn't remember the man's name. He thought it was Antonio or Luigi. Something as predictable as that.

'What's wrong?' Gallardo asked.

'I made a mistake,' Murani replied in a low voice. 'I was followed. Or I was spotted.'

'Someone is here?'

'Yes. Across the building. Up against the back wall.' Murani was afraid that Gallardo was going to turn, but he didn't.

'Will anyone at the Church know who I am?'

'I don't know. But if the story comes out later about what happened in Moscow, I could be asked a lot of questions.'

Gallardo reached an instant decision. His face turned hard. 'Okay, we don't want that. Give me the keys.'

Murani's stomach flip-flopped. Even if the junior priest ran to the Pope and the Pope didn't worry about the meeting any further, the Society of Quirinus might. They protected their secrets zealously, and if they saw him as a risk they would cut him off from the information. He couldn't have that.

He dropped the keys into Gallardo's palm.

'Now get into the car,' Gallardo ordered while he unlocked the vehicle. 'On the passenger side.'

Murani went around the car and got in. Gallardo put the transmission into drive and reached under his jacket for the pistol he carried there. As he pulled out into the lane, he slid the pistol under his thigh.

'What are you going to do?' Murani asked.

'I'm going to take care of your problem.' Gallardo watched the young priest take flight and pressed down harder on the accelerator.

The priest ran, obviously in fear for his life. His robes flew around him as he ran out of the exit. Gallardo zoomed after him, tyres squealing as he cut sharply to the right to follow his fleeing prey along the pavement.

The prey was in full panic mode. He ran for all he was worth.

Gallardo sped up. He passed the fleeing priest and cut him off. Pedestrians backed away.

The priest was trapped. His face, features taut from fear, was only inches on the other side of Murani's window. For a moment, the cardinal faced his subordinate. Then the priest pushed away and ran down the alley. Gallardo shoved the transmission into reverse briefly, backed up and pulled the shift lever to drive again. The tyres clawed for traction. The car shot forward and careened against a stack of rubbish.

Before he could ask what Gallardo planned, Murani knew. Gallardo's foot hit the accelerator harder. The vehicle gained speed and overtook the priest. When the car caught up to him, the bumper struck the back of his legs and knocked him off his feet.

The priest disappeared beneath the car. His body turned into a series of speed bumps as the airbags deployed. The impact hit Murani in the chest with bruising force and knocked him backwards. Chemical smoke and the stench of gunpowder from the explosive charge that detonated with the airbag filled the air.

Haunted by the crunching sound the tyres had made as they'd ploughed over the priest, knowing he'd never forget it, Murani turned in his seat and stared out at the broken body of the man where he lay still and silent.

Gallardo braked the car, shoved the transmission into reverse, and backed over the priest. He stopped, burst the airbag with a knife, and got out with the pistol in his fist.

Murani had to slide across on the driver's side to get out. He knees wobbled as he followed Gallardo.

Miraculously, the priest was still alive. The side of his head was mashed in from the contact with the ground and one eye was missing. Blood was everywhere. He struggled to lift his head and fought for breath, but failed at both. In seconds he slumped to the ground.

Gallardo knelt and felt for a pulse. He wiped his bloody fingers on the priest's garments.

'He's gone,' Gallardo said. He stood and looked at Murani. 'Can you handle this?'

For a moment Murani didn't know what the other man was talking about.

'Take out your cellphone,' Gallardo directed him calmly as he shoved his pistol back into the shoulder holster. 'Call the police. Report that you were just involved in a carjacking. Tell the police when they get here that you were in the car. That a man with a gun forced you over and took your car. You fought with him and the carjacker ran over a pedestrian.'

Murani fumbled for his phone.

'Do you have that?' Gallardo asked.

'Yes. But are they going to believe me?'

Gallardo struck without warning. His big fist caught Murani on the jaw and nearly spun his head around. As he stumbled back, Gallardo hit him again. The second punch landed squarely on his nose. Blood filled his mouth and his legs turned to water. For a moment he thought Gallardo had knocked him unconscious. He fell forwards and Gallardo caught him.

'You're more believable already. They'll know you were in a fight.' Gallardo grinned. He stood Murani up against the car. 'Make the call. Keep it short. Now you're going to sound believable, too. I've got to get clear.'

As if he were out for a Sunday constitutional, Gallardo shoved his hands into his pockets and walked away. In seconds he had disappeared into the night.

Murani made the call and waited in the alley with the dead man. This wouldn't be the end of it, he knew. The stakes had been raised. After a moment, when he was sure he could move without falling, he crossed to the young priest's body and began administering the last rites.

14

Max Planck Institute for Social Anthropology
Halle an der Saale, Germany
3 September 2009

Lourds found a drawing of the cymbal on Wednesday afternoon. Despite the seemingly endless days of sorting through the wealth of material the institute had on the Yoruba people, he'd maintained hope that something would be there. What he regretted most, though, was the search for a specific something. Although he was somewhat aware of the Yoruba people and the impact they'd had on West Africa and beyond, he hadn't truly known the extent. He hadn't known how well developed the city-states had been. In his opinion, the Yorubans had rivalled their European counterparts. Even though they'd been ruled by monarchies, the rulers ruled by the will of the people and could be ordered by the senators to abdicate the throne.

Not exactly the savages they were reputed to be, Lourds thought grimly. The Yoruba had been governing at that level for hundreds of years before the Europeans started raiding the African nations for slaves.

Unfortunately, the Yoruba – generally known as the Oyo empire at that time – gave in to the easy wealth that could be made from the slave trade. They'd waged wars against other kingdoms and city-states to capture slaves.

Several extensive documents from the eighteenth and nineteenth centuries tempted him. Lourds would have loved to have read them, but there was no time. So, with Fleinhardt's permission, he uploaded several of the files to the off-site server he used at Harvard.

Of course, that server was already overflowing with material he intended to get around to. Some days it got frustrating simply acknowledging how much he *wasn't* going to get to know no matter how hard he strived. Life just wasn't long enough to satisfy his curiosity.

But he read about the cymbal and he grew even more certain that they'd only touched the tip of the iceberg.

Radisson SAS Hotel Leipzig
Leipzig, Germany
3 September 2009

By eight o'clock, Lourds was settled in to dinner with his companions. Leslie had insisted on him getting at least one proper meal and bringing them up to date with his research.

They ate in the hotel's restaurant. Generally it was empty enough so they could get a table in the back and quiet enough so they could talk in relative privacy.

'You found the cymbal?' Leslie's eyes gleamed with excitement.

'I believe so.' Lourds took his notebook computer from his backpack and placed it on the table well away from the wine glasses.

They'd all become accustomed to eating and talking about their work – illustrated by computer when needed – at the same time, but they continued to draw curious glances from the restaurant's other patrons and the waiting staff.

'This is a drawing of the cymbal. Not a picture. But I think it's close enough.' Lourds tapped the keys and brought up the digital image of the cymbal he'd downloaded from the institute's archives. In the drawing, the cymbal looked like a flat disc with an inscription on it. The man holding the cymbal wore a long cape and a crown.

'I'd guess he's the king,' Gary said blithely.

'More than a king, actually,' Lourds said. 'That's a representation of Oduduwa.'

'Easy for you to say, mate,' Gary cracked.

'He was the leader of an invading army who came to West Africa from Egypt or Nubia, according to the Yorubans. Muslim sources document that Oduduwa came from Mecca. He was supposed to have been fleeing the country over a religious argument.'

'What argument?' Natashya asked.

Lourds shook his head. 'The records I looked at don't say. He could have also been outrunning an invading army. The point is that he fled with the cymbal.' He smiled. 'Interestingly enough, Oduduwa is thought to be descended from the gods.'

'The bell was found in Alexandria,' Leslie said.

'Do you think that's where the cymbal came from?'

'Do you mean, was it there?' Lourds asked. 'Given the legends I've uncovered, I'd say it was there once. But I'm not satisfied that we've yet found the land of its origins.'

'Because the languages don't match anything from those areas,' Natashya said.

Lourds nodded and smiled. 'Exactly.'

'What if the instruments were planted there? Intentionally put there.'

That thought hadn't struck Lourds, and he found it highly interesting. He took a moment to mull it over.

'Wait,' Leslie said, 'what makes you think anyone planted the bell and the cymbal there?'

'Because they don't fit,' Lourds said, carrying on with Natashya's insight. Her idea made everything fall into place so much better. 'They don't spring from that culture. The materials used. The work that went into them. The languages. All of them jar with what we know of that area.'

'If they wanted the cymbal to disappear, why attribute it to a god? Or a near-god? Or whatever O-dude is supposed to be?'

'Maybe they didn't do that. Maybe that story followed the O-guy out of Egypt,' Gary said.

'It's possible,' Lourds said. 'According to the legend, Oduduwa was sent by his father, Olodumare –'

'That name's on a Paul Simon album,' Gary said, interrupting. 'It was released in the early 1990s. It was called *Rhythm of the Saints* or something like that.'

'No way,' Lourds responded.

'Way, mate,' Gary replied. 'You get Wi-Fi in here, right?'

Lourds nodded.

'Lemme borrow your computer.'

After pushing it across, Lourds turned his attention back to his meal. As chief speaker during the debrief, he was usually the one who ended up eating cold food.

In minutes, Gary smiled in triumph. 'And Bob's your uncle, mate.' He spun the computer back around and displayed the song lyrics.

The reference to Olodumare was in the eighth line down.

'Olodumare is smiling in heaven,' Gary said.

'You're turning out to be a fount of information,' Lourds said. 'Why didn't you ever go to university?'

'I tried. It was too boring. A lot of the time I knew more than the professors did. One of the first things you learn at university is that the professors aren't a whole lot smarter than you are, and sometimes they don't even know as much.' Realizing what he'd just said, Gary held his hands up defensively. 'Wasn't referring to you, mate. You've been right impressive, you have.'

'I'm glad to know that. Let me see if I can impress you a little more.' Lourds sipped his wine. 'The Yorubans refer to themselves as Eniyan or Eniti Aayan. The literal translation of this reference is "The Chosen Ones to bring blessing to the world".'

'Do you think the cymbal was supposed to be a blessing?' Leslie asked.

'The question did enter my mind,' Lourds admitted. 'After all, it did arrive there in the hands of a near-god.'

Cambrigeport
Cambridge, Massachusetts
3 September 2009

The best time to burgle a home wasn't at night. It was during the day. At night nobody was supposed to be around and anyone who was stuck out. But during the day, people came and went and were around all the time.

Bess Thomsen was a professional thief. She'd been breaking into other people's homes since she was eleven. Now, at thirty-three, she was an old hand at the game.

She was five feet five inches tall, with brown hair, brown eyes and a face that was mostly forgettable. In other words, she was totally nondescript in her appearance. But she had a figure. Part of that was from working out so she could do her job. Part of it was that it kept people's eyes off her face. But today she kept that figure disguised beneath loose orange coveralls.

Her partner for the burglary was a twenty-something named Sparrow. She'd brought him along in case they had to do any lifting. Sparrow was six-two and over two hundred pounds. Bess was convinced 90 per cent of it was attitude. She'd never met a more arrogant person.

He slouched in the van's passenger seat and flicked cigarette ash out of the window. Stubble turned his cheeks and jaw line into sandpaper. His surfer-blond hair was cropped to his shoulder line. Cool blue sunglasses covered the upper part of his face. Earbuds filled those orifices, though Bess had thought about shoving them in other orifices. Even with his earbuds blocking some of the sound, Sparrow played his music – hard-driving rock – loud enough for Bess to want to scream.

She checked the phoney work order for the address one last time and pulled into the driveway of the house. She leaned under the sun visor and studied the structure.

The house was a generous two-storey building. Not overly large, but more than was necessary for the single occupant she'd been told lived there. Cambrigeport was mostly residential, with single-family homes as well as rental properties since Harvard University and access to the Charles River were nearby. It was a good walking neighbourhood for those so inclined. That was another reason to do the job in the daytime as opposed to at night.

The notes Bess had on the job were sparse. The homeowner was supposed to be a university professor currently out of the country. Bess had taken down the notes, but she didn't count on that. People got back at the oddest times.

It would have been better if the prof had been at work in the city. Steady hours on the job were a lot better than counting on an occasional vacation.

She got out of the van, took her hard hat from the seat and put it on. Clipboard in hand, she walked to the door. Sparrow fell in beside her.

The lock was a good one, but it took her less than thirty seconds to pick her way through. As soon as she entered the front door, she heard the *peep* of the burglar alarm fire up. According to the alarm company reports she'd hacked out of the system, they had forty-five seconds to get to the keypad in the foyer to shut the alarm down. She made it with time to spare, then entered the code she'd also got from the files.

She turned to Sparrow. 'Did you lock the door?'

He frowned at her and folded his arms across his chest. His tool belt, all the tools untouched in case he had to run for it, dangled at his hip.

'Screw you.' Sparrow took out the earbuds. 'I got the top floor,' he said. 'See you when I see you.' He headed in the direction of the stairs.

Bess cursed him and his arrogance out. Both of them were big enough to merit their own time, and both of them were deserving of the epithets.

She locked the front door and did a walk-through of the lower house to make sure she was alone. Once she was satisfied, she returned to the office area on the ground floor and powered the computer up.

'You've heard about the dig in Cadiz, haven't you?' Lourds asked.

'The one where they're looking for Atlantis?' Gary asked.

Leslie sipped her wine and watched Lourds. She found she'd missed him during the days he spent at the Max Planck Institute.

Don't go there, she told herself. *This isn't the time or the place.*

'I don't know if they'll find Atlantis there,' Lourds said. 'A half-dozen places have potentially been Atlantis. Greece claims a submerged Atlantis just off the coast. So does Bimini. There have even been claims for an Atlantis site off the coast of South America.'

'I hadn't seen anything about that one.'

'The South American claim comes in because a man named J. M. Allen postulates that Atlantis was actually on the Altiplano, a Bolivian plain. According to research Allen has done, it's not unusual for that area to become flooded. In fact, they did surveys and found out that the plain was flooded in 9000 BC.'

'Why are you talking about Atlantis?' Natashya asked. 'Has there been anything in your research that's indicated anything should be related to Atlantis?'

Witch, Leslie thought. Things hadn't been as much fun since Natashya had joined them. When it had been her and Lourds going to Moscow – with Gary in tow, even – things had been potentially interesting. Now it was hard to get five minutes of conversation with the handsome professor without the Russian cop butting in.

Leslie felt sorry about the loss of Natashya's sister, of course. But she still didn't see why the woman had to invite herself along.

'Interestingly enough,' Lourds said as he leaned back and stretched out, 'the topic of Atlantis did indeed come up during the research. Some theories say that Yoruba might have been Atlantis.'

'No way, mate,' Gary said.

'Way,' Lourds said.

Leslie smiled at that. The stoner banter probably would have been condemned at Harvard. Lourds didn't seem to care. That was what she most liked about the professor. He seemed *real*.

'Ile-Ife is a Yoruba city located in Nigeria. The documents I looked at claimed the city has existed at least as far back as 10,000 BC.'

'That fits with the time frame that's been established for Atlantis,' Gary admitted.

'Some historians believe that Yoruba was once a mighty sea power,' Lourds went on. 'I've seen documents that suggest the existence of a great fleet of ships that were destroyed during an oceanic cataclysm that came far inland.'

'Like the sinking of an island?'

266

'And the resulting tsunami.' Lourds nodded. 'The society was known for its traders who dealt in goods and services. The Aromires were admirals and Olokos were merchants who usually travelled for a year at a time. Scholars think they travelled to Asia, Australia and North and South America.'

'What does any of this have to do with the cymbal that my sister was killed for?' Natashya demanded.

That sobered up the two men. Leslie resented the ease with which Natashya had taken control of the conversation. She always had to be so calm and cool.

'There was an interesting fact I turned up during my studies,' Lourds said. 'I digressed. But here it is: during those early years of Ile-Ife, only a few people could read and write their language. The Yoruba scribes kept such knowledge out of the hands of everyone except a select few.'

'Do you think the inscriptions on the cymbal and bell are Yoruban?'

'It's possible.' Lourds yawned. 'I've got more research to do now that I've ferreted out this much. According to Yoruba legend, Oduduwa and his brother Obatala – who was also the son of Olorun, the sky god – created the world. Obatala created humans out of clay and Olorun breathed life into them.'

'Creation myth,' Gary said. 'Every culture has them.'

'And it's fascinating to see what all those myths have in common,' Lourds said.

'You're going to continue to search the institute

for any inscriptions that may match those on the cymbal and bell?' Natashya asked.

'That's the plan.'

'How long will that take?'

Lourds shrugged. 'I don't know. The problem is that I'm getting close to exhausting the material these people have.'

'What happens if you do?'

'Then we need to think about taking a look at the source material.'

That caught Leslie's attention. 'You mean travel to West Africa?'

Lourds looked at her and nodded. 'If it becomes necessary, yes.'

Cambrigeport
Cambridge, Massachusetts
3 September 2009

Bess was working in the office when the operation turned ugly. She'd booted up the victim's computer and was downloading everything on the hard drive to the external drive she'd brought with her. She was also going through the paper files in the filing cabinet, but most of the folders there concerned presentations and class course lectures.

That was when the front door opened and someone entered.

Bess went into motion at once. She stepped toward the office doorway and flattened herself against the wall. Her heart rate barely elevated. Over the years she'd had people walk in on her before. Today she looked like a natural-gas employee.

Sparrow wasn't so cool. He came down the stairway with the earbuds in and didn't see the man until it was too late. Sparrow was also carrying a pack over his shoulder, looking like an evil Santa. Evidently he'd swiped one of the pillowcases from the target's bedroom and filled it with whatever had caught his eye.

That hadn't been part of the plan.

Unprofessional and worse, inexcusable, since they were doing this on the Q-T. Bess promised herself that she'd never work with him again.

The man who'd just entered the house was in his forties and a little overweight. He wore khaki shorts, a golf shirt and sandals.

Judging from the casual shoes, Bess figured him for a neighbour. Nobody'd be stupid enough to walk very far in those things. He was probably just watching the house for a friend.

'Who are you?' the man demanded.

Bess stepped around the corner. 'We're with the gas company. Someone reported a gas leak in the area.'

The man looked at the pillowcase stuffed with stolen loot on Sparrow's back. 'I don't believe you.' He took a cellphone from his hip.

That was one technological advance that had been put into the hands of almost everyone, and that made a professional burglar's job even harder. Every idiot on the street could report a crime almost immediately these days.

Sparrow reached to the back of his waistband and took out a revolver.

Bess didn't know what kind it was. She never worked with guns and she never stole guns. There was no telling where some mark had gotten a gun, or how he'd used it, and the last thing she wanted to do was get picked up for breaking and entering then get charged for someone else's murder. But before she could stop Sparrow, he fired.

The pistol's detonation filled the house and sounded incredibly loud in the enclosed space.

The neighbour staggered, put a hand to his chest that came away bright with blood, and went down.

Bess didn't waste time checking to see if the man was alive. She didn't waste time cursing Sparrow. She looked at him.

'Get out of here now,' she instructed.

Sparrow stood frozen for a moment.

'Get out!' Bess ordered more loudly.

Sparrow went, but he couldn't take his eyes off the fallen man. 'He was going to call the police. I had to . . .'

Bess ignored him and returned to the office. She unhooked the external drive she'd brought to download the computer's files onto. At least the program had finished running. Whatever the target had had on his hard drive was now mirrored on the hard drive she had.

The job was accomplished.

She skirted the man on the floor, left the house, and pulled the door closed behind her. Sparrow sat in the van's passenger seat.

Bess slid into the driver's seat, started the engine, and pulled out onto the street. She pulled a disposable phone from her coverall. Before every job she bought one in the hopes of never having to use it.

She dialled 911, reported the shooting and hung up.

'Why did you do that?' Sparrow asked.

'That man might still be alive. He shouldn't have to die just because you got greedy.' Bess drove methodically as she wound through the streets.

'Hey, what I got wasn't all that much. This job didn't pay –'

'It paid fine,' Bess said. 'The man who hired us didn't want any complications. That, just so you know for future reference, was a complication. *Big* complication.'

Sparrow slumped against the seat and folded his arms over his chest like a petulant child.

'Give me the gun.' Bess held out one gloved hand.

'Why?'

'The gun,' Bess said.

'It's *my* gun.'

'Now.'

Sullen, Sparrow gave it up.

Working one-handed, Bess wiped the gun down. She even opened the cylinder and wiped the cartridges. Thankfully the gun had been a revolver. Nothing had been left behind but the bullet.

She chose her route deliberately and drove over

the Longfellow Bridge. A Red Line train was crossing the tracks in the centre as she drove across.

Midway, Bess had Sparrow roll down the window and she threw the pistol into the Charles River as they headed into Boston. She hoped that would be the end of it.

Radisson SAS Hotel Leipzig
Leipzig, Germany
3 September 2009

Leslie's cellphone rang while she was staring out over Leipzig. The caller ID showed that it was her producer. It was 11.18 p.m. This wouldn't be a good call.

She debated answering between the second and third rings, then muted the television and pressed the TALK button.

'Hello,' she said.

'Tell me you've got something.' Philip Wynn-Jones didn't sound like a happy man.

'What would you like me to tell you?'

'Don't be flip.'

'I'm not. We're in Leipzig –'

'I knew that the moment the credit-card bills started coming in on the hotel. Tell me something I don't know.'

Leslie stared out at the cityscape and tried to think calm thoughts. 'We're still on the trail of those missing instruments.'

'But are you getting anywhere?'

'Lourds is beginning to think we may need to go to West Africa.'

There was silence on the phone for a moment. *'West bloody Africa? The four of you?'*

Leslie decided not to pull any punches. Gary was a given, and – even though she didn't care for Natashya Safarov – the Russian policewoman had skills and access to information that she couldn't get. Yet.

'Yes. The four of us.'

Wynn-Jones let out a long breath and followed it almost immediately with an equally long string of curses.

'You're breaking my bloody balls here, Leslie. You know that, don't you?'

'You've got to give us a little more time.'

'Time is money in this business, love. You know that.'

'I also know that exposure means money.' Leslie turned back from the window because the traffic in the streets below was too distracting. She looked at the television.

She'd turned to the Discovery Channel out of habit. The programmes there could offer ideas and markets for what she wanted to do, as well as give her an idea of the competition she faced. Bizarrely, given the dinner conversation, tonight featured one of the documentaries on Atlantis. With the excavation going on in Cadiz, the whole world was thinking about Atlantis.

But the programme gave Leslie's mind, fuelled by

desperation because she felt certain Lourds would proceed on without her at this point, an idea.

'The remnants of a prehistoric band isn't going to be worth much,' Wynn-Jones protested.

'Not prehistoric,' Leslie said automatically. She knew she was mentally channelling one of Lourds' lectures over the last few days. What was that phrase he'd used?

'What?'

'Prehistoric refers to a time before there were any written records. The bell and the cymbal are definitely from . . .' she fumbled for the term '. . . the historic period.'

'Great. You're getting an education. Not exactly what I had in mind when you and the professor went haring about the world.'

Leslie's eyes focused on the television screen. Stock footage of great crystal towers from some cheesy science-fiction movie rolled. After a moment, tides swept over the city and shattered it into a million pieces.

'What if,' Leslie said, 'I can give you Atlantis?'

Wynn-Jones snorted. 'In case you haven't noticed, they've found Atlantis. It's in Cadiz.'

'What if they're wrong?' Leslie said.

'The Roman Catholic Church is backing that dig.' Even though Wynn-Jones remained a naysayer, interest sounded in his voice. 'They're seldom wrong about things like that.'

'They're wrong all the time. Think of the sexual attitudes of their priests.' Before Wynn-Jones could say anything, Leslie hurried on, 'The bell and the cymbal have writing on them that Lourds has never seen before. He's tracked the cymbal to the Yoruba people – who live in West Africa, hence the need to go there – and found indications that the artefacts are remnants of the civilization of Atlantis.'

'They came from Spain?'

'No. It's beginning to look like Atlantis was off the coast of West Africa. Or part of the coast of West Africa.' Leslie thought that was how Lourds had explained the situation.

'They're pretty certain about Cadiz,' Wynn-Jones said.

But Leslie knew she had the man thinking. Both of them were driven to grab attention to themselves if they could.

'What if they've got it wrong?' Leslie asked. 'What if, given time, we can deliver the true location of Atlantis?'

'That's a tall order.'

'Think about it, Philip. International media has been making love to this story since it began. Remember all those headlines we laughed about?'

They had laughed about those, but they'd also grudgingly admitted they wished they had gone to work on the story.

'The public's appetite has been whetted for this story,' Leslie pointed out. 'If Lourds can get us into part of that story, we'd be a smash. But if we could steal it away from them . . .'

She left the rest unsaid. She knew Wynn-Jones. His mind would cycle through the possibilities.

'All right,' Wynn-Jones said. 'I'll give you West Africa. But you'd better hope there's a bloody story there.'

Leslie did. She didn't know if it was Atlantis, but she was certain there was enough to mollify her bosses when the time came. If there wasn't, she might be out of a job. But that was the risk. Playing it safe wasn't going to get her anywhere. And she planned on going places, big-time.

After thanking Wynn-Jones, she rang off and started to punch in Lourds' room number to let him know they'd been cleared for Africa. But she was still slightly flushed with the wine. There was also that itch she had to contend with.

She decided to deliver the message in person. She opened her handbag and took out the spare key for Lourds' room. He hadn't thought anything of the fact he'd only been given one key.

Smiling, feeling hopeful, she headed out the door.

Natashya stepped out of the elevator in time to see Leslie walk past. Suspicious, still bothered by how easily Patrizio Gallardo and his men seemed to find them in Odessa, Natashya followed.

After dinner had broken up, she'd taken a cab to a club a few blocks away and checked in with Ivan Chernovsky. She didn't want him to know what hotel they were staying at. He hadn't been at home. His wife had told Natashya that he was working on a murder.

That news had made Natashya feel guilty. Chernovsky was out on the streets, possibly facing danger, and she wasn't there to cover his back. His wife, Anna, had let Natashya know she was concerned about her. Evidently Chernovsky had been talking to her about everything. Natashya had assured Anna that she was fine and asked her to tell Chernovsky that she would call again soon.

Although Natashya stayed well behind, if Leslie turned to check, she would be caught. Thankfully, her room was also this way. She had an excuse. But Leslie didn't turn once from her destination. She headed straight for Lourds' door. She halted there and raised her hand to knock. Then she reached into her handbag and took out a card. She swiped the card and watched as the light flashed green. Then she went inside.

Natashya never broke stride, but she felt deeply disturbed. The thing that bothered her most was she didn't know why she felt that way. It had been apparent from the beginning that Leslie had a crush on the professor. Natashya wondered, though, if Lourds would be vain enough to think it was anything more than that.

That could be a problem. Natashya needed Lourds up and thinking correctly if she was going to have a real chance at finding Yuliya's killers. But Natashya was also aware that on some level she didn't like the idea of Lourds being with another woman. *Another.* She caught that quirk in her thoughts and was unhappy with herself.

She thought about going to Lourds' door and

crashing the party, then decided that was too juvenile. Instead, she went to her room and ordered a bottle of Finlandia vodka. It gave her a small sense of satisfaction to put it on the room's tab and know that Leslie was going to have to account for it.

Excitement burned through Leslie when she heard the running water and saw the steam coming out of the bathroom. Lourds was in the shower. It wasn't exactly what she had in mind, but it would be fun. She felt a smile spread across her face.

The television was on and tuned to CNN. The computer was open on the desk and she could see that he'd been working.

Leslie hesitated, though. *Okay, you're in or you're out*, she told herself. She took a quick breath, dropped her handbag, kicked off her shoes, and peeled her clothes off.

Totally starkers, she stepped into the bathroom.

Lourds lay in the deep bathtub with his head back and his eyes closed. At first Leslie thought he was asleep. But when she moved toward him and her shadow tracked across his face, he snapped his eyes open.

When he saw her, he didn't try to cover up or act modest. He just lay there and looked at her. Then he smiled.

'I don't suppose you accidentally ended up in the wrong room,' he said.

Leslie giggled. *That* she hadn't expected. But one of the things she'd come to appreciate about Lourds over the last nineteen days she'd known him was his sense of humour.

'No,' she said. 'I didn't.'

But he didn't invite her in, either.

'Do you mind?' she asked as she pointed to the bath.

'Not at all. Although seating could be a little difficult.'

Leslie stepped into the bath with her feet outside Lourds' legs and sat across his thighs. For a moment she didn't know how interested he was going to be in what she had in mind. *If he wasn't intrigued he would have sent you away.* Then his interest manifested, hard and insistent, as it glided up between her thighs and pressed against her lower stomach.

'Well, now,' Lourds said, grinning. 'To what do I owe this pleasure?'

'It's not pleasure,' Leslie said, 'yet. But I think it will be.' She leaned into him and kissed him deeply. The heat of his body lit flames inside hers. Her mind swirled and her thoughts shattered into a kaleidoscope of sensory overload.

He smelled of soap and male musk. His lips tasted like wine. Leslie could hear her heart beating inside her head as his rough hands roved freely over her body. He gripped her hips and pulled her in for a tighter fit, but he didn't try to penetrate her. His proximity was maddening, though, because it was right *there*.

Leslie rolled her hips and tried to capture him so he would slide into place. He flexed his thighs and avoided her intimate embrace.

'Not yet,' he whispered against her throat.

'I thought you were ready,' she said.

'I am,' he told her, 'but you're not.'

She started to object and tell him that she was ready. If anyone would know she was ready, it was her. And she was more than ready.

His hand slipped in between her legs as they kissed. He bit her lips as he touched her gently. She doubted that he'd find what he was looking for. That bloody spot – the one that felt so good – was never in the same place twice. At least, that was the way it seemed.

But he did. His fingertips rubbed just hard enough to rob the breath from her lungs. She bent her back and leaned away from him so she could press her clitoris against his fingers. She rocked with him and couldn't believe he'd so easily found what she sometimes got frustrated searching for. He bent toward her and kissed her face and neck. But she was so locked into the vibrant need coursing through her that she couldn't respond.

In the next instant, warmth flooded her loins as her hips jerked toward him. She bucked and rocked as she rode his hand. The world came to a quiet and gentle stop. She took a shuddering breath.

'Wow,' she whispered. She leaned into him when he drew his hand back. His chest felt warm and solid against her breasts.

'Wow, indeed,' Lourds agreed.

'Am I ready now?'

'I think you are.' With surprising strength, Lourds

stood in the tub and stepped out. Leslie kept her legs tight around him.

He deposited her on the floor, then briskly towelled her dry. Even that contact sent her senses reeling. It was made even worse when he leaned in to kiss her, but somehow avoided her own efforts.

'You're a tease,' she accused.

'I hardly think so.'

She towelled him off too, but was more direct with her attentions. She dropped to her knees and took him into her mouth. That caught him by surprise but he resisted her best attempts to bring him over the edge. That was more than a little frustrating, but she looked forward to breaking down his resistance.

'Okay,' he said in a thick voice. 'That'll be enough of that.'

'For the moment,' she agreed.

Lourds bent and picked her up in his arms, cradling her like a child. She luxuriated in feeling small and defenceless in his embrace, though she knew she was anything but. The hunger in her belly fired anew as he carried her to the bed.

He laid her on it gently, then climbed aboard with her. She looked up into his eyes as she felt his hand nudge between her thighs and start caressing her again. She had no doubt that he could bring that to a successful conclusion again, even though that was surprising, but she wanted more.

She rolled him over onto his back, threw a leg across his hips, and pushed herself on top. She teased him for a moment, raking her slick loins against his erection, but figured out that he could handle any amount of teasing that she wanted to dish out.

Leslie laughed.

'What's so funny?' he asked.

'You,' she said. 'I hadn't thought you would have this kind of control.'

'Not control,' Lourds said. 'Consider it a compliment. I want you to enjoy yourself.'

'I am.' Leslie canted her hips a final time and eased him into her, claiming his flesh as her own. 'But I like it best when I'm in control.' She settled onto him, found the rhythm of the bed, and proceeded to grind him into dust.

15

Base Camp
Atlantis Dig Site
Cadiz, Spain
4 September 2009

Father Emil Sebastian roused when he heard his name called. When he looked up from the cot where he slept, he saw a hooded figure looming over him. Panic nearly throttled him because the figure reminded him of the nightmares he'd had for the past few weeks since his descent underground.

Then the figure adjusted the flame inside the lantern he carried.

Demons wouldn't need a lantern, Sebastian thought. His fear subsided. How could he have thought such a thing? If he hadn't already been seeing disturbing images when he slept, though, he might have blamed the horror movie some of the dig workers had watched on DVD last night. He hadn't intended to join them, but he loved a good scary story. He'd been fond of the genre since he was a kid – it was a childhood thrill he couldn't put away in spite of his fifty-six years.

'Are you awake, Father?' the young man asked politely. The lantern revealed his features then. They were angelic, not demonic. His voice was almost too soft to be heard over the constant throb of the diesel generators that supplied the base camp with electricity.

'I'm awake, Matteo.' Sebastian fumbled on the tent floor beside his bed and found his glasses and watch. It was 3.42. AM.

'Has something happened?'

There had been three cave-ins so far, but – *thank God!* – none of them had yet proven fatal. Four men had gone to the hospital with broken bones, though.

'Nothing bad, Father,' Matteo said. 'What's happened is good. Come and see.'

'Help me find my shoes.' In the darkness and with his night vision so impaired, Sebastian had trouble finding things. Worse yet, he couldn't actually remember where he'd taken his shoes off.

Matteo played the lantern around and pointed to Sebastian's feet.

'You're still wearing them, Father,' the young man said.

'Ah, so I am.'

'You've got to stop doing that,' Matteo told him. 'You'll get fungus.'

Sebastian knew that from the countless warnings they'd been given since the entrance into the cave system had been revealed during the underwater quake that had dredged up a new shoreline from under sixty feet of water. The cave system, after having been underwater for so long, remained a wet environment. Bacteria and fungus could grow rapidly.

During the first few months of the operation they'd had to build retaining walls against the sea and pump the water from the caves. It remained that way for each new cave they opened. When Sebastian had gone to bed – or, to cot – the pump team had still been working on draining the cave they'd found two days ago.

Sebastian stood and stamped his feet to check his circulation. Sometimes when he'd slept in his shoes his feet had turned completely numb.

'You should at least change your socks,' Matteo said.

Grudgingly, Sebastian knew the boy was right. He sat back down, took a pair of fresh socks from the duffel near the bed, took off his shoes and put them on. Then, grimacing with disgust, he put his shoes back on again.

'So why did you come for me, Matteo?' he asked as he stood once more.

'They've drained the cave. They think they've found another.'

'We expected there to be another cave.' In fact, they still expected a number of caves. Whatever had sundered the original coastline had also wreaked havoc with the catacombs that had undermined the ancient city.

Surrounded by the sea as it had been nine or ten thousand years ago, the original builders had taken steps to compartmentalize the catacombs. If one area flooded they could shut down the next.

'Yes, but not like this.'

Sebastian clapped the young man on the shoulder. 'Then let's go and see what they've found.' He stepped through the tent flap, but paused long enough to pick up his rechargeable flashlight from the charging plate. He didn't relish the idea of getting lost in the dark twisting maze of the cave system.

Outside the cave, three of the Swiss Guard assigned to the excavation team stood to attention. They wore casual clothing suited for exploring in the chill of the caves and they carried pistols.

Sebastian had protested at the presence of the weapons, but he hadn't been able to convince their captain to relinquish them. So far there hadn't been any incidents where they'd proved necessary, but the Guard didn't accept the idea that that meant there wouldn't be such incidents eventually. The men were well trained and polite, but they remained ever watchful.

The base-camp area smelled of diesel and salt water. The tang of dead fish remained as well. When the sea had given up the coastline and revealed its secret, and when the caves had been pumped dry, sea creatures had been marooned. They'd died by the hundreds and their rotting corpses had to be removed.

Sebastian had been told the fish apparently made good fertilizer. At any rate, they had disappeared from the camp.

As they passed the food tent, Sebastian stepped inside momentarily to retrieve two bottles of water and a pastry. He admitted the pastry was optional, but he needed the water. No one was supposed to walk anywhere without water in case they became lost. That had happened a few times as men, drawn by their curiosity, had gone off exploring on their own.

They still hunted riches, Sebastian knew. All the stories of Atlantis had filled their heads with hopes of fabulous wealth.

For himself, Sebastian didn't know what to think. He'd expected *something*. Instead, all they'd found so far were artefacts that carbon-dated back many thousands of years, proving them interesting in their own right, but nothing that really spoke of the civilization that had been there.

Much of the city had been lost. When the waves had drunk Atlantis down, the sea had purged the city. Torn asunder in the cataclysm – whether it was the fabulous towers shown in the illustrations Sebastian had seen, or whether they were only huts – the city had been shattered and spread across the sea bottom.

Whatever remained of it was buried beneath thousands of years of accumulated silt. Unless the sea chose to give it up, it might not ever be found.

Sebastian slid the bottles of water into the pockets of the long coat he wore against the chill of the caves. He followed Matteo's lead as they trailed along the yellow nylon rope that marked the path.

Strings of electric lights hung from the cave walls, but every time Sebastian left the base camp he was aware of entering the darkness waiting in the interior of the earth.

Radisson SAS Hotel Leipzig
Leipzig, Germany
4 September 2009

The strident ring of a cellphone woke Lourds amid
a tangle of soft limbs and seductive curves. In the
dim glow from the clock-radio on the nightstand he
saw the blonde highlights of Leslie's hair.

So it wasn't a dream.

He smiled at that. He'd been so tired last night
that he hadn't been certain he hadn't just dreamed
the encounter.

Gently, he disentangled one arm and reached for
the phone.

'Is it mine?' Leslie asked in a soft voice.

Lourds looked. There were two cellphones on the
nightstand.

'No,' he said. 'It's mine.'

'Good.' Leslie rolled off him and curled up in the
blankets.

As he punched the TALK button and brought the
phone to his ear, Lourds admired the smooth expanse
of her back and the supple curve of her naked derrière.

'Lourds,' he answered.

'Thomas?' The woman on the other end of the
connection sounded panicked.

Lourds focused immediately. He knew the voice
but he couldn't remember who it –

'This is Donna Bergstrom. Professor Marcus
Bergstrom's wife.'

'Yes, Donna.' Professor Bergstrom also taught at Harvard. He was in the palaeontology department. His wife was a professor of economics. Since he was a neighbour as well, Bergstrom watched over Lourds' house whenever he was out of the city. They often had cookouts and invited Lourds over.

'Something terrible has happened. Marcus was shot.'

Lourds swung his legs over the bed and sat up. 'How is he?'

'He just got out of surgery a few hours ago. The doctor says he's going to be fine. He's strong and he's a fighter.'

'He is that,' Lourds agreed. Bergstrom played soccer as well. 'What happened? Was he mugged?'

'The police say it was a home invasion,' Donna said.

'I'm sorry to hear that.' Lourds felt Leslie shifting behind him. He glanced at her and found her sitting cross-legged on the bed with a sheet around her hips. 'Did they do anything to your house?'

'It wasn't our house,' Donna said. 'It was yours. Marcus saw a gas van at your house. So he went to see what was going on.' The woman broke down in tears. 'They shot him, Thomas. Shot him for no good reason at all.'

Lourds tried to placate the woman, but the whole time he felt certain that his friend hadn't been hurt for no reason at all. Lourds had inadvertently left them in harm's way. The guilt was almost overwhelming.

*

Seated in the passenger seat of the corporate helicopter, Patrizio Gallardo peered down at the Radisson SAS Hotel.

'Ready?' the pilot asked over the headset.

'Ready,' Gallardo responded. He glanced over his shoulder at the eight men in the passenger area. All of them were dressed in black suits that hid the silenced pistols they carried. Briefcases carried spare magazines.

DiBenedetto sat smoking despite the pilot's desire for him not to. His blue eyes burned bright with the drug coursing through his system. Farok sat calm and resolute with his hands between his knees. Pietro and Cimino looked a little tense. Getting into and out of the hotel wasn't going to be easy.

The helicopter swooped down to the hotel rooftop and hovered only inches above. Gallardo opened the passenger door while DiBenedetto and Farok opened both side cargo doors. The nine men, with Gallardo in the lead, dropped to the rooftop and streaked for the access.

Cimino used a shaped charge that didn't sound any louder than a firecracker to blow the lock on the door. By the time the helicopter had cleared, they were inside the building and heading down to the seventh floor.

Lourds would never know what hit him.

Murani stared at the book he held. It represented both promise and condemnation. It was the only book outside the Bible he knew that truly did that.

Oversized and leather-bound, the book was an illustrated manuscript with obscure origins. It was written in Latin, and he believed it had been written in Rome at the height of the empire. After Rome fell, however, and the Germanic tribes rode through her walls and into her streets, libraries had burned in their wake. Some of the books had been taken out to the Netherlands where they were copied by the Irish monks and kept alive.

Murani wanted to believe the copy he had was the original. He didn't like the idea that other copies might exist in the world. Once a secret spread, it was hard to control.

He sat at one of the antique tables deep in the stacks and breathed in the aroma of dust, old paper and leather. He could still remember the excitement he'd felt when he'd first been permitted entrance into the room after becoming a member of the Society of Quirinus.

The library shelves were piled high with books. The saddest realization he'd ever come to was knowing that he'd never be able to read them all. At least, not in this life.

He still had hopes for the next.

The trick, then, had become to read the best ones. He'd started with some of the books the other Society members had recommended. There were so many secrets to choose from, so many things the Church struggled to keep secret from the rest of the world.

And the Society of Quirinus wanted to keep them secret from everyone.

In the end, though, Atlantis had called out to Murani. That, in his own estimation, was the biggest secret God and a few men had ever kept from the rest of the world.

When he'd first been told of the secret texts and the story that went with them – of the Garden of Eden and what had truly transpired there – he hadn't accepted it. Then, when he had, he'd wanted to know for sure that everything had happened exactly as he'd been told.

He stared at the page that showed the five instruments.

The bell.

The flute.

The cymbal.

The drum.

The pipe.

They were the five instruments that could unlock the secrets waiting within Atlantis. Exactly how they were supposed to do that he still wasn't certain.

But he had two of the instruments. The Society of Quirinus didn't know that.

Murani smiled there in the quiet darkness of the

library. If they had known he possessed them, they would have been frightened.

All that power, the power to remake the world, and it was nearly at Murani's fingertips. He traced the images on the page.

As part of the restricted collection the book was never allowed to leave the library. So he'd had to hide it in plain sight. The library caretakers were careful to let no books out of the library, but they weren't fastidious in keeping everything in order. There was simply too much to keep proper track of if people who read the books weren't exemplary in their upkeep of the system as well.

So the book had remained Murani's secret for four long years while he had searched for the instruments. Then the bell had shown up in Alexandria.

When that had happened, Murani had taken it as a sign. Afterwards, when the cymbal had come to light in Russia, he had begun to feel more hopeful.

'Cardinal.'

Unaware that anyone else was nearby, Murani looked up.

The old librarian was stooped with age. His grey whiskers stuck out in all directions. He walked with a cane.

'Good evening, Beppe,' Murani said politely, then hoped that the old man would simply go away.

'Good morning is more like it,' Beppe replied.

'Then good morning.'

'What happened to your face?' Beppe touched his own.

Murani wasn't surprised that Beppe hadn't heard the story of the carjacking that had claimed Antonio Fenoglio's life. The older librarians and caretakers rarely went anywhere outside the areas they supervised.

'I was in an automobile accident,' Murani answered. His face was still livid with purple and green bruises that were only now starting to yellow with age.

'That's why I never ride in those things,' Beppe said. 'I'll leave you to your reading. I've got a lot of things to do. Books that need mending and tending.' He shuffled off.

Murani returned to the wonder and the promise of the book. Surely everything would be revealed soon. Then he could set out on the mission God had chosen him to undertake.

Cave #41
Atlantis Dig Site
Cadiz, Spain
4 September 2009

'Father Sebastian.' Ignazio D'Azeglio, the night foreman on the dig, stepped forward and greeted the priest. He was a well-built man in his forties who was going grey at the temples and in his goatee. He had dark, swarthy Mediterranean skin, laughter lines, a broad nose and honest eyes. 'I hope you can forgive me for sending for you.'

'Matteo tells me you think you're about to break through into another chamber,' Sebastian said.

D'Azeglio nodded and handed Sebastian a yellow hard hat. 'We are. I've sent for Dario as well.'

Dario Brancati was the construction head of the excavation team. He'd worked on archaeological digs in the Middle East and in Europe.

D'Azeglio grinned. 'He hasn't yet arrived. I don't think he's as easy to wake as you are, Father.'

'Dario works much harder than I do.'

'No one works harder than you.' D'Azeglio shook his head. 'I think you've spent more time in a hard hat than anyone here.'

'Only because I'm not governed by the work guidelines your people are.'

'Come over here and let me show you what awaits us.' D'Azeglio led the way toward the wall where the team worked with drills and small loaders to shovel rock and debris out of the way.

Several dumper trucks, bulldozers and backhoes stood ready. All the earth that had been removed from the caves had been trucked out and used to build the bulwarks that kept the sea out.

The cavern was almost two hundred yards across and sixty or seventy yards high. Most of it lay in darkness. The further they went into the interior, the harder it became to power all the lights. Until they could maintain proper ventilation, no one wanted to risk any more carbon monoxide build-up than there already was.

The catacombs had demonstrated the same

circular compartmentalization that Plato had written about when describing the lost city. Sebastian didn't know if it was a design to give them a certain appearance or if it had been done to stabilize the underground tunnels and caves. He also wasn't certain if the underground area had been constructed first or if the city had. The city had been smashed almost beyond all recognition but perhaps they'd find records down here, where so much more was still preserved.

D'Azeglio walked over to an area lit by floodlights and pointed. 'We think another large chamber is behind that wall.'

Sebastian nodded. He'd already been briefed about it but D'Azeglio didn't know that.

The foreman took Sebastian back to the van where all their computer equipment was stored. Sebastian knew from earlier talks that the excavation team was using seismic reflection. They'd originally tried using ground-penetrating radar but had rapidly discovered the rock was too dense for the machine to handle, and that the caverns they were searching through were too large.

The seismic reflection required the use of dynamite or an airgun to set off shockwaves that could be mapped by the sensitive equipment. Once those shockwaves were set off, they were tracked and a picture was built up by the computer program.

D'Azeglio showed Sebastian the images they'd captured during earlier testing. Even though Sebastian knew the principle, he still struggled to see what was revealed.

'The cavern behind this one is huge,' D'Azeglio said.

'Maybe the biggest one we've found so far,' another man said.

Sebastian turned and found Dario Brancati standing behind the van. Brancati was a big man a couple of years older than Sebastian. His beard had turned solid grey and his bushy eyebrows almost surrounded his deep-set eyes. He was a friendly man, but he ran a tight ship.

'Sorry to wake you up, boss,' D'Azeglio apologized. 'But I knew you'd want to be here for this.'

'I do. I knew you guys would be hitting this about now. I sacked out once I left.' Brancati surveyed the wall. 'We all set up?'

'Yes. Charges are all in place. We're just waiting to get a green light.'

'You've got it,' Brancati said. 'Let's get it done.'

Radisson SAS Hotel Leipzig
Leipzig, Germany
4 September 2009

Lourds, dressed in a T-shirt, shorts and tennis shoes, knocked on Natashya's door. He felt awkward, but the phone call from Donna Bergstrom had left him feeling upset beyond bearing. He didn't believe for a moment that the home invasion had just been a random act. As he waited, he adjusted the backpack over his shoulder.

'What do you want?' Natashya demanded from inside.

'I need to talk to you.'

'Why aren't you still *talking* to that bottle-blonde airhead in your room?'

That surprised Lourds. Natashya had seen that?

'I didn't think at your age you would still be alive after she got her claws in you,' Natashya declared.

An older man passing by in the hallway looked at Lourds with disdain.

Lourds felt the need to defend himself but he knew that was insane. He didn't know the man and he hadn't done anything wrong.

'Maybe we could not talk about this out here?' Lourds suggested.

'We're not going to talk about it in my room.'

Lourds couldn't for the life of him figure out why Natashya seemed so angry. He hadn't gone after Leslie. True, he hadn't turned her away either. But they were two consenting adults looking for a little down time. There was nothing more to it. He was certain Leslie felt the same way. Then again, they hadn't talked about it and Lourds wasn't exactly a mind reader. He'd been involved with women before who hadn't understood the ground rules. His passion would always be his work. He wasn't going to be bereft of female companionship, but he wasn't going to let it change his life either. He had the impression that Leslie was a kindred spirit in that regard.

'Leave that be for now. Something more important has come up. Someone broke into my house,' Lourds said. 'A friend of mine got shot when he checked it out and is now in the hospital. He almost died.'

For a moment he didn't think Natashya was going to answer the door even after he told her that. Then, just as he was about to walk away, the door opened.

'Come in.' Natashya stepped back from the door dressed only in a too-big T-shirt that clung to her high breasts and ended well above mid-thigh.

Lourds knew he shouldn't have noticed. He tried not to, in fact. There were times he could go whole days at a time without noticing such things. At least, without letting them have an effect on him. The problem was that once his libido was aroused it remained rampant till it had burned itself out. That could take a while. His blood was definitely still running hot now.

Lourds entered the room and closed the door behind him. Light from the television monitor created a bubble of grey-blue illumination in the centre of the room. Evidently he hadn't caught Natashya sleeping.

'Having trouble getting some shut-eye?' Lourds asked in Russian.

Natashya stood with her arms folded over her breasts. 'You have a story. Let's hear it.' She spoke in English.

'My house,' Lourds repeated. 'Broken into.'

'So?'

Lourds ignored her, even as he wondered why she was in such a mood. He opened his backpack and took out his computer. After placing the computer on the desk, he opened it and booted it up.

'I've got a program on my computer that allows

me to access the security camera system in my house no matter where I am,' Lourds said.

'So you're going to show me your house?'

'I'm going to show you what bothers me about the break-in.' Lourds brought the program up. A series of windows spread across the screen as the cameras came on-line. 'This feature also allows me to go back twenty-four hours. Anything more than that and I have to access the security provider.'

'You have a picture of who broke into your house?' Natashya seemed a bit more interested.

'Yes.' Lourds tapped keys. 'Granted, it's possible that my house could have been broken into at random. I've been gone for about three weeks or so. But it seemed awfully coincidental.'

'Maybe you're only being paranoid.'

'With everything that's happened, I think that's the only way to be.' Lourds reversed the digital film to the point where he was watching one figure in orange coveralls in his den while the other raided his entertainment equipment from the bedroom.

'She's backing up your hard drive to the external one she brought,' Natashya said.

'Yes.' Lourds was uncomfortably aware of how the T-shirt material stretched across Natashya's breasts when she bent closer. She also, he discovered, smelled nice. He had to clear his voice to speak. 'Doesn't seem like something your typical burglar would do.'

'Do you keep anything important on your computer?'

'Notes. Projects I'm working on.'

'Important projects?'

'I work on the same kind of thing Yuliya did. None of it's going to make me wealthy or be worth much to anyone else.'

'No. What about credit cards and financial matters? Are those on your computer?'

'No. I'm too leery of that, I'm afraid.'

'Says the man who can look into his own bedroom from another country.'

'I thought it was pretty cool, actually. I'd never done it before today except when my friend installed it. I wouldn't have done it today if Marcus Bergstrom hadn't been shot.'

Natashya stood straight again and Lourds was sorry to miss the view.

'They were professional. The woman took data off your computer while the man upstairs attempted to make it look like a common burglary.' Natashya took a breath. 'This just means that Gallardo hasn't forgotten about us.'

'I thought maybe Gallardo had given up after Odessa.'

'Apparently not.' Natashya looked at the computer screen. 'They're hunting us now.'

'Why?'

'You tracked the cymbal back to the Yoruba people. I'm willing to wager they haven't done that.'

'They?'

'A man like Gallardo operates by a simple profit-and-loss statement. He does a crime and he immediately benefits from it.'

Lourds nodded. 'He stole the bell in Alexandria, so he must have had a buyer.'

'We have to find out. In the mean time, you need to leave.'

'I do?' Lourds was startled at how quickly she brushed him off.

'Yes. I don't want –'

There was a knock at the door.

Quietly, Natashya slid her hand under a pillow on the bed and brought out a pistol. Lourds started to speak but quieted at once when she put a finger to her lips. Silently, Natashya crossed to the door and peered out the peephole.

Then she sighed in disgust. Russian women, Lourds was willing to acknowledge, were champions at sounding disgusted when they chose to.

'*This*,' Natashya said as she opened the door, 'is what I didn't want.'

The door swung open and revealed Leslie standing there fully dressed. The young woman had her arms crossed and looked just the slightest bit challenging.

'I thought I'd come see what was taking so long,' Leslie stated. 'I was wondering if maybe you'd been distracted.'

For a moment Lourds thought Natashya might shoot Leslie. Though he wasn't sure why.

'Trust me,' Natashya said as she walked back to the bed, 'when I bed a man, I'm much more than a distraction.' Without another word, she slipped the pistol back under the pillow and lay on the bed. 'You people need to leave. I must get some sleep.'

Lourds started to do just that. He felt awkward enough as it was without getting into the middle of a catfight that he didn't quite understand. When he opened the door, though, he saw a man he recognized and quickly stepped back into the room.

'We can't leave,' he said.

The women looked at him with scathing stares.

'Patrizio Gallardo and his men just passed by in the hallway.'

Cave #1
Atlantis Dig Site
Cadiz, Spain
4 September 2009

'Fire in the hole!'

Crouched down behind one of the big bulldozers, Father Sebastian barely heard the warning shout of the demolitions crew chief rip through the cavern on the PA. The ear protectors muffled nearly all sound.

A moment later, the explosives blew in a rapid series like popcorn popping.

Dust and debris filled the cave. The full-face filter mask protected Sebastian's eyes and lungs. Tremors ran through the ground and reminded him of being on a ship's deck. Not for the first time did he think of the sea waiting outside the bulwarks they'd built to keep the cave dry.

He remained down until D'Azeglio slapped him on his hard hat.

'We're okay, Father,' the construction man said as he lifted one of the ear covers. 'Everybody's okay.'

D'Azeglio looked like some kind of freakish insect in the filtration mask and hard hat. His voice was muffled and strained. He offered a hand up.

'Thank God,' Sebastian said as D'Azeglio helped him to his feet. He took off the ear protectors. 'These explosions always make me nervous.'

'I've been around them for years, Father. When you're under this much rock, it never gets any easier.'

'No water,' someone called out. 'No water. The next cave is dry.'

A cheer went up. The water-filled caves they'd encountered so far had slowed them down considerably. Days had been lost with all the necessary pumping.

Excitement flared anew within Sebastian. Since he'd been a boy following around his archaeologist father, he'd always loved the idea of seeing things that hadn't been seen in hundreds or thousands of years.

When he'd been pulled to the cloth, he'd feared those days were over. But he thanked God, in whose infinite wisdom he'd been allowed to take up not only the Bible and cross as a priest, but also the pick and shovel of an archaeologist.

It was a good life.

High-intensity spotlights played over where the wall had been. Now it was only a jumble of rock in the opening to another cave. The opening at the top was perhaps four feet high.

Brancati ordered the scholars to stay back while some of the more able climbers surveyed the area. Sebastian watched the four men climb up the rock and reach the pinnacle. They wore miner's hard hats with built-in lights. They carried other lights in their hands. Brancati remained in constant contact with them by radio.

After a few minutes, the men descended the other side. Shortly after that, Brancati came over to Sebastian.

'Father, do you think you can make it up that rock?'

Sebastian was surprised by the question. Brancati had taken pains to make certain he was kept out of harm's way.

'I think I can manage,' the priest replied.

'We'll help you. It's important that you see what's in that cave.'

'What is it?'

Brancati's expression was solemn. His voice was low when he spoke. 'They think it's a graveyard.'

The announcement sent a chill through Sebastian. It wouldn't be a graveyard in the traditional sense. While travelling with his father as a young man, Sebastian had been present when such discoveries had been made. Simple men were always humbled.

And frightened.

'Let's go,' Sebastian said. He started forward, but his mind whirled with the implications. Were they about to see Atlanteans for the first time?

16

Cave #42
Atlantis Burial Catacombs
Cadiz, Spain
4 September 2009

The long climb robbed Father Sebastian of his breath and reminded him that he wasn't as young as he remembered. Despite the daily constitutionals he took, he too often found himself in library stacks rather than dig sites during the course of his working days. Reading was not the most aerobic of activities. But he managed the task in hand. He made it all the way up the sloping pile of broken stone and debris, even if he didn't do it quite so quickly as his younger colleagues.

The halogen light one of the men raked across the interior of the next cave lit up the catacombs. The cave had been carved from solid rock and hollowed out to make room for the dead. Aisles wove through the walls that stood floor to ceiling like huge bookcases and reminded Sebastian of an old coil radiator.

'Looks like an apartment village of the dead,' one of the construction workers said quietly.

The wreckage and the debris had been spread on

the other side of the opening as well. Rocks had tumbled down between the walls of graves.

Atlantis.

The word whirled through Sebastian's brain. Atlantis was the most fabled of all lost worlds. And it seemed to him that at least a piece of its past was spread out before him. It was a truism in both his fields of expertise that the soul of a culture revealed itself in the way it treated the dead.

Sebastian turned so quickly he almost fell on a loose rock. One of the Swiss Guards reached out reflexively to steady him.

'I need to get down there,' Sebastian said. 'I need to see. Help me.'

'Father,' one of the Guards said softly, 'the way doesn't look safe.'

'I'm afraid we can't allow you down there,' one of the construction men said. 'The boss told us we could bring you this far, but that's it.'

'Then I need to speak to Brancati,' Sebastian said to the nearest construction worker. 'May I borrow your radio?'

'Mr Brancati's a stubborn man,' the worker said. 'But you're welcome to try.'

After the man showed Sebastian how to use the radio, the priest keyed the microphone. 'Mr Brancati? Dario?'

'Yes, Father,' Brancati replied.

Sebastian stared into the darkness that swathed the final resting places of the people who had once made the city above them teem with life. His conservative estimate was that there must be at least a thousand bodies within the crypt.

'I need to go down there,' Sebastian said.

'Wait,' Brancati said. 'Let my team make sure everything's safe.'

'Just for a short visit.' Sebastian knew a pleading note had entered his voice and it embarrassed him.

'I don't want you to get hurt.'

'I did not believe that our excavation would play out this way,' Sebastian admitted. 'I feel like the men who unearthed King Tut. I need to see what we've discovered.'

'You should remember what happened to those men. Couldn't you wait till –'

Sebastian interrupted. 'Dario, I'm going to be on the phone with the Pope in a few minutes. We already know that we have leaks within the crew. We're not going to be able to keep this secret. I don't want to tell the Pope that we don't yet know what we have. Do you?'

Brancati was silent for a moment. 'All right, Father. But be careful. Down and up, and you're out of there.'

'Of course.' Sebastian handed the radio back to the construction worker. 'You heard?'

The man nodded but didn't look particularly happy about the situation.

'You can either lead or follow me,' Sebastian said.

'I'll lead, Father,' the young man said. 'But you have to do what I say. I want both of us to stay safe.'

Sebastian nodded and prepared to follow.

Natashya took command of the situation at once.
With Gallardo and his people just outside the door,
there was no time to lose.

'Call Gary,' she directed, and hoped that the young
man wasn't already a casualty. 'Tell him to get out of
his room. Tell him to take the nearest stairwell. We'll
find him there.' She swept her T-shirt off and revealed
her nudity beneath. Although Lourds and Leslie both
stared at her, she ignored them. She wasn't modest
about her body. 'Do it!'

Lourds reacted first and crossed to the telephone.

'Let's hope they go for your room first, Professor.
It's what I would do. And it will buy us time.'
Natashya kept her pistol in hand as she located her
jeans and pulled them on without benefit of panties.
'Leslie, call the front desk and ask for security. Tell
them someone is trying to break into your room.
You're next door to Lourds.'

Lourds talked quickly but Natashya felt his eyes
on her as she pulled on a light knitted top. If they
hadn't been in fear for their lives, she might have felt
a little smug about that. She noticed that Leslie was
definitely aware of where Lourds' attention was.

Unfortunately, her jealousy might get them all killed.
Leslie was still standing there, not following commands.

'Move it!' Natashya said.

Shocked into action, Leslie used her cellphone to call the desk. She was asking for security while Natashya found a pair of tennis shoes and pulled them on. Natashya abandoned the rest of her wardrobe. She took a fanny pack from her suitcase containing extra magazines for her pistol – bought from a local black-market dealer the day they'd arrived in Leipzig – and strapped it around her waist.

Lourds put the phone down. 'Gary is going to meet us in the lobby.'

'Security's on the way,' Leslie said.

Tension rattled through Natashya's stomach. It would have been better if she hadn't been the only one here with security experience and wasn't the only one with a weapon.

'We'll go now,' Natashya said. 'Once we're through the door, head for the stairwell at the other end of the hallway. Move fast but don't run. We don't want to call attention to ourselves. And don't go to the elevator.'

'It's seven flights of stairs,' Leslie said.

'You wish to be a target to save a few steps, it is fine by me.' Natashya shrugged. The woman's plan suited her just fine in her present mood. 'You go for the elevator. You can decoy them. Try not to get killed too quickly.'

Leslie was shocked into silence by the blunt words.

Lourds reached out and took Leslie's hand. 'No elevators. We'll go to the stairwell.'

'I wish I had a gun, too. I'd feel a lot better,' Leslie said.

'You couldn't have got it through the airports, much less customs,' Lourds said.

'She managed to find a weapon,' Leslie pointed out.

'As soon as we have time, I'll tell her to take you shopping,' Lourds said. 'For now, let's get moving.'

'All right then,' Natashya said.

A knock sounded on the door.

Cursing, not even thinking about looking through the peephole in case Gallardo's men chose to shoot first and verify identities later, Natashya flung the door open and swung it wide. The move caught the two men outside flatfooted. They had their hands on their weapons beneath their jackets but hadn't yet drawn them.

She aimed her pistol at the lead man's face but knew the man behind him could see it as well. 'Touch your weapons and you die,' she said in English, hoping that they spoke the language. 'Get your hands up.'

She wasn't certain if it was English the men understood or the blank, naked threat of the pistol. Either way, they lifted their hands.

'Inside. Quickly.' Natashya wiggled the gun to lead the way. She plucked their ear/throat headsets from their heads, then had Lourds search them and take their pistols. Both of them were silenced.

Both of the men scowled.

'Down on your knees. Cross your ankles. Hands behind your head,' Natashya ordered as she took the pistols one at a time from Lourds. She shoved her own at the back of her waistband, then held one of the thug's silenced pistols pointed at them. It would be justice if they were killed with their own weapons, she thought.

Neither of them moved.

'Okay, we try this again,' Natashya said. 'And I'm going to shoot any of you who don't speak English.'

Lourds rattled off something in Italian. The men quickly got into position.

Okay, Natashya thought, *perhaps they really don't speak English.*

At the end of the hall Natashya heard a door break. They were running out of time.

'Let's go.' Natashya opened the door again and motioned for the others to precede her. She kept her gun trained on their captives.

'I will shoot the first one of you who comes out of this door,' she said, and hoped they understood her intent, if not her words.

Then she stepped out into the hall and followed the rest of the crew to the stairwell. She kept one of the silenced pistols out of sight along her leg, and kept her eyes on the door they'd just exited. The men they'd left in her room weren't going to stay there long. She knew that. Less than six steps into their escape, she heard the door open behind her.

'Gallardo!' one of them yelled.

Natashya brought the silenced pistol up. She fired two rounds. Both of them struck the door within inches of the man's face.

He ducked back inside the room as the low-velocity bullets failed to penetrate the door. But the damage had already been done.

Even though the rounds were silenced, Gallardo heard her.

At the other end of the hall, Gallardo and his men stood in front of Lourds' door. Gallardo turned at the sound of the coughing noises the pistol made and the *slaps* of the bullets against the door.

By that time Lourds had reached the stairwell door. He opened it and went through.

Natashya took advantage of the cover provided by the stairwell door to get off enough shots to make them duck. 'Go!' she shouted over her shoulder. 'I will hold them back.'

Lourds hesitated.

'Go!' Natashya ordered, then ducked herself as bullets struck the wall and the door.

Leslie pulled Lourds into motion and they started down the steps.

Pressed against the doorframe, Natashya waited a moment, then whirled around. She tried to keep herself calm and collected, but it was hard. Even when she and Chernovsky were on the streets, she hadn't faced these kinds of odds in a gunfight. There were occasional instances where they chased a team of criminals, but usually they sought only one man. Never more than three. She'd counted at least five in the hallway.

She sighted on the man closest to the hallway door and fired at his centre mass. He was twenty feet out and running hard. She fired her captured pistol dry and saw the slide lock back. The man she'd shot stumbled and fell headlong into the floor. He twitched and spasmed. The other men in the hallway flattened in a doorway. A hail of gunfire drummed the door.

Natashya dodged back inside and tossed the empty pistol away. She drew the other silenced one she'd seized and flipped the safety off. Studying the door, she saw that none of the bullets had penetrated the metal shell. Her enemies' low-velocity silenced rounds had less power than her primary weapon had.

Every nerve in her body screamed at her to run. Instead she reached overhead and raked the pistol's long silencer through the fluorescent lights. Glass rained down as the tubes exploded and the stairwell landing dimmed. With lights above and below, the area didn't go completely dark.

She forced herself to squat down in the corner by the stairwell. Far below, she heard Lourds and Leslie running. Their footsteps echoed in the stairwell. They seemed to be making good time.

The door opened cautiously. Natashya held the pistol steady.

Come on, she thought. She didn't like ambushing anyone, but when it came down to her survival and the completion of her sister's goals, she wasn't going to hesitate. She owed Gallardo and his men for Yuliya. There was no mercy in her as she waited.

A man looked around the door. She shot him between the eyes. She was in full flight before his body hit the ground. Seeing the dead man in the doorway would hopefully give the others pause before they followed.

She ran as if her life depended on it – it probably did.

Five floors down, Natashya caught up with Lourds and Leslie. Lourds was leading the way and struggling to keep Leslie on her feet. That surprised Natashya. She'd expected the professor to be struggling, not Leslie. He was in much better shape than she'd thought. And Leslie was crumpling under the pressure. Or was it that simple?

Lourds opened the lobby door and moved to step through.

'Wait,' Natashya said. She ran up to the professor. Listening to Leslie gasping for air left her secretly pleased, and she was surprised she could still be that vindictive while running for her life.

Hiding the pistol behind her back, Natashya peered out into the lobby. She couldn't see the front desk from her position, but she could see no one waiting for them.

'We'll leave the car and take a cab,' Natashya told Lourds and Leslie. 'In case Gallardo has managed to hack into the hotel's database and get information on us, he won't be able to trace us by the licence plate.'

Lourds nodded.

'Go,' Natashya said. 'I'll cover you.'

Around the next corner, two men in suits held pistols out.

'Hotel security!' one of the men said in German. 'Put the weapon down!'

Cave #42
Atlantis Burial Catacombs
Cadiz, Spain
4 September 2009

Once Sebastian climbed through the initial barrier of rocks and debris, the going got much easier. He trembled with excitement and terror as he stepped among the graves. If this place was what he supposed it to be, he had cause to be cautious.

The two Swiss Guards stayed at his side. They carried flashlights as well.

Drawn by the eerie sight of the dead lying in their simple graves, Sebastian knelt before the nearest stack of them and gazed into the hollow spot. The hole had been hand carved. Rather than being merely hacked out, though, the corners of the niche were rounded off and the measurements were equal. It was a carefully prepared receptacle for the remains and artefacts that occupied it.

All of the graves showed the same care and skill.

Sebastian gazed at the body that lay there. Judging from the bones, it was a man. The girth of the pelvis revealed that. They poked against the shroud. Sebastian judged that the man had been nearly six feet in height, quite tall for the presumed period of the burial. The formation of the skull and features looked normal, there was no bone binding or alterations in dentition or other small changes to the human form he'd seen in his countless digs across the world.

He shone his light over the remnants of the shroud. He wanted to tear it off and see what lay beneath, but he knew he couldn't. Before anything was done in the burial vault, everything had to be digitally recorded, then measured, then catalogued as the examinations took place.

But he could see bits and pieces through the holes in the shroud. The man had worn a grey or black or dark blue robe. It was hard to judge the colour after so long. The teeth looked like they had been in very good condition at the time of his death. That was odd because most humans who had lived to adulthood that long ago displayed dental issues. Tribes that had eaten millet and other coarse grains usually showed wear and tear to the teeth from the constant grinding it took to process their food. Tribes that ground their grains also showed wear and tear – the stones used to process the grains left grit in the flours, and that wore away at the dental enamel almost as much as eating unground grains. This man had teeth a modern actor would have been proud to display.

Metal gleamed at the dead man's neck under his crossed hands.

Leaning into the grave a little more, Sebastian used a pencil from his pocket to gently shift the shroud to reveal the prize beneath. It belonged to a necklace made of white gold or silver. The pendant was in the shape of a man with his right hand offered in friendship. He carried a book in his left hand.

'Oh, God,' Sebastian said as recognition of the image seared through his mind. 'Forgive us. Forgive what we have done to You and Your Son.'

It was true. All of it.

And if this was true, then the story of the secret texts had to be true as well.

Sebastian reached for the necklace with a shaking hand. He touched the metal and felt a small electric shock at contact, but he didn't know if the sensation was real or imagined.

The skeleton's arm leapt up and brushed his as if trying to grab it.

Sebastian cried out in fear and jerked back. The back of his head slammed against the side of the grave and nearly knocked him out. The pain left him dazed as he sat heavily on his posterior.

In the next instant, the skeleton leapt from the alcove and fell against his legs.

Only then did Sebastian realize that the whole cavern was shaking. The skeleton wasn't moving under its own power. He looked down the row of crypts as several other skeletons vacated their premises and clattered to the stone floor. Embalmed corpses fell, too, with a sound much different than the crack of hard bone against the stone floor.

Lights in the hands of the other men whipped around the cavern's interior. The panorama of illumination presented a dizzying light show.

Then someone cried out, 'Flood! *Flood!*'

It's happening again, Sebastian thought. *The sea's reclaiming Atlantis and the Garden.*

The Swiss Guards grabbed him under the arms and yanked him to his feet as inches of water suddenly covered the stone floor. They ran and pushed him back towards the opening they'd come through. With every step, though, the water swirled higher and higher.

Radisson SAS Hotel Leipzig
Leipzig, Germany
4 September 2009

Confronted by the hotel security staff, Natashya froze for just a moment as she tried to figure out what to do. She didn't want to get embroiled with the local security people, and she couldn't just put down her weapon because then they'd be sitting ducks for Gallardo's people.

At that moment Gary stepped out of the lobby area and walked up behind the security men. He leaned over the first man's shoulder and whispered something.

'Horst,' the first man said as he slowly raised his arms, 'he has a gun on me. Surrender.'

The second guard hesitated for just a moment. Then he raised his weapon, too.

Natashya rushed forward and took both men's weapons. 'Down on your faces,' she ordered.

As they got down, Gary flashed her a sickly grin

and showed her the ballpoint pen he'd used for his bluff.

Spare me Americans and Brits and their macho television shows, Natashya thought.

'You could have been killed,' she whispered to Gary.

'I kind of planned not to,' he replied hoarsely. 'And it wasn't like I had a lot of time to figure things out.'

'Go.' Natashya pushed him into motion toward the main entrance. Glancing back over her shoulder, she saw Gallardo come down the fire stairs.

She lifted the pistol and fired rapidly. Her bullets drummed the door and wall. The small inset window emptied in jagged pieces.

Gallardo ducked back and cursed loudly.

By then Lourds, Leslie and Gary had reached the main entrance. They were through it by the time Natashya arrived. They ran into the street and tried to flag down a passing taxi, but it kept going.

The next taxi had its light off and obviously had no intention of stopping. Natashya stepped out, drew her own pistol because it wasn't silenced, and fired into the air. The flat report echoed across the street and the muzzle-flash reflected in the windshield. Natashya aimed the pistol at the taxi driver.

The taxi screeched to a stop in front of Natashya. Keeping her weapon trained on the driver even though she had no intention of shooting him, she made her way to the driver's side door.

'Get out,' she told the driver in German.

He got out while Lourds helped Leslie into the rear seat. He didn't join her, though. Instead he sat up front with Natashya. Gary got in on the other side.

As soon as they were aboard, Natashya put her foot down on the accelerator.

'Where are we going?' Lourds asked.

'I don't know,' Natashya replied.

'The airport,' Leslie said. 'I contacted my supervisor earlier and cleared us for a trip to West Africa.'

Natashya looked at the woman sharply. 'You did what?'

'Professor Lourds . . .'

Now we're back to Professor Lourds? Natashya wondered. *After you've bedded him?*

'. . . has said that he thinks he's got all the information that was possible at the Max Planck Institute,' Leslie continued. 'He thinks there are more complete records and ties to our missing artefacts in Africa.'

As she drove, Natashya said, 'You've been talking to your supervisor this whole time? Telling him what we are doing?'

'Yes.' Leslie looked sullen. 'I have to. The company has been paying for everything. They deserve to know what we're up to.'

Natashya looked at Lourds and couldn't help feeling that part of this was his fault. 'You do realize that's how Gallardo has been keeping tabs on us? Through the BBC's financial support?'

To his credit, Lourds looked guilty. 'No. I didn't know that.'

'Well, you know it now.' Natashya turned away from him, too angry to speak for the moment. Nothing good would come out of her mouth, and she didn't want to say anything she'd feel guilty about or regret later. She concentrated on her driving as she looked for a place to dump the taxi. They couldn't take it all the way to the airport. Surely the driver had already called in his stolen vehicle. It was time for new wheels.

'The woman stopped a taxi in front of the hotel. I will track her through the streets.'

Until she abandons the vehicle, Gallardo thought as he ran back up the seven storeys to the roof. His legs burned from the effort and panic started to set in when he thought he might not make it.

'No,' Gallardo huffed as he dragged himself up the last flight of stairs. DiBenedetto and Farok followed him. Pietro and Cimino were both down, dead or wounded too severely to survive. The sounds of pursuit – footsteps ringing on the steps – echoed after them. 'We have bigger problems right now.'

Up on the roof, Gallardo ran and waved his flashlight. He watched the helicopter approach the rooftop and hang in the air only inches from the surface. He ran toward the craft and pulled himself into the passenger seat.

'What about the others?' DiBenedetto asked from the rear section.

'They're not here,' Gallardo said. 'They're not coming. You wish to die or be captured while we wait for them?' He pulled the headset on and gave the pilot a thumb's up.

The pilot lifted the helicopter immediately and swung to the west. The emergency plans were clear: to get out of the city and drop the helicopter in the trees. Air-traffic control might be able to track the chopper, but the police wouldn't be able to catch them before they drove away in the cars stashed at the staging area outside the city.

But right now Gallardo was less concerned with where they were going than he was with where they'd been.

Back on the hotel rooftop, the doors from the stairwell opened again and two of Gallardo's hired help rushed out. They stood and stared after the departing helicopter.

Only seconds later, hotel security staff flanked by Leipzig police officers came through the door. Muzzle-flashes lit up the night briefly as the two men exchanged fire with the police and security guards. When it ended, both of Gallardo's hired men were down.

Quietly, Gallardo damned Lourds. The linguistics professor was having an incredible run of luck. But there would be an accounting. No one's luck lasted for ever. He turned to DiBenedetto.

'Did you get the chance to raid the professor's room?'

DiBenedetto nodded and handed over the book bag holding all the papers and books he'd been able to get from Lourds' hotel room.

Gallardo searched through the bag. Most of the information seemed to be centered on West Africa, and on a single tribe. He smiled. At least they had a probable destination to check out if the professor disappeared.

'Natashya has a point,' Lourds said quietly. 'Gallardo and his men have managed to dog our heels. Your continued contact with your employer could present a danger to us.'

Leslie glared at him in exasperation. 'I understand that she has a point. Truly I do. But I also have a point: Without the backing of my company, we wouldn't be here. And we won't be able to continue. Unless you think we can hitchhike to Dakar?' Spots of colour darkened her face as they sat in an all-night diner.

Gary was at the counter flirting with the female cashier. She'd been drawn to the concert T-shirt he was wearing that featured a German speed-metal band. Lourds thought the cameraman was definitely having a better time than he was.

'No,' Lourds said finally. 'I don't think we could hitchhike to Dakar.'

'Good. At least that's something.'

'I don't think she was accusing you of betraying us –'

'Trust me,' Leslie said, 'I know an accusation when I hear one. That was definitely an accusation.'

'Do you really think she would believe you would risk your own life by telling Gallardo and his minions where we were?'

'Maybe you should ask her. She's the one with all the answers. Maybe she believes I think getting shot at serves some special, twisted kink I have.'

Lourds frowned. He hated getting in the middle of a war of wills between women. On the one hand it could be dangerous for everyone. On the other, they could join forces at any moment and come after him together. In many ways, he worried about that danger more than he worried about getting shot at.

'Perhaps you might ask your supervisor to see if he couldn't get us the money he agreed to let us use in a different fashion.'

Leslie crossed her arms over her chest. 'Maybe you could call Harvard and ask them for the money to fund an expedition to Dakar?'

Lourds sipped his green tea and thought about that. He almost laughed. He'd have a better chance of hitchhiking to West Africa. Especially since he couldn't tell them what the expedition was really about.

'No,' he said. 'You're right.' He paused. 'We're not in a good spot. The question is whether we should continue, knowing these people are trying to kill us.'

'Could you actually walk away from this thing right now? Just forget about it after we've come this far? Do you know what kind of story this is going to be?'

'This isn't a game, Leslie. Those people murdered one friend of mine and almost killed another. And that doesn't count all the other corpses they've left scattered in their wake. Remember how they killed your producer?'

'Do you want them to get away with that? Do you want them to get whatever it is they're after? Don't you want to save the artefacts?'

'This is too big for us,' he said. 'We need to get help.'

'We went to the police. In Alexandria, remember? They didn't do anything. The only police that seems to be interested in acting on this is Natashya.'

'She has a vested interest. They killed her sister.'

'So do you. They've been shooting at you for days. They nearly killed your neighbour. Just think, if you hadn't been there the day they took the bell, we wouldn't have had a clue about what was going on.'

'We still don't.'

'Then why are we going to Dakar?'

Lourds didn't answer. She had a point, but he didn't have to admit it.

'I don't think it's just because you'd like to go to West Africa,' Leslie said. She leaned in closer to him. 'You believe there's an answer there.' Her eyes held his. 'You *believe* it.'

Seeing the desire for knowledge in her eyes, Lourds felt his own need to know fanned to a fever-pitch. 'Maybe.'

'Why do you think something's there?'

'Because the Yoruba culture is the oldest we've yet encountered. Because I've seen hints that they had these instruments at one time. If these instruments all came from one area, it stands to reason that they came from the oldest known civilization.'

'Then we need to go there.'

'Those men may be waiting,' Lourds pointed out.

'And they may be waiting back home for you as well,' Natashya said.

Glancing over his shoulder, Lourds found her standing there. He hadn't even heard Natashya approach. It was another grim reminder that he was clearly out of his element while dealing with dangerous felons.

'As I was telling Leslie, we should go to the police.'

'The police are seeking to detain us. They've got witnesses who have seen us shoot at armed men. It doesn't inspire trust in a municipal police department to have that happen. The radio is full of our descriptions and the news that we are wanted.'

'That's just absolutely brill,' Leslie grumped. 'I suppose you know that getting out of the country by airline, train, ship or bus is absolutely out of the question if what you say is true.'

'I do. However, I was able to secure a car so we can get to France.'

'Why France?' Leslie asked.

'We're not wanted in France,' Natashya replied. 'The EU has open borders. We won't be stopped entering France if we drive. From France we should be able to book passage to Dakar.'

Gary wandered over from the counter. He looked slightly nervous. 'I was just watching the telly. You were right. We made the news.'

Looking at the television mounted above the counter, Lourds watched as hotel surveillance-camera footage of the gunfight at the Radisson rolled. So far police and hotel management weren't releasing any details, but four men were confirmed dead at the scene.

'You said you only killed two,' Leslie accused.

'I did,' Natashya replied.

And that exchange drew attention from nearby patrons.

Lourds gathered his backpack and eased out of the booth. 'On that note, ladies and gentleman, I think it best if we adjourn somewhere else. Before the police arrive.'

Restricted Library Stacks
Status Civitatis Vaticanae
4 September 2009

'Cardinal Murani? Yes, he's here.' Beppe's hoarse voice carried in the quiet library.

Seated at the table, Murani gazed at the drawing of the man offering his right hand while holding a book in his left. The figure had occupied his thoughts for years.

No, he corrected himself, *not the figure. The book.*

Footsteps headed in his direction.

Cardinal Giuseppe Rezzonico followed the old librarian to Murani.

'Cardinal,' Beppe bared a toothless grin, 'you have a guest.'

'Thank you, Beppe.' Murani waved to a chair on the other side of the table.

Rezzonico seated himself. He looked like he'd just got out of bed and wasn't too happy about it. 'Father Sebastian's excavation team just began exploring the new cavern they found.'

'Cave number forty-two.' Murani nodded. He'd been keeping up with the exploration of the catacombs.

'It turned out to be a burial vault. A large one.'

Murani couldn't hold himself back. 'Who was buried there?'

'We don't know. The Swiss Guard relayed us digital images over the internet.' Rezzonico passed over a digital camera. 'I downloaded them to this.'

Murani took the camera and quickly flicked through the images.

'This is them,' Murani said hoarsely. 'The Atlanteans. Those who lived in the Garden.'

'Perhaps.'

Murani couldn't believe it. He stared at Rezzonico and anger filled him. 'How can you doubt this? If your faith were as strong as it should be, you'd know this for what it was.'

'It's a burial vault,' Rezzonico said. 'That's all I know for certain.'

After checking the size of the digital files, Murani discovered they were almost five megabytes each. They could be blown up considerably.

Without a word, Murani got up from the table and walked to the back of the room. High-tech digital equipment occupied a small area in the stacks.

He sat at the desk and popped out the SD-RAM

memory chip from the camera and inserted it into the reader slot on the front of the computer. It only took a few keystrokes to bring up the images.

'This isn't why I came here,' Rezzonico protested. 'We need to talk.'

'I'm listening. But let's look while we talk.' Murani examined each of the pictures in turn. Slowly, he followed Father Sebastian into the crypt.

'The council wants to talk to you. They don't believe that you had nothing to do with Father Fenoglio's death.'

For a moment Murani couldn't remember who Father Fenoglio was.

'They know the Pope had Father Fenoglio following you,' Rezzonico said.

'The Pope should feel guilty about that. Not me. I didn't put Fenoglio in harm's way.' Murani glanced up at Rezzonico. 'Furthermore, why didn't the council see fit to tell me that the Pope had someone following me?'

'They thought Fenoglio would be more circumspect.'

'Why would the Pope assign someone to spy on me?'

'Because he doesn't trust you.'

'I've proven myself very trustworthy for years.'

'Not to this Pope. He believes you're far too interested in the secret texts for your own good.'

'I'm here, not in Cadiz,' Murani snorted. 'I couldn't be much further removed from the secret texts. The Pope has already seen to that.'

'Yet here you are,' Rezzonico said, 'prowling through the stacks dedicated to the secret texts and all that pertains to the Garden of Eden.'

Murani took a deep breath and let it out. 'I should have been the one to go to Cadiz. I should be the one heading up the excavation. No one knows more about the secret texts, the Garden of Eden and Atlantis than I do. *No one.*'

'The Society didn't want to fight the Pope.'

'The Pope *isn't* right in his approach to the Church!'

Self-consciously, Rezzonico glanced around. 'Please keep your voice down, Stefano. I beg you. You're already in enough trouble.'

'What trouble?'

'Didn't you hear me? The council suspects that Fenoglio's death was no accident.'

'Of course it was no accident. The carjacker ran him down. I know. I was there. I nearly was killed myself – the bruises haven't fully faded yet.'

'*And* the car backed over him, according to the police report.' Rezzonico's gaze remained level. 'That was something *you* didn't report.'

Murani realized he hadn't mentioned that. At the time it had seemed like it would draw too much attention to the incident. He had forgotten about the forensic work that could be done. 'I was in shock. It all happened so fast.'

'The police say there was no blood in the car's interior.'

'The carjacker hit me again and again when I got

out of the car,' Murani said. 'He didn't want me to escape and identify him.' That was an easy adjustment to make to the story.

Rezzonico was quiet for a moment. 'The only reason the police haven't questioned you further in this matter is because we have interceded on your behalf.'

'We?' Murani showed the older man a mirthless smile. 'Now the Society protects me?'

Rezzonico frowned. 'Your disrespect grows insufferable, Stefano.'

'No,' Murani growled, 'the stupidity shown by the Society – and you – deserves my derision. The Society protects me to protect itself. If I were to be arrested for Fenoglio's murder, do you think I would continue to protect the secrets the Society of Quirinus has been covering up for generations?'

'If you loved the Church –'

'The Church is the bride of God. She's supposed to serve God. She isn't serving God by growing weaker and more tolerant every year. She's supposed to be strong and run God's house here in this world. She has a mission –'

The newest image on the computer caught Murani's attention and froze his diatribe in mid-word.

A necklace lay revealed in the image. It showed a man offering his hand while his other hand held a book.

'Sebastian found it,' Murani whispered in disbelief. 'Look here.'

'So I see. And he may have lost it,' Rezzonico said.

'Shortly after this cave was found, after the images were relayed to the Society, there was a collapse. Water flooded the burial chamber. No one knows if Sebastian or the men in that room are still alive.'

17

ATLANTIS DROWNING AGAIN?

The headline on CNN *Headline News* caught Lourds'
attention as he sat in the boarding area awaiting the
flight to Dakar, Senegal.

Leslie's production company had, though grudgingly, set up a separate accounting to foil whoever had
been spying on the travel expenses. They'd also sent
her a bundle of traveller's cheques instead of credit
cards to pay expenses. The familiar FedEx envelope
had been a welcome sight to the rest of them. But it
hadn't had a positive effect on Leslie's mood. When
she'd finished the negotiations that accomplished this,
she'd returned to their hotel in Paris in a particularly
foul mood. At present she sat wrapped in a light jacket
and slept in the row of seats across from Lourds.

Gary lounged in another seat nearby and played a
video game player that he seemed totally absorbed
by. Earphones trapped him totally in whatever virtual
world he was experiencing through the tiny game
platform.

Lourds didn't know where Natashya was. He was fairly certain, aside from brief catnaps here and there, that she hadn't slept. He was also certain that being bereft of her weapon inside the airport was driving her slightly insane.

There was nothing he could do about any of it. He turned his attention back to the broadcast.

'Nearly thirty hours ago, the Cadiz excavation site – which has received international media coverage for the last few months as myths of sunken Atlantis have surrounded it – suffered a serious setback,' the young black news anchor said.

The scene cut to stock footage of the Cadiz dig site. Dumper trucks and baskets trundled earth from the open mouth of the excavation area to the coastline less than a hundred yards away. Great earthen bulwarks held back the tide.

'Early on the morning of the fourth of September,' the anchor continued, 'Father Emil Sebastian led explorers into a new cave that had just been opened up.'

More stock footage rolled. It showed Sebastian talking to crews inside the base-camp cavern. The media – according to the *Time*, *Newsweek* and *People* articles Lourds had read in the airport – hadn't been allowed past the base camp, and hadn't been allowed there often.

'We've received unconfirmed reports that the explorers were examining a burial vault filled with dead.'

'Cue scary music,' Gary said.

Glancing over at the cameraman, Lourds discovered the young man had put his PSP away and was focused totally on the story playing on the television.

'Decided to leave the cyber realms?' Lourds asked.

Gary grinned. 'If I had my way, mate, I'd still be there. Freaking batteries are dead. I gotta go charge 'em.'

Gary looked around for a power source, and Lourds focused on the screen.

'Although those reports have been unconfirmed by the excavation team,' the anchor said, 'we do have a report from an undisclosed source inside the work party who stated that bodies *were* found in the cavern. We also have a picture that shows the cave with the alleged graves carved into the side of a wall.'

A picture showed up on the monitor. It was splotchy and too dark. But it did look like an ancient burial chamber with a wall of graves. The image was too fuzzy for Lourds to identify any iconography or scripts.

The camera switched back to the anchor. 'We're told that two men drowned in the accident before they could be rescued.'

Pictures of a young man and a middle-aged man formed on the backdrop behind the anchor's head. Neither of them was Father Sebastian.

'Father Sebastian has stated that the newest cavern has been nearly flooded by the water,' the anchor said. 'The mishap has put the excavation behind schedule, but Father Sebastian says they will continue their work there. The Vatican, which has funded the excavation, has offered no comment when contacted.'

'I'm telling you, mate,' Gary said, 'the blokes crawling around in the guts of the earth like that have got some bloody big balls on them. You wouldn't catch me that far underground with the sea just waiting to pounce in on me.'

'Not even for a chance to see a new culture?' Lourds asked.

'Not for love nor money.' Gary shook his head. 'Truth to tell, I shouldn't even be haring about with you, Leslie and Natashya the Terminator.'

Lourds frowned. 'I don't think Natashya would like hearing you refer to her in that manner.'

'Prolly not. That's why I don't do it around her.' Gary shot him a crooked grin, then got up to go connect to a nearby wall outlet.

Lourds took a last glance at Leslie, feeling troubled all over again but realizing there was nothing he could do about the way things were between them. Resolving to let matters lie until he could manage them better, he turned his attention to the Yoruban documents he'd copied at the Max Planck Institute.

He paid particular attention to the legend of the five instruments: the cymbal, the drum, the flute, the bell and the pipe. If he'd translated everything right, he might be on to something.

Pope Innocent XIV's Study
Status Civitatis Vaticanae
6 September 2009

Father Sebastian stood on the balcony of the Pope's private study and peered out over Vatican City. After spending months in Cadiz, rarely journeying outside the base camp and the small town that had sprung up nearby to cater to the excavation team's needs, the city felt claustrophobic to him.

But it didn't come close to how he'd felt that night in the burial vault when the cavern had flooded. If not for the Swiss Guards who watched over him, he would have died.

No, he told himself, *not just the guards. If God hadn't saved you from harm, you would have died. Never forget whose hands you're ultimately in.*

'Emil,' a boisterous voice called in greeting.

Turning, Sebastian saw the Pope approaching.

'Your Holiness,' Sebastian said as he dropped to one knee and bowed his head.

Pope Innocent XIV helped his old friend to his feet and they embraced.

Sebastian could never get over the fact that his dear friend had become the Pope. They'd never even joked about such a thing when they'd worked together in the Church libraries.

The Pope, back when he'd been nothing more than a parish priest, had been fascinated by Sebastian's stories about journeying with his father. He'd even read all of Sebastian's journals from those times.

'I'm glad you're all right,' the Pope said. 'When I first heard about the cavern collapse and thought you were lost to us, I prayed for your survival. I felt guilty for sending you there.'

'Nonsense.' Sebastian waved that away, then wondered if such a gesture was permissible now that his friend was pope. 'You've given me back my life, Your Holiness. I love the work of uncovering the past. It is something my father, God rest his soul, would have loved to do. This excavation has brought me back to him – and to myself – after too many years.'

'I'm glad you feel that way. Especially in light of everything that's happened. The flooding . . . I heard what the news channels said, but they dramatize everything. How bad is it?'

'Bad, but perhaps not permanent. Dario Brancati insists that he can pump Cave Forty-Two dry in two weeks or possibly three. After that, we can resume exploration.' The idea filled Sebastian with cold fear. He had yet to walk back into the cavern after the collapse, and truthfully didn't know if he could.

'Where's the water coming from?'

'Brancati's divers believe it's from another chamber deeper in the catacombs. They're searching for the source now. We're fortunate that the air pressure equalized as quickly as it did.'

'What do you mean?'

'When we opened the burial vault, the air that had been trapped there escaped. The change allowed the water to break through a compromised wall in the cave system. It could have been much worse. The whole system could have become submerged. Had such been the case, there would have been many more casualties. I certainly wouldn't be standing here.' Sebastian paused as a chill ghosted over him. He believed his escape could only have been due to divine intervention. 'You have to remember, Your Holiness, all the Atlantic Ocean waits close by, ready to reclaim those caves.'

'I know.'

Silence stretched between the two men for a time. Sebastian could tell by the strained look on the Pope's face that his thoughts were as troubled as his own.

'Even though we were lucky, we lost two men this time, Your Holiness,' Sebastian said.

The Pope sighed and shook his head. 'You're wondering if what we're doing is worth those lives.'

Sebastian remained silent. He couldn't bear to put his fears into words.

'I told you when I first put you in charge of this excavation that this was possibly the most important work any of us could be doing at this time.'

'You mean, the graves?'

'More than that. I mean the necklace you found.'

'You mean, this?'

Taking his hand from his robe, Sebastian opened his fingers and released the pendant. The shining figure, one hand stretched forth and the other holding the sacred text, spun in the ambient light.

'May God have mercy,' the Pope whispered. He reached for the pendant with trembling fingers.

'After everything mankind has done to reject God's gifts, I don't know how He could possibly have any mercy left for us.'

The Pope cradled the pendant tenderly.

'Do you think it still exists down there, Your Holiness?' Sebastian couldn't even mention the name aloud. 'The sea has destroyed so much.'

'Everything God created is eternal.' As if torn by some emotion too strong for words, the Pope squeezed the pendant so fiercely the skin of his knuckles turned white. 'When you get to the end of your journey down in that dig of yours, my friend, you'll find the Garden of Eden. But you'll also find the greatest danger that God ever set forth in the world.'

Dakar, Senegal
6 September 2009

Lourds sat in the passenger seat of the Land Rover they'd rented at Dakar-Yoff-Léopold Sédar Senghor International Airport and stared out at the afternoon sun that baked Dakar. Heat waves shimmered on the hot pavement even through the sunglasses he wore.

The city was the westernmost on the continent of Africa. They travelled the highway leading from the airport. The Atlantic Ocean spilled across the white sand beaches that led up to modest houses flanked by pockets of scrub trees that offered scant shade. Fishermen and tourists plied the water.

Dakar was a mix of the old and modern. Tall buildings stabbed at the sky, but small houses ringed the city. Many of them were without modern utilities. The future and the past sat side by side.

'So,' Gary said good-naturedly, 'I assume Gorée Island is an island and we can't drive there.'

'We'll take the ferry,' Lourds said.

'But you haven't mentioned why we're going there.'

'Ile de Gorée, as the island was once known, has an infamous past. It held the large slave markets that supplied the whole world with African slaves. Thousands of men, women and children were funnelled through there and auctioned off to bidders from nearly everywhere. Even though England and a few other countries eventually outlawed slavery on their home turf, there were always men willing to buy slaves here and sell them in America and the Caribbean.'

'Doesn't explain why we're going there, though.'

'During the long years of the slave auctions,' Lourds went on, 'Ile de Gorée also became a repository for documents and artefacts, ships' logs, African carvings, pottery, jewellery. Everything that came out of Africa was put on display there.'

'Surprised they didn't sell it.'

'Actually, they did. For a profit. Much of what once existed in the lands where whole tribes were decimated by the slavers has now disappeared. Whole cultures were lost to time and greed.'

Seagulls and egrets span out over the grey-blue

water. Farther out a few cruise ships and fishing boats departed and arrived at the port.

'But that's an old story,' Lourds went on. 'Everywhere one civilization has risen in power over another, that's happened. In England, the Picts were routed by the Romans and all but destroyed. They were forced to retreat to the Scottish highlands. In the Americas, it was the Native Americans. Many tribes were wiped out entirely as European settlers swept over the continent, and even today the ones who remain are struggling to hang on to their cultural identity. Cultural destruction is most complete when the cultures being flattened have only oral histories instead of written ones. When you kill the storytellers of a tribe without written language, you kill the culture for ever.'

'So what are you hoping to find on that island?' Gary asked. 'Storytellers?'

'I want to follow up on an interesting legend I read about while at the Max Planck Institute.'

'What legend?' Natashya asked in Russian.

Ah, the language barrier, Lourds thought. *Bi-linguals can always use that to isolate themselves from others. And to point out the differences between* us *and* them.

'There's an ancient legend,' Lourds answered in English, 'that involves a set of five instruments – a pipe, a flute, a drum, a bell and a cymbal – and how they were divided among cultures after a flood.'

'Our bell?' Leslie asked in English.

'The cymbal Yuliya was working on?' Natashya asked in Russian.

'Which flood?' Gary asked.

'Good questions, all of you. I don't know if it's the bell and cymbal we've come in contact with,' Lourds admitted. 'But I think this was the direction Yuliya was pursuing while she was researching. Remember, she knew that the cymbal hadn't been made in Rus.'

'She believed it had been brought there by traders,' Natashya said in English. Evidently she had decided to join the others in their language since Lourds wasn't going to acknowledge hers.

'Correct.'

'Except that it didn't make sense because the cymbal wasn't worth anything.'

'Also correct.' Lourds paused for a moment. 'Technically. But what if the instruments had a worth that wasn't tied in to their intrinsic value? What if they were all tied to a common disaster?'

'The flood?' Gary asked.

'One of the most common archetypes of the universal mythic base found in all cultures is that of the flood. Besides the story of Noah, you'll find tales of deluges in Sumerian, Babylonian, Norse – though those concerned a deluge of blood from the frost giant Ymir – Irish, Nahautl spoken by the Aztecs and many other languages. The Greeks feature stories about the world ending in flood *three* times.'

'Including the one that sank Atlantis,' Gary said.

'Actually, those flood tales don't include Plato's yarn about the sinking of Atlantis,' Lourds amended. 'That was a different story entirely. In it, the world survived, just not Atlantis. The flood story with the instruments was bigger. Much bigger.'

'You think the instruments were linked to the great ancient flood?' Natashya asked. 'The Hebrew flood that God sent to wipe evil and wickedness from the world?'

'The legend I read wasn't clear. I don't know. Possibly. But it's just as possible that it's another flood entirely. The world has – at one time or another – undergone major floods that inundated most of the major land masses. Much of the United States was once under the sea. Archaeologists constantly find evidence of prehistoric marine life in the deserts and wastelands of the west. Much of Europe has been underwater, too. They've found a whale skeleton half-way up a mountain in Italy.'

'But the instruments . . . You think they're tied to that flood?' Leslie asked.

'I don't know. It's an old legend from an oral tradition that was almost lost. It doesn't matter what they're tied to. I just want to confirm the myth that talks about those instruments. If I can, I'd like to find out if there's any more to that tale than the bit I know. I think it might be important.'

Sacred College of Cardinals
Status Civitatis Vaticanae
6 September 2009

Even though Murani had arrived for the meeting early, he was the last to enter the room. He wore his cardinal robes, laying claim to the power of his office through the virtue of God's armour.

The underground room was not well-known throughout the Vatican. Only a handful of people had keys to the two doors that allowed entrance to it. Due to the size of the labyrinth carved out beneath the Vatican over the course of the thousands of years the site had been occupied, some of it now in disrepair, it was easy for such rooms to exist without the knowledge of the general populace. In fact, it was easy for such spaces to exist where no one knew about them at all.

There was probably no more private space on earth.

Wall sconces held candle lanterns that lent a golden glow to the stone walls and the burnished wood of the long table in the centre of the room. Someone had clearly wiped it off when they brought in the lanterns. A thick layer of dust coated the cobblestone floor and the cobwebs in the corners. This wasn't a space on the itinerary of the cleaning roster. The chamber hadn't been used much, and never since Murani had taken office.

All of the twenty-three men around the table were members of the Society of Quirinus. Since not all of the members were there, Murani had to assume that some of them weren't available.

But Cardinal Lorenzo Occhetto had come. He sat at the head of the table in all his regalia, so frail and aged he looked like a well-dressed corpse. He waved a hand at the empty chair to his left.

'No, thank you,' Murani said. 'If this is to be an inquisition, I'd prefer to remain standing.'

His comment drew baleful looks from the other cardinals.

'Your impropriety is out of place here,' Occhetto said in his dry whisper.

'Actually,' Murani said, choosing to be defiant, 'impropriety is out of place everywhere. That's part of what makes it impropriety.'

'Don't seek to amuse yourself at our expense,' Occhetto rebuked him.

'I'm not amused,' Murani told them. 'I'm angry.' He folded his hands behind him and walked around the table. He met the gaze of every man there.

'Sit down,' Occhetto commanded. But his weak voice failed to carry authority.

'No.' Murani remained defiantly upright at the end of the table. 'This is a farce, and it's gone quite far enough. I will not allow it any longer.'

'*You* will not allow it?' Cardinal Jacopo Rota exploded. He was in his early fifties and was known for his temper. A hulking man who'd done manual labour in his youth and retained the muscles to prove it, he rose threateningly from his chair at Occhetto's right hand.

'No,' Murani said in a calm voice. 'I will not.'

'You murdered poor Fenoglio,' Rota said. 'You will account to God for that.'

'To God, perhaps,' Murani said, though he didn't believe that. 'But not to you.'

'Then you admit it?' Occhetto asked. 'You admit to the murder?'

'Is Fenoglio's death the first committed by the Society of Quirinus to protect all those precious secrets you covet?' Murani demanded.

'We did not order his death. We do not murder,' Emilio Sraffa said. He was barely thirty, the youngest of them, and – in Murani's opinion – the most innocent.

'Yes,' Murani said, 'we do. You've just not been made part of it yet.'

Sraffa looked around the rest of the table for someone to deny the charges. No one did. No one even took their gaze off Murani. The rest of them knew.

'Those lives that we ordered taken,' Occhetto said, 'were –'

'Ones you deemed obstacles to what you desired,' Murani interrupted. He waved the old man's further comments away and rode right over his words. 'Justify it any way you want to. Say that you only killed men who had no true souls before God. I don't care. You have killed before. Often.'

'You murdered a priest,' Rota accused him.

'Your precious Pope put Fenoglio onto me,' Murani said, 'while I've been doing what all of you are afraid to do.'

'We're not afraid to do anything,' Occhetto said.

'Oh, no? Then tell me why Father Sebastian is heading up the excavation instead of one of us?'

No one had an answer for that.

Filled to bursting with energy and anger and his sense of mission, Murani paced around the table. 'You sit here in the dark like scared old women instead of taking control of the Church.'

'It isn't our place –' Occhetto began.

'It *is* your place,' Murani said loudly. 'Who else has been entrusted with the secrets you've been given custody of? The Pope you elected wasn't even one of us. He didn't know about the sacred texts. He didn't know what really happened to the Garden of Eden until you told him.'

'We couldn't elect one of our own,' the old cardinal said. 'We don't hold enough votes in the Sacred College. We –'

'Don't want to get caught out in the light,' Murani said viciously. 'I know you. You scurry for the safety of the darkness like cockroaches.'

'We have always worked from the shadows,' Occhetto declared. 'For hundreds of years, through dozens of popes, we've kept the necessary secrets locked away.'

'Your actions, your choices, have weakened the Church,' Murani accused them. 'You weren't protecting the secrets; you were protecting your own lives.'

'You go too far,' Rota stated. 'Now, you're either going to sit down and listen to what we have to say or I'm going to sit you down.'

'No.' As the man moved to stand, Murani banged his fist hard against the table, shocking all the men gathered within the hidden chamber. 'Sit!'

Rota's dark eyes blazed with defiance, and he remained where he was, halfway to standing.

'I said, *sit*!' Murani said. 'You should listen to me. You know what I am capable of. Think of Fenoglio. Think of what you're accusing me of. Do you think one body more will matter?'

Scowling, Rota sat.

Murani kept his back to the nearest door, but stood to one side so he could see if it opened. This meeting was secret, but he didn't know what words his fellow Society members had let slip through the years. The Swiss Guard was always about.

No place, no matter how secret, was truly safe.

'While you've been sitting safe in Vatican City, nattering like children,' Murani said, 'I've been working. I've been out in the world. I have deciphered some of the passages regarding the sacred texts.'

That caught them all by surprise.

'You lie,' Occhetto accused.

'No. I speak the truth. The five instruments will open the final vault where the sacred texts are kept,' Murani said.

'We all know that.'

'I have two of them,' Murani said.

Instantly the voices of the cardinals filled the room. Occhetto raised his hands and quieted them all. Slowly, order returned.

Murani gazed at the men before him. Pride and

fear ran through him like an electric current. He'd never dared to say so much so openly before. None of them had.

'Where are the instruments?' Occhetto asked.

'Safe,' Murani said. 'Where I can get to them.'

'Those are not yours to control.'

'They are now. And soon the other instruments will be mine, too.' Murani was convinced that Lourds would lead Gallardo to the others, or perhaps he could use the bell and the cymbal to locate the remaining instruments. God's will would not be denied, and Murani was certain he was following God's will.

'You don't know what you're doing,' Occhetto said. 'If you have the instruments, then you must give them to us.'

'Why? So you can lock them away in the dark and they can get lost? Again?'

'They aren't supposed to be together. Everything we've read tells us that God intended those instruments to be apart.'

'Then why didn't God destroy them? Why did he leave them here for me to find?'

'This is heresy,' Rota said.

'This is God's design,' Murani said. 'I am His divine force come to bring the Church back to power.'

'How do you propose to do that?' Occhetto asked.

'Through the power of the sacred texts.'

The cardinals objected loudly. Murani ignored them all.

'Those texts destroyed the world once,' Occhetto said. 'Possibly even twice. They could do the same thing again.'

'They won't,' Murani said. 'They're going to help re-make the world. They're going to empower the Church in a way that's never been seen before.' He glared at them. 'I will find them. And you can't stop me.'

'We can,' Rota said. 'Don't forget yourself.'

Murani smiled at the big man. 'You're talking about the Swiss Guards?'

No one said anything.

'Your handpicked crews among the Guards have been doing your dirty work for hundreds of years,' Murani said. 'One more murder, done in the name of the Society of Quirinus, wouldn't be that much, would it?'

'It wouldn't be murder,' Rota said. 'It would be justice.'

'None of you that sit in this room have clean hands,' Murani accused. 'You've all been involved in some bit of treachery and death.'

Sraffa looked troubled. He was weaker than Occhetto assumed. He still had a conscience. He didn't give everything over to God's hands.

'Not murder,' Occhetto said. 'Not really.'

'So if you had me killed?' Murani asked. 'Would that be murder then?'

'No,' Occhetto said. 'It would be justifiable homicide, a mercy killing in the name of the Church.'

'Perhaps.' Murani strode toward the old cardinal.

'It would also be foolish. It would destroy you and wound the Church you profess to love.'

Occhetto quavered and closed his eyes. Murani knew that the man was afraid.

'I'll tell you why,' Murani said. 'I've written down your names. I've written down your deeds. I have recordings and documents to prove them. You were fools, to keep records of such things. You covered up my dealings with Fenoglio. Now you are all involved in that crime, accessories to murder. I've given all the evidence to a man who will mail the undeniable proof of it to the proper authorities and to the world's press, should something happen to me. Do you think the Church can handle a scandal like that, on top of everything else that has become public in the last few years? Do you think the Pope or your red robes will protect you?' A gasp in the room confirmed the accuracy of the intelligence he'd paid for. 'Yes, I know your secrets well. And the world will share them, should anything happen to me.'

Outrage showed in Occhetto's eyes. 'You can't do this, Murani.'

'It's already done,' Murani said in a cold voice. 'If you touch me, I'll touch you back. Just try it.'

Silence filled the room.

'Here's how we're going to handle this,' Murani said in a soft, deadly voice. 'You're going to stay out of my way from this point on, or I *will* have you destroyed.'

'You're a madman,' Occhetto whispered.

'No,' Murani argued. 'I'm a man of faith and

353

conviction. God has revealed to me what must be done. And I'm going to do it. We all want those secret texts. I'm the man who will stop at nothing to get them.'

He looked at all the cardinals sitting there. Without hesitation, Murani turned his back on them all and walked toward the door.

No one followed him.

He took out the flashlight that he'd used to reach the room and started back through the underground maze the way he'd come. He felt certain that the Society of Quirinus hadn't finished with him, but he now had more breathing space than at any time before.

They feared him. And they would not act against him.

Everything was going according to Murani's – and God's – plan.

Ile de Gorée
Dakar, Senegal
6 September 2009

From the ferry, Lourds spotted Ismael Diop standing on the landing. Lourds recognized the man from photographs he'd seen on the internet.

Diop was black and thin to the point of emaciation. In his seventies now, according to the biography Lourds had read, he still got around to conventions on African history and the Atlantic slave trade in particular. He also published regularly, despite being retired. He was a professor emeritus from the University of Glasgow.

He wore white twill shorts, a khaki shirt with the sleeves hacked off and a battered Panama hat festooned with fishing lures. Grey stubble showed on his cheeks and chin.

Beyond Diop, the setting presented a picturesque view of the harbour. It looked like a tourist postcard, in fact. Pirogues, small canoes, knifed through the water carrying tourists, teenagers and fishermen. The brightly coloured houses stood out against the blue sky and white sand. Canopies on stilts shaded patches of the beach for tourists and vendors. Papaya and palm trees shared space with lime and sandbox trees. Lourds recognized them from the research he'd viewed concerning the Ile de Gorée.

When the ferry put in to the pier, Lourds waited till the ship was still, the lines were made fast and the gangway was lowered. Then he stepped onto the pier. Leslie was behind him while Gary and Natashya brought up the rear.

Diop stepped forward. A big grin split his face and he offered his hand.

'Professor Lourds,' Diop greeted him.

'Professor Diop,' Lourds responded.

'No,' the old man said, waving a hand. 'Please. Call me Ismael.'

'There's a famous line in there,' Lourds observed with a smile.

'Indeed there is. But trust me when I tell you I've

heard it before.' The old professor's voice was softly melodic with just a hint of a British accent.

Diop stood and shook hands as Lourds introduced the others.

'This heat and humidity make speaking out here unbearable,' Diop said. 'I took the liberty of securing a room at a local tavern if that's all right with you all.'

'Cold beer?' Gary asked as he wiped at his face with a towel. 'I'm in.'

Diop laughed. 'Yes. This way, then. It's only a short walk. It's not a big island.'

Lourds followed Diop through a narrow alleyway lined with bushes and bougainvillea. The bright purple, red and yellow flowers made the area seem festive. Blossoms of a mango tree added to the colour and the shade was a welcome relief from the punishing glare of the sun.

'This is beautiful,' Leslie said.

'It is,' Diop agreed. 'We have colour all year round. But I'm afraid that means we also have to suffer the heat.'

At the end of the alley, they came out onto a place that fronted a large pinkish building with sweeping staircases that coiled towards each other. A small balcony stretched between them over a large wooden door.

'Is that the slave house?' Gary asked. He stepped off to capture video of the house.

'Yes.' Diop stood and waited patiently. 'The French called it Maison de Esclaves. The House of the Slaves. They passed through the door beneath, which they called the Door of No Return, and waited – shackled – in the holding areas within till they were brought out and sold.'

'Grim.' Gary frowned and put the camera away.

'Very grim. If those walls could talk, they'd fill your ears with horrors, I'm sure.' Diop stared at the building. 'Still, if it weren't for the Atlantic slave trade, no one would have thought this area important enough to try to save. A lot of information we have now would have been lost.' He paused. 'Including the information you came for, Thomas.'

'It's always fascinating to see how the bones of history get preserved longer when guilt is involved,' Lourds commented.

'And how quickly the truth of it is all forgotten,' Diop said. He nodded toward the children playing in the open area. 'The young people here know of the history, but, for better or for worse, it exists as something separate from them. It has no true impact on their lives.'

'Except for the fact that they can make money from the tourists,' Natashya said.

Lourds looked at her unhappily, thinking perhaps she'd transgressed politeness.

'It's the same in my country,' she went on. 'Westerners come to Moscow and want to see where the Communists lived and where the KGB were located as if it was a movie set, not a matter of life and death in Russia for nearly a century.'

'Too many James Bond films, I suppose.' Diop smiled.

'Far too many,' Natashya agreed. 'We don't set out to be a stereotype, but I think sometimes we end up as one to outsiders. Especially to Western eyes. Perhaps that building is the same.'

Diop nodded. 'I think perhaps you're right.'

The beer came to their table in bottles so cold they iced up in the humidity then immediately started to sweat it off. Thick lime wedges blocked the open necks, but only temporarily.

Lourds removed the lime and drank deeply.

'I wouldn't do that, if I were you,' Diop said.

Lourds started to ask what the old professor was referring to, then the brain freeze almost shattered his mind. He closed his eyes and suffered through it.

'Ouch. Got it. I'll go slower in the future.'

Diop laughed gently. 'I brought us here because the beer is cold and the food is excellent. I didn't know if you'd had the time to eat.'

'No,' Leslie said. 'I'm famished.'

'Perhaps we could talk over a meal,' Diop suggested. 'It is traditional, yes? The breaking of bread among friends?'

They all agreed.

As he sipped his beer more cautiously, Lourds noticed that Natashya had immediately taken the seat with her back to the wall. She never went off guard. *Like an Old West gunfighter*, he thought.

The tavern was small. Hardwood floors showed the scars from decades of use and abuse. The tables and chairs were all mismatched. Wicker-bladed fans swept slowly round overhead but did little more than stir the thick air. Bougainvillea dripped from ceramic pots and planters. The fragrant blossoms filled the air with scent.

Diop waved a young woman over and quickly ordered in French. Lourds only paid a little attention as he opened the Word document on his iPAQ where he'd made a list of the questions he wanted to ask the professor once he tracked him down.

The waitress brought another round of beers over and quickly departed.

Diop took his hat off and tossed it at the hat rack against wall. The Panama sailed elegantly and came to a rest on one of the pegs.

'Good shot,' Gary complimented.

'Either you're very good with that little trick,' Lourds commented, 'or this is a favourite place.'

'It's a favourite place.' Diop ran his long-fingered hands across his shaved scalp. 'And that hat and I have been together for years.' He paused and looked at Lourds. 'I was sorry to hear what happened to Professor Hapaev.'

'Did you know her?' Natashya asked eagerly.

'No. Other than a few emails there at the end.'

'She was my sister.'

'My condolences.'

'Thank you.' Natashya leaned slightly across the table. 'I don't know exactly what Professor Lourds has told you about why we're here.'

'He said you were looking for more information

about the cymbal Professor – your sister – was working on.'

'I'm also looking for my sister's killers.' Natashya took her identification from her pocket and laid it on the table.

Diop reached out and quickly folded the ID closed. 'This is not a place to be flashing badges. Many of the people here still pursue quasi-illegal business. And a number of other people don't want to deal with authority figures. Do you understand?'

Natashya nodded, but Lourds had the impression that she'd known exactly what she'd been risking. She put the ID away.

'While you're here,' Diop said seriously, 'it might be better for you to forget you are a policewoman. That could get you killed on the mainland. Here, it could get you worse.'

18

Chez Madame Loulou
Ile de Gorée
Dakar, Senegal
6 September 2009

'What do you know about the bell and the cymbal?' Diop asked. He held the 8 x 10 photos of the two instruments that Lourds had directed Gary to make. He'd taken a pair of glasses from his pocket for the close-up work.

'Not enough. They're part of a set of five instruments,' Lourds replied. 'The other three still missing are a pipe, a flute and a drum.'

Diop studied Lourds over the glasses for a moment. 'Do you know where any of these instruments are?'

'No. I know where two of them have been.' Lourds quickly relayed the story of the bell and the cymbal and how they'd been taken from him.

The young woman had returned with fried plantains and pastels – a Portuguese-style stuffed pastry that was deep-fried. She'd also brought fresh beers. Natashya opted for water instead and Lourds knew it was because she didn't want to risk getting intoxicated. He doubted she ever let her control slip enough to indulge.

'Patrizio Gallardo,' Diop mused. Then he shook his head. 'A number of artefact dealers – legitimate and black market – ply their trade here and on the mainland. The past is always for sale to collectors.'

'Do you know anyone who's been looking for these instruments?' Lourds asked.

'No.' Diop handed the pictures back.

'I've read your work.' Lourds put the photos into his backpack. 'What have you heard about them?'

'There's an old Yoruba tale about five instruments,' Diop said. 'Perhaps it's about the same five instruments you're searching for. I don't know. I've concerned myself more with the history of this place than the fables of the various cultures that have passed through here.'

'But you have heard the story?' Leslie asked.

'Yes.' Diop shrugged. 'It isn't so different from a lot of creation myths.'

'Can you tell it to us?' Lourds asked.

'Once, long and long ago,' Diop said, 'the Creator – call him whatever you wish according to your own religious beliefs – grew angry with his children here in this world. In that time, they lived only on one land.'

'What one land?' Gary asked.

'The legend doesn't say. It merely calls it the "beginning place". There were some scholars I tipped a few beers with who insisted that the land might have been the Garden of Eden. Or perhaps it was Atlantis. Or Lemuria. Or any of other countless supposed lands of wonder that disappeared into the dark recesses of time.'

'When you put it that way,' Leslie said, 'it sounds like pure hokum.'

Lourds glanced at the young woman briefly. Was she really beginning to lose faith in what they were searching for? Or was she only saying that to needle him? Or maybe it was to challenge Diop. Lourds didn't know. He tried to keep from being irritated, but he wasn't altogether successful.

Evidently Diop took no offence. He grinned. 'If you stay around Africa long enough, Miss Crane, you'll hear all kinds of things. But if you stay around even longer than that, you'll find that many of those things – each in their own way – have a kernel of truth.'

The waitress returned again, followed by two others. All of them carried huge platters of food. Diop quickly explained what they were about to eat. *Thieboudienne* was the traditional Senegalese dish, consisting of marinated fish prepared with tomato paste and an assortment of vegetables. *Yassa* was chicken or fish simmered in onion with garlic, lemon sauce and mustard added to enhance the taste. *Sombi* was a sweet milk rice soup. *Fonde* was millet balls rolled in sour cream.

Eating and talking, Lourds noted, didn't bother Diop. The scholar left the conversation at appropriate places for questions to be asked while he ate.

'After his anger had passed, the Creator saw what he'd done to his children and he was sorry,' Diop said. 'So he made them a promise that he would never destroy the world again that way.'

'Sounds like the covenant of the rainbow,' Gary said. 'Or the whole lost ark business with Indiana Jones.'

'As I said, many of these tales are similar,' Diop agreed. 'Even the animal stories – such as how the bear lost his tail – are similar in regions that have long had those animals.'

'So you think a bear actually used his tail to go ice fishing?' Gary asked. 'Then froze it off in the ice?'

Diop laughed. 'No. I believe the bear was lazy and tricked the kangaroo into digging for water. As an act of vengeance, the kangaroo used his boomerang to cut the bear's tail off.'

Gary grinned. 'Now that one, mate, I had not heard.'

'The Australian aborigines tell it.' Diop forked up some spicy couscous and ate. 'The point being, every culture tells stories to explain things they don't know.'

'But there's more to this story,' Lourds said. 'I've seen the bell. And I've seen digital images of the cymbal. They both share a language that I can't decipher.'

'Is that so unusual for you?'

Lourds hesitated a moment. 'At the risk of sounding egotistical, yes, it is.'

'Ah, no wonder you're so intrigued by these things.'

'Some other intrigued person killed my sister for that cymbal,' Natashya stated flatly.

'But you have the name of one of the men who

364

murdered your sister,' Diop pointed out. 'You could pursue him.'

Natashya didn't say anything.

For the first time, Lourds realized that. He was amazed that he hadn't noticed that fact himself.

'Of course, if Gallardo and his people are truly searching for the same five instruments that Thomas is,' Diop said, 'it only makes sense to stay with the professor. Sooner or later they'll come to you, eh?'

Natashya's eyes remained frozen like ice even when she smiled. 'Sooner or later,' she agreed.

Gallardo nursed a beer while he leaned against the Auberge Keur Beer guesthouse and watched the festivities taking shape in the courtyard. Children played soccer with home-made balls while men wrestled in the sand and women pounded millet. Vendors sold baguettes and iced drinks to the tourists and locals.

Tired from the long trips he'd taken lately, Gallardo longed for a soft bed and plenty of time to rest. He didn't know how Lourds and his companions kept going.

He stared at the table where Lourds sat with some black man. It irritated Gallardo that they sat there with impunity. All of them . . .

All of them?

For the first time Gallardo realized the Russian woman had disappeared from the table where Lourds and the others sat under a broad umbrella. Candle-light played over their faces and showed they were deep in conversation.

Dammit. The woman was missing. Where the hell was she?

He finished his beer, left the bottle sitting on the nearby windowsill, and stepped back into the shadows. His hand dropped to the back of his waistband and closed around the handle of the 9mm gun he'd purchased from a black-market dealer soon after his arrival in Dakar. He continued sweeping the area for the woman but didn't find her.

'I know a man,' Diop said as they sat at the table, 'who might be able to help you with this legend. But it will take you a few days to reach him. He lives in the old Yoruba lands.'

'Where?' Lourds asked.

'In Nigeria. Ile-Ife. It's the oldest Yoruba city that anyone knows of.'

Leslie looked up from her beer. 'How far away is that?' she asked.

'You can get there by plane in a matter of hours,' Diop said.

'Who's the man?' Lourds asked.

'His name is Adebayo. He's the Oba of Ile-Ife.' Diop pronounced the title as *orba*.

Lourds recalled from his reading that Oba meant king. The bearer of the title was the traditional leader of a Yoruba town. The title might be traditional, but the position still carried weight. Obas were often consulted by present-day government bodies – they said more out of respect and an effort to keep the peace than to acknowledge any power they might have. But, in fact, it acknowledged what really shaped the society they were dealing with.

'He knows the story?' Lourds asked.

Diop grinned. 'More than that, Thomas. I believe Adebayo has the drum you're looking for.'

'What makes you think that?'

'Because I've seen it.'

Natashya hated being without a gun. She was better with one. She'd left her weapons behind before the flight. Still, that situation might remedy itself in the next few moments.

She paused in the shadows next to the bed and breakfast overlooking the courtyard. The mortar in the stones was loose and had crumbled away under the attack of years, vines and salt spray. Plenty of finger and toe room existed between the stones.

In the darkness, she stepped out of her shoes and peeled off her socks. Then, knife clenched between her teeth, she started her assault on the side of the building up to the window where she'd spotted the man watching Lourds and the others. There were other men. She knew that from studying the darkness and seeing them move.

Only moments ago she'd excused herself from the table. She'd barely drawn the attention of the others because they'd been so rapt in their conversation with Diop. When none of the watchers had followed her, she figured she'd eluded them as well.

Her arms and legs strained a little under her weight. It was one thing to use arm and leg strength to assault a vertical climb, but it was another to use only fingers and toes. She breathed in and out rhythmically and worked to clear her lungs of carbon dioxide build-up.

Soon enough, still under the cover of darkness, she reached the fourth-floor balcony and gradually shifted her weight over to it.

The man she'd spotted lounged in the darkness and watched Lourds and the others.

They wouldn't last an hour on their own, she thought. Moving slowly, she hauled herself over the side and silently crossed the terraced balcony floor. Only two chairs, a potted palm and the watcher shared the space. She took the knife from her teeth and gripped it tightly in her hand.

The man stood almost six feet tall. He was European, pale white in the night. He smoked a cheap cigar that stunk so badly Natashya could have found him by the scent of that alone. At the last moment, he turned as if he sensed something. Dormant sense from a less-than-civilized lifestyle came on-line.

But it was too late.

Natashya slid behind him, gripped his chin in one hand, and put the point of her blade against the side of his neck with the other.

'Move,' she whispered in English, 'and I'll slit your throat.'

The man froze but she could feel him quiver in terror.

Heart thumping wildly as she battled her own fears, Natashya reached under his shirt and relieved him of the 9mm pistol in his shoulder holster. He carried another at his waistband. She took it as well.

The radio receiver crackled at his ear. Someone spoke in Italian.

'What does he want to know?' she asked the man.

'He wants to know where you are,' the man replied.

The fear intensified inside Natashya. She removed the knife and placed the barrel of one of the 9mms she'd just acquired against the back of his head.

'Don't shoot me,' the man whispered hoarsely. 'Please don't shoot me.'

'What is he saying?' Natashya asked.

'He's noticed that you're missing,' the man added.

'Is it Gallardo?' Natashya asked.

The man nodded.

'Give me the radio.' Natashya held out her hand.

The man handed it over.

Natashya keyed the SEND button. 'Gallardo.'

There was a moment of silence, then a man's voice demanded, 'Who is this?'

'You killed my sister in Moscow,' Natashya said. 'One day soon, I'm going to kill you.'

'Not if I kill you first.' His voice was hard and arrogant.

'I hope you can get off the island tonight,' Natashya said. 'Otherwise you're going to be answering a lot of questions from the police.'

'Why?'

Without betraying what she was about to do, Natashya shoved the man over the low balcony. The fall was a short one by some standards, with nicely tilled garden soil at its end. She doubted that it would kill him, but he screamed on the way down. Then he stopped – abruptly.

Natashya stayed back from the balcony's edge and resisted the impulse to look down. The rush of conversation below let her know that the man's fall had drawn a crowd.

She walked back into the room, emptied a small suitcase on the bed, and found two boxes of ammunition for the pistols. There was also a small package containing what looked suspiciously like marijuana. The drug wouldn't cause too much of a disturbance on the island, but it would make for a long question-and-answer session with the Gorée police until payment could be arranged to buy the man out of trouble.

She left it and the clothes behind.

She dumped the ammunition and pistols into the suitcase, zipped it closed, and walked out of the door in her bare feet.

'I think he's broken his leg,' someone said.

'What happened?' another asked.

'He fell from the balcony.'

'Is he drunk?'

'If he isn't, I'm betting he wishes he was about now.'

Standing on the outside of the crowd of tourists that had gathered around the man writhing painfully on the ground, Lourds glanced around. An uneasy feeling dawned in the pit of his stomach.

'Where's Natashya?' Leslie asked at his side.

Lourds shook his head. 'I don't know.'

'Do you think she . . . ?' Leslie hesitated.

'Wasn't her,' Gary said. 'I've seen her work. She'd have shot him.'

'Not if I simply wanted to create a disturbance so we could get out of here.'

Lourds turned and found Natashya standing behind them. She held a suitcase.

'Where did you get the suitcase?' he asked.

'From his room.' Natashya nodded toward the man curled into a foetal position on the ground.

'You did that?'

Natashya returned his gaze without guilt. 'I considered shooting him. But I doubt we would have been able to walk away without answering a lot of questions.' She shrugged. 'As it is now, it simply looks like a tourist had an accident.'

'I don't suppose he's a tourist.'

'No. Gallardo is here. I hope dumping his minion over the balcony will attract enough law enforcement attention to chase him into hiding for now. Meanwhile, we need to go into hiding ourselves.'

Lourds marvelled at how coolly and calmly she handled everything. She hadn't even worked up a sweat facing an armed man and overpowering him.

'You're lucky you weren't injured or killed,' he said.

'You're lucky Gallardo doesn't want you dead.' Natashya nodded towards a nearby alley at the foot of the bed and breakfast the man had fallen from. 'We needed a diversion to get out of here.'

Diop shook his head in wonder. 'Well, then, that's certainly what I'd call a diversion.' He glanced back at Lourds. 'You certainly do keep interesting company, Thomas.'

You don't know the half of it, Lourds thought.

'I'd also suggest we not spend the night on the island,' Natashya found her shoes in the alley and stepped into them, 'in case the police decide they want to talk to us as well. Gallardo's little friend might be persuaded to give up information about us as well as his employer.'

'I know a man who has a boat,' Diop said. 'He can take us to the mainland tonight.'

'Good,' Natashya said. 'The sooner the better.'

Atlantic Ocean
East of Dakar, Senegal
6 September 2009

Gallardo stood in the stern of the rented powerboat as it beat a hasty retreat back toward Dakar. The trip was twenty minutes by ferry. The powerboat cut that time considerably.

Unfortunately, the powerboat also made him stand out as an outsider. When the Gorée Island police started looking into the life of the man who had ended up in the middle of the courtyard, as Gallardo was certain they would – and he knew the Russian woman had guessed that as well – they were going to track him back to Gallardo in short order.

If the man didn't give Gallardo up outright, he would certainly have to own up to the relationship when challenged by the boat-rental person or the black-market dealer who sold him the weapons he carried.

Gallardo cursed his luck and stared out bleakly across the moon-kissed white curlers rolling across the sea. His sat-phone rang. He knew who it would be and he thought about whether or not he should answer.

In the end, though, there was no choice.

'Yes,' he said.

'Did you find him?' Murani's voice sounded coldly efficient and much closer than Gallardo would have wanted.

'I did, and if you'd let me deal with him as I wanted it would be done by now.'

'No. He's still of use to us.'

Gallardo paced the short length of the boat. 'Only if we can keep him under observation.'

'What happened? Where are you?'

'On our way back to the mainland. There was a problem.'

'What problem?'

'The Russian woman saw us. She made it impossible for us to stay in position.'

Murani was quiet for a time. 'Keep after them. Things are getting hard for me, too. I need you to stay on Lourds.'

'I know. I'm trying. If it weren't for the woman, he wouldn't even have known we were there.'

'Have you figured out what he's doing there?'

'The man he met with today is a professor of history. The kind who specializes in African studies.' Gallardo had got that from the street talk he'd paid for in the bars while his men had watched Lourds over on Ile de Gorée.

'Ah. Lourds is searching for the other instruments.'

'What other instruments?' Gallardo didn't like the fact that Murani was withholding information. Especially when that information might get him killed.

'Three other instruments go with the bell and the cymbal,' Murani said. 'It's possible that they were all in that area at one time.'

'Why didn't you mention this before?'

'Because I didn't know. I keep researching. I'm still learning about them.'

Gallardo swallowed an angry response. Murani usually knew everything when he put him into the field. The fact that he didn't this time meant that the stakes must be higher than they'd ever been before.

'Find Lourds,' Murani coaxed. 'Stay with him. I don't want him harmed. Yet.'

The phone clicked dead in Gallardo's ear. He folded the device and put it away. He turned back to the west. In the distance he saw the lights of the city. He hadn't expected it to be so big. Dakar was new to him, but the movement of the black market was the same. He was good at his work. No matter where Lourds went, Gallardo was confident he could trail the professor.

And when the time came to kill the man and his companions – especially the red-headed Russian bitch – he was looking forward to it.

Sofitel Teranga Hotel
Dakar, Senegal
6 September 2009

Lourds laboured over the languages. He had enough pieces of the puzzle to start putting them together. Assuming that he had the right legend and assuming that the three different languages were all talking about the same event, then he could attempt to replace some of the words/symbols with words he had to assume were in those texts.

He kept a short list of words that he exchanged throughout the text.

Flood.

God.

Danger.

Cursed.

Those all ought to be in there somewhere.

The Russian encryption method provided for plain text to be rearranged before the encryption process, so headers, salutations, introductions and other standards in texts were all pulled out. That process mixed up the written language enough that decrypting the finished result without a key was almost impossible because it reduced the redundancy that normally took place in encrypted messages.

Lourds sighed and stretched. He tried in vain to find a comfortable position, but his back and shoulders ached fiercely. He glanced at the television set tuned to ESPN but silent. He used the images to rest his eyes and change the distance of his focus.

Someone knocked at the door.

Remembering the man Natashya had caused to plummet to the cobblestones on Ile de Gorée, Lourds got up cautiously. In a way, it gave him a sense of déjà vu. He crossed to the closet and looked for an iron. The one the hotel provided was skeletal and had no heft. It was a sorry weapon at best.

The knock was repeated, more insistently this time.

Lourds peered through the peephole. Leslie Crane stood in the hallway with her arms folded, looking a little put out.

For a moment Lourds debated whether to answer the door. It was almost midnight. He could claim that he'd fallen asleep. Then again, she could – as she had last time – have kept one of his room keys. He hadn't checked this time either.

He gave in and opened the door, but he didn't step back.

'Yes?' he asked.

'I thought maybe we could talk,' Leslie said.

Lourds crossed his arms and leaned against the doorframe.

'Well?' Leslie demanded.

'Well, what?'

'Are you going to ask me in?'

'I thought I might find out what kind of mood you were in first.'

'I'm in a fine mood,' Leslie said crossly.

'Fine. You can come in. But the ground rules are that if you become unpleasant, you're leaving. Even if I have to carry you out myself.'

Leslie bristled at that. 'You weren't so quick to throw me out a few nights ago.'

Lourds smiled. 'On that night I found you quite fetching.' He stepped back. 'Lately, not so much so. But, please, come in.'

Leslie entered the room and glanced around. Her gaze landed on the computer.

'You were working,' she said.

'Yes.' Lourds closed the door and locked it. Having assassins creep into the room – even though the hotel was rated five stars – would be embarrassing. Not to mention deadly.

'Are you having any luck?'

'I don't know yet. Breaking languages, especially when you have so little to go on, is a laborious process.'

'Do you think Diop knows what he's talking about? About the drum?'

'I certainly hope so.' Lourds sat on the couch and gazed at the young woman. He tried to keep his mind on business. It was too easy to remember what she'd been like naked and in his arms.

Leslie paced for a moment. 'I'm getting a lot of pressure from my superiors. They want more of the story.'

'We don't have anything more to tell them.'

'My job is on the line here.'

'I realize that. If you want to part company from me now and declare it a loss, I'll understand. I've got some money put by. I can continue this for a while.'

She stopped pacing and gazed at him. 'You'd do that, wouldn't you?'

'Yes.'

'Why? Because of Yuliya Hapaev's death?'

'Partly, although I see that as work for the police rather than a linguistics professor. But it would be nice to give them everything they need to put Yuliya's killers behind bars.'

'That isn't where Natashya wants to put them.'

'No, I suppose it's not.'

'She's going to get us into trouble.'

'As I recall,' Lourds said, 'Natashya's been far more apt to get us *out* of trouble than into it.'

'She kills people.'

'I know. I can't say that it's something I would do, but if I were to meet those people under the same circumstances –'

'But you have. *We* have.'

'And if people's lives were on the line, I don't know if I wouldn't do the same thing.'

Leslie shook her head. 'You're not like her. She's cold and detached.'

'When she chooses to be, I have no doubt of that.' In fact, he was sure of it. Pushing a man from a fourth-storey window into the street was pretty callous.

'You couldn't do it.'

'I don't know. I might surprise you,' Lourds said softly.

'You already have.' Leslie's voice also softened. Without another word, she approached Lourds and pushed him back onto the bed.

She kissed him. At first Lourds wasn't going to respond, not certain at all about what he was getting into. And not at all certain that the flesh wasn't too weak. But then, when he found out the flesh was responding just fine, he decided to go for it.

Their hands pulled at each other's clothing.

Exhausted and running on fumes, Natashya forced herself out of the too-comfortable bed and paced the floor. She didn't trust herself not to sleep too deeply in the plush bed. And she didn't trust Gallardo not to break through the hotel security. He'd already shown he was capable and willing to do such a thing in Leipzig. In the end, though, she knew she was going to need a few hours of sleep. There was only one place she could think of to get it.

She picked up the suitcase containing the guns she'd taken and left the room. Across the hall, she knocked on Lourds' room. After a few moments, the peephole darkened.

Lourds opened the door and looked at her. 'Is something wrong?'

Natashya took one look at the dishevelled clothing and hair, then noticed the lingering scent of Leslie Crane's perfume, and knew exactly what was going on. When Leslie stepped into view behind Lourds wearing only her blouse which barely covered her modesty, there was no doubt.

'You,' Natashya declared fiercely in Russian as she felt anger and embarrassment sting her cheeks, 'are a *goat*.' She reached out and pulled the door shut.

Cursing to herself, Natashya walked to Gary's room. She knocked.

A moment later, he let her in. Thankfully he was still clothed. He carried his PSP in one hand. Aliens danced across its little screen.

'Hey,' Gary said. 'What's going on?'

'I need a place to sleep,' Natashya declared. She brushed by him and entered the room.

'Okay. Sure.' Gary closed the door behind her. 'I guess that's cool. Got two beds in here.'

Neither of the beds had been used. Evidently Gary had been playing video games for a while.

'Let me have three hours sleep while you stay awake,' Natashya said. She laid back on the bed and kicked off her shoes. Taking the pistols from the suitcase, she held them in her hands, which she crossed over her breasts. 'After that you can wake me and then you can sleep.'

'Sentry duty, huh?' Gary asked.

'Yes.' Natashya closed her eyes and felt them burn with fatigue.

'Maybe I should get a gun.'

'No.'

'Oh? Why not?'

'Because I said so. Now be quiet and let me sleep. And there's one thing further.'

'Yeah?'

'If you try to touch me while I'm sleeping, I'll shoot you through the head.'

Then sleep dragged her off into a welcome darkness.

Cave #2
Atlantis Burial Catacombs
Cadiz, Spain
7 September 2009

The excavation crews played lights over the waters roiling in the cave as the pumps worked.

Father Sebastian stood to one side and listened to the pumps and generators fill the cavern with noise. Fear rattled inside him. Even though the excavation foreman, Brancati, had told him the structural integrity was sound, Sebastian knew that if the patchwork they'd done to the breached wall gave way again they might all drown.

Along with the water, though, the excavation crews also brought out the bodies of the ancient dead. They lay like sunbathers on top of body bags. Their clothing was much the worse for wear, but that was no surprise. The experts on the dig staff seemed to feel that the materials could easily be restored. But many more of the crypt's occupants had been shattered by the flood waters and now lay in pieces. The Atlanteans had apparently had superb techniques to preserve the bodies of their dead, but even so, the unleashed power of an ocean had been too much for them.

It would be years, perhaps many years, before all of those bodies would be returned to sacred ground.

Sebastian couldn't help but pity them, even as he knew that studying them would open new windows into humanity's distant past.

Even then, Sebastian thought, *we won't know your names*.

The loss was monumental. Somewhere in the recesses of the burial vault, or perhaps the caves beyond – if, indeed, any caves yet existed – there might be a record book that listed all of the dead. Perhaps there would be a history with those names as well.

Were you Adam and Eve's true sons and daughters? Were you really the last of those who lived in the Garden of Eden? Did you taste immortality only to have it stripped away for daring too much against God?

As he stared into the darkness of the flooded cave, Sebastian remembered all the old stories from the book of Genesis. As a child, he'd imagined what it must have been like to walk with God and see first hand all the wonders he'd wrought. The illustrations in his childhood Bible had shown thick, lush forests filled with animals that had no fear of Adam. He'd roamed freely among them and given them their names. God had also given Adam Eve to be his wife. And she had been tricked by Satan in the guise of a serpent who had persuaded her to eat from the Tree of Knowledge of Good and Evil. When God had found out they had done the one thing he had forbidden them to do, he drove them from the Garden and placed a cherub with a flaming sword to guard over it.

Would the cherub still be there?

The question haunted Sebastian. If this was indeed the Garden of Eden, as Pope Innocent XIV believed it was, what would he do if God blocked the way? Sebastian shook his head. Merely thinking the question was sacrilege. If God blocked the way, then the way would be blocked. There would be no going past that.

'Father Sebastian.'

Recognizing his name amid the thunder and crash of the big machines operating around him, Sebastian turned. One of the young men from the construction crew stood before him.

'Yes?' Sebastian said.

'You need to put your hat on, Father.' The young man pointed to the hard hat now cradled in Sebastian's hands.

'Of course. You're right. I was just thinking about God. I never stand before him with a hat on.' Sebastian pulled on the hard hat.

'In the future, you might want to do your thinking about him in a safer area.'

Sebastian nodded but didn't say anything. The young man went on his way. After a moment more, Sebastian turned his attention back to the flooded cave.

Soon, he told himself. Maybe only days remained

before they could re-enter the cave. In truth, though, he didn't know whether to look forward to that or be fearful of it.

Outside Ile-Ife
Osun State, Nigeria
8 September 2009

'Have you been to Ile-Ife before, Thomas?' Ismael Diop asked. He sat beside Lourds in the middle seat of the forty-year-old Jeep Wagoneer.

Natashya sat up front with the young Yoruba driver Diop had negotiated for them after they'd touched down in Lagos the day before. While they'd been in Lagos, Natashya had outfitted herself with a hunting rifle and holsters for the pistols. She'd been mildly insulted that none of the rest of the party wanted to carry weapons.

Leslie and Gary occupied the rear seat.

The old 4 x 4 rode better than Lourds had expected after seeing it. Most of the paint and the wood-grain sides had been lost over the years, but the engine and transmission sounded strong.

'Once,' Lourds admitted. 'A long time ago. Shortly after I graduated from university I was asked down here by a linguistics professor I had. She had come from Nigeria.'

'She asked you to come for further study?'

Lourds grinned at the memory. 'You might say that. She was a very strict professor. No dating the students. Graduates were an entirely different matter.'

He glanced over his shoulder and made sure Leslie was still occupied with Gary. She was pointing out spider monkeys and brightly coloured birds. The tall forest was alive with animals. It was still early morning and breakfast was the first order of the day for the wildlife.

The occupants of the car had already taken care of their morning meal. They'd struck camp early that morning, had a hasty breakfast and got on the road. During the night, Leslie had learned a lot about manoeuvring around in a sleeping bag. She'd left Lourds' tent before Gary had woken, so their trysting was still presumably secret from him. But Natashya had been at the campfire and given them both scathing looks of disapproval for their nocturnal activities.

'Ah. I see,' Diop said. 'So after you graduated you were – fair game for this professor?' Diop's eyes crinkled in merriment.

'Exactly.'

'How long were you here?'

'A month. Five weeks. Something like that. Enough for us to find out that we were compatible. We had a good time together.'

'But not enough of a good time to form a more permanent arrangement?'

'No.' Lourds shook his head. 'I'm not the marrying kind. I love my work too much.'

Diop nodded. 'I understand. I found myself in similar straits. I married and I tried to make the best of it, but I often found myself torn between my family and my work. In the end, my wife left me for someone who was more inclined to stay at home.'

'That's too bad.'

'Actually, I think it was for the best. We were both happier for it. And now I have three beautiful daughters and seven grandchildren to visit when I feel the need for family. I believe they understand me more than their mother ever did.'

Spider monkeys leaped from treetop to treetop. Antelope stood at the roadside with twitching ears, then shied away as the jeep roared past. A short distance further on, the driver had to swerve to avoid hitting a forest elephant that wandered out onto the dirt road leading up into the bush country.

'The man we're going to see,' Diop went on. 'The Oba of Ile-Ife.'

'Adebayo,' Lourds said.

Diop nodded. 'Yes. You have a good memory. Anyway, this man is very much taken with the old ways. He is lately come into the office he holds, but he's always been protector of the drum.'

'The drum isn't part of the office of Oba?'

'No. The drum has been handed down through his family for generations.'

'For how many generations?'

Diop shrugged. 'To hear him tell it, since the beginning of the Yoruba people.'

'For many hundreds of years, then.' Excitement sang within Lourds. Despite the knowledge that Gallardo was on their trail, but buffered by the fact that they hadn't seen the man since leaving Ile de

Gorée, Lourds felt hopeful. 'Do you believe him?' Lourds asked.

'I believe him more now having seen those pictures of the bell and cymbal. Although I'm no expert, I think the writing on the drum is related to those.'

Lourds shifted restlessly in the seat. They'd travelled most of the day yesterday, by plane and then by jeep. Last night's encounter with Leslie had been relaxing, but he was consumed with curiosity. His impatience today was escalating.

'Do you speak Yoruba, Thomas?'

'Passably,' Lourds said. 'My professor was Yoruba, and we worked with Yoruba artefacts.'

'That's good. Adebayo speaks a little English and more Arabic, as many need to in this region to conduct their business affairs, but the process is painfully slow. Besides, he'll be more impressed if you speak his language.'

'How much further is it?'

'Not so much. We're not going into Ile-Ife proper. Adebayo lives in a small village north of the city. He travels into town when he needs to in order to let his voice be heard. But don't let that fool you. He's an educated man.'

'Stay back,' Gallardo instructed DiBenedetto, who drove the Toyota Land Cruiser they'd purchased back in Lagos. 'I don't want to get too close.' He gazed at the notebook computer screen on the lap of the man next to him which showed the Nigerian terrain they traversed. A blue triangle marked Lourds' position.

One of the computer geeks Gallardo hired for jobs had hacked into Lourds' cellphone and was able to track the GPS locator as long as it remained on. They'd also hacked into Leslie Crane's phone service. They hadn't yet been able to get the Russian woman's.

The red square following the blue triangle marked Gallardo's own progress. A small satellite receiver mounted on a pole on the Land Cruiser's bumper connected them to the geo-synchronous satellites that orbited the earth and painted their position.

DiBenedetto nodded and reduced his speed.

Gazing behind him, Gallardo looked at the three other vehicles that carried the small army of mercenaries he'd hired back in Lagos. They were white, black, Chinese and Arabic, a real global collection. Men like them were always for hire in the right bars. Africa remained torn by wars and greed. The dogs of war stayed close to the battles.

All of the new men were armed to the teeth.

Gallardo settled back into the seat and felt the day heating up around him. He felt certain it wouldn't be long now. He'd get the instruments. Then that redheaded bitch was going to get what was coming to her.

19

North of Ile-Ife
Osun State, Nigeria
8 September 2009

The village was a scattering of huts and small houses made of whatever their occupants could lay their hands on. There were a few tin roofs, but most of them tended to be made of bundles of grass. Goats, chickens and sheep wandered around the houses. Laundry hung on tree limbs behind them.

The driver pulled the 4 x 4 to a stop in the centre of the village. A little girl no more than four or five years old ran from a young woman and yelled for her father's attention.

'See?' Diop said quietly. 'These are the things you miss if you never have a family.'

'It wouldn't be a good idea for me to have a family yet,' Lourds replied. 'I'm still not through with my childhood.'

Diop's eyes sparkled. 'No. And I suspect you never will be. You'll always find one adventure or another that will call your attention away.'

Lourds thought again of the Library of Alexandria. He hadn't given up hope that all the books and scrolls had not been lost. He wanted to find them. Perhaps that want would haunt him all his life.

He got out of the vehicle feeling stiff and sore. Part of that was from the sleeping bag, he knew, but part of it was from his amorous adventures with Leslie. He was getting a bit too old for romps on the bare ground.

The men, women and children of the village all circled them excitedly. They talked in a handful of dialects, each one trying to find a means of communication that worked for the newcomers. They finally picked English, but they had only a rudimentary grasp of the language. Still, they did much better with English than the standard English-speaker would do with the Yoruba dialect.

But Lourds wasn't standard. He chatted easily and amiably with them in the Yoruba tongue. Even though it had been years since he'd last spoken it, the language came back to him almost naturally. He'd always known he'd been gifted when it came to languages. Not only did he generally have a quick grasp for them, but he also had a tendency for almost photographic recall when he needed them again, no matter how long it had been since he'd used them.

The villagers made only a token attempt to get to know Natashya. She'd shaken her head at them and smiled at their many questions, but her attention remained riveted on the surrounding forest. She carried her hunting rifle slung over one shoulder and pistols at her hips. She wore her long hair back in a ponytail and a cowboy hat shaded her face. Ice-blue sunglasses hid her eyes.

She looked more dangerous than any of the forest predators.

As Lourds talked to the villagers, he wondered again at how Yuliya's sister could be so different from her. Then again, he had to be grateful that she was. Without her, they'd all be dead.

His attention was drawn away from Natashya as the crowd parted before an old man dressed in khaki shorts, sandals and a white golfing shirt. He carried a staff in his right hand. Grey-white cottony hair covered his head and face.

The man stopped before them.

'Thomas, I'd like you to meet Oba Adebayo,' Diop said.

Lourds walked forward and met the man's gaze.

'Oba Adebayo,' Diop said, 'this is Professor Thomas Lourds. From the United States.'

Adebayo looked from Diop to Lourds. 'What do you want?' he asked in heavily accented English.

'Only to talk to you,' Lourds said in the Yoruba tongue.

The old Oba's eyebrows crawled up his forehead in surprise. 'You speak my language.'

'Some,' Lourds admitted. 'Not as much as I'd like.'

'It has been long and long since I have heard a white man speak my language so well,' Adebayo said. 'What do you wish to talk about?'

Lourds had given much thought as to how to bring up the subject of the drum. He could have forestalled the discussion, but he'd figured that anyone wise enough to run a village and serve as a king to one of the oldest existing African cities would see through that ruse.

Instead, Lourds shrugged out of his backpack and sat it on the ground. 'Let me show you,' he said. He knelt beside it, unzipped one of the outer pouches, and took out the pictures of the bell and the cymbal.

'These,' he said, handing the photographs over.

After a moment, Adebayo took the photos. He studied them in quiet contemplation as the livestock milled about and the children continued talking excitedly.

Then he looked up at Lourds. 'Where are these things?'

'I don't know.' Lourds stood and slung the backpack over his shoulder again. 'But I want to know.'

'Why have you come here?'

'To hear the story.'

'You have wasted your time. You have come to the wrong place.' Adebayo handed the photographs back and turned away.

'Have I truly come to the wrong place?' Lourds asked softly. 'I haven't been able to translate much on those instruments, but I've found a warning on them. Beware the gatherers.'

Adebayo kept walking back to his small house. It had a tin roof and walls that had been covered in children's drawings that Lourds assumed had come from Yoruba legends.

'Someone is gathering those instruments,' Lourds said. 'Someone very ruthless. One of my friends was killed when it was taken. Whoever is behind that theft isn't a good person.'

The old man pulled aside the vinyl curtain that hung over the doorway.

'He – or she – knows more about the instruments and the gathering than I do,' Lourds said. 'I know that gathering the instruments is dangerous, but I don't know why.' He paused. 'I need help.'

Adebayo disappeared into the house. Lourds started to pursue him. Immediately half a dozen young men stepped in front of the hut to block his path.

Helplessly, Lourds looked at Diop. The old historian only shook his head.

'If Adebayo doesn't wish to speak to you,' Diop said, 'then he won't speak. Perhaps another day.'

Disgusted with himself, Lourds tried to think of something to say or something he could do. He looked back at the photographs of the bell and the cymbal.

'You're supposed to protect the drum,' Lourds said. 'I know that. But you're also supposed to be a wise man. That's why the messages are written on the instruments. You're supposed to hand knowledge down to those who would take your place as the drum's protector.'

The young warriors came forward and chased the children and animals back.

'You will go,' one of them said in English. He had a hand on the knife at his belt.

'Someone else will come,' Lourds said as he

reluctantly gave ground before the warriors. 'Soon. Someone else will come and take the drum from you. Can you stop what happens when the instruments are gathered?'

Adebayo's head poked back out the door. 'Can you?'

'I don't know,' Lourds admitted. He had to be honest, even if it was to plead ignorance now. The 4 x 4's fender pressed into his hip and blocked any further movement backward.

'Do you know what the writing on the bell and the cymbal say?' Adebayo asked.

'No. I was hoping you could help.' Lourds felt the tiniest trickle of hope in the air, but he dared not reach for it.

Anger showed on the old man's face. 'Let him pass,' he growled to the warriors. 'I will talk to him.'

Gradually, the warriors pulled back.

'Come,' Adebayo said. 'I will tell you what I can of the Drowned Land and the God Who Walked the Earth.'

Hidden by the brush over a thousand yards from the village, Gallardo kept watch on the proceedings through high-powered binoculars. For a moment it had looked like Lourds and his companions were about to be given the boot.

If that had happened, Gallardo wasn't sure what he would have done. He still wasn't certain what Lourds was doing here so deep in the forest. He pulled his hunting rifle up to him and took the protective caps off the scope lenses. Peering through the scope, he sighted in on the Russian woman's head.

Killing her would be easy.

After a moment, he slid his finger over the trigger and started to squeeze. At that moment she moved and disappeared entirely from the scope's field of view.

Gallardo cursed quietly.

Then he heard Farok laughing softly.

Turning to the man, Gallardo scowled.

'This woman,' Farok said without making any attempt to hide his amusement, 'has really got under your skin, hasn't she?'

'Yes. But she won't stay there. Not for long,' Gallardo promised.

Inside the small, one-room house, Lourds found only sparse furnishings. The old man sat in a rocker and left Lourds and Diop straight-backed chairs that looked, and were, uncomfortable. Shelves lined the walls and held little knick-knacks that could have been purchased at a tourist store. There were also maps and several American and British magazines years out of date.

'Tell me about the bell and the cymbal,' Adebayo said.

Lourds did, but he compressed their story and that of the trail that had ultimately led him to Nigeria to the bare-bone facts. As he talked, a young woman brought in freshly squeezed mango juice and Jollof rice.

Lourds had enjoyed the food before while he'd visited West Africa with his professor. The rice was flavoured with tomatoes, tomato paste, onions, chilli peppers, salt and curry that coloured the end product reddish. Thin slivers of roasted chicken, beans and a vegetable and fruit salad filled the plate.

The aroma of the food awakened Lourds' hunger when he didn't think he'd be hungry. Breakfast had been hours ago.

'You have related the stories on those instruments to the great deluge,' Adebayo said.

'Yes.'

The old man ate as he talked. 'You know many peoples talk about the flood that God called down to destroy the world to erase the wickedness he found here.'

Lourds nodded.

'God has many names for many different peoples,' Adebayo said. 'Call him what you will, but for many people the stories are all the same.' He paused and pointed outside the door. 'Once my people were great fishermen and traders. They were proud and mighty. When they sailed, they sailed to all parts of the world. Did you know that?'

'No,' Lourds said.

'Well, it is true. I hear how some of the white teachers begin to talk about these things again, but many of them don't like the idea that the African man would know so much. Part of my people's banishment to this place was their downfall from that. When the water drank down the Drowned Land, most of my ancestors and their ships drowned as well.'

'What happened?'

'The people on the island angered God.'

'How?'

'They wanted to be gods themselves and they refused to be his children any longer.' Adebayo sipped the juice. 'In those days, all the people were one. They shared one tongue.'

'One language,' Lourds said. The thought excited him. With the prevalence of the internet in the world and the interface provided by the binary language and translation interfaces, the world had nearly reached that point again. As a linguist, he rejoiced in the openness, even as part of him mourned for the unique languages that were fading from the human consciousness.

Adebayo nodded. 'This is so. God caused the ocean to rise up and take down the land where all the people lived. But he was merciful and spared the lives of some of them. This is how the Yoruba people came to these lands.'

'What of Oduduwa?'

'He was the ship's pilot. The man who brought us to these lands. He was also the first protector of the drum. Men fought over the drum, though. Oduduwa took his army south and west of where their ship had landed in the north. My grandfather told me that Oduduwa landed somewhere in what is now known as Egypt. That is where the first war for the instruments was fought.'

'There was a war over the instruments?'

'Yes. Many men died to possess them. Oduduwa did as God bade him and kept the drum separate. Four other peoples,' Adebayo held up four crooked fingers, 'were also given instruments.'

'Who were those people?'

'Those who became known as the Egyptians kept the bell. More people spread to the frozen north.'

'Russia,' Lourds said.

Adebayo shook his head. 'I do not know these names. These names did not exist in those days. And no one was supposed to talk to each other after the instruments were given out.'

'Why?'

'The instruments have the power to unlock the way,' the old man said.

'The way to what?'

'The Drowned Land.'

Lourds thought about that. 'But if God caused those lands to sink into the sea, how would people reach them again?'

'I hear many stories,' Adebayo said. 'I hear that men have walked on the moon and on the bottom of the sea.'

'On the moon, yes,' Lourds replied. 'And on the bottom of the sea. But we haven't been able to go everywhere.'

'Maybe the Drowned Land is not in the deepest part of the ocean.'

'Which ocean?'

'What is now called the Atlantic Ocean. In those days, it had another name.'

'Not the Indian Ocean or the Mediterranean Sea?'

'The sea to the west,' Adebayo confirmed. 'The story has always been told so.'

'Who made the instruments?'

'God made five men come together. He gave them their own language which they could not teach to others. He said that the five instruments they created under his direction would become the key to reopen the Borrowed Lands.'

'How?'

Adebayo shook his head. 'God did not give them that knowledge. He told them only that when the time came, a way would be made for them to reach that which was hidden from the eyes of men.'

'What was hidden?'

'Power,' Adebayo said. 'The power to destroy the world again, and this time God would not save them.'

'Why didn't God simply take the power away?'

'I don't know. My ancestors have suggested that God would not destroy that which he created.'

'But he destroyed the world.'

'Not completely. You and I are here now as proof of that.' Adebayo sipped at his juice. 'My ancestor told me the story also goes that God left the power here to test his children again. That he sowed their own seeds of destruction among them.'

'To see if they had learned?'

Adebayo shrugged. 'Perhaps.'

'But this story,' Lourds said incredulously, 'isn't even known.'

'Many of the people who knew this story spread

lies about it so that others would not hunt for the instruments and no one would believe it. They stripped the faith in God away so they would be the only ones who knew. Many wars are fought in this world over the name of God.'

Lourds silently agreed with that.

Adebayo continued. 'Two of the instruments, the bell and the cymbal, were lost in early times to men who wanted to claim the power left in the Drowned Land. The Yoruba people have always protected the drum.'

'Do you know where the flute and the pipe are?'

'We are not supposed to know.'

Lourds thought for a moment. Something wasn't ringing true. There was some conflict that was in front of him that was evading his grasp. Then his mind closed on it.

'You knew that the bell and the cymbal were lost,' Lourds stated.

'That was many years ago.'

'But . . . you . . . knew,' Lourds said.

Adebayo said nothing.

Lourds decided to take another tack. He took the pictures of the bell and the cymbal from his backpack again. 'These instruments both have two inscriptions on them. One of the inscriptions on both is in the same language.'

'I know.'

'Can you read either of them?'

Adebayo shook his head. 'It is forbidden. To each people there shall be an individual language.'

'Then what is the language of the inscriptions that are in the same language?'

'That,' Adebayo said, 'is in the language of God. It shall never be known to his children.'

The announcement stunned Lourds. The language of God? Could it really be? Or was it simply a language that had been forgotten?

'Do you have the drum?' Lourds asked.

'Yes.'

'May I see it?'

'The drum is a holy relic,' Adebayo said. 'It's not some tourist trinket.'

'I know,' Lourds said as patiently as he could under the circumstances. Every nerve in his body screamed at him to make Adebayo turn the drum over to him so he could see it. 'I've come a long way to see that drum.'

'You are an outsider.'

'So are the men hunting these instruments,' Lourds argued in a soft voice. 'Those men are trained killers. They won't stop at anything to get what they want. They know about the five instruments.'

'No one knows about the five instruments except the Keepers.'

'Someone knows about them. Someone has been looking for them for a long time.' Lourds took a deep breath. '*I* know about them. I know enough about languages to know that the cymbal had a language on it that came out of Yoruba.'

'That can't be. The languages were different.'

'These were later markings,' Lourds said. 'And

they were written in a Yoruba dialect. That's how I came to be here.' He nodded at Ismael Diop. 'The fact that you had shown him the drum made finding you even easier. When more than one person is involved, secrets tend not to last.'

Adebayo didn't look happy.

'You've protected the drum for a long time,' Lourds went on, 'but the secret is coming out again. Somewhere, somehow, someone knows more about this than I do. They're searching for the instruments systematically. It won't be long before the killers find you too.' He took a short breath. 'They may already have.'

A troubled look filled Adebayo's eyes. 'I know who the other Keepers are. We have been in contact with each other, as our ancestors were, for a long time. Since almost the beginning. That's how I knew the bell and the cymbal were lost.'

Lourds waited quietly and found himself scarcely able to breathe. *So close, so close.*

'We had believed the bell and the cymbal destroyed,' Adebayo said. 'For generations we've protected the instruments but didn't fear that the wrath of God would ever be turned loose in the world again.' He paused. 'Now you say it is almost upon us.'

'Yes. The time has come to take action before it is too late. The message on the instruments needs to be translated,' Lourds said. 'Maybe that will help.'

'No Keeper has ever been able to read the inscriptions.'

'Perhaps no Keeper has ever before been a linguistics professor,' Ismael Diop suggested. He reached out and clapped Adebayo on the knee. 'For ever and always there has been talk of prophecies. Yet, every now and again, one of them has to come true. Perhaps, my friend, it is time for this one to come true.'

'Even if it destroys the world?' Adebayo asked.

'We can't let that happen,' Lourds said. 'God willing, perhaps we'll prevent that here and now. But if we don't do anything, our enemies will.'

Adebayo knelt down on the floor near the woven sleeping mat. Placing both hands against the wall, he pushed and slid a section of it away. Only then did Lourds realize the wall was over a foot thick. The hiding place was cleverly disguised.

A drum and a curved striking stick sat inside the wall. Lourds recognized it at once as a *ntama*, an hourglass-shaped drum. It was also called a 'waisted' drum due to its unique shape. Usually the drum cores were made out of wood carved into the hourglass-shape then hollowed out.

This one was made of ceramic material. As with other *ntama*s, it had a drum head at either end that would be struck with the curved drumstick as needed. Lourds didn't know if the heads were made out of goatskin or fishskin. The hoops that formed the drum heads were tied together with dozens of flexible leather cords.

Lourds had seen men make the drums 'talk' the last time he'd been in West Africa. By placing the *ntama* under the arm and squeezing to relax or tighten the leather cords and the drum heads, the drummers could dramatically change the tone produced.

None of them had been made of ceramic, though.

'May I?' Lourds held his hand out for the drum.

'Be very careful,' Adebayo said. 'The ceramic body had proven very resilient over the years, but it is fragile.'

All of the instruments were, Lourds reflected. How any of them had survived thousands of years was beyond him. Yet the 8,000 terracotta soldiers and horses that had been buried with Qin Shi Huang, the first emperor of China, had lasted over 2,000 years. Of course, they hadn't gone anywhere, and some of them had broken. But they had survived a revolution in which rebels broke into the tomb and stole the bronze weapons they'd been armed with.

It seemed to Lourds that the only explanation for the instruments to have survived, as unscientific as it was, was divine providence.

He studied the ceramic core, turning the drum gently in his hands and peering through the leather cords, to find the inscriptions he knew had to be there.

He wasn't disappointed. At the sight of them, remembering all that Adebayo had said about the Drowned Land and the story of God's wrath, the hair on the back of Lourds' neck stood up.

It was true. All of it.

Having to relieve herself *au naturel* in the forest was one thing Leslie Crane swore she'd never get used to. Nor did she ever want to.

She squatted down in the bush and let her bladder go while trying to hold her pants out of the way. It wasn't easy. There was a whole balancing problem that wasn't an issue on a proper toilet. Men definitely had a much easier time when they were roughing it.

She couldn't wait to get back to the city. A proper toilet, a bubble bath, and a good meal would set her to rights. And maybe another evening in Professor Lourds' bed. That man had an uncanny ability to satisfy her, and he stayed longer in the saddle than she'd expected for a man of his years. Honestly, she'd been hard-pressed to keep up, and that wasn't something she was used to.

She liked being with him.

Trekking through the bushes with him was simply horrible, though. The whole time she'd felt like someone was watching her.

Maybe someone was.

Dirty, pathetic pervert, she thought as she used the roll of toilet paper she'd brought.

As she hiked up her pants, she caught a flash of motion from the corner of her eye. Someone *had* been watching. Anger boiled through her. The first inclination that struck her was to find the peeping Tom and give him a good piece of her mind. Then she realized she didn't speak the language well enough to really take him down. Nor did she know exactly what one of the Yoruba tribe would do if he suddenly found himself face-to-face with a flamingly furious European woman.

That was when she caught sight of the man back

in the bush. It was only for a brief second. Hardly more than a glimpse, actually. But it was enough to know that his skin colour was a swarthy tan, not black. *She* wasn't being spied on, she realized. All of them were.

Fear pricked the back of Leslie's neck. She held onto the toilet paper and made herself walk back to the village as calmly as possible when every instinct she had screamed at her to run.

When she arrived back at the 4 x 4, Leslie found Gary seated in the back with his feet propped up. His attention was focused solely on his PSP as his thumbs drummed across the buttons.

'Any snakes?' he asked when she fired the toilet paper into the back of the vehicle.

'No, but I found a peeping Tom or two.'

Gary grinned. 'Is it the native lads, then? Going to grow up to be mashers, are they?'

'No.' Leslie forced herself to be calm. 'It was not. Maybe a sun-tanned white man. Maybe Chinese or Arabic. But definitely not black.'

That caught Gary's attention. He looked up from the game. 'What're you saying, love?'

'I'm saying Gallardo has managed to find us out here.'

Gary cursed and brought his feet down. 'We need to tell Lourds.'

'Do you think?' Leslie asked sarcastically. She looked around. 'I don't want to tip off Gallardo's goons. Where's the Russian witch? This is her area of expertise.'

Gary looked around as well. 'Don't know. She was here a moment ago.'

'Well, this is absolutely brill.'

'I can look for her.'

'Maybe you could run up a flag and announce to Gallardo that we're on to him while you're at it.' Leslie sighed. 'No. Stay put and stay ready. I have a feeling we're going to be getting out of here very quickly.' She headed toward the house where Lourds and Diop had gone.

Gallardo watched the young blonde woman through the rifle's sniper scope. Something felt off. She seemed more tense and driven than she had been while tending to the call of nature.

He pulled away from the scope and searched the village with his binoculars. 'Farok.'

'Yes,' the man responded.

'Have you seen that Russian she-devil?'

'No.'

'How long has she been missing?'

'Ten, fifteen minutes.'

Gallardo thought that over. If, like the other woman, she'd gone to the bathroom, she was taking her sweet time about it. When she wasn't visible, she was more dangerous than at any other time.

'What do you think Lourds and that old man are talking about?' DiBenedetto asked. His pupils were pinpricks and Gallardo knew he was riding a cocaine high.

'I don't know.'

'Lourds wouldn't have come out here for nothing.'

Gallardo grunted. He picked up his radio and pressed the TALK button. 'Stay alert. The Russian woman has dropped off the radar.' He kept thinking about how she'd caught his man off-guard on Ile de Gorée two nights ago. 'When you see her, let me know.' He started to put the radio away and thought better of it. 'If you get the chance to kill her – quietly – get that done. There's a bonus in it for the man who succeeds.'

Lourds' sat-phone rang as he watched Adebayo place the *ntama* into a protective airline case with a high-impact liner. He glanced at the caller ID, wondering who would be calling him now.

'Lourds,' he answered.

'Gallardo and his men are encamped around the village,' Natashya said without preamble in Russian. 'He's hired an army. I think they're waiting for us to leave before they try to stop us.'

Anxiety vibrated through Lourds. He walked to one of the windows and peered out.

'That's great,' Natashya said in disgust. 'Go and stand at the window so you'll make a great target.'

Lourds stepped back hurriedly. 'Where are you?'

'Out in the bush with them. I intend to be your diversion when you make your break.'

'When am I going to do that?'

'Five minutes ago.'

Lourds thought about it. The idea of being caught out in the open out here by Gallardo and his men wasn't appealing. Nor did it promise much in the way of life expectancy.

'They're still tailing us,' he said.

'Yes.'

'Although Leslie's no longer staying in contact with her production team.'

'So Gallardo has found another way. At this point he might be tailing us through the phones.'

'He can do that?'

'It's possible, if he can buy off the right people. A good computer geek could do it – though these goons don't strike me as the type to be hackers. At this point I'm inclined to think that he's attached to some deep pockets that aren't going to stop at anything.'

The fear inside Lourds stepped up a notch. 'If you have a suggestion, I'm listening.'

'Keep calm. Walk out like nothing has happened. Get in the car and get out of there. Do it quickly. Put your foot down on the accelerator and don't let up until you reach Lagos. The city is full of armed men. We should at least be safer there with the police and military all around.'

'What about you?'

'I'm fine. I'll meet you there.'

The phone clicked dead in Lourds' ear just as Leslie entered the room.

'We've got to go,' Leslie said.

'I know.' Lourds picked up his backpack. 'Gallardo's found us.'

A perplexed look darkened Leslie's face. 'How could you possibly know that?'

'Natashya just called,' Lourds explained. 'She's out there with them. I think she's about to attack.'

Leslie's eyes widened. 'I don't know how she does that.'

'Just be glad that she does.' Lourds turned to Diop and Adebayo and spoke in Yoruba. 'Our enemies have found us again. We have to go.' He looked at the old man. 'If we leave you here, they may try to take you.'

'I will go with you. Besides, you will need me to speak to the other Keepers.'

Lourds flashed him a smile. 'Good. I will be glad of your company. I think you'll be safer that way.' *But probably not by much.*

'They're leaving,' Gallardo said into the radio handset. 'Everybody stand ready. We're going to take them on the road back into Lagos when there's less chance of interference from all those villagers.'

'It would be better if we took them here,' Farok commented. 'Once they start moving, everything becomes more fluid.'

'We can handle this,' Gallardo said. 'We have the upper hand.'

DiBenedetto smiled. 'Of course,' he said, 'we could kill the Russian here. Maybe freak the others out a little more and make them easier to manage in the long run.'

The idea appealed to Gallardo for a number of reasons. He'd been hoping for the opportunity to personally end the bitch's life. He reached out for the rifle and brought it close to him. Then he began searching for the red-haired woman as Lourds slid behind the old wreck's steering wheel and started the engine.

Lourds took off hell-for-leather and scattered a platoon of chickens and goats when he laid on the horn.

The woman wasn't with them. The realization caused Gallardo to worry. Then he thought furiously. If the woman wasn't with Lourds, that meant she was outside the village. He scanned the brush quickly.

'Find the Russian woman,' he ordered. 'She's out there. She's spying on us.'

Farok and DiBenedetto began searching.

'Check in with the men,' Gallardo said. 'See if anyone is missing.'

Then he spotted her. But only because she was aiming at him with a rifle of her own.

Gallardo framed her in the sniper scope for a split second. It wasn't even long enough to slide his finger over the trigger. She was smiling in anticipation. Her head was tilted behind the sniper scope as she looked at him through her viewfinder.

Abandoning his rifle, Gallardo rolled to the side. 'Look out!' he shouted, sending Farok and DiBene-detto diving for cover as well.

Natashya knew from the way Gallardo disappeared just *before* the powerful hunting rifle thumped against her shoulder that she'd missed. He'd seen her just in time to dodge away. She cursed and worked the bolt-action to slide another cartridge smoothly into place.

She stood beside a gnarled baobab tree that had a trunk nearly four times as wide as she was. The thin limbs looked arthritic and twisted, as if stunted from giving up everything they might have had to make the trunk so thick.

Even though Gallardo had evaded her, Natashya still had targets marked in her mind. She hadn't confirmed for certain how many men Gallardo had brought with him, but she knew where nine of them were. She'd hoped to take Gallardo out of the action.

Calmly, she settled the cross hairs over a man firing at Lourds' car. The shooter's rifle bullets chopped into the ground slightly behind the vehicle, which told her that he was trying to blow out the tyres.

Too bad for him.

She squeezed the trigger and rode out the recoil. The bullet punched the man down to the ground. She worked the bolt-action again and sent the empty brass flying before seating another round.

A pair of jeeps loaded with armed men roared out of the underbrush. Natashya had missed them in her headcount. She'd accounted for two other vehicles she'd found.

With careful deliberation, she focused on the driver of the first pursuit car as he screamed off after her allies. Her finger slid onto the trigger, took up slack, and squeezed through. The bullet caught the driver in the side of the head and slammed him over against the passenger, covering him in blood spatter and brains. Immediately the jeep went out of control and crashed into a baobab tree. Two men flew free of the wreck.

She took aim at the second jeep, but it was moving fast and nearly out of range.

She'd get to them later.

Natashya worked the action and moved to her next target. She barely got the shot off, knocking the man out of position with a centre-mass shot, before a dozen rounds chopped into the tree she was using as cover.

Stay here and you're dead, she told herself. Her impulse was to stay, though. She wanted Yuliya's killer. If she stayed, he'd certainly come after her. She could kill him then. But that wasn't going to happen yet.

She slung the rifle over her shoulder and skidded down the small drop behind the tree. She'd chosen the man she'd taken out first with care. He was one of the few who had driven an Enduro motorcycle. And he was the only one who'd taken up a position by himself.

At the bottom of the incline, Natashya hauled his motorcycle up on its tyres and thumbed the electronic ignition. The big engine warbled to life and shuddered between her thighs. She paused only long enough to pull on the helmet, knowing that while it wouldn't stop a direct shot, it might at least serve to turn a glancing blow from a bullet.

She dropped her left leg onto the gearshift lever and pressed it down into first gear when she pulled in the clutch. Twisting the accelerator, she released the clutch and felt the rear tyre bite into the earth.

Staying low, she roared up over the rise and changed gears as she accelerated quickly in pursuit of Lourds.

Gallardo ran through the forest and used his rifle to knock branches and brush out of the way. When one of his motorcycles roared past with the Russian woman astride it, he paused to fire, but all three shots went wide of her.

Then she was gone, speeding through the dust cloud left by the military-style jeep chasing Lourds' vehicle.

Setting himself into motion again, Gallardo ran for the area where they'd left the vehicles. He cursed the decision he'd made to leave them so far from the village, but at the time it had seemed the wisest thing to do. By the time he reached the Land Cruisers, he was out of breath. He stumbled to the SUV and hauled himself behind the wheel.

'Keys!' he yelled to DiBenedetto, who was right behind him.

DiBenedetto fished the keys from his pocket and threw them across. Then he stopped and shook his head. 'The keys aren't going to do you any good. We're not going anywhere.'

Gallardo got out of the vehicle and looked down. All four tyres had been slashed.

'She found the vehicles first,' Farok said in grim appreciation. 'This woman you've decided to hate so much, Patrizio, is worthy of your attention.'

She was also thorough. Even the spare tyres had been slashed. And the fuel lines. All Gallardo could hope for was that the jeep she'd missed would catch Lourds.

'Come on,' he shouted. He jogged back towards the road and the sound of roaring engines. It was a long way to run, but there was nothing else to do.

As he drove, Lourds checked his rear-view mirror for any signs of pursuit. He silently cursed himself for not taking a weapon when Natashya had offered one. But guns weren't his weapon of choice. He preferred using his mind.

Except you can't really do a lot with your mind in situations like these, he told himself grimly.

Leslie sat in the passenger seat. She was turned around, peering behind them anxiously. Gary, Diop, and Adebayo sat in the back seat and hung onto their safety belts. The old man had his arms wrapped protectively around the *ntama* case.

At least they'll have to be careful of the drum, Lourds thought. *If they know we have it.* But that still wouldn't prevent them from killing everyone.

'They're coming,' Leslie said softly.

Lourds glanced at the rear-view mirror in time to see a jeep pull onto the road after them. He tried to press the accelerator down harder, but his foot was already on the floor, pedal to the metal. The engine whined in protest. As he watched, the jeep began to gain ground. So far they weren't shooting, but he expected that would change soon enough.

A bullet took off the side mirror and dropped it away from the 4 x 4 in a swarm of flying pieces.

Leslie yelped and ducked. The others crouched down as well.

Two other rounds pounded the back glass from the vehicle. One of the bullets, or a third – Lourds wasn't sure – ripped through the front windshield and left a hole that he could fit his thumb through.

In the next moment, a motorcycle raced through the swirling dust clouds left by the speeding vehicles. It caught up with the jeep easily. The rider pointed a pistol in her left hand at the driver.

As Lourds watched, the driver's head jerked violently. Then the vehicle lost control. The passenger scrambled for the steering wheel, but the motorcycle rider shot him as well. The passenger on the rear deck tried to get his rifle into play, but the jeep pulled hard to the left, causing the motorcycle rider to nearly lose control. The jeep rolled on the roadside, skidded across the ground and bounced like a pinball between the trees.

If anyone had been left alive after Natashya's attack, Lourds doubted they were still breathing now.

Natashya – and Lourds knew it *was* her now from the clothing she wore – accelerated and pulled alongside the 4 x 4. She opened her helmet's faceplate and shouted across to him.

'I think that's all of them. Gallardo's still alive, but he and the rest of them won't be able to pursue us any time soon.'

Lourds nodded. He didn't know what to say, but he knew he had to say something. 'Thank you.'

'I'm going to check up ahead and make certain the

way is clear.' Natashya closed the faceplate again and shot ahead of him.

'Great,' Lourds said, not that she could hear him.

'That's a most incredible woman,' Diop said from the back seat.

'I'm just glad she's on our side,' Gary commented.

Lourds silently agreed.

20

Rage gripped Murani as he listened to Gallardo trying to explain how Lourds and his companions had escaped again. He paced his private room and stared at the television monitor broadcasting the latest coverage of the excavation in Cadiz.

The efforts to pump the submerged cave dry were ahead of schedule. Father Sebastian had shot footage of the cave's interior and given copies to the news media. He was even granting a few interviews as though he was a celebrity. His actions supremely irked Murani. Now it was no longer enough to simply take over the excavation from the old fool. Murani wanted Sebastian dead for defiling God's work.

'We almost had them,' Gallardo protested.

'But you don't, do you?' Murani demanded. 'And now they have the drum.'

'If it's the right drum. We only got a glimpse of it.'

'It's the right drum or Lourds wouldn't have been there. He wouldn't have taken it. That man is on the trail of the instruments.' Murani went to his closet and took out a suitcase. He carried it to the bed, fumbled with the latches, and opened it.

'Even if it is the drum, he doesn't have all the instruments. You have two of them. Lourds can't do anything. You said you needed all five.'

'We do need all five. Do you know where those missing instruments are?'

Gallardo was silent for a moment. 'No.'

'Neither do I. But I'm willing to bet Professor Lourds has a clue.' Murani took clothing from his closet and began packing. Staying in Vatican City was no longer possible.

Although he felt safe from the Society of Quirinus – not only because he'd threatened them, but because they ultimately had some of the same goals he did – the Pope was paying closer attention to him. Murani had received a summons to see him in the morning.

Murani didn't intend to attend that meeting. The next time he returned to Vatican City, it was going to be when he was pope. Things were about to change for the better in Vatican City. He was going to see to it.

'Where are you now?' Murani asked.

'On foot. We're having to hike into Ile-Ife to arrange transportation.'

'How long will that take?'

'Hours. I don't know if we'll make it before dark.'

'Then you'll be heading back to Lagos?'

Gallardo hesitated. 'Travelling through this area at night is dangerous.'

'Get to Lagos. You're already behind Lourds. I want that man found. I want to know what he knows. I want that drum.'

'All right.' Gallardo didn't sound happy. 'I've talked to the man I paid to hack into their phones. He says they're all off-line.'

Murani slammed the suitcase lid. 'Then they've figured out how you found them.'

'That's what I was thinking.'

'You'll need another way to find them.'

'I'm open to suggestions.'

If there was any sarcasm in Gallardo's voice, Murani couldn't detect it. 'Keep the phone trace active on Leslie Crane's director. She's a reporter. By now she realizes she has a huge story to tell. Besides the pressure she's getting from her studio, there's got to be a need inside her to capture the limelight. She'll call him, tell him what is happening. We'll find them then.'

'All right.'

Murani forced himself to remain calm. 'Get Lourds this time, Patrizio.' He watched the footage of the excavation inside the Cadiz cave. 'We're running out of time.'

'I will.'

Murani ended the call and pocketed the phone. He picked up the suitcase and headed for the door. When he stepped outside, two Swiss Guards stood at attention. Both of them looked at the suitcase in Murani's hand.

'I'm sorry, Cardinal Murani,' the younger of the

men said. 'His Holiness has asked that you remain in your quarters for the evening.'

'And if I refuse?'

The younger of the men grimaced. 'Then I am to make sure you stay in them.' He hand dropped to the pistol at his hip.

The thought that Pope Innocent XIV had confined him to quarters brought Murani's anger to a boil. If he could have struck the Guard dead that moment he would have.

'Go easy, Franco,' the older Guard admonished his colleague. He was thicker and more taciturn. 'This is Cardinal Murani. He has always been a friend to the Guard. Proper respect should be shown.'

Franco cut his gaze to the older man for a moment. 'I'm being respectful, Corghi. I've apologized.' His gaze swivelled back to Murani. 'But we're also here by the Pope's orders. You can be polite, but you must also be firm.' He paused. 'Please, Cardinal Murani. Return to your quarters. If you need anything, we will gladly arrange for it.'

'Insufferable, blind fool,' Murani growled.

Franco put a hand out to restrain Murani. In disbelief, he looked at the other Guard who took a hypodermic from his jacket and swept it toward the younger man in a swift arc. Alerted by the *hiss* of clothing as the older man struck, Franco tried to draw his weapon. Corghi grabbed his hand and trapped his arm against his side, then shoved him into the wall beside Murani.

'What are you doing?' Franco demanded. 'You can't –'

Corghi drove the hypodermic into Franco's neck and depressed the plunger. Franco opened his mouth to yell. For a moment Murani thought the Guard might manage it. But Corghi rammed his forearm into Franco's face and blocked the scream.

A few seconds later, as the men strained against each other, the chemical acted. Franco's eyes rolled up into his head until only the whites showed. He slumped and would have fallen if Corghi hadn't caught him.

'I was beginning to wonder if you'd changed your mind, Corghi,' Murani said.

'No, Your Eminence,' Corghi said. 'Now, if I may borrow your rooms.'

'Of course.' Murani opened the door and watched as Corghi tossed the other man's unconscious body inside the room. Normally no one but cleaning staff and friends were ever allowed inside the rooms. However, Murani had no intention of returning to them. He had his eyes on far grander quarters.

Franco hit the floor loosely and remained there.

'He should be out for a few hours,' Corghi said as he closed the door. He reached down and picked up Murani's luggage. 'Even if he can't talk, though, the Pope will know you're gone. Search groups will be sent out.'

Murani nodded and set off down the hall. 'By that time we'll have gone and it'll be too late.'

'Yes, sir.' Corghi fell in behind him. 'I'm going to get you out of Vatican City, Your Eminence. There's a way through the catacombs.'

Murani didn't tell the man that he already knew that. He'd been the one who had established the escape route with Lieutenant Sbordoni. Vatican City, the Church, the Swiss Guard and the Society of Quirinus had all existed long enough to establish factions within those organizations.

Shortly after being invited into the ranks of the Society, Murani had found a few others who believed as he did regarding the Church's place in the world. However, few of them were willing to act as boldly as he was. He'd found more like-minded men among the warriors of the Swiss Guard. Over the years, a few of the Swiss Guard had been restrained or even removed from office for their zealous efforts to enforce the Church's power. None among them had the knowledge that Murani had, and only a few times before had a cardinal acted with the guardsmen.

It was difficult splitting that group. Many of them remained loyal to the Pope. Some of those who had still held allegiance to the office of pope had come under Murani's sway after Innocent XIV was elected. They had seen the same weaknesses in the man that Murani had seen.

And they recognized the strength in you, Murani reminded himself. After he had stepped forward and made his trepidation known to the cardinals, the Swiss Guard had learned of Murani's doubts as well. Guardsmen had quietly come forward to offer their support.

'Will Lieutenant Sbordoni be joining us?' Murani asked.

'Not inside the city, Your Eminence.' Corghi took the lead briefly and stepped into the small public study where the residents sometimes met to confer. 'He'll be joining us in Cadiz.'

Murani nodded. 'He'll take command of the men we have on site there?'

'Yes, sir.' Corghi pressed the hidden release along the back wall. A section of a bookcase turned sideways and allowed entrance into the hidden space beyond.

Murani took a flashlight from his robes and switched it on. Some of the catacombs had power lines through them, but the section they were going to use was decrepit and hardly travelled. He followed the beam into the darkness.

Anticipation filled him to overflowing with every step he took toward his destiny.

Outside Lagos, Nigeria
8 September 2009

By the time Natashya held up a hand and signalled for a stop, Lourds' back and shoulders were knotted with tension and his eyes burned from fatigue. Sitting hunched over a steering wheel, especially along a rutted and bumpy road while travelling at excessive speeds, was nothing like sitting hunched over a computer or manuscript in need of translation. Dirt and bug entrails only blunted some of the sunset as they'd driven into it.

The motorcycle's brake light flared ruby in the gathering dusk that pooled in the forest. Natashya swung her leg off the bike as Lourds pulled in behind her.

'What's wrong?' Leslie woke in the passenger seat. She'd gone to sleep only a couple of hours ago and Lourds hadn't had the heart to wake her.

'Natashya wanted to pull over,' Lourds said.

'It's about bloody time,' Gary commented. 'My bloody back teeth are floating. I thought I was going to burst a kidney on those bumps.' He opened the side door, got out and trotted for the tree line.

Diop and Adebayo got out as well. The old man carried the tribal drum with him.

As Lourds watched the oba move into the forest, he grew anxious that he might not see the man again.

'He'll be back,' Leslie said.

Lourds looked at her.

'That's what you were worried about, right?' Leslie asked.

Lourds nodded and smiled. 'I guess my interest is pretty transparent.'

'Solution of a mystery. Dead languages. And the possibility of the world ending.' Leslie shrugged and smiled back. 'I'm pretty interested, too.' She glanced towards Natashya, who was approaching them. 'Probably more interested than others I could mention.' She walked away before Natashya could join them.

Instead of stopping, Natashya walked to the rear of their 4 x 4 and unstrapped one of the jerry cans of gasoline. A dark splotch of blood showed on her right shoulder.

'What are you doing?' Lourds asked.

'The motorcycle is out of petrol.'

'You could ride with us.'

Natashya shook her head. 'Two vehicles give us a better chance to react if Gallardo had another vehicle around that I didn't see.'

'He hasn't followed us thus far.'

'That doesn't mean he's not out there.'

Lourds had to silently admit that was true. Gallardo had managed to keep finding them at every point in the journey so far. His uneasiness grew by the heartbeat.

Natashya turned to grip the jerry can.

'Let me get that,' Lourds offered.

'I can do it,' Natashya insisted stubbornly.

'I've no doubt of it.' Lourds stepped up to take control of the jerry can as it came free. For a moment he thought Natashya was going to hit him. Then she turned on her heel and walked back to the motorcycle.

She took a water bottle from one of the saddlebags and drank deeply.

Knowing the woman wasn't going to talk until she was ready to, Lourds put the jerry can down and opened the petrol tank. A quick rap on the side told him it was running on fumes. He hefted the can and topped the tank up without spilling any of the fuel.

'I had him in my sights,' Natashya whispered.

Lourds placed the cap back on the tank. 'Who?'

'Gallardo. I had him in my sights and I missed.'
Natashya tucked a length of lank hair behind her ear.

Lourds didn't point out that she might well have another opportunity. That would hardly be comforting. Although there hadn't been any signs of pursuit, he wasn't willing to rule out the possibility. Like a bad penny, Gallardo had a way of continuing to turn up.

'He killed Yuliya,' Natashya said.

'You don't know that,' Lourds said softly. 'Not for sure. There were many men involved in that attack.'

'I know it here.' Natashya put a fist to her heart. 'In the part of me that is Russian, I know it.'

'Let me have a look at your wound.'

She shook her head. 'It's nothing.'

'In this heat, with all the dust and grime we're facing, not to mention the local flora and fauna, it's dangerous to let it go untended. Infection could set in.'

She shrugged. 'Do whatever you wish. But make it fast. We need to keep moving.'

Lourds called out to Gary, who had returned to the vehicle, to bring the first-aid kit over. Lourds took out a pen flash and a bottle of antiseptic.

'Need any help?' Gary asked.

Before Lourds could answer, Natashya said, 'No.'

'Okay. Cool. I'm just going to be over by the jeep if you need anything.' Gary left the first-aid kit and retraced his steps to the vehicle.

'Feeling anti-social?' Lourds asked.

'If I hadn't been concerned about all of you,'

Natashya told him, 'I would have stayed behind and killed Gallardo.'

Lourds said nothing. Her way of dealing with her sister's death was very different to his. He wanted to carry Yuliya's work on. Natashya wanted to dispatch her sister's killer. He couldn't imagine cold-bloodedly killing someone. On some of his international hunts for artefacts and manuscripts, he'd sometimes crossed paths with professional soldiers. To a degree, he'd understood their mentality, but he'd never once believed he could have been one of them. But Natashya had made him realize that there was a place for such people in this dangerous world.

'Well, I'm glad you were concerned about us.' Lourds pulled at her blouse sleeve and realized he'd never be able to roll it up high enough to clear the wound. 'Can you take off your shirt? I can't . . .'

Natashya slipped a lock-back knife from her pocket, flicked the blade open with her thumb, and sliced through the material.

'Thanks.' Lourds ripped the material further to give himself access to the wound. He played the light over her shoulder and quashed the queasiness that blossomed in the pit of his stomach.

'It's nothing to worry about. The bullet only grazed me,' Natashya said.

Not trusting his voice, Lourds nodded. The ragged tear across the top of her shoulder looked nasty and painful, but it didn't look life-threatening. However, he couldn't help thinking how much different things would have been had the bullet been six or seven inches to the left. It would have smashed through Natashya's throat. If the wound hadn't killed her outright, she would have drowned in her own blood.

And she was acting as if it were nothing.

She was amazing.

'This may sting,' Lourds warned.

'If I can't bear it, I'll let you know.'

That was what Lourds was afraid of.

Lourds poured antiseptic over the wound and flushed the blood away. He cleaned the area up as best he could without pulling at the edges because he didn't want to risk starting it bleeding again.

Natashya never said a word.

Once he was satisfied that the wound was as clean as he was going to get it, he applied an anti-bacterial ointment and a bandage. He taped everything in place.

'Where do we go from here?' Natashya asked as he taped the ragged edges of her blood-stained shirt together.

'I don't know. We've got to make contact with the other two Keepers.'

'Are they like the old man?'

'His name is Adebayo,' Lourds replied. 'And I don't know. I think all people tend to be products of their culture rather than of the assignment they've been handed down.'

'Do you know where they are?'

'Not yet.'

'Staying here in Nigeria wouldn't be a good idea.'

Lourds nodded. 'I agree. We're flying to London.'

Natashya frowned and shook her head. 'She'll have all the power there.'

Lourds knew there was no question who Natashya referred to. 'It'll be safer there. For all of us. Leslie's been able to arrange a temporary visa for Adebayo through the British Consulate.'

Natashya looked at him. 'She's been on the phone?'

'Yes. She also arranged flights for us that will –' Lourds discovered he was talking to Natashya's back.

Natashya bent down and hefted the jerry can without a word. Then she walked over to the edge of the forest where Leslie stood with her sat-phone pressed to her ear.

Lourds hurried to catch up. The situation suddenly didn't look good.

'Give me the phone,' Natashya demanded.

Leslie glared at her, then looked at Lourds for help. When it wasn't forthcoming – and Lourds knew for sure he didn't want to step into the buzz saw that existed between the two women – Leslie glared at Natashya again.

Behind Leslie, Gary, Diop and Adebayo all stepped back out of harm's way as if of a single mind.

'The phone,' Natashya demanded again.

'Excuse me,' Leslie said, 'but I happen to be on the phone this moment trying to negotiate –'

Natashya reached for the phone. Leslie blocked the attempt only because the Russian woman reached with her wounded arm and was slower than normal.

'You cheeky cow!' Leslie exploded. 'How dare you try something like that!'

Lourds inserted himself between the two women, and immediately decided it was one of the more foolish gestures he'd ever made in his life. Before he could do anything, Natashya chopped him in the throat with the edge of her hand and kicked his feet out from under him. He fell gracelessly and landed on his back hard enough to knock the wind out of his lungs.

Natashya drew her pistol and pointed it between Leslie's eyes.

'The phone,' Natashya said. 'Now.'

Unbelievably, Leslie threw herself at Natashya. She swung the phone like a club toward Natashya's face. The Russian woman blocked the blow with her pistol and knocked the phone from Leslie's grip. Before it hit the ground, Natashya caught it easily.

Leslie came at her again but Natashya spun aside and tripped her. Leslie sprawled on the ground beside Lourds, who still hadn't regained his breath.

Natashya hunkered down and took Lourds' satphone, too. Then she demanded Gary's and Diop's. Both men, faces tense and astonished, handed their phones over.

'Gallardo and his people have been tracking us,' Natashya said as she threw the phones onto the ground. 'This is how they find us. They know where we are through the global positioning satellite signatures of these phones.' She scowled at Leslie. 'Most probably yours, with the way you've been on it all the time.'

Leslie said something totally unladylike and uncomplimentary.

Natashya ignored her and reached for the jerry can. 'Personally, I'd love another chance at Gallardo and his people. But I don't think you'd live through another assault.' She sloshed gasoline over the phones.

'What are you doing?' Leslie screeched in disbelief.

'Making sure they can't follow us anymore.'

Lourds took his first real breath since he'd been knocked over as Natashya knelt down and started the pyre with her lighter. The flame lapped at the gasoline quickly and blazed in the gathering darkness. In seconds the phones started to melt and caught fire.

'What if we need help?' Leslie demanded as she pushed herself to her feet. 'Did you happen to think of that?'

'If we need help,' Natashya said. 'We help ourselves.' She walked back towards the motorcycle. 'We're more likely to need it if Gallardo finds us again. Get back in the truck. We must put as much distance between us and this place as we can, as fast as we can.'

Gingerly, wondering if something had been broken, sprained or torn Lourds got up. He stood for a moment and felt the heat of the fire.

'You brought her along,' Leslie accused.

Lourds knew that wasn't exactly true, but he wasn't

going to argue the point. 'Maybe we should get moving.'

Natashya didn't give any signs of waiting for them. She got on the motorcycle and pushed the ignition switch to start the engine. The low rumble vibrated through the forest and chased away the night sounds. A moment later the headlight came on and burned through the darkness.

Lourds picked up his dusty hat, slipped it on and kicked enough dirt over the burning phones to put them out. He slid behind the old 4 x 4's steering wheel. Diop, Gary and Adebayo climbed into the back.

Leslie stood for a moment at the side of the truck with her arms crossed. She looked as stubborn as a child.

Natashya roared ahead.

'It's a long walk back, Leslie,' Lourds commented. 'Even from here. And you wouldn't like the neighbourhood.'

Cursing, she opened the door and swung herself inside. She sat in the seat with her arms crossed and glared at the disappearing motorcyclist.

'She's not my boss,' Leslie said petulantly.

Lourds didn't comment. He put the truck in gear and let out the clutch. They gained speed as they followed the motorcycle. He just hoped that Leslie would see that he wasn't interested in having this conversation. It wouldn't do any good to talk about it. No matter what they said, the phones had been burned and what had happened still would have happened. Natashya was the most trouble-ready among them. Not following her was stupid.

'Why didn't you do something back there?' Leslie demanded.

Despite his efforts to intercede, which had collected him a nice assortment of bruises, Lourds knew it wouldn't do any good to point out now that he'd tried.

'I can't believe you let her set my phone on fire.'

It's going to be a long trip back, Lourds realized.

Cave #42
Atlantis Burial Catacombs
Cadiz, Spain
8 September 2009

'Are you all right, Father?'

Father Sebastian looked at Dario Brancati. The construction foreman stood beside the priest and looked as worn and haggard as Sebastian felt.

'I'm fine, Mr Brancati,' Sebastian replied. 'I'm just tired, that's all. It's nothing that a few more hours' sleep won't cure. You look as though you could use some sleep yourself.'

'I'll sleep when we're finished with this,' Brancati said. 'I apologize for the early hour.'

According to Sebastian's watch, it was almost three in the morning. He'd barely had four hours' sleep even though he'd promised himself he would get to bed earlier.

'I would have waited,' Brancati said, 'but I thought perhaps you'd want to see this for yourself.'

'I do.'

Brancati handed him a fresh flashlight and a new hard hat.

'I've already got a hat,' Sebastian said. He held the old hat up.

'How fresh are the batteries in that?'

Sebastian hesitated, then shook his head. 'I don't know.'

'That's why you need a new hat.'

The two Swiss Guards accompanying Sebastian also got new hats. Sebastian struggled to remember their names – Peter was the one with the small scar over his eyebrow. He'd got it in a fight with his brother as a boy, some mix-up over a coveted toy. And the other, Martin, had a cleft chin. Good men, both. They'd insisted Sebastian wear a lifejacket with handgrips on it in case they had to get him out of the cavern in a hurry. Together, they followed Brancati and his team into Cave #42.

Nervous energy filled Sebastian as he carefully waded into the waist-deep water. The pumps growled incessantly as they removed the water from the cave. Most of it was gone, but the crews remained vigilant in case another leak sprung up. The ground radar had confirmed the presence of water on the other side of several walls. They walked through a rock bubble that hung 150 feet below the level of the Atlantic Ocean.

The floor was treacherous. Bodies and parts of

bodies were mostly submerged beneath the oil-black water. Once Sebastian felt something strike his leg and saw a skull float up for a moment before disappearing once more.

'We should have the rest of the water out of here in the next few days, Father,' Brancati announced. His voice carried in the cavern, but it was almost buried in the throb of the vacuum engines pulling water from the cave.

'That's good.' Sebastian followed the man through the burial crypts. Only a few of them had tenants at the moment.

'We didn't see it last time because we weren't in here long enough before the cave gave way,' Brancati said. 'Even when it was found this time' – he shook his head – 'nobody believed we'd found it.'

A few minutes later, Sebastian gazed up at Brancati's find.

The door was immense. It was at least fifteen feet across. The oval shape gleamed in the reflected light and had a metallic cast to it. Strange symbols covered the surface. As Sebastian watched, the symbols shimmered and wavered. In only seconds he could read what was there.

KNOW YOU OUR HONOURED DEAD.
THIS PLACE IS PROTECTED, KEPT SAFE BY
THE HAND OF GOD.
THESE PEOPLE ONCE LIVED ON GOD'S
HOLY GROUND.
LET THEM SLEEP WELL.

Sebastian read the inscription again. When he tried to concentrate, he didn't see the writing. He only saw the symbols. But he was certain what he'd read.

In the centre of the door, though, was depicted the same figure he'd seen hanging from the dead man's necklace. He stood tall and handsome, the book under one arm and the other offered to help whoever wanted it. Below him was a seal Sebastian recognized from the materials Pope Innocent XIV had given him. It showed a glowing hand on an open book with flames leaping from the pages.

He felt cold, shock rang through him until it nearly stopped his heart.

'It's some kind of metal alloy,' Brancati said. 'But we haven't determined what kind yet. The way it's built into the rock is way ahead of the time period we're talking about. We couldn't do it today. Not like that. I don't have an explanation for it.'

'It's just lost tech,' one of the construction workers said. 'Just like the way the Egyptians built the pyramids. We can guess how they did it, but we don't know for sure.'

'Oh my God,' Sebastian whispered hoarsely as he stumbled forward. He would have fallen if one of the Swiss Guards hadn't caught him. He reached out and touched the seal.

It was still well-defined and hard-edged, gleaming as though it had been struck yesterday.

It's true. All of it. Sebastian ran his trembling hand over the seal.

'Father,' the Guard who held him, young Peter, said softly.

'I'm all right.' Sebastian pulled at his arm. 'Please. Release me.'

With obvious reluctance, Peter did so, but he remained close at hand.

Cold fear twisted through Sebastian. It had nothing to do with the depths of water waiting outside the cave walls to drown them. The fear that flooded the priest now focused solely on the figure on the great door ahead. Sebastian dropped to his knees and felt the cold brine he'd waded through climb to his chest.

He put his hands in front of him and prayed for mercy and salvation, not just for himself, but for all the souls who had been lost when Atlantis had been gathered by the ocean.

God hadn't been merciful then. He wouldn't have been. God's loss of His Son and the effrontery shown by the priest-kings of Atlantis had been inexcusable.

That was why he had pulled the island continent beneath the sea.

But why is this here now? To test us again? Is that what you want, God? A test?

If it was a test, Sebastian feared that they would fail once more. He feared even he might be tempted by what lay beyond the strange metal door.

And if he was, the world might be doomed again.

Lourds referred to the notebook computer screens where the images of the bell, cymbal and drum were open, but he worked on the lined yellow legal pads he'd bought on the way to the hotel. Natashya hadn't been happy about the shopping, but he'd explained he'd needed the pads.

His brain was on fire as he compared the four languages represented on the three instruments. He worked feverishly, exchanging values and words, ideas and guesses that had come to him during the long drive back to Lagos.

Even fleeing for his life hadn't turned off that part of his mind that so loved puzzles of language and culture. This was where his passion lived.

Upon their arrival at the hotel, they'd checked in and gone to their rooms. Leslie had managed to get them all on the same floor. There hadn't been any sense of camaraderie, though. Each of them – except for Diop and Adebayo, who acted like long-lost friends – had elected to trudge off to their room separately.

Lourds hadn't wanted to deal with the women, and he still wasn't exactly sure where his loyalties lay in handling them. Leslie had managed to bring him this far, and there was the intimacy factor, but Lourds had never let sex get in the way of his job. He suspected

Leslie was very much the same in that respect. Sadly, both of them were also driven by the same desire to excel at their jobs. And that put them on different sides of the fence regarding the instruments.

Natashya had her own agenda – to avenge her sister's murder. Lourds suspected that need came not only from the personal aspect of Yuliya's murder, but also out of whatever motivation had prompted Natashya to become a police officer in Moscow to begin with.

The problem was, Lourds was near to bursting with ideas about what they were ultimately searching for. He needed a sounding board, someone he could talk to about everything that was buzzing through his head.

And it didn't seem fair not to share it with Leslie.

Except that he couldn't.

He looked at the notes he'd made and knew that he was going to drive himself crazy if he didn't talk through what he suspected to be true. It was decision time. Ultimately, it came down to needing the most dispassionate listener. He judged that Leslie wouldn't be. If he told her what he believed was true, she would feed off of it and push him into making even wilder leaps. He needed to be grounded to complete his work.

He left the notebook on the bed, went to the refrigerator and took out two beers. He was fresh from the shower and dressed in khaki shorts and an old soccer shirt. For a moment, he stood at the door and tried to debate whether he needed an audience, but he knew he did. Having to explain things, just focusing to put everything he was thinking into perspective and an oratory summary, allowed him to see and think more clearly. Perhaps that was caused by the nature of the teacher within him, but he also believed it was because speaking caused him to think more linearly.

He needed that now.

He glanced back at the legal pad lying on the bed. The name ATLANTIS was underlined, circled and starred. He really, really needed that now.

Feeling some apprehension, he left the room.

Lourds knocked on the door. He waited a moment outside in the hall, feeling ridiculous and vulnerable all at the same time because he knew she would be watching him through the peephole.

And probably putting the safety back on her pistol, he told himself.

He started to knock again, thinking maybe he'd caught her in bed. It was a few minutes after five a.m. locally.

Then she asked, in Russian, 'What do you want?'

'I come bearing gifts.' Lourds tried a smile and held up the two beers.

'I have my own refreshment bar. Go away.'

Some of Lourds' confidence waned. He dangled the beers at his side. 'I need to talk.'

'About what?'

'I've deciphered some of the inscriptions on the instruments.'

441

'Good. We can talk about it in the morning.'

'I want to talk about it now.'

'There's nothing we can do about it now. Get some sleep.'

Lourds hesitated, knowing he was sounding like a petulant child. 'I can't sleep.'

'Drink those beers. You'll sleep. You've had a big day.'

Lourds tried to think of another argument and couldn't. Frustration chafed at him. 'I need to know if I'm on the right track.'

'I'm not a linguist. I can't help you with that.'

Unable to argue that point, Lourds apologized for waking her and turned to go. He hadn't gone three steps before she opened the door and called his name. He stopped and turned.

Dressed in pyjamas, her hair free, Natashya looked beautiful. Of course, the pistol in her hand clashed with the demure appearance.

'Come in,' she sighed. 'But if you try to get fresh with me after the day I've had, I'll shoot you.'

Lourds paced as he talked. He couldn't help it. The more he talked, the more energized he felt. Every word he spoke seemed to feed the fire raging inside him.

Natashya sat on the bed with her knees up to her chin. Her pistol rested on the pillow beside her. She hadn't been sleeping either, Lourds had realized. She'd been sitting there in combat mode.

She sipped her beer as he talked, but his just grew flat and warm on the nearby table as the rising sun

442

started to warm the window on the other side of the drapes.

'The inscription talks about an island kingdom,' Lourds said. 'I think what it's actually referring to is Atlantis.'

'Atlantis,' Natashya repeated, and sounded as though she didn't believe it for a second.

'I think so. Though they don't call it by that name in the inscriptions.'

'What name do they give it?'

Lourds shook his head. 'I'd have to know more of the language to understand that. What I have to do is substitute words and ideas for the symbols on those inscriptions. I can use the name they refer to the island as Atlantis, and even call the people Atlantean, but that doesn't necessarily mean that they are.'

'Then why was the island called Atlantis?'

'That was the name Plato identified it by in his discourses. Subsequently, the ocean the island presumably sank in was called the Atlantic.' Lourds tried to frame everything in his mind. 'Allow me for the moment to simply call the place Atlantis.'

'You do realize that the Roman Catholic Church believes they've found Atlantis? It's been in all the news.'

'It doesn't matter if they did or didn't,' Lourds said. 'They're not going to find anything there worth having.'

Natashya smiled at him and shook her head. 'You sound awfully sure of yourself.'

443

'I am. It's been buried under the sea for nine or ten thousand years. That can be hard on artefacts – though in the right circumstances much can survive. Pottery, carved stone, gold. But I doubt they will differ much from other artefacts from the time. Do *you* think they're going to find anything?'

'I've found, Professor Lourds, that the world is made up of many strange occurrences. Take this situation. I have always known I could get killed in the line of duty. It's the nature of my work. But the thought that Yuliya might be killed because of some object she dug up never crossed my mind.' She paused for a moment, but Lourds didn't say anything. 'More than that, the world also has a number of things that have existed for thousands of years and continue to exist: the pyramids, the tombs of the pharaohs, ancient documents you've undoubtedly read.'

'Yes, but that site in Cadiz has been underwater for thousands of year till the tsunami lifted it from the sea bottom.' Lourds shook his head. 'They're not going to find anything new or different there.'

'Then why is Atlantis so important?'

'I don't know. But I know this – it just happens to be the place where everything on those inscriptions happened.'

'What did happen?'

'A cataclysm.'

'The island sank.'

'Yes. But from what I've translated, the authors of the inscription believed God sank the island.'

'You don't?'

Lourds sighed. 'I've not been a big believer in God involving himself in our lives. I'm sure he's got plenty of other things to do than answer prayers.'

'I don't think those people prayed to have their island sunk.'

'Probably not.' Lourds frowned.

'Did the inscription say why God sank the island?'

'He was angry with the people.'

'In the Old Testament, he seemed to be angry a lot.'

'Not exactly a new story, is it?'

'Why are you excited about it?'

'Because it fits in with what Adebayo told me about the Drowned Land. His name for the world that was sunk.'

'I didn't hear what he had to say.'

Realizing there hadn't been time to tell Natashya the story during the trip back to Lagos, Lourds did so. 'The thing that interests me is that Adebayo said all the people spoke the same language in those days. No one knew another language.'

'Isn't there a biblical story about that?' Natashya asked.

'A famous one. The Tower of Babel.'

'I remember. Men decided to build a tower to ascend into Heaven and join God. Seeing this, God destroyed the uniformity of man and caused them to split off from each other, each speaking a different language.'

'Exactly. The Tower of Babel was believed to have

been built in Babylon,' Lourds said. 'That's supposedly part of the reason Babylon is named that. The name comes from the Akkadian language and roughly translates into "Gate of the God".'

'Why are you discussing the Tower of Babel? I thought this was about Atlantis.'

Lourds sighed. His mind was working overtime these days. Instead of slowing down, it seemed to be speeding up. 'Because if you have one place where one language reigned supreme among all its people, it stands to reason that it would be on an island.'

'What about the Fertile Crescent area? Mankind was supposed to have come from there.'

'The archaeology to date seems pretty clear, so I'm not going to dispute that. What I'm going to propose is that a group of those people set sail and found a wondrous island out in the Atlantic Ocean and set about creating a society like none that had been seen before.'

'Why?'

'Because Plato said that's what the nation he called Atlantis was like.'

'Some people also say that Atlantis is pure imagination.'

'Maybe it was,' Lourds responded. 'But this island, the one that generated these artefacts, according to the inscriptions I've translated, was real. If anyone was going to do any ambitious building back in such ancient times, the kind of building that would raise up a tower so high that it threatened God, why not Atlantis?'

'What are you saying?'

'I'm proposing that an advanced civilization on the island that produced these instruments might also have built the Tower of Babel there.'

'The dig site doesn't seem to have any skyscrapers hidden in the rubble. Nothing like that has come up in the news stories,' Natashya said.

'From what I've seen, they haven't found much in the way of a city on top of that area,' Lourds pointed out. 'When the island sank, it could have lost everything on the surface. And they haven't found much in the caves either.'

'They found a door,' Natashya said.

Lourds looked at her. 'What door?' He hadn't turned on the television in his room.

Natashya reached for the remote control and switched the set on. CNN came to life, and the topic of discussion was the discovery of the strange metallic door down in the caves.

As Lourds watched, his incredulity grew. The camera locked on the door. He gasped, unable to believe his eyes.

'The door is clearly shown here in the footage we've received from Father Sebastian's public information team,' the news reporter was saying. 'As yet, the excavation team hasn't been able to progress beyond the door. My sources tell me that the archaeologists fear the possibility of potential collapse as the excavation crews continue their work. For now, they are proceeding cautiously, if at all.'

Lourds grabbed a pen and paper from the nearby

desk. Standing in front of the television, he started writing furiously.

'What is it?' Natashya asked.

'That writing on the door,' Lourds said hoarsely, 'is in the same language and character set that I'm deciphering on those instruments.'

You really shouldn't be doing this, Leslie Crane admitted to herself as she swiped the key card through Lourds' door lock. But she'd known she was probably going to do it the minute she'd kept the extra key card for Lourds' room.

She'd tried staying mad at him for not stopping Natashya from burning her phone, but that hadn't worked. In the end, Lourds was the story she'd sold to the production studio, and she had to have the story. Lourds was going to hand her a professional triumph. More than that, she wanted the man himself for personal reasons. She'd slept just enough on the journey back so that she hadn't been able to drift off to sleep. There was nothing like sex to take the edge off her emotions when she was feeling the way she was.

She stepped into the room and found all the lights on. She'd expected the professor to be at the desk or in bed. She'd thought that he would spot her the minute she came through the door. They were all a little jumpy after their adventures the past few days. Having him see her walk in would have taken some of the surprise out of the equation of a meeting, but she didn't think it would lessen any of the desire they felt for each other. She and Lourds were good in bed together. She was confident that he felt the same way.

Only he wasn't there.

Irritation filled Leslie when she thought he might be prowling around the hotel after Natashya had given them all such stern warnings about keeping a low profile. Was the man out risking his neck and her story?

She started clearing off the bed. When he got back from wherever it was he'd gone, he could find her there and they could have make-up sex. It was nearly always the best kind. She didn't think he had been overly distraught about the rancorous feelings she'd harboured toward him just lately, but that didn't dampen her enthusiasm.

Then she spotted the yellow legal pad covered with Lourds' neat handwriting on the desk. One word jumped out at her:

ATLANTIS

Mesmerized, she picked up the pad and flipped through the pages. Atlantis was mentioned several times, as if Lourds kept coming back again and again to the same answer.

Island kingdom. Drowned Land. Defiance of God.
One language.
Atlantis.

Her sexual cravings forgotten, Leslie grabbed the pad, took it to her room, and shot pictures of the pages with her digital camera. Her heart thudded frantically in her chest as she worked. She expected Lourds to return to his room at any instant.

When she finished, she took the pages back to his room. Her thoughts raced in circles within her mind. This was even bigger than she'd imagined. What she had was pure gold. If she could link Lourds' name to the Atlantis dig site, somehow tie the bell they'd found on her show to it, the ratings for the programme would go through the roof. Not only that, but she might be able to sell another series. Maybe even for BIG bucks. If the Atlantis dig in Spain turned out to be anything important, and it was getting more interesting with the discovery of the mysterious door, she could own a piece of that with the artefacts they were tracking.

Her excitement grew. So did her desire for sex. She settled onto the bed and waited. Impatiently.

After another hour, Lourds had finally talked himself dry. The excitement still bubbled within him, though, and the idea of the massive door Father Sebastian had discovered wouldn't let him go.

He couldn't believe Natashya was still awake.

'So what are we to do?' she asked.

'Diop and Adebayo have called the other Keepers,' Lourds said as he sat on the edge of the desk across the room. 'We're going to meet them in London.'

'They're bringing the instruments?'

'Yes.'

'They're showing a lot of trust in us.'

'No.' Lourds shook his head. 'Wrong dynamic. They're showing a lot of desperation. Gallardo and his employer have two of the instruments. If he's able to decipher them, and there's no reason that he won't be able to –'

Natashya flashed him a teasing smile. 'You're admitting that someone else might be as linguistically gifted as you are?'

'Whoever it is,' Lourds pointed out, 'has known more about what we're chasing than we have.'

'Do you think he knows about Atlantis?'

Lourds didn't hesitate. Now that she'd asked the question, everything seemed clear to him. 'Probably.'

Natashya's brows furrowed. 'Have you given any thought to the Church's position in this?'

'The Church? The Catholic Church?' Lourds shook his head. 'Why would they –'

'Be funding and directing a dig site at a place that might be Atlantis?' Natashya interrupted. 'I asked myself the same question. What possible interest could the Roman Catholic Church have there?'

Lourds considered what was because connecting the two events – Atlantis and the Church excavation with the instruments – had truly never occurred to him. However, in light of the potential links to Atlantis – and knowing that the Church had a wealth of documentation at their beck and call – how could the Church not know?

Uneasiness filtered through him when he considered the ramifications. The Church had a network that spanned the world. If anyone could search for something for hundreds of years, the Roman Catholic Church could do that.

'I think we're getting ahead of ourselves,' he said.

'Do you?' Natashya arched a brow.

'You're talking about a conspiracy.'

'I see conspiracies all the time in my job. Conspiracy to commit murder. Conspiracy to commit robbery. Conspiracy to commit fraud. Something's being hidden here, and it's been hidden for possibly thousands of years. Now that it's starting to come out, don't you think someone would want to control it?'

What she said made perfect sense – from the logistics of knowing about the research involved – and it rocked Lourds back on his heels.

'No one could have counted on the tsunami pushing that piece of land back to the surface in Spain,' Lourds said.

'Maybe someone was counting on it never coming back up,' Natashya said. 'When someone puts a body into the Moskva River, they don't expect that body to show up again. But sometimes they do.'

'You're talking about a murder,' Lourds said. 'After a century or so, everyone concerned with it will be dead.'

'I'm talking about an event. You mentioned the sinking of Atlantis. The destruction of the Tower of Babel. Those are some pretty far-reaching events. And those are only the ones you know about right now. What if there's more?'

Lourds thought about it. There was more. There

had to be more. If the instruments didn't matter to *someone*, then why had Yuliya been killed?

'We'll keep looking,' he said.

'Expect more resistance,' Natashya replied. 'I'm sure that whoever is behind Gallardo didn't intend for you to find out this much.'

Lourds nodded, then pushed himself up. 'You're probably right.'

'I'm certain I am. That's why Gallardo and his men have been trying to kill us.' Natashya wrapped her arms around her knees.

'I'd best be going.' Lourds started for the door. 'Perhaps you can get a few hours' sleep before we catch the flight this afternoon.' He had his hand on the door when she called him back.

'I'm not sleepy,' she said.

Lourds looked at her for a moment as he wondered about the implication in her words.

'Unless you'll feel you're being disloyal,' Natashya said.

'No,' Lourds said as he stepped toward the bed. Since Leslie hadn't come to bed with him since they were in Nigeria. And she wasn't any too happy with him lately. He figured that was pretty much that.

Natashya met him with open arms.

Harsh knocking woke Lourds. He was still groggy as Natashya disengaged herself from him and came up with her pistol over him. The sheet slid off her and revealed her naked body.

Then the door opened and Leslie barged through.

'It's after eleven,' she snapped. 'If you don't get up, you're going to miss the flight.' She glared at Lourds. 'You are a proper bastard, aren't you?'

Lourds didn't know what to say, so he said nothing.

'I could shoot her,' Natashya said in Russian. She made no move to cover herself.

'No,' Lourds croaked as his mind span freely and he tried to find some purchase on his thoughts.

Without another word, Leslie strode from the room and barrelled through Gary, Diop and Adebayo. The two older men tried to hide their amusement.

'Man,' Gary said, 'that's bloody harsh. I tried to get her not to use that extra key card. She just wouldn't listen after she worked out where you were.'

'Could you close the door?' Lourds asked.

Gary gave him a brief salute and did just that.

Natashya heaved herself out of bed and started towards the shower.

Lourds lay there feeling like the unwanted prize in a fierce competition. If it hadn't been for the fact that he'd enjoyed himself, he might have felt badly about it. But he watched the suggestive roll of Natashya's bare flanks till she caught him staring.

She grabbed his shirt from the desk and threw it at him. 'Get dressed.'

'We could shower together,' Lourds suggested. 'It would save time.'

Natashya looked back at him and grinned. 'If last night was any indication, we'd be even later.' She closed the bathroom door.

Lourds groaned and forced himself from bed. It promised to be a long flight back to London given the circumstances. Thankfully he had a toehold on translating the inscriptions. If everything went right and his present luck didn't hold, he might have it translated by the time they landed.

2 1

Murtala Mohammed International Airport
Lagos, Nigeria
9 September 2009

'Hey.'

Alerted by Gary's voice, Leslie flicked her eyes up to his reflection in the glass. She'd been looking out at the planes on the runways. Her father's business had often taken him out of the country. She and her mother had always driven him to Heathrow to see him off. Planes held a fascination for her. People were always coming and going.

'What?' Leslie asked.

Gary shrugged self-consciously. He looked like a dork standing there. iPod earbuds hung around his neck. Then she realized how unkind she was being to him. Unfortunately, at the moment, she didn't care. But she knew she would later, so she curbed biting observations that immediately came to mind.

'Just wanted to make sure you were all right,' Gary said.

'I'm fine.'

Gary nodded. 'I figured you would be.'

'I'm a big girl,' Leslie said and tried to keep the

bitterness out of her voice. 'It's not like he broke my heart. We were just having sex.'

'Yeah. I know. I've been there a few times myself.' Gary showed her a lopsided grin. 'Funny how you start off telling yourself that it's just a physical thing and you don't care.'

'I *don't* care.'

'But you get in a twist anyway when it ends.' Gary looked more uncomfortable. 'I just wanted you to know you're not alone.'

'Are you feeling particularly big brotherly today?'

'Maybe a little.'

Leslie glared at the reflection of Lourds and Natashya in the seats by their departure gate. The professor worked on the legal pads. The Russian cow sat reading a magazine and sipping water. None of them were talking to each other.

'Then, as my big brother, shouldn't you go and beat Lourds up for me?' Leslie asked.

Gary frowned. 'I don't think that would be a good idea.'

'Why not? Surely you're not afraid of him. He's just a university professor. A rough and tumble lad like yourself shouldn't have any trouble with the likes of him.'

'Lourds doesn't worry me. I'm more afraid of his new girlfriend. She could kick my arse without blinking. And that's if she didn't kill me first.'

'Some big brother,' Leslie muttered.

A pained expression twisted Gary's features. 'I just

wanted to let you know I was here if you needed anything.' He turned and walked away.

Leslie sighed. *You needn't have been so harsh with him. This isn't any of his fault.* She sipped her sports drink and resumed watching planes. Later she'd apologize to Gary for being bitchy. But for the moment she needed to stay angry.

Being angry was the only way she was going to stay selfish enough to betray Lourds' confidence and look after her own career. She knew that was what she had to do. Besides, after finding him in Natashya's bed this morning, it was what he deserved.

A few minutes later, the flight began boarding. Leslie watched Natashya and Lourds gather their things. Diop and Adebayo continued talking about whatever they'd been discussing all morning as they shuffled along. Gary had found a pretty young woman to chat up.

Steeling herself, Leslie turned and dropped the empty drink container into a waste receptacle. She headed for the phones over by the toilets.

After she swiped the company credit card she carried, she punched in her supervisor's phone number.

'Wynn-Jones.'

'Philip, it's Leslie.'

Wynn-Jones's voice immediately took on a note of severe irritation. 'Where the bloody hell are you?'

Any other time, Leslie might have been in fear for her job. But not today. The story she had to tell was simply too big.

'In Nigeria,' she answered.

Wynn-Jones cursed spectacularly. 'Do you know how much this little foray is costing us?'

'Haven't a clue,' Leslie replied honestly. She'd given up keeping track after she'd seen bills for the first few thousand pounds they'd spent.

'You've gone far beyond anything I can cover. When you get back here, you might as well start writing your CV. And you're bloody lucky we're going to fly you back home.'

'You'll be lucky if I don't demand a pay raise.'

That set off another round of curses.

'Philip,' Leslie said as the final boarding call pealed through the public address system, 'I can give you Atlantis.'

The curses stopped.

'Did you hear me?' she asked.

'Yes.' Wynn-Jones sounded cautious.

'What we've been following up – the bell in Alexandria, the cymbal that was found in Russia and a drum here in Nigeria that I've not had time to tell you about yet – it's all connected to Atlantis. Lourds came through. I can prove it.'

Wynn-Jones sat silently at the other end of the connection for a time. 'You're not just desperate, are you? Or mad with some disease from over there?'

'No.'

'Or pissed in some bar?'

'No. I'm in an airport. We're heading to London.'

'Tell me about Atlantis,' Wynn-Jones said cautiously.

'Lourds has translated the inscriptions on the bell, cymbal and drum,' Leslie said. She felt excited and depressed at the same time. She didn't like betraying confidences, but this was all about self-preservation. She loved her job. She didn't love Lourds. Not at all. Not ever. She could hear the bitterness echoing in her head. She turned her attention to what she wanted to say.

'I've got the story of a lifetime here,' she said.

'I didn't mean that business about the CV,' Wynn-Jones backtracked, almost whining in his desire to regain her confidence. 'We'll have to weather some heat, but I'm certain I can keep your job for you. The BBC likes your work.'

Leslie smiled at that. 'Good. Then you won't mind telling them that I want a piece of this one.'

'What?'

'You heard me. I want a percentage of the final product. The television rights. The book rights. The DVD sales.'

'That's impossible.'

'So was proving Atlantis.' Leslie smiled now and some of the sting at finding Lourds in bed with Natashya went away. She was about to relaunch her career in a big way. 'Make it happen, Philip. I've got to run.'

She hung up the phone and shouldered her carry-on as she strode toward the entry gate. She was being a real bitch and she knew it. But she excused herself. Not just for her career and personal advancement, but because being a bitch was the only way to make

Lourds remember her. Men always remembered women who struck back.

She was selfish enough to want him to remember her too.

The Hempel
West London, England
11 September 2009

The last of the Keepers arrived in the late evening. Lourds had offered to pick him up at the airport, but the man had declined.

When Lourds opened the door to the private suite at the Hempel Hotel Leslie had surprisingly arranged for them, he was taken off-guard for a moment by the man's appearance. He was of medium height and athletic build. His skin was dark but his eyes were hazel. A silver headband held his long black hair from his face. He wore stonewashed jeans and a chambray work shirt under a fringed leather jacket. He might have been all of twenty-five years old.

'Professor Lourds?' the young man inquired in a polite voice.

'I am,' Lourds acknowledged.

'I'm Tooantuh Blackfox. Call me Jesse.'

Lourds shook the proffered hand. 'It's a pleasure to meet you, Jesse. Come in.'

Blackfox stepped easily into the room. His eyes, though, roved the suite instantly and took in everything.

'Have a seat.' Lourds gestured to the long conference table he'd had brought up to the room. Diop, Adebayo and Vang Kao Sunglue, the other Keeper, sat at the table.

Natashya stood near the windows. Lourds didn't doubt that she'd already gone 'shopping' for weapons to replace those she'd had to give up in Nigeria. A long jacket reached to her thighs.

Gary and Leslie sat to one side. Lourds had forbidden any filming, but he hadn't had the heart to ban them from the meeting. They'd come a long way together. Leslie had also provided a touch-pad projection computer set-up that Lourds was currently using. He was familiar with the system from university.

Brief introductions were made. Thankfully they already shared a common language and some history through their exchanged letters.

Vang was an old man, more withered and ancient than Adebayo. He wore black slacks and a white shirt with a black tie. He was of Hmong descent, one of the tribal people in Vietnam the United States had recruited to fight their war against communist North Vietnam. He'd carefully slicked back his wisps of grey hair.

According to what he'd told Lourds, he'd been a lawyer in Saigon. But that was before it had fallen and been renamed Ho Chi Minh City. Now he lived once more out in the mountains as his people had always done. There he was a shaman. As a Keeper, he cared for the clay flute that had been handed down for thousands of years through his family. He had been loath to leave Vietnam with the instrument. The flute had never been risked before.

But they were all, Lourds knew, curious about the heirlooms they'd been guarding all those years.

'Ladies and gentlemen,' Lourds said as he stood at the front of the conference table, 'we've all taken part in a remarkable journey during the last month.' He looked at Adebayo, Blackfox and Vang. 'Some of you have been on this journey for much, much longer. Let's see if we can bring it to a close. Or at least head in that direction.'

Lourds tapped the keyboard in front of him. Images of the inscriptions on the instruments appeared on the large screen behind him.

'Those instruments each come with two inscriptions,' Lourds said. 'You've told me that you can't read either one of them. As you know from your conversations with each other, all of you have been told the story of an island kingdom where many wondrous things were. That, according to the tale, is where the five instruments come from.'

All eyes focused steadily on him. The room was entirely quiet.

'According to the stories you were told, God chose to strike down the island in His holy wrath,' Lourds went on. 'I'm here to tell you that one of the inscriptions on each of the instruments confirms that story.'

'You translated the inscriptions?' Blackfox asked.

'Yes.'

'You've seen the other two instruments?' Blackfox hadn't been there for the briefing Adebayo and Vang had received.

'Yes, and I suspect that the inscription on the pipe you're in charge of will have the same inscription.'

'It does.'

Lourds looked at the young man. 'How do you know that?'

'Because I translated it.'

Leslie saw the surprised look on Lourds' face and smiled a little. *You're not the only brainiac in the group, are you, Professor?*

Then she caught Natashya looking reproachfully at her and dropped the smile.

'How did you translate the inscription?' Lourds asked.

Blackfox shrugged. 'What do you know about the language of my people?'

'The Cherokee were an advanced society,' Lourds replied. 'The popular misconception is that Sequoyah invented the Cherokee syllabary.'

Blackfox smiled. 'Most people refer to it as the Cherokee alphabet.'

'Most people,' Lourds replied, 'are not linguistics professors.'

Gary held his hand up just like he was in class. Leslie snorted quietly.

'Yes, Gary?' Lourds said.

'I don't know what a syllabary is, mate.'

Lourds leaned a hip against the conference table and folded his arms across his chest. Looking at him,

Leslie felt again why she'd been attracted to him. He was smart and handsome, and his passion for his work and teaching was obvious. Stealing him away from that work was almost like cheating his mistress.

Watching him work was a total turn-on. Except that she knew now he was a hound dog. Still, she'd been warned, and the whole physical relationship between them had been due to her manipulations, not his. It almost made her feel sorry for him when she thought about what she was going to do.

'A syllabary is a system of symbols that denote actual spoken syllables,' Lourds said. 'Instead of letters, symbols are grouped together. It's pure phonics-driven and many words are differentiated by tone. The written syllabary doesn't reflect the tone, but readers know what it is from the context in which it's presented. Clear?'

'Sure.' Gary nodded.

'There are eighty-five symbols in the Cherokee language,' Lourds said.

'Do you speak the language?' Blackfox asked.

'I can when pressed to do so. Reading it is harder.'

'They got it wrong when they thought Sequoyah invented the syllabary.'

'I know,' Lourds agreed. 'The Cherokees had a priesthood called the Ah-ni-ku-ta-ni that invented writing and guarded the knowledge of it zealously. From what I've read recently, the Cherokee priests oppressed their people and were finally killed in an uprising.'

'Most of them were killed,' Blackfox agreed.

'Several of their descendants, young men who still knew the language of the priests, hid among the people. They kept their society secret and intact. Sequoyah was one of them. The outrage against the priests was so strong that a written language wasn't allowed for hundreds of years.'

'How does the inscription on the pipe you've been protecting compare to the Cherokee language?'

'It's very similar.'

'May I see it?'

The pipe was a straight barrel of fired blue-grey clay with six holes. It was little over a foot in length. The inscriptions were there as well but it would take a magnifying glass to make them visible.

Lourds ran his fingers over the instrument's semi-rough surface. 'You've read the inscription?'

Blackfox nodded. 'It tells the same story that you're telling. There was an island kingdom, a place where our people came from, that was destroyed by the Great Spirit.'

'But you haven't been able to translate the other inscription?'

'No.'

Lourds took a quick breath and refused to be disappointed. The other language would fall prey to his skills soon. He was confident of that, but impatient.

'Did Sequoyah know about the pipe?' Lourds asked.

Blackfox hesitated. 'He'd never seen it. That wasn't permitted.'

'But he'd known it existed.'

'Possibly.'

Lourds stood and paced. 'I think someone did, and I think that someone was looking for the instruments in the 1820s or 1830s.'

'Why do you think this?' Vang asked. He had been very quiet and conservative in his speech since his arrival yesterday.

'Have you ever heard of the Vai people?' Lourds asked.

Vang shook his wizened head.

'They are people who live in Liberia,' Adebayo said.

'Exactly,' Lourds said, smiling. 'They didn't have a written language. But in 1832 a man named Austin Curtis moved to Liberia and married into a Vai tribe. As it turns out, Curtis was just part of a group of Cherokee immigrants who moved into the area.'

'You think they were looking for the pipe?' Diop asked.

'Possibly.'

Diop shook his head. 'That may not be so. In 1816, Reverend Robert Finley proposed the American Colonization Society and James Monroe, who had already been elected President of the United States, helped found it. Under this society, freed slaves were returned to West Africa. This man Curtis may have simply been involved with that.'

'Whatever the case,' Lourds said, 'we know that Austin inspired the Vai people to adopt their own written language. Which they did. It's very similar to the Cherokee written language. The actual Vai syllabary is attributed to Momolu Duala Bukare.'

Lourds handed the pipe back to Blackfox. The young man put it back in its protective case.

'I believe people have been searching for these instruments since they were first made,' Lourds said. 'Many thousands of years ago.'

'Who?' Blackfox asked.

'I don't know. We've been discussing it for days now.' Lourds felt fatigue hovering over him. Only his self-discipline, excitement, and the certainty that he was about to crack the final language kept him going.

'The inscription also says that the instruments are the keys to the Drowned Land,' Blackfox said.

'When I first translated that,' Lourds admitted, 'I didn't believe it. I thought perhaps there might have been a way once, but not when an island has been underwater for thousands of years. Salt water even leeches away silver over time. Turns it into an unrecognizable lump of oxidized metal. I couldn't imagine doors made of gold. Much less this.'

He turned to the display and tapped the keyboard. Immediately the image of the massive door down in Father Sebastian's dig in Cadiz filled the screen.

'I don't know what this door's made of,' Lourds commented, 'but it doesn't look like gold. However, after being on the sea bottom – or near to it – that door appears to be unblemished.'

'That's Cadiz,' Blackfox said. 'I've been watching this story.'

Lourds nodded. 'It is.'

'Do you think that was the Drowned Land?'

Tracing the inscriptions across the vault door, Lourds said, 'This is the same writing as the transcription I haven't – yet – been able to translate. I'd say it's a safe bet.'

'Do you think we need to go there?'

'No,' Adebayo said. 'Our stories tell us that the seeds of man's final and eternal doom lie in that place. God must have his vengeance and we must not seek out his wrath again.'

'It's possible that we need to destroy the instruments,' Vang said.

The idea of that – which had most emphatically *not* been discussed before – horrified Lourds.

'No,' Adebayo said. 'We were given these instruments by our ancestors. We were told to protect them, as they were told by their ancestors before them, and I believe we should do that or anger God again.'

'But,' Blackfox said quietly, 'if the inscription is correct, if the Drowned Land – or Atlantis or whatever you want to call it – does hold a temptation that could destroy the world again, shouldn't we remove that temptation?'

'I think so,' Vang said.

'And what if we incur God's wrath by destroying those instruments?' Adebayo asked.

Neither Blackfox nor Vang replied.

'Man is shaped by his belief and his resistance to temptation,' Adebayo said. 'That is why God has provided the mountains to make our way hard, and the oceans to make it look like some journeys are impossible.'

'We could save the world by destroying those instruments,' Vang said. 'Even one of them. The ancestors say all five must be used.'

'I don't think destroying them would be so easy. The cymbal and the bell have been lost to us for thousands of years,' Adebayo said. 'How do you account for the fact that even under trying circumstances they still exist?'

No one answered.

'I propose to you,' Adebayo said, 'that you've already seen God's will in motion. He has preserved these instruments, and he has sent Professor Lourds to bring us together. For the first time, the Keepers are joined.'

Lourds didn't know how to feel about that. He'd never pictured himself as a divine instrument.

'There's something else to consider,' Natashya said.

The men looked at her.

'If you destroy the instruments, your enemies – whoever they are – win. You lose. You will have failed the task you had set before you.' Natashya paused. 'Not only that, but your chance to strike back against your enemies will be gone.'

Her words hung over the group.

'And one further thing,' Lourds said, not wanting the potential future of the world to hang on a chance at vengeance – which he didn't personally see as a positive thing. 'It's possible that the people looking for the instruments might know more about them than you do.'

'They have already proven themselves our enemies. They won't tell us anything.'

'If we get to negotiate with them at some point, we might learn something.'

'We won't give up the instruments,' Blackfox said quietly.

'No one's asking you to.' Lourds made his voice stronger. 'You won't have to do that.'

'You could go to Cadiz,' Leslie said.

'No,' Lourds said immediately. Going to Cadiz meant losing the instruments. His chance to translate the language would be stripped from him. He wasn't afraid of losing the fame – he didn't believe in that anyway – but challenge was everything. Besides, the bit about the end of the world worried him, even though he hated to think he was driven by superstition. 'That's a bad idea.'

Leslie frowned in displeasure. She obviously wasn't happy about that.

'Just give me a little more time,' Lourds said. 'I can crack the last inscriptions. I know it. Time. That's all I'm asking for.' He glanced at the men. 'Please.'

'Are you sure about this?' Gary asked.

Leslie almost cursed him out. She would have, too, if she could have been certain she could have found another cameraman in five minutes or less.

'Yes,' she snapped. 'I'm certain.' She smoothed

her blouse to make sure it was wrinkle-free. 'Let's do this. I want to get it to Wynn-Jones as soon as possible.'

She stood out in the street in front of the Hempel Hotel. Night had fallen and the West End was alive behind her.

Despite her angry words to Gary, she was hesitant about what she was doing. But she thought she was owed it. She'd put her job in jeopardy by believing in Lourds.

Gary stood in front of her with his camcorder over his arm.

'Okay,' Leslie said. She took a deep breath. 'Let's do it. On my mark. Three, two . . .'

Strident ringing dragged Lourds from sleep. He flailed for the room phone and finally dragged it to the side of his head. Whoever was speaking – angry and quick – sounded garbled. Then he realized he had the headset upside down. He reversed it.

'Hello,' Lourds said. He cracked an eye open to read the clock radio. It was 11.41 p.m. The voice on the other end of the phone was American. There was a five-hour time difference between England and the East Coast.

'Professor Lourds,' the crisp, perfectly enunciated voice spat, 'this is Dean Wither.'

'Hello, Richard. Good of you to call.'

'Well, maybe you won't think so in a minute.'

That brought Lourds up short. Dean Wither hadn't been cross with him for years.

'I thought you were in Alexandria filming a documentary for the BBC,' Wither said.

'I was,' Lourds replied. He swung himself around and sat on the edge of the bed. He was still fully dressed. When he'd got up from the computer an hour ago, he'd been going to lie down for just a moment to rest his eyes.

'Now you're in London?'

That woke Lourds entirely. He hadn't called anyone connected to the university and let them know where he was.

'How did you know that?' he asked.

'Because you're on CNN. Right now.'

'What?' Lourds scrambled for the remote control and switched the television on. He flipped through the channels till he reached CNN. He recognized his face staring out at him from the screen. Below him, a text line read: HARVARD LINGUISTICS PROFESSOR DISCOVERS ATLANTIS CODE.

'Did you?' Wither demanded.

'Did I what?' Lourds asked.

'Discover an Atlantis code?'

Lourds wasn't sure how he was going to answer that. He stared at the television and wondered how CNN could possibly have gotten the story.

'Something turned up in Alexandria,' Lourds said weakly. 'We've been following it.'

'We?'

'Miss Crane and I. And some others.' Lourds didn't know how he was going to explain everything he needed to explain in such a short time. 'We found an artefact with a language on it I couldn't read.'

'You?'

'Yeah. Precisely,' Lourds said.

'Many of you may recognize Professor Lourds' name,' the young male anchor said. 'A short time ago he translated a manuscript that has become known as *Bedroom Pursuits*.'

The particularly lurid cover that graced – and wasn't that a poor choice of words? – the trade paperback edition showed on the screen. The pose was straight out of the *Kama Sutra*.

'Oh, God, not again,' Wither said.

Lourds winced. When he'd done the reading at the dean's house, it had been something of a sensation. However, once the translation got out into the publishing world – and hit the *New York Times* extended bestseller list – Dean Wither hadn't been happy. He'd often said . . .

'If I was going to have this university remembered for anything,' Wither said, 'it wouldn't be for pornography. How many times have I told you that?'

'I honestly can't remember,' Lourds responded.

'Now it appears that Professor Lourds has channelled his incredible mind into a new pursuit,' the CNN anchor said. 'Here to tell us about the Atlantis Code is Leslie Crane, hostess of *Ancient Worlds, Ancient People*.'

'So you're in on this together?' Wither accused. 'The BBC may find humour in this, but I assure you that I don't.'

'I didn't know about this,' Lourds objected.

The video showed a street corner in front of the Hempel Hotel. Leslie stood looking radiant with a microphone in her hand.

'I'm Leslie Crane, hostess of *Ancient Worlds, Ancient People*,' Leslie said. 'Many of you have heard of Professor Thomas Lourds. His bestselling translation of *Bedroom Pursuits* remains a favourite in bookshops. While we were filming a segment for my show, *Ancient Worlds, Ancient People*, Professor Lourds discovered an ancient bell that has led us around the world. But it was here, in London, that Professor Lourds finally cracked the code that has hidden the last secrets of Atlantis.'

The television cut back to the anchor. 'Miss Crane has promised us further information as it becomes available. But until then it remains to be seen if Father Sebastian and his team will manage to open the mysterious door to the caverns they claim are linked to Atlantis, or if Professor Lourds' research will put an entirely new spin on the efforts there.'

Lourds switched the television off. He didn't need to see any more. His very soul ached.

'You didn't know about this?' Wither asked.

'No,' Lourds replied. 'I didn't.'

'Did you find an Atlantis code?'

'I believe so.'

'So the story is true?'

'As far as I know, yes.'

'But you didn't know she was going to talk to CNN.'

'No. If she'd said, I would have asked her not to. I think she knew that, though.'

'Then why did she do it?'

'To get back at me.'

'Why would she –' Wither stopped.

Lourds knew he'd said too much.

'Oh, Thomas,' Wither groaned. 'Tell me that you didn't sleep with her.'

Lourds didn't say anything.

'My God, man, she looks young enough to be your daughter.'

'Only if I'd started having children really early,' Lourds pointed out in his defence.

'So I've got that scandal to look forward to as well?'

'It won't be a scandal.'

'Of course it will be. How could it not be? You're the only professor I've got who is personable enough to be on *Good Morning, America*, quick enough to swap barbs with Jon Stewart on *The Daily Show*, and still manage to plummet to the pits of puerile interests and juvenile shenanigans on *The Jerry Springer Show* with your sexual indiscretions.'

Personally, Lourds didn't feel sex had to be discreet. And he believed he'd always been accountable for his part in his dalliances. But the dean's admonition truly surprised him.

'I wasn't aware that you watched *The Jerry Springer Show*,' Lourds said.

Wither took a deep breath and audibly counted to ten. 'You need to be very glad you have tenure here, Professor Lourds.'

'I am. And some days I'm amazed.'

'You do realize that this is going to look like you're trying to horn in on all the media attention the dig site is promoting, don't you?'

'I do.'

'Well?'

'Well what?'

'Is this connected to Atlantis?'

'I believe so.'

'Much as I hate to say this, then get out there and prove it. You can't back off this horse in mid-stream.'

Lourds was pretty certain Wither had mixed his metaphors in there somewhere, but he was too tired to sort it all out. 'All right.'

'Make sure you do this properly,' Wither cautioned. 'We could swing a lot of enrolments from this, and additional funding.'

Lourds shook his head. That was what most things came down to for the dean. He said goodbye and started looking for his shoes. He had to find Leslie, and then he was going to –

He stopped there because he honestly didn't know what he was going to do.

Lourds met Natashya in the hall. The Russian woman looked angry enough to kill someone. Lourds had a sinking suspicion he knew who that was.

'You have seen the news, yes?' Natashya demanded in Russian. She strode down the hallway toward Leslie's door.

'Yes,' Lourds replied. 'Maybe I should talk to her.'

'We will *both* talk to her,' Natashya declared. 'By revealing this story now, she could have scared off the people who are responsible for Yuliya's death.'

Lourds really didn't think that would be the case. Gallardo and his cronies had proven willing to kill over and over again. He didn't think a little thing like CNN would worry them at all.

'Those men won't run from a fight,' Lourds said.

'No, but they will scatter in all directions like cockroaches in the light. They will be harder to find.' Natashya stopped in front of Leslie's door. She rapped her knuckles hard against the door. 'We should have left her in Africa.'

Lourds stood beside her and waited. The whole thing was getting entirely out of hand. He could almost *feel* his opportunity to translate the inscriptions sliding away from him.

'Or Odessa,' Natashya said. 'We could have left her in Odessa.' She rapped again, louder than before. She glared at Lourds. 'What could you have ever seen in her?'

That question took Lourds aback. He was certain that no matter how he answered it would blow up in his face. He tried to stand there and look wise and experienced.

Natashya snorted at him angrily. 'Men.' She said it like a curse word. Or maybe like it was a take-away container that had been left in the refrigerator for months, rotting and stinking up the space. She rapped again.

Heads popped out of the next room and two on the opposite side of the hallway.

'Maybe you could keep it down out here,' a balding man suggested.

'Police matter, sir,' Natashya spoke in English. Her voice carried that officious police tone effortlessly. 'Please go back inside.'

The people grudgingly disappeared back into their rooms.

Natashya hit the door again and Lourds would have sworn it jumped on the hinges after each impact.

Just then Gary poked his head out of his room. 'Hey.'

'Hey,' Lourds said.

'What's going on?' Gary asked.

'Where's the harpy?' Natashya asked.

Gary blinked. 'Uh, she's not here. She went home.'

'When?'

'After we shot the trailer for the new series she's suggesting to her director.'

'It was just on CNN,' Lourds said.

'No way,' Gary said.

'Way,' Lourds said.

'It wasn't supposed to be on television. Leslie's gonna have a cow.'

'At least she'll breed true,' Natashya said, 'and it'll probably have a doctorate from Harvard.'

Ouch, Lourds thought.

'She made that trailer to show her boss, Philip Wynn-Jones. If this Atlantis thing pans out, she thinks she can get you another series to do for the BBC in addition to the one you're already doing.'

'On Atlantis?'

'Yeah. She sent that trailer to her boss via the internet. It was supposed to have just been for corporate use. To get him some leverage for all the money they've spent transporting you guys around. He must have double-crossed her.'

'Why would he do that?'

'To drum up some additional publicity for Leslie and you.'

'Where does she live?' Lourds asked.

Bookman House
Central London
12 September 2009

Patrizio Gallardo sat tensely in the van across the street from Bookman House. The neighbourhood was average for the area, small homes and close access to the Tube station. It was the kind of place a young professional woman of modest means trying to make it on her own would live. The streets were dark enough to make it dangerous, though.

They had got Leslie Crane's address from her personal files at work. When they'd discovered she'd checked out of the Hempel Hotel, Gallardo hoped she would put in an appearance at home. After all, how many places would she be welcomed?

'I see her,' Cimino declared. He sat behind the steering wheel and watched the street through night-vision goggles. He nodded in the direction of the Tube station.

Gallardo took Cimino's word that it was the woman. In the darkness he couldn't be certain. She looked the right shape. He wondered if Lourds would still feel anything for her after the way she'd screwed him with the CNN interview. Murani was still fit to be tied over that. Time was moving inexorably against them.

Even Murani could not stop time.

'All right,' Gallardo replied. He tapped the radio headset he wore. 'Do you have her in sight?'

DiBenedetto answered immediately. 'Yes.'

'Then bring her in.' Gallardo watched through the window as Farok and DiBenedetto stepped out of the shadows and flanked Leslie Crane as she worked the locks on the door. The woman froze for a moment. Then she nodded. DiBenedetto took her by the elbow and guided her toward the waiting van. Anyone who saw them would probably mistake them for lovers out for a late walk.

Gallardo checked his watch. It was 12.06 a.m. A new day had begun. He felt satisfied. Now there was only one more deal to make. Fortunately, he was holding all the cards.

DiBenedetto opened the van door and escorted Leslie inside. Then he roughly shoved her back into a seat.

'Good evening, Miss Crane,' Gallardo said in English.

'What do you want with me?' Leslie tried to act defiant, but Gallardo saw her lip tremble.

'You,' Gallardo said good-naturedly, 'are going to

481

make a phone call for me.' He turned in his seat and looked back at her. 'Then we'll let you go.'

'Do you expect me to believe that?'

Gallardo gave her a hard look and put menace in his voice. 'If you don't make that call, I'm going to gut you and throw you in the Thames. Do you believe me now?'

'Yes.' Her voice broke. Tears gathered in her eyes but she somehow held them back.

'Your little stunt on television has angered my employer,' Gallardo said. 'The only way you're going to live is to cooperate.' He took out his cellphone and handed it over. 'Call Lourds.'

Leslie's hand was shaking so badly she almost dropped the phone. 'He's not going to talk to me.'

'You'd better hope he does.'

Lourds was in his hotel room just zipping his backpack up when the phone rang. He debated whether or not to answer it but finally gave in. Dean Wither wouldn't be calling again tonight.

He rounded the bed and lifted the receiver. 'Hello.'

'Thomas.'

Lourds recognized Leslie's voice immediately. Anger blazed through him in a white-hot flash. 'Leslie, have you any idea –'

'Please. Listen.'

The near-hysteria in her choked voice silenced Lourds. His door opened as Natashya let herself into the room with the key card he'd given her. She looked at him with mild irritation. She was obviously ready to go.

'They've got me, Thomas,' Leslie whispered hoarsely. 'Gallardo and his people. They kidnapped me.'

Lourds felt as though the floor tilted out from under him. He sat on the edge of the bed because his knees suddenly felt like they would no longer support him.

'Are you all right?' he asked.

That caught Natashya's attention. She approached him and mouthed, *Leslie?*

Lourds nodded. He asked again, 'Are you all right?'

'They haven't hurt me.'

Who has her? Natashya asked.

Gallardo, Lourds mouthed back.

'What do they want?' Lourds asked.

'I don't know. Thomas, I just want you to know that I didn't have anything to do with that CNN coverage. That wasn't my idea. I got –'

A moment later, a man's voice came on the line. 'Professor Lourds, I'm in a position to make you an offer.'

'I'm listening.'

'My employer wants the three instruments you've located.'

'I don't have –'

The sound of flesh striking flesh cut Lourds off. He could hear as Leslie yelped in shock and pain, then she started crying.

483

'I know you know where those instruments are,' the man said. 'Every time you lie to me, I'm going to cut off one of her fingers. Do you believe me?'

'Yes.' Lourds barely heard himself because his voice was so tight. He repeated his answer.

'Good. Act fast and you can save Miss Crane's life. You have one hour to get the instruments and meet one of my associates in front of your hotel.'

'That's not enough time,' Lourds protested.

The phone clicked dead in his ear.

'What?' Natashya asked.

Lourds cradled the handset. 'Gallardo just gave me one hour to get the instruments to him or he's going to kill Leslie.'

Anger darkened Natashya's face. For a moment Lourds feared that she'd tell him to let them kill Leslie. He'd learned that Natashya could be very forceful in her opinions. He didn't know what he was going to do if that happened.

'We'll get the instruments,' Natashya said.

Lourds knocked on Adebayo's hotel door. He had to repeat the knock. The whole time he stood in the hall he thought he was going to throw up. It helped that Natashya stood beside him and was so calm.

Adebayo answered the door. 'Yes?'

'I'm sorry to barge in on you,' Lourds started.

Beside him, Natashya sighed in disgust. 'We don't have time for this.'

'What has happened?' the old man asked.

'Gallardo. The man who's been chasing us has

kidnapped Leslie. He's threatening to kill her if I don't give him the instruments.'

'That is too bad,' Adebayo lamented. His big eyes looked sorrowful. 'But you can't give him the instruments.'

Lourds watched in disbelief as the old man started to shut the door. 'What? You can't just let them kill –'

Natashya stepped forward and jammed her foot in the door before it could close. She put the barrel of her pistol between the old man's eyes.

'Open the door,' she ordered.

'You would shoot me?' the old man asked.

'If I have to, yes. I don't have to kill you, but getting shot is very uncomfortable.'

Adebayo backed away from the door. He looked at Lourds. 'You can't let her do this.'

Natashya spoke to him without looking at him. 'Do you want to try to save Leslie or not?'

Her harsh tone broke Lourds out of his frozen state. 'Of course.'

'Then let's do it.' Natashya tossed him a roll of tape. 'Put him on the bed. The least we can do is make him comfortable.'

'Sorry about this,' Lourds apologized as he taped the old man's hands after helping him onto the bed.

Adebayo said nothing. He just collapsed and made Lourds feel guilty the whole time.

Forty-seven minutes later, Lourds left the hotel with all three musical instruments. He had put them on a luggage trolley because it was too awkward to carry them all.

Personally he felt he needed an even bigger cart for the guilt he was feeling. Jesse Blackfox had fought. He'd punched Lourds in the eye and it was now partially swelled shut. After that, Natashya had dropped Blackfox with a chokehold. No one had come to investigate the sounds made during the struggle.

Vang had cried when they'd taken the flute he'd protected for so long. The Keeper had received the instrument when he was hardly more than a boy. His father had been killed and his grandfather had died young. That had been the hardest for Lourds. He had broken Vang's heart as well as taken his flute.

'Can I help you with that, sir?' a porter asked as Lourds waited at the street.

'No, I'm good,' Lourds replied. 'Thanks anyway.'

The young man returned to the stand.

Only a few moments later a van pulled to the curb. The driver reached across and pushed the passenger door open.

'Professor Lourds,' the man said. 'You will come with me.'

'Where's Leslie?' Lourds asked.

'Alive for the moment.'

'I want her released.'

The man lifted a pistol from between the seats and pointed it at him. 'Get in. Otherwise I'll shoot you and hope those cases contain what I'm looking for. You have been irritating. It would be good to shoot you.'

Another man leaned into view from the cargo area of the van. He also had a pistol. 'I'll take the instruments.'

Lourds almost glanced over his shoulder. He knew that Natashya was there somewhere. But she couldn't stop the man from shooting him.

Without a word, Lourds handed the instruments to the man in the van's cargo area. When he was finished, he expected the van to simply pull away and leave him standing there like an idiot.

Only it didn't.

The driver moved the pistol slightly. 'Get in, Professor Lourds. I was told to bring you as well.'

'Why?'

'So I don't have to kill you right here. Would you not rather come quietly than die in the street?'

Reluctantly, Lourds climbed into the vehicle. The man in the back reached around with a length of rope and tied Lourds' arms to his sides and his body to the seat as the driver pulled into traffic. In seconds Lourds was unable to move.

'Is Leslie still alive?' Lourds asked.

'Sit back and try to enjoy the drive, Professor Lourds. You'll have the answers to your questions soon enough.'

Lourds stared blearily through the bug-smeared window. He was so tired and adrenaline-charged by now that he saw words and symbols in the insect detritus. He glanced occasionally into the rear-view mirror for any sign that Natashya might be following him. They hadn't hired a car, but she'd always seemed resourceful.

The headlights gradually faded away as they left London behind. Lourds' hope of rescue faded as well. He was also pretty sure that Gallardo had killed Leslie and dumped her in the first convenient alley. The thought made him almost physically ill. But no matter what, his mind kept turning again and again to the final words he hadn't been able to fully translate on the five instruments. He had most of it. He was convinced of that.

A few moments later, the van turned off and drove down a pothole-filled road under massive oak trees. Then they stopped and the sound of silence filled the van.

'What are we doing?' Lourds asked.

'Shut up,' the man instructed. He shook out a cigarette and lit up.

A short time later, a helicopter descended from the black sky and landed in the nearby field. The two men who had taken him captive climbed from the van, cut Lourds free and marched him through the tall grass to the waiting helicopter.

Lourds recognized Gallardo at once. The brutish crook sat in the rear compartment of the helicopter. Another man handcuffed Lourds and shoved him into a seat.

'Where's Leslie?' Lourds demanded.

Gallardo laughed mirthlessly. 'You and that little witch have been a problem since the beginning. The

488

only good that's come of it is that you found all the instruments for me.'

Pain lanced Lourds' heart. He'd enjoyed Leslie's company and it hurt him to think something awful had happened to her.

'We had a deal,' Lourds croaked as the helicopter powered up and leaped into the sky.

Gallardo spoke more loudly. 'I give you part of the deal. She's still alive.' He shifted and revealed Leslie collapsed on the seat beside him. She was handcuffed as well, but fast asleep. He saw her pulse beating at her throat.

Thank God, Lourds thought. *She really is alive.*

'But how long she stays alive depends on your cooperation.'

Fear gripped Lourds all over again when he realized the implications of what Gallardo had said. 'Why do you need my cooperation?'

'You'll find out soon enough.' Gallardo nodded.

The man beside Lourds leaned in with a large hypodermic. The needle sank into Lourds' neck. He felt the prickling pain for only a moment, then warmth gushed through his head and he fell through himself.

Getting to Cadiz proved harder than Natashya had at first believed it would. When she'd seen Lourds step into the van from her observation point on a second-storey balcony, she hadn't tried to follow. Gallardo's men were professionals. She knew when to hold back and use her head instead of going on a mad dash into danger.

She knew where they were going to take Lourds. At least, she hoped she knew. He might not make it there alive. There was always the chance that Gallardo or his mysterious employer would simply get whatever they wanted from Lourds and kill him somewhere along the way.

But she trusted her instincts.

Instead of following the van, she'd woken Gary and gone to Heathrow to hire a private pilot. She'd intended to use Gary to hire the pilot so there wouldn't be any questions about her ID. As it turned out, Gary had a friend who was a pilot and who was only too glad to take them.

That problem, at least, was easily solved.

Gary sat up front with the pilot and talked about some of the craziness he'd been through during the past month. Of course he lied about the women he'd had and his role in the dangerous side of things. It was typical male bonding between two old friends.

Natashya merely rolled her eyes when the embellishments got too outlandish.

She sat in the small passenger section as the plane jumped and danced through the treacherous dark night. She felt certain that Gallardo wouldn't try to get Lourds onto a conventional flight to Spain. If that was true, she'd arrive in Cadiz before him.

It wasn't much of an edge, but it was all she had.

She made herself comfortable in the seat and willed herself to sleep, but she was plagued by nightmares. She could see and hear Yuliya, but her sister couldn't hear her any more no matter how loudly she yelled.

Cave #42
Atlantis Burial Catacombs
Cadiz, Spain
12 September 2009

'We're through!'

Father Sebastian sat with a blanket snuggled around his shoulders to stave off the unrelenting cold inside the cave. Most of the water had been pumped away, but the process of clearing the disturbed bodies continued. They'd taken to stacking them up on pallets like cargo and freighting them out of the caves.

The large metal door had proven to be a problem. Whatever it was made of, Brancati had never seen anything like it. In the end they'd had to drill through the locking mechanism. They kept wearing out even the diamond-bit drills. Getting through the lock had taken days.

Sebastian pushed himself to his feet. Dizziness swam through his head for a moment, then gradually dissipated. *You haven't been getting enough sleep*, he chided himself. *You've got to take better care of yourself.*

'I think they've got the locking mechanism cleared away,' Brancati said. He looked worn as well. 'If you're ready, Father.'

Sebastian nodded, but fear filled him when he thought of what they were going to find.

A cable from a small earthmover was attached to the door. Gradually, as the winch revolved and filled

491

the immediate vicinity with mechanical noise, the slack in the cable disappeared.

Then loud grinding filled the cavern.

All of the men looked nervous. No one knew for certain about the integrity of the walls, and none of them could forget about the merciless sea waiting somewhere outside.

Stalactites fell from the cavern roof and caused a minor furore as they exploded against the stone floor and splashed in the remaining pools of water. One of the stalactites smashed against the protective cage of the earthmover. Startled, the driver put his foot too hard on the accelerator. The machine roared backwards, struggling against the weight of the door and finally found traction. Then the cable snapped and flicked across three of the workers. They fell like rag dolls and bled furiously.

But the massive door swung open.

22

The screams of the wounded men filled the cavern and barely penetrated the sense of unreality that flooded Father Sebastian's mind. Ignoring the huge door now several feet ajar and filled with the inky blackness of the dark cave, he went to help the nearest man lashed by the snapping cable.

Brancati yelled at his workers to tend to the men as well, then joined them as first-aid kits arrived. It was a brutal, bloody business for several minutes.

Thankfully, none of the men had been killed outright. Given the situation, it could have been so much worse.

That no one died . . . The Lord was at work here to save them all, Sebastian thought. *May His mercy reign over us all as we proceed.*

After he'd finished his work with the wounded, he cleaned his hands with a sterile cloth. He'd refused to wait until gloves were available to begin giving first aid. By the time the workers had passed out surgical gloves, he'd already attended to several of the most serious injuries.

'Do you believe in evil portents, Father?' Brancati asked.

'I believe in everything that proceeds from the hand of the Lord,' Sebastian answered. 'But I also believe in accidents. The men here are tired and stressed from everything we have dealt with. We must proceed carefully.'

'I agree.' Brancati passed Sebastian one of the big flashlights the men carried in addition to their helmet lights and led the way into the next chamber.

Sebastian stayed close behind. The two Swiss Guards, Peter and Martin, flanked him.

The next cave was even larger than the last. It was a gaping maw of stone. Stalactites and stalagmites looked like wicked teeth as the flashlight beams swept across them. The cavern was dry, indicating that the chamber had been airtight until they'd opened the door.

'Maybe we'd better let the cave breathe a little while, Father,' Brancati suggested. 'In case the change in air pressure creates a problem like it did in the last cave.'

Sebastian made himself nod. He didn't want to leave the room but he knew that was safest.

'Father Sebastian,' a man called.

Sebastian turned toward the voice. He spotted two men playing their flashlights over an inscription carved into the wall. Drawn by the words, he made his way over to them. For a moment, the words were almost impossible to make out. Sebastian squinted and tried again. This time he could read the message.

MAKE A JOYFUL NOISE UNTO THE LORD

Sebastian couldn't understand the meaning of the message. He stared at it for a long time, then turned and surveyed the huge cavern again.

'Over here!' someone else yelled. 'Father Sebastian, over here!'

Hurrying to the voice, aided by Peter and Martin, Sebastian found a long line of walls that had been chipped smooth then engraved with pictures. The engravings were spaced like the leaves of a giant stone book. The intricate work represented several lifetimes' effort by the people who had carved it.

The first picture was of a huge forest. A man and a woman stood naked in a clearing. Numerous animals lay at their feet or nearby. Birds filled the branches of the trees around them.

'Blessed Mother,' Sebastian whispered. Hypnotized by what he saw before him, he stepped forward and ran his trembling fingers over the beautifully carved surface.

'What is this?' Brancati asked quietly.

'It's the Garden of Eden,' Sebastian croaked. 'Adam and Eve in the Garden of Eden.'

Several of the men crossed themselves and took off their protective helmets till Brancati growled at them to put them back on.

'Are you trying to tell me that this place was the Garden of Eden?' Brancati asked.

'No,' Sebastian said. 'This place wasn't the Garden of Eden. This place was a part of Atlantis. Or whatever the people who we know as Atlanteans called themselves.'

'Why carve these pictures into the walls?'

'So they wouldn't forget. So they wouldn't follow Adam and Eve into folly.' Sebastian shone his light farther back and found another picture. This one showed God's hand fashioning Adam from clay.

'The whole story is here,' Peter said. 'These images tell the story of creation.'

'Is this God?' Martin asked reverently.

Sebastian strode through the twists and turns of the cavern and found him standing in front of a picture of Adam and Eve in the jungle. In the drawing, a second man stood near the couple. He held a thick book in one hand. A glowing halo hung over his head.

'No,' Sebastian said. 'It's not God.'

'Then who is it?' Martin asked.

'I'm not sure. But I think that's His Son.'

Outside Cadiz, Spain
12 September 2009

Hunched over the notebook computer, Cardinal Stefano Murani studied the live video coming out of the dig site only a few miles away. He'd arranged the safe house in case he needed a bolt hole. It was one of the small houses in the area that were sometimes rented out to tourists. It didn't afford him the kind of luxury that he was accustomed to, but it was within a few miles of the dig and the Atlantic Ocean.

When he saw the pictures deep within the centre of the new cave beyond the massive metal door, Murani watched with growing excitement. Sebastian was close to the goal the Pope had hoped he would reach.

Are these wall carvings illustrations from the Book? Murani asked himself. He flicked through the downloaded images. The work that had gone into the finished pieces was astounding.

The answer, for the moment, was that he didn't know. He needed to be inside the caves.

His cellphone chirped for attention. He flipped it open and answered. 'Yes.'

'We'll be there in five minutes or less,' Gallardo said.

'I'll see you then.' Murani closed the phone, disconnected the computer from the internet, and shut it down. He walked to the front door and passed the security set-ups the Swiss Guard who had chosen to follow him had put into place. Cameras watched over the surrounding terrain.

Lieutenant Milo Sbordoni sat in a chair on the covered porch. In his thirties, Sbordoni was a handsome man with chiselled features and a fierce black goatee that flipped up at the end. Like the other guardsmen under his command, he wore tactical armour festooned with weapons. There had been no doubt that they would take over the Cadiz dig after Gallardo had Lourds.

'Cardinal.' Sbordoni got to his feet. Oil glistened on the pistol and rifle he carried.

'It's time,' Murani said.

'Good,' Sbordoni said. He smiled, then passed orders to his men to assemble.

The Swiss Guard rose to readiness. They passed out even more weapons. A large cargo truck out on the street rumbled to life.

'I'll need a word with your men,' Murani said.

Sbordoni quickly gave the command. The men assembled around Murani. Due to their size and the armour they wore, Murani was dwarfed by them. Still, they acknowledged his office and stood quietly while he addressed them.

'You are my brothers in arms,' Murani said. 'You are the best that the Swiss Guard at the Vatican has to offer. More than that, you have also recognized the holiness of God's word in ways that many of those in that place have forgotten.

'The Church has grown weak. We must strengthen her.' Murani paused. 'Some of you have known for years about the Society of Quirinus and how the cardinals in that group have chosen to work with past popes to recover things that have been lost over the past thousands of years. A few of you who have been blessed by God have had the chance to assist in locating and taking custody of some of those things.'

Those men nodded. Sbordoni was among them. All of them carried scars from those battles. The

Church wasn't the only entity that searched for powerful artefacts. And the Society of Quirinus hadn't always succeeded in obtaining what it sought. At times the treasures had been lost again, or had fallen into enemy hands.

'What we're after tonight is the most important artefact God has ever delivered to his chosen people,' Murani said. 'It has the power to remake the world.'

Sbordoni's eyes met Murani's. He nodded in anticipation.

'It was used once before,' Murani said, 'by unbelievers and those corrupted by the lust for power. The wanted to be like God.' He paused. 'This is God's holiest work, and it must be used by those who love God. I know you love God as I love God. Together, we will make this world once more into the place that He intended for it to be.'

'Praise God,' Sbordoni said.

Murani asked them to bow their heads while he prayed to Mary for her protection.

Lourds sat handcuffed in the canopy-covered back of a truck. His head felt like a balloon and he was groggy from the after-effects of the drug he'd been given.

Beside him, Leslie looked bleary-eyed as well. 'Where are we?' she asked.

'I don't know.' Lourds swept his gaze over the night-darkened coastline visible through the opening at the rear of the truck. Moonlight shone on the rolling waves. 'Near the sea.'

'When did they get you?' Leslie licked her lips and tested the handcuffs.

'After they got you,' Lourds told her. 'They told me they'd kill you if I didn't come to them.'

'Your new girlfriend didn't stop them?'

Lourds sighed. Being taken captive was dangerous enough, but being held captive with a young woman with an axe to grind over amorous misadventures was worse.

The drug she'd been given had made her talk while she'd been unconscious. She hadn't been generous in her references to Lourds. The offensive comments had provided tremendous entertainment to Gallardo's minions. Lourds was just thankful he hadn't recovered too much earlier than she had.

'I'm not the only thing they used you to get. Gallardo told me if I didn't give him the instruments he was going to kill you.'

'You gave them the instruments?' she shrieked.

'Yes. He meant it. That part about killing you, I mean.'

'I bet *that* didn't go over well with the new girlfriend. The part about you giving up the instruments for me.'

'Natashya isn't my new girlfriend,' Lourds said.

'Don't tell me she decided to just use you and lose you?' Leslie feigned sympathy.

'Why are you worried about my love life?' Lourds held up his manacled wrists. 'Has it occurred to you that we might be in some trouble here?'

'You have a point.' Leslie took a look at the hard

faces of the men guarding them. 'Okay. You're right. The good thing is that they haven't killed us.'

'That,' Lourds said, 'might not be as good a thing as you think.'

The truck rolled to a stop. One of the men grabbed a fistful of Lourds' shirt and yanked him to his feet. He hauled Lourds to the rear of the truck, then over the tailgate. It hurt like fury. His captors didn't seem to be too worried about bruising the merchandise.

Lourds tripped and fell heavily to the ground, his breath rushing out of his lungs. Spots whirled in front of his eyes. Before he had a chance to recover, the man in charge of him yanked him roughly to his feet. Pain burned through Lourds' wrists. He pushed himself upright as quickly as he could.

An elegant man in cardinal's robes stepped in front of Lourds. A small army bristling with weapons stood behind him.

'Professor Lourds,' the man said, 'I'm Cardinal Stefano Murani.' He smiled.

The priest's expression sent chills down Lourds' spine.

'Under the circumstances, I can't say this introduction is exactly a pleasure,' Lourds said.

Leslie pressed close to him. In the face of so many foes, she wasn't quite as unforgiving of his past trespasses in the boudoir.

'Not a pleasure at all,' Murani said. 'But you have been something of a surprise. A pleasant surprise for me, but I'm afraid it could end unpleasantly for you.'

Lourds didn't say anything, but cold, unrelenting fear wormed through his stomach.

'Have you worked out the riddle of the instruments?' Murani asked.

'No.'

Murani's eyes never flickered. 'Lieutenant Sbordoni.'

A lean man with a jutting goatee stepped forward and unholstered a pistol. 'Cardinal?'

'The woman, I think,' Murani said.

Immediately the man pointed his pistol at Leslie. Lourds stepped between them. She gripped his shirt and held him firmly in place in front of her. It wasn't exactly the reaction Lourds had hoped for, but he couldn't blame her.

The bearded lieutenant Murani had called Sbordoni barked an order. Two men stepped forward and grabbed Leslie. She yelled, kicked and screamed as they pulled her away.

'Thou shalt not kill,' Lourds shouted. 'That's one of the top ten edicts from God, isn't it?'

Murani's soldiers pressed Leslie to the ground. The lieutenant stood over her with his pistol aimed point blank into her face.

'That commandment is not applicable when soldiers have to go out and fight holy wars for God,' Murani said. 'And this is a war. You have become our enemy. God will forgive us the trespasses we make in His name today. We're here to rid the world of evil. The instruments you located are our weapons.' He stared at Leslie on the ground. She'd curled into a foetal position, but her hands over her face wouldn't stop bullets. 'You will help us. I'm willing to have the girl killed to prove to you how serious I am in this regard.'

'I haven't figured out the riddle of the instruments,' Lourds said as truthfully as he could. There hadn't been a riddle in what he'd translated yet. 'I'm still working on the inscription. I've got most of it. But there's no mention of a riddle.'

Murani looked at him.

'I swear to you,' Lourds said. 'I'll help you do whatever you want to do. I don't want her to die. I don't want to die either.' Blood roared in his ears as his heart hammered frantically. 'I'll try again. That's the best that I can do.'

The cardinal's gaze never wavered. Finally, when Lourds was growing more certain that Murani was going to have Leslie killed anyway, Murani looked at the lieutenant and said, 'Bring her along.'

Thank God, Lourds thought. He let out a breath. Somehow, it didn't seem to ease the tightness in his chest.

'Load them into the truck,' Murani commanded.

Hard hands grabbed Lourds again. He gritted his teeth against the pain and endured.

Lourds sat on the metal deck between two long benches full of black-suited warriors. He believed the men were Swiss Guards from the Vatican. He'd deduced most of that from the conversations he'd overheard.

A short length of chain connected Lourds' manacles to the truck bed. No running to safety this time. He rocked and surged as the truck travelled over the uneven terrain.

Flaps hanging across the rear opening of the truck kept most of the view outside at bay, but there was enough swaying on the journey so they were occasionally open to the view outside. The course they were on shadowed the coastline. Lourds' attention was torn between Leslie, Murani and watching for landmarks he could use to let police know where they were.

Leslie sat beside Lourds. Her body bumped softly against his and brought back memories of more pleasant times. It also reminded Lourds how vulnerable she was. Despite the apparent willingness of these men to kill for Cardinal Murani, Lourds didn't think they would rape Leslie. At least she was safe from that. He hoped. Gallardo and his crew sat among the guardsmen, too. Their hot gazes often travelled to Leslie. Lourds found it uncomfortably easy to read their intentions.

'Thomas.'

Lourds looked at Leslie. 'Yes?' he asked.

'I'm sorry.' Unshed tears glimmered in her eyes.

'For what?' Lourds felt sorry for her. She hadn't been trained for something like this. Neither had he. Truthfully, he felt sorry for both of them.

'For being such a bitch.'

'Look, the night with Natashya . . .' Lourds stopped, unsure what to say. The night with Natashya had been incredibly wonderful. So had the nights with Leslie. But he didn't think he owed anyone an apology. He'd been upfront about his intentions the whole time. He liked women. He wasn't ready to settle down with any one woman. And he hadn't pursued either of them. They'd made themselves available.

'You didn't do anything wrong,' she said.

Lourds relaxed. A little. Sometimes when women faced trying or difficult times they said things they thought they were supposed to say but it was not what they truly felt. He'd learned that the hard way.

'At least, not *really* wrong. You're a guy and you have some basic limitations. And you aren't, as a species, terribly loyal.'

In the corner of the truck, Gallardo and one of his men listened to this conversation and grinned.

'Perhaps there would be a more appropriate time for us to discuss this,' Lourds suggested.

'There may not be another time for us,' Leslie said. She looked exasperated. 'This isn't exactly an "oops" situation where we're going to be inconvenienced for a while then returned to our normal lives.'

'I was rather hoping it would be.'

Leslie rolled her eyes at him. 'We're sitting in a truck full of bad guys and you want to go Pollyanna on me?'

Lourds suddenly realized she was on the verge of getting mad at him all over again.

'We're not bad guys,' Murani said.

'Yeah, right.' Leslie shifted her attention to the

cardinal. 'Like kidnapping people and threatening to shoot them is so heroic?'

'I'm trying to save the world,' Murani protested. 'I'm not the villain.'

Anger surged through Lourds when he thought how Gallardo – or one of the other men in Murani's employ – had killed Yuliya, and shot at Leslie's team back in Alexandria. No matter what the man said, Murani was a villain.

'And how do you propose to save the world?' Leslie demanded.

Murani sighed. 'Through God's word. Now be silent or I'll have you gagged.'

Leslie quieted, but she leaned more heavily against Lourds.

'Anyway, I'm sorry,' Leslie said to him in a whisper. Lourds nodded.

She looked at him with irritation. 'Aren't you going to tell me you're sorry, too?'

Lourds froze. What was he supposed to be sorry for? He took a guess. 'I'm sorry I convinced you to go along with me.'

Leslie growled at him and shifted away. 'You,' she declared, 'are an *idiot*.'

Gallardo and his men laughed out loud. Even Murani seemed somewhat amused.

Lourds couldn't believe he was supposed to fear for his life and feel guilty about his relationships with women at the same time. If he wasn't so curious about what they were going to find at the Cadiz dig, he figured he'd have gone mad by now. He concentrated on remembering the inscription. He rebuilt the language again in his mind so he could translate it once more.

Later, although how much time had passed Lourds couldn't be certain, the truck stopped. Voices sounded outside. A glance through the open flaps before one of the guardsmen tied them together revealed that they were undoubtedly at the dig. Media vehicles ringed the area.

Desperation flared through Lourds. Surely all he had to do was yell for help and people would –

'Don't,' Murani said coldly. 'Stay silent or I will kill your friend. I need that brilliant mind of yours for a little while longer. But Miss Crane's company is merely a convenience for you, one you retain solely based on your good behaviour.'

Lourds subsided. He heard Leslie take a deep breath beside him. Almost immediately one of the guardsmen slapped a hand over her mouth. She squealed behind the hand, but the sound was mostly trapped.

The truck's engine rumbled and they got underway again.

Natashya stood in shadows that ringed the site and surveyed the two trucks that pulled through the gate in the hurricane fence. The fence had been erected at the beginning of the dig in anticipation of world interest and media coverage. Ten feet tall and topped with razor-wire, the fence wouldn't be proof against an armoured division, but it held out journalists, the curious and those who had larceny in mind. Searchlights patrolled the rocky terrain.

To the right, the Atlantic Ocean beat against an eight-foot-high retaining wall that had been constructed to keep the sea at bay during high tide. The wall wasn't meant to be permanent, but she could see it was the best money could buy. The Roman Catholic Church hadn't spared any expense in making certain their people were safe.

Thinking of going down into the caves still left Natashya feeling slightly sick to her stomach. Even the subway tunnels under Moscow left her feeling that way. She didn't like the idea of being trapped underground. The possibility of being drowned while underground was even more terrifying.

She focused her binoculars on the two trucks rolling through the gate. It was 2.38 a.m. She couldn't imagine a late-night delivery coming in, but it was possible.

'Well?' Gary whispered as he stood beside her.

Natashya didn't make a reply. Gary was proving inept at patience.

'Is it them?' Gary persisted.

'I don't know,' Natashya replied. 'There wasn't a list of occupants printed on the outside of the truck.'

Gary cursed. 'What if you're wrong?'

'Then Lourds was wrong. He's the one who did the translation and felt certain the instruments were leading us here.'

'He could have been wrong, you know. Even if he was right about the translation talking about Atlantis, this might not be the Atlantis the instruments referred to.'

'I know.'

'We could have lost them.'

'I know.' Natashya only kept the conversation going because it relaxed Gary to a degree.

He cursed some more. 'Maybe the Roman Catholic Church is wrong about this being Atlantis. If you'd read the materials that have been written about it, you'd know that prospective sites for Atlantis have been located all around the world.'

'Not my problem. Lourds said they were coming here.'

'If Lourds is wrong, then we've lost them.'

'Try not to think like that. I believe he was right.' Natashya watched as the trucks stopped in front of the throat of the cave system. The passengers in the back disembarked.

'How else am I supposed to –'

'He was right. They're here.' Natashya focused on Lourds as he stumbled from the truck.

'I knew they would be,' Gary said. 'Lourds is a really smart guy.'

'Certainly.' Despite the danger that still faced them, Natashya couldn't help smiling. Partly because of Gary's ridiculous about-face, partly because Lourds and Leslie Crane were still among the living, but the biggest part was because vengeance for Yuliya was at hand.

She could hardly wait to dispense it.

The group walked into the cave and disappeared inside.

Now for the hard bit.

'We've got other problems,' Natashya said.

'What?'

'Gallardo's people got into the cave easily.'

'So?'

'That means they already have people here who know them,' Natashya said. 'They've already infil-trated the security.'

'So?'

'They're in charge, they're well armed, and they outnumber us a hundred to one.' Natashya pointed out, as to a small child.

'That's never stopped you before.'

Murani walked down into the caves with Sbordoni on one side of him and Gallardo on the other. It was strange thinking that if the two men had met each other separately they wouldn't have liked each other.

Yet he was able to use them both for his own purposes.

Gallardo watched nervously as the arriving group of Swiss Guards met the teams already on site as security. He hadn't been aware that so much of the invasion into the cave system would be so easy.

'Were you thinking we'd shoot our way in?' Murani asked.

'Me?' Gallardo asked. 'I was hoping more for the "slide in the back door" strategy.' He looked tense. 'There's something else I've learned over the years: just because you walk into a place doesn't mean you can walk back out.'

'We can walk back out,' Murani said. He was confident about that. All of the Swiss Guards on site had sworn allegiance to the Society of Quirinus and believed in keeping the Church's secrets. Those who didn't know Murani planned to use the artefact Father Sebastian undoubtedly was on the verge of finding wouldn't find out until it was too late.

'Just so you know,' Gallardo said, 'if this thing goes south, I'm not going to hang around.'

'It won't go south.' Murani stared at the caves and at the base camp.

Most of the workers were asleep in their tents. The few who were up only watched with mild curiosity as Murani and his people passed through. Everyone knew the Swiss Guards went armed, and there had been threats against the site. Murani was sure that the presence of guardsmen at the base camp just told interested spectators that security was being increased.

'How far is the cave where Sebastian is?' Gallardo asked.

'Almost two miles.'

Gallardo looked back at the cave entrance uneasily. 'That's a long way underground.'

'Personally,' Murani said, 'I was thinking it was a long way to get where I want to go. I can't wait to get there.' He just hoped that Sebastian hadn't found the Book before he arrived.

Under direction of one of the Guards, Lourds clambered aboard a trailer that had been converted to haul supplies and construction workers through the caves. Long wooden benches provided seats.

Leslie sat beside him.

'I don't like caves,' Leslie said.

'Some of them are quite fascinating,' Lourds said. He'd seen several of them himself while studying prehistoric drawings for any sign of rudimentary language. The idea of how mankind had lived in them for a time captivated him.

'You like the weirdest things.'

Lourds grinned at that. 'I suppose I do.'

'That's one of the things that makes you interesting.'

'I'll take your word for that.' Lourds struggled to keep up with Leslie's way of thinking. He didn't know if she found him primarily charming or offensive. Right now, he was astonished to discover that what she thought mattered to him.

Instead of worrying about her, he directed his

attention to the base camp. It had been set up in much the way a support area on a mountain climb would have been arranged. Food, medical care and amenities were all provided for. Television and video games, powered by the throbbing generators that filled the caves with a giant's heartbeats, were even included.

The truck jerked the trailer into motion. Lourds whipped into Leslie for a moment. He gazed at the Guards sitting across from him and couldn't help thinking that if this was a James Bond film it was here that 007 would swing into motion and overpower his captors. Then he'd save the world.

At least James Bond knew what he was saving the world from, Lourds thought sourly. He still only had a general idea of what they were going to find.

But the lunacy of the idea of jumping one of the guards and taking his weapon away filled him before he acted. He was silently thankful for that. He could just imagine himself being shot to pieces and Murani still torturing his dying body with red-hot pliers or something to get the inscription translated.

The truck picked up speed as it descended into the bowels of the earth. Lourds discovered the dig crew had followed pre-existing tunnels, but had been forced to enlarge some of them. The headlights cut through the darkness, but bulbs strung against the naked rock that framed the tunnels marked the way to their destination.

Lourds felt Leslie shivering against him. He considered putting an arm around her. Even with the handcuffs he could manage that. But he didn't know if she'd allow that contact. So he sat in silence and anticipated with dread what he was about to find at the other end of this journey to Atlantis.

'These were the catacombs beneath the city,' Father Sebastian said as he wandered through the large stone carvings that depicted so much of the history written in Genesis. He paused at one that was undoubtedly illustrating the birth of the universe and the parting of the darkness and light. God stood, a glowing presence, with his arms raised wide as the light from the sun surrounded him. 'They probably built them as they'd built the city.'

'We haven't found anything up top,' Brancati said.

'Mightn't earthquakes and incoming waves account for the loss of the city above?' Sebastian ran his hand over a carving showing a huge ziggurat being built at the centre of a fantastic city far in advance of anything that should have been out in the world at the time they believed Atlantis plunged into the ocean.

'Yes. I've seen earthquake sites that were shaken relatively clean of rubble in rural areas. That doesn't happen so much in cities like the ones we have now. Too many utility hook-ups and underground systems – like this one, I suppose – exist for them to simply disappear.'

'But many thousands of years ago?'

'You've seen the circular walls on the surface. They argue for the possibility that this *is* Atlantis.'

Sebastian nodded. He pointed at the carving before

him. 'Biblical scholars and historians were wrong about the Tower of Babel. It wasn't built in Babylon. It was built here in Atlantis.'

'Do you think so? I hadn't expected that.'

Recognizing the voice but not having any idea what its owner would be doing here, Sebastian turned to face Cardinal Murani. Murani walked at the front of a small army of Swiss Guards.

'What are you doing here?' Sebastian demanded.

Murani stopped in front of the carving and studied it for a moment. Then he turned to Sebastian. 'I'm here doing God's true work. I'm going to bring knowledge of His word and truth back into the world. I'm not going to cover it up and continue to help make Him powerless.'

'You're not supposed to be here,' Sebastian said.

'No,' Murani agreed. 'I'm not. But the man who commands me is useless. The new Pope is going to be just as weak as those who have gone before him. He's insisting on burying what is found here. He is wrong. I'm not going to do that.'

Terror flooded through Sebastian as he watched the cardinal. It was obvious that something had gone terribly out of control in the man. The priest's eyes were as crazed as his voice was certain. Sebastian glanced at Peter and Martin.

They stepped back from him.

Brancati stepped forward. 'I don't know what the hell you people —'

A rough-looking man beside Murani slammed his rifle butt into the construction foreman's forehead and knocked him out. Brancati hit the ground in a loose sprawl. Blood leaked from a small cut over his left eye.

The members of the construction crew surged forward to protect their supervisor, but the weapons brandished by the Swiss Guard chased them back. The warriors barked commands and the construction workers dropped to their knees with their hands behind their heads. Guardsmen quickly bound their hands with disposable plastic cuffs. When they were all taken captive, some of the Guards took them into the outer cave. No one fought against them this time.

Murani smiled. He came close enough to Sebastian so that his voice went no further. 'You can't stop me, old man. All you can do is struggle against me and die. If you want to die for God, go ahead. I'm willing for you to make that sacrifice. I applaud it, in fact.'

Sebastian made himself stand fast in spite of his fear. 'The Book isn't here.'

Murani glanced around. 'I believe that it is.'

'It destroyed Atlantis.'

'Because the priest-kings in those days wanted to be the equal of God,' Murani said. 'I only want to bring Him back into this world. I want to bring the fear of God to everyone's attention. Including that ineffectual bungler in Vatican City. Especially to him. I have plans.'

Sebastian trembled but said nothing. He couldn't believe this was happening. The Swiss Guard owed their allegiance to the Pope, not to anyone else. Yet they followed Murani as though he *was* the Pope.

'Where's the Book?' Murani demanded.

Sebastian shook his head. 'I don't know. If I did, I wouldn't tell you.'

A nervous tic flared to life under Murani's right eye. 'Careful. I'm not going to suffer rebellion quietly. I'll bury you here if I need to.'

'So you're going to add murder to your list of atrocities?'

'Too late. It was added long ago,' Murani said coldly. 'All I can do at this point is compound my work. And it's not murder when I take a life pursuing God's purposes.'

'This isn't God's work.'

'*You* don't recognize it as God's work,' Murani said. 'I do.'

'I won't help you.'

Murani smiled. 'I don't need your help,' he snarled. He raised his voice. 'Professor Lourds.'

Lourds stumbled forward across the stone floor as one of the Guards shoved him. He noticed then how worn the stone was between the large carved murals. Thousands of years ago, he realized, people had spent a lot of time walking between these images.

'Come here,' Murani ordered.

Reluctantly, Lourds approached the cardinal. He'd seen the conversation between Murani and Father Sebastian, but he hadn't been able to hear it over the throbbing generators in the next room. But he could tell from the expressions on both men's faces that neither of them was happy with anything that had been said.

Murani gestured at the image carved in stone before him. 'Do you know what this is?'

Lourds looked at the stone and thought that maybe the cardinal was trying to trick him. The image was stark. There was no mistaking what it was.

'This is Atlantis.' Lourds gestured with both hands, since they were bound together, at the ziggurat. 'That's the Tower of Babel. They were building it to ascend to Heaven and be with God.'

'Yes,' Murani said. He directed Lourds' attention to the sections of stone that were covered with the same language that was on all the instruments. The picture, though, was different. Two men and a woman were shown in the forest with animals around them. 'Can you read this?'

Lourds studied the writing for a moment. He was aware of Father Sebastian's intense gaze on him.

'Don't help him do this,' the old priest said softly. 'You don't know what he intends to –'

Uncoiling like a striking snake, Murani struck Sebastian in the face with the back of his hand. Sebastian cried out, staggered and dropped to one knee. Blood streamed from his nose and split lips.

Some of the Swiss Guards started to come forward, including a young man with a scar on his face who looked particularly upset. Only the barked commands from men who were evidently their superiors held them in place. Obviously whatever agreement existed within the group meant different things to different members. The Swiss Guards weren't all of the same mind.

Lourds didn't know if that was a good thing or a bad thing. One thing he did know – all of them were armed. A rebellion among them could have massive casualties, and bystanders weren't likely to be spared. He decided that setting them against each other wasn't a sound plan right now. Maybe later, if he got desperate.

'Can you read this?' Murani asked.

Lourds examined the text. 'I don't know. I just learned how to translate this language last night.'

'What does it say?'

Glancing at the man, Lourds wondered if Murani could read the inscription.

A smile curved Murani's thin lips. 'Let me paraphrase this section for you. After God created the Heaven and the Earth, after the oceans and the skies, when He finally created man and woman from His rib shortly thereafter, He sent down His son to walk with Adam and Eve.'

'That can't be right,' Lourds said. During the whole recital Murani hadn't looked at the inscription.

'It's right,' Murani replied.

Lourds turned his attention from Murani to the story written in the stone. Even allowing for mistakes and misinterpretation, that was what the stone recorded.

'But that's wrong,' Lourds said. 'The Bible states that Jesus was born to Mary thousands of years later, and that He was God's only Son.'

'That's what the Church would have you believe,' Murani agreed. 'That's just one of the secrets they've protected all these years. God had *two* Sons. *Two*. God sent both His Sons to earth. Mankind killed them both.'

Lourds looked at Father Sebastian.

Sebastian's silence was eloquent.

'If you can read this, why do you need me?' Lourds asked Murani.

'Because I *can't* read it,' the cardinal answered. 'I only know what the story deals with. I know only part of the secret. I need you to tell me the rest. God's first Son came to earth, to the Garden of Eden, and He brought a wondrous gift: the Book of Knowledge.' Murani smiled. 'It wasn't a tree or a fruit at all. That was another thing the Church hid. It was a Book. That Book is God's word and it has the power to reshape our reality.' He paused. 'It was that Book that destroyed Atlantis.'

23

Carefully making her way through the shadows, Natashya crept up to the side of the hill where the hurricane fence butted up against the rock. The cave's throat blossomed light only a few feet away.

Gary followed her. She was thankful for the lax security. If anyone had been really listening, she was certain they would have heard Gary as he stumbled through the dark. He stayed behind her and sucked in air.

Hunkered down against the hillside, Natashya took out the sat-phone she'd bought in Cadiz after she'd landed. She'd arranged it through the same black-market dealer from whom she'd procured the two 9mm pistols she carried in the pockets of her trench coat.

'This next part is going to get dangerous,' Natashya told Gary as she punched buttons on the sat-phone. 'You might want to reconsider coming along.'

Gary looked tense. He swallowed hard and shook his head. 'I can't let you go on alone.'

Natashya stared at him for a moment and saw his

resolve reflected in his eyes. She nodded as she pressed the TALK button. She stared out at the coastline where the retaining wall held back the thunderous surf. The noise of the breakers striking the wall rolled continuously over the area.

It took a moment for the call to go through the international operator.

Ivan Chernovsky answered on the first ring, however. 'Chernovsky.'

'It's Natashya.'

'So then. You *are* still alive.'

'For the moment,' Natashya admitted.

'I had been wondering,' Chernovsky told her. 'It appears that Professor Lourds and other members of your entourage have been busy.'

'Somewhat.'

'Running gun battles in Odessa, Germany and West Africa. You've had quite the itinerary.'

'I knew you would know about Odessa, but how did you know about the others?'

Chernovsky sighed. 'I have been answering many calls from other countries about my partner. Our supervisor feels that I should know everything about you. He put those people directly in touch with me. After telling me to deny everything and that my job hangs in the balance, of course.'

'I apologize. I never intended for this to cause you problems.'

'Eh.'

Natashya could imagine Chernovsky shrugging in his office.

'We'll get through this, Natashya. We always do. So where are you? The reporters in London seem to think you're not there any more. Many people have wanted to speak to Lourds, and the company that employs Miss Crane has announced that she's gone missing.'

'Cadiz,' Natashya answered. 'We're in Cadiz.'

Chernovsky was silent for a moment. 'So it was true? Atlantis was there?'

'I don't know. Lourds was abducted in London. I escaped before they could catch me. I knew they would bring him here, and they did.'

'Why?'

'Because of the instruments.'

'The musical instruments Miss Crane alluded to in her interview.'

'Yes.'

'Is there any truth in that?'

Natashya hesitated for a time. She thought again of Yuliya and how interested she'd been in the ancient cymbal she'd been working on.

'I hope so,' she finally answered.

'But you called about something else,' Chernovsky said.

'Things have become more complicated here. Evidently the Roman Catholic Church has been hiding more than they've been showing. Lourds and the woman have been taken into the caves by the people who captured them.'

'What are they after?'

'I don't know.'

'Does Lourds?'

'Possibly.'

Chernovsky paused and Natashya heard the rasp of his hand across his stubble. She knew if he hadn't been shaving that he had been under tremendous stress.

'He must know, Natashya. There's no other reason for these men to kidnap him and bring him here.'

'That makes sense. But I do not know what he knows.'

'What do you need me to do?'

Natashya smiled a little. 'At this point I'm wanted for questioning, yes?'

'Yes.' Chernovsky's reply was cautious. 'In several places. What are you thinking?'

'I'm thinking,' Natashya said, 'that you should notify the local authorities and let them know that a potential terrorist threat is in the area.'

'You?'

'Me.'

Chernovsky was silent.

'Ivan,' Natashya said, 'we don't have a lot of time.'

'What you're suggesting is very dangerous. Especially for you.'

'I know.' Natashya watched the front of the cave. So far she hadn't seen any guards at the entrance. Trucks and mobile buildings sat outside the cave mouth. No one appeared to be guarding those, either. 'But I need to save Lourds and I need to do it right now. I'm out of choices. I need help. And I think things are already dangerous. If what Lourds believes is right, whatever destroyed Atlantis is still here.'

'After thousands of years underwater?'

'So he says. The Catholic Church is here. In force, I might add. And some of them have been pursuing us all along.' Natashya studied the fence. 'I have to go. Tell me that you'll make the call.'

'I will.'

'And wish me good luck.'

'Good luck, Natashya.'

Natashya thanked him and closed the phone. Then she stood.

'I didn't understand a word you were saying,' Gary said.

'I called my partner. He's going to phone the Spanish authorities and get them to intercede.'

'Cool. Then we just stay out here and keep watch?' Gary seemed happy with that.

'No. We go inside. Now. The men he is sending are going to be looking for us. We could still be killed, possibly by friendly fire.'

Gary frowned.

'I told you this wouldn't be easy. Or safe.' Natashya looked at him. 'You should stay behind.'

He shook his head. 'I can't. I'm in.'

'Then follow me.'

Natashya turned back to the fence and climbed over it.

Lourds read the inscriptions aloud as he walked. He held a powerful flashlight to scan the words. Even though he was operating at gunpoint, lecturing to an audience headed by a madman, part of him still felt proud of his ability to decipher the long-dead language.

He hadn't had a large amount of language to work with on the instruments' inscriptions, but the translations had proven fairly simple and straight-forward after he'd broken it. He didn't recognize all the words in front of him now, but he was able to make educated guesses to fill in the gaps in his knowledge. His voice sounded loud in the walkway between the pictographs.

'Adam and Eve and their children grew to be selfish even in the Garden of Eden. With the world laid at their feet, they wanted more. The First Son walked with them and tried to teach them the ways of God, but He didn't teach them all of God's holy knowledge and they faulted Him for it. In the end, they decided to take the knowledge for themselves.'

The next image was disturbing. It showed a man in a deep stream beneath a waterfall. Men on both banks kept him from the shore with long poles.

'Adam's sons with the darkest hearts took the First Son to the stream that fed Eden and drowned Him. This is what caused God to drive them from Eden and to later drown the wickedness in the world.'

On the next stone, men held the Book of Knowledge high in obvious exultation.

'Adam's children took the Book of Knowledge. They celebrated their triumph, but they did not admit their ignorance. Though they studied the Book, they could not understand it. Three days after His death, the First Son rose again.'

The next scene showed the First Son dressed in robes with a glow around his head as he walked through the forest filled with cowering men and women. Around them, animals were poised to attack.

'When the First Son returned, He carried His Father's wrath. No weapon made by Adam's children pierced him. No stone bruised Him. Adam's children lay in fear before Him. He . . .' Lourds hesitated as he tried to decipher the word.

'He alienated the animals from Adam's children,' Father Sebastian said.

Lourds glanced at the priest. 'You can read this?'

Sebastian nodded.

'Where did you learn the language?'

The old man shook his head. 'I've never seen it before I came here.'

'You're a linguist?'

'No. I'm a historian. Languages have never been my strength. I can barely manage Latin.'

'But you can read this?'

Sebastian nodded.

'How do you explain your ability to read it?'

'I can't.'

Lourds regarded the old man curiously. *There's no way I'm going to start believing in divine intervention at this point.* But how else could he explain what the old priest claimed? Lourds doubted that Sebastian was lying.

Turning back to the last image in the series, Lourds said, 'Adam, Eve and all their children were driven from the Garden of Eden.'

The image on the stone looked a lot like the interpretation in several illustrated Bibles Lourds had seen. A winged angel with a flaming sword blocked the way back. But this time the First Son was with the angel.

'In his righteous anger, God left the Book of Knowledge among men,' Lourds went on. 'He gave warning that if it was found it was to be kept – unread – until He took it back from this world.'

'But the Book of Knowledge wasn't lost,' Sebastian said. 'One of Adam's descendants hid it for generations. He brought his family out here, to found Atlantis and begin the civilization that would draw God's greatest wrath.'

'How do you know that?' Lourds asked. At that moment he was so lost in the excitement of deciphering the story that he hardly noticed Murani and the armed warriors surrounding him.

'Because that story is here.' Sebastian led the way through the stones. His flashlight whipped over other stones with more writing.

Lourds followed, and Murani and the Swiss Guard trailed behind.

Gary's heart banged inside his chest as he followed Natashya.

Mate, you're going to get yourself killed. You should drag your bleeding arse right on out of here.

But he couldn't. He needed to do something to help Lourds and Leslie. And he'd grown up on hero-driven fiction and videogames. He had always wanted to be a man of action. Kill the bad guy, get the girl and all that. He'd learned over the last few weeks, though, that being heroic wasn't that easy. Heroes were more likely to bleed to death than throw victory parties.

But that wouldn't stop him.

He followed Natashya to one of the temporary buildings in front of the cave mouth and slipped inside. Racks of overalls like those most of the construction crew wore against the chill of the caves were stacked near the cave mouth.

'Get dressed,' Natashya ordered quietly in the darkness. She threw him a pair of work boots. 'Put those on as well.'

'They're kind of clunky,' Gary objected.

'Too bad. We have to fit in. Criminals often get caught because they don't change their footwear.' Natashya shrugged into her overall and pulled it over the twin pistols she carried. 'Supervisors probably check for work boots and hard hats. If you're not wearing them, you're going to get noticed.' She thrust a hard hat at him as well. 'I don't want that to happen.'

'Neither do I.' Gary put the hard hat on and kicked his shoes off. 'The boots are still clunky.'

Natashya ignored him, put her hair up, slapped the hat on top of it, and headed back out the door. Gary had to hurry to catch up. He fell in beside her as she strode into the cave.

'One question,' Gary said quietly. 'Do you have a plan?'

'I do,' Natashya said. 'We find Lourds and Leslie.

We get whatever it is everybody is after. We get out. During that time, we stay alive.' She looked at him. 'Is that clear?'

'Crystal,' Gary replied. 'Especially the part about us staying alive.'

'Good. Don't make me kick your arse for getting killed.'

Gary couldn't think of a heroic reply, so he followed along silently.

'The man who had the Book of Knowledge founded the island that became known in legend as Atlantis. With the power he expected to get from the Book, he knew the other men in the world would try to take it from him.'

Lourds came to a stop beside Father Sebastian. The priest's flashlight beam illuminated the stone in front of him alone for a moment, but the beams of the others quickly joined them.

The image showed a king seated on a throne overlooking a vast empire.

Drawn by the words, Lourds began reading again. 'Stripped of Eden, Adam's children began making their lives in the outer world. One of those children, Caleb, founded the island kingdom of . . .' He couldn't make out the word. He turned his attention to Sebastian.

'I see it as Heaven,' Sebastian whispered, 'but that can't be what this place was. The founder chose to name this place that.'

'Caleb continued his work to read the Book of

Knowledge. Years passed and he gave the task to his children. They passed it on to their children. They didn't forget about God's power. They lusted after the power. Instead, they chose to forget about God.'

The next image showed a ziggurat under construction. Hundreds of men laboured to haul rock and build the edifice that was supposed to reach the heavens.

'Under the priest-king, Caleb's son, a great tower was built. The people intended to live in Heaven and become gods themselves. They believed all they had to do was climb into the sky to reach God's paradise.'

The next stone showed the tower's destruction. Bodies littered the ground.

'God saw the evil, selfish ways of the people and rained His vengeance –'

'Wrath,' Sebastian interrupted.

'And rained down his wrath,' Lourds amended, 'upon the people and destroyed their tower. He also destroyed that which bound all men together when He took away their language. Even the language they had carried with them from the Garden of Eden was lost.'

Lourds tried to imagine what that had been like. All of the men who had shared so many things suddenly couldn't talk to each other. Even the core language, which he had to assume this was, had been taken.

'In time, they spoke to each other again, in a multitude of tongues. In time the language in the Book of Knowledge was decoded,' Lourds said. 'The priest-kings began to read the Book. God called the sea up and destroyed the island.'

The next image showed a huge wave crashing against the island's coastline. People stood in horror as they watched the approach of their impending doom.

'Only those who took shelter in the caves . . .'

'Catacombs,' Sebastian said.

'Catacombs,' Lourds made the adjustment automatically. The words drew him as he chased them with his flashlight, 'survived the flood. Afterwards, when the sea rolled back, the survivors locked the Book of Knowledge away in the – home of . . .' He stopped, unable to go on.

'In the Chamber of Chords,' Sebastian said. 'That's where we are now.'

Lourds shone his flashlight over the stone wall.

'The Book of Knowledge is here?' Murani asked.

'I don't know,' Lourds said.

Leslie yelped in surprise and pain.

When Lourds turned to face her, he saw that Murani had grabbed her by the hair and forced her down to her knees. He took a pistol from one of the Swiss Guards.

'What are you doing?' Lourds demanded. He stepped toward her.

Murani slammed the pistol into Lourds' temple.

Pain exploded in Lourds' head. Dizziness swept over him and he dropped to all fours. He barely kept his face off the stone.

'*Where* is the Book?' Murani yelled.

Lourds barely kept from throwing up. Bile bit into

the back of his throat. 'I don't know. It doesn't say. That was written thousands of years ago. For all we know, someone already got the Book. The stories you heard could have been lying.'

Murani turned to Sebastian. 'Tell me where the Book is.'

'No,' Sebastian said. 'I'm not going to help you, Murani. You have disgraced yourself, your Church, and your God. I'll be no part of this.'

Murani pointed the pistol at him. 'Then you'll be dead.'

For a moment Lourds thought Murani was going to shoot the old priest.

Sebastian held his rosary and prayed in a voice that only cracked a little.

Murani pointed the pistol at Leslie. 'I'll kill her. I swear to you, I'll kill her.'

Sebastian opened his eyes and looked at Leslie. 'I'm sorry.'

Furious, Murani turned his attention back to Lourds. 'Keep reading. Find that Book. If you don't, I'm going to kill this woman. You have ten minutes.'

Weakly, Lourds pushed himself to his feet and stood swaying. Then he picked up his flashlight and staggered back to the wall of images. He moved down to an image of the five musical instruments.

Lourds blinked his eyes and tried to clear his double vision. 'The survivors lived in fear of God. They locked the Book of Knowledge away in the . . . Chamber of Chords. The key was divided among five . . . *instruments* – I'm guessing, but it fits.'

'Keep going,' Murani ordered.

Lourds wiped sweat from his eyes. He moved to the next pictograph. 'The secret was hidden within. The five instruments were given to five men who were called . . . Keepers.' He chose that term because it was what Adebayo, Blackfox and Vang had called themselves. 'The Keepers were chosen from among those who now spoke different languages. They were given the parts of the key and sent out into the world. They were never to be together again until God called them together.'

When he moved on to the next section, Lourds found that it was blank. He played the flashlight over it, then turned back to Murani.

'There's nothing more,' Lourds said in a thin, quiet voice. He fully expected Murani to shoot him out of frustration.

'The secret's in the musical instruments,' Murani said. 'Find it.'

At Murani's gesture, Gallardo and his men brought the music cases forward and deposited them on the ground.

Lourds hesitated. The challenge was difficult, and the conditions were impossible. But he wanted to save Leslie. He wanted to be the hero. He wanted to rise to the occasion.

'Don't do this.'

Lourds swivelled his head in Father Sebastian's direction. The old man stood there with his rosary in hand.

'The Book of Knowledge was hidden away,' Sebastian said. 'God had it hidden for a reason. It destroyed this world.'

Lourds thought about the images of destruction captured on the stone walls. They only scratched the surface of the true horror that had overtaken the island kingdom.

'You're not supposed to do this,' Sebastian said.

'Shut him up,' Murani snarled.

Gallardo punched Sebastian in the throat. The priest collapsed to one knee as he coughed and gagged. Without mercy, Gallardo kicked the old man in the side and knocked him over.

One of the Guards, the one with the scar, made a small sound of protest. Gallardo turned and stared him down. But he backed away from the old priest.

Murani pulled the gun away from Leslie's head and crossed to stand in front of Lourds'. Lourds wanted to step back. The threat emanating from the cardinal was a palpable force. Sickness twisted in Lourds' stomach.

'You *are* supposed to do this,' Murani said in a low, fierce voice. 'You didn't even know about any of this. Yet here you are. Do you believe in God's will, Professor Lourds?'

Lourds tried to answer but couldn't force his voice through his fear-constricted throat.

'I think,' Murani said, 'that you're here by God's will. I believe that He wanted you here. To serve in this fashion.'

'Don't do it, Thomas,' Leslie entreated.

'Think about the knowledge,' Murani said. 'Could

you go to the grave without knowing this?' His dark eyes searched Lourds'. 'You are so close. There's every chance that I won't be able to read what's written in the Book of Knowledge. I need you for that as well. You find the Book, you get to live.'

Lourds wanted to say no. Everything good and decent within him did *not* want to cooperate with the crazed zealot before him. But an insistent voice in the back of his mind wouldn't shut up. He *wanted* to read that Book. He *wanted* to know what had been written there.

'How can you walk away now?' Murani asked.

'Don't let him sway you,' Sebastian croaked. 'Don't let him tempt you.'

But the temptation was too great. This was the best and finest thing Lourds had ever been part of finding.

And it wasn't found yet.

Without a word, he turned his attention to the musical instruments.

While Natashya had waited for Gallardo and his crew to arrive she had familiarized herself with the dig site as much as possible. She'd read newspapers and magazines that had been scattered around the media camp. Gary had helped her gather them. They'd also watched some of the news video the journalists had broadcast. The dig had featured heavily on the news channels. According to everything she'd learned, the cave with the mysterious door was located two miles in from the entrance.

She walked to the motor pool inside the first cave where the heavy equipment was kept. She spotted a small pickup sitting by itself in the darkness beyond the reach of the security lights. The truck was locked up tight. Natashya supposed it was more habit on the part of the driver rather than to prevent theft. Who would make it over the fence to cause trouble with the equipment?

'Locked, huh?' Gary said. 'Maybe there's another . . .'

Natashya opened the toolbox in the truck bed, took out a small crowbar and smashed the driver's side window. Cubes of safety glass cascaded to the stone floor.

'Bloody hell.' Gary glanced around nervously. 'Do you think maybe a more subtle approach would be better?'

'Subtlety takes time.' Natashya unlocked and opened the door. 'We don't have time. It could be too late even now.'

'I think someone's onto us.' Gary nodded.

When she glanced over her shoulder, Natashya spotted three construction workers approaching them. She slid in behind the steering wheel and unlocked the passenger door.

One of the men called out, but Natashya didn't understand the language. She slipped her knife from her pocket and scraped the ignition wires. Then she used the small crowbar to tear away the steering-wheel casing and the locking mechanism to free the wheel.

'Do you understand what he's saying?' Gary asked.

'Probably wants to know what we're doing.' Natashya touched two wires together and the truck's engine rumbled to life.

'What if he's saying something more along the lines of, "Get away from the truck or I'll open fire"?' Gary asked.

'We'll know in a minute.' Natashya shifted the transmission and put her foot on the accelerator.

The three men broke into a run as they yelled and waved their arms.

Gary ducked down in the seat, obviously anticipating the worst. 'You know, a problem occurs to me.'

Natashya swerved through the maze of heavy equipment and roared toward the lighted arch that led more deeply into the cave system. 'Only one problem?'

Evidently tension robbed Gary of his appreciation for sarcasm. 'Some of these security guys are good guys. They're just here to do a job. They're not hooked up with the bad guys. How are you going to tell the good guys and bad guys apart?'

'They're going to have to choose sides.' The truck bounced over the harsh terrain. 'If they get in my way, they are bad guys. And the only good guys down here might just be us.'

'Great.'

When she checked the rear-view mirror, Natashya saw that at least two other vehicles had taken up the chase.

'So much for the stealth factor,' Gary said dismally.

A bullet speared through the back window and smashed out of the front one.

'Bloody hell!' Gary ducked down and cradled his head in his hands.

Natashya concentrated on driving. She had a loose map of the cave system in her head, but the darkness was complete except for the security lights that barely marked the way. Her headlights only pierced the darkness a short distance at a time. The cave walls seemed to come up faster and faster as she drove. Once her bumper grazed the wall and spewed out a torrent of sparks.

She hoped that Chernovsky had placed the call to the Spanish authorities. She hoped that half the Spanish police force was on its way here. And maybe half the army, too. And she hoped she didn't smash this truck into a cave wall. She also hoped that they arrived in time to save Lourds.

Lourds studied the instruments spread out before him. He gave serious thought to smashing them. It would be easy enough to do. But he didn't know if that would prevent Murani from finding the Book of Knowledge.

And it felt like sacrilege.

'If you try to destroy the instruments, I promise you that you'll be begging to die before I kill you.' Murani knelt opposite Lourds. The cardinal held a pistol in one hand.

'I can read better if you don't point that gun at me,' Lourds said. 'And you're blocking my light.'

The crazed priest backed away, but he didn't put down the gun.

Again and again, Lourds read the inscriptions. They told of the destruction of Atlantis and of the decision to send the key to the 'drowned land' out into the world in five pieces.

And the final line was: Make a glad noise.

'Make a glad noise,' Lourds said aloud. 'Does that mean anything?' He'd thought it had something to do with the instruments, but he'd played them and nothing had happened.

Murani hesitated only a moment. 'Make a joyful noise unto the Lord, all ye lands.' Psalm one hundred, verse one.'

'What does that mean?'

'Men should praise and rejoice God.'

'You knew just where to find that?'

'All bishops used to be required to memorize the Book of Psalms.' Murani shook his head. 'So many crucial Church practices have passed by the wayside. I am something of a traditionalist.'

Lourds wanted to ask, *Do those practices include murder?* But he decided it would be too inflammatory.

'Does that passage have any special significance to the Book of Knowledge?' Lourds asked.

'Not that I'm aware of.'

Carefully, Lourds touched the instruments again. The answer had to be there, but it eluded him. He racked his brain. The solution had to be hidden, but it would also need to be attainable. After all, if a Keeper was lost too early, those who followed would have to know how to figure everything out.

Taking up his flashlight, Lourds returned to the image of the Keepers being given the five instruments. Murani accompanied him.

In the image, the five men held the instruments high. They stood in a row, each with the instrument held in a certain way.

Lourds memorized the sequence of the instruments. He returned to the instruments and put them in that order. Drum, bell, pipe, flute and cymbal. Was there significance to the order? Or was he fooling himself?

He used the flashlight and studied the surfaces closely. Symbols he hadn't noticed before, carved into the drum's side so they looked like scratches, suddenly caught his eye. They were faint and loose, nothing like those on the inscription. After thousands of years it was a wonder they remained.

Excited now, Lourds rolled the instruments around until he found symbols on each of them in turn. Together they formed a sentence.

'Break make a joyful noise.' Lourds translated it again. It didn't make sense. Surely he had it wrong.

'What do you see?' Murani asked.

Lourds told him.

'What are these symbols?' Murani asked. He picked up only a few of the symbols with his flashlight.

'Make a joyful noise.'

Murani aimed his flashlight toward a nearby wall. 'These symbols are there as well.'

Looking up, Lourds saw that the symbols were repeated. Excitement screamed through him. He stood and crossed to the wall. Bending down, he picked up a rock and smashed it against the wall.

A hollow noise came back.

Lourds pounded again. 'There's an empty space back there.' He slammed the rock against the wall again. This time the rock broke through.

Murani, Gallardo and some of the others surged forward and attacked the false wall with their rifle butts. It shattered and fell to the floor.

On the other side of the wall, an elegant and pristine cavern filled with stalactites and stalagmites lay before them. The sound of the blows echoed almost melodically inside the cavern.

Before anyone could stop him, Lourds crossed the broken wall and stepped into the cavern. The air seemed fresher here. The noise quietly died down, but he couldn't help noticing how this space held the sound like a stage. The wall to Lourds' right held a carved image of the First Son standing with the Book of Knowledge.

The inscription below the First Son read:

Make a joyful noise unto the Lord.

24

'What does it mean?' Murani asked as he played his flashlight beam over the stone that captivated the linguistics professor's attention.

'I don't know,' Lourds replied.

Their words floated into the emptiness of the cave and echoed back.

'It's the same as the one that was on the wall, right?' Murani's impatience grew. He was on dangerous ground now. The Swiss guardsmen recognized the authority of the Society of Quirinus for the moment, but their paths were divergent and Murani knew it. They would baulk at killing Lourds, Sebastian and the others. The Guards who had been with Sebastian were already ripe for rebellion. Murani would not suffer them to live. That was why he'd brought Gallardo and his people here. Perhaps Lieutenant Sbordoni and his men would follow orders, including murder, but many of the Swiss Guard who had been on site at the dig wouldn't.

Murani would deal with that complication when

the time came. For now, he needed Lourds to spill his knowledge. Murani swore it would be his last opportunity to do so.

'It's the same,' Lourds confirmed.

'The last wall was fake.'

'I don't think this one is,' Lourds said.

Murani gestured to Gallardo. The man slammed his rifle butt against the stone wall. The metal struck fire and broke loose a few stone chips.

The loud *clank* echoed within the chamber.

'Solid,' Gallardo grunted.

Lourds cocked his head and listened.

Murani supposed he was listening to the echoes but he didn't know why. The professor surprised the cardinal. He'd expected the man to be begging for his life by now. Instead, Lourds seemed to be more fascinated than ever by what was going on.

For himself, it was all Murani could do to keep his impatience in check. He'd been thinking about the Book of Knowledge for years since he'd first discovered the existence of the five instruments in the book that the other members of the Society of Quirinus hadn't found in their own archives.

He took a fresh grip on the pistol he carried. The weapon felt awkward in his hand, but he knew enough about it to use it. And he knew enough about himself to know that he would use it if he felt he had to.

For a moment, he wondered if Lourds were stalling. If he was . . .

'Hit the wall again,' Lourds said. His eyes never left the wall.

'Hit it yourself,' Gallardo replied.

Impatient, probably wondering if he'd thrown in with the wrong person, Lieutenant Sbordoni struck the wall with his rifle. Again, the sound echoed through the cavern.

'This place is like a sound stage,' Leslie said.

The moment she said that, Murani remembered that it had reminded him of that as well. Or an antechamber in a church.

'Once more,' Lourds directed.

Sbordoni struck the wall again.

'Hit another area.'

The lieutenant drew back his rifle and did it again.

This time Murani heard the double-cadence of the blow as well. The cave amplified the noise so well that the sound was discernable.

'Help me.' Lourds shone his flashlight over the wall. 'There has to be an artifice here somewhere. A release lever or something.'

'Why?' Murani asked.

'There's trapped space behind this wall,' Lourds said.

'Another cave?'

Lourds shook his head as he felt along the lines of the engraving. 'There's not that much space. This sounds like a void.'

'No more than a few inches,' Sbordoni said searching as well. 'Do you think it's hidden in the picture?'

'Step back. Give me as much light on the engraving as you can.' Lourds stepped back also.

All of them stood in silence for a time. As they did, they heard a gentle susurration against the stone.

'What's that?' Gallardo asked.

'It's the sea,' Father Sebastian said. His voice was scratchy and rough from the blow Gallardo had dealt him. 'The stone walls of the caves are the only barrier that keep the Atlantic Ocean from filling this place up. Break through and you'll drown us all.'

That sobering thought made many of the Swiss Guards nervous. Gallardo and his men didn't seem to appreciate their circumstances either.

'The walls will hold,' Murani said. 'He's just trying to scare you.'

But he knew the scare tactic was working. These men lacked the faith in God and in the mission that he had.

'Have any of you seen this picture before?' Lourds asked.

'I have,' Murani answered. It was like the one in the book in the archives.

'Did you bring it?'

'No.'

Lourds looked disappointed. 'It would have been good to have something to match this one against.' He studied the wall and Murani could see that he was totally absorbed by the problem, forgetting all about the threats to his life.

Bemused by Lourds' preoccupation, Murani searched for any differences in the image. It looked the same as the one in the book.

Except there was one difference.

'The book,' Murani said. 'The book in the First Son's hand.'

'What about it?' Lourds stepped closer to examine the book.

'In the picture that I saw, it was closed, not open.'

Lourds touched the book with a forefinger. 'I need a knife.' He held a hand out.

'No way,' Gallardo said. 'You're a captive, not a guest.'

'Give him the knife,' Murani ordered. 'You have your rifle. What's he going to do with a knife against your sharpshooters?'

Gallardo handed over a knife with a five-inch blade.

Lourds opened it and started scratching at the outline of the book. Without warning, the blade slid into the engraved line. Smiling, Lourds shoved the knife forward.

Something within the wall clicked. The sound echoed within the chamber. Then angry grinding started behind the wall and filled the cave with noise. Abruptly, the cave wall recessed and revealed hidden demarcations that dust had filled. The wall slid back six inches, then slid again to the left. Behind the wall was another engraving. This one showed the five instruments again but they were in a different order. Below the engravings were ten squares. Lourds pressed one. Something ratcheted in the wall and almost immediately a loud, musical *bong!* filled the chamber.

Lourds was already on the move with his flashlight in hand as he strode into the darkness.

'Press that button once more.'

Murani waved at Sbordoni to follow Lourds and told Gallardo to press the square again.

The *bong!* pealed again.

Lourds altered his direction and shone the flashlight overhead. 'Again,' he yelled as the echoes died away.

Bong!

Murani heard the noise almost directly overhead. His light trailed Lourds' up against the cave roof.

'Again,' Lourds called.

This time Murani saw a hammer strike the stalactite above. The hammer was compact and looked as though it was made of bone. A gold wire connected to it ran up into a hole in the cave ceiling.

'Again.'

The hammer moved and struck the stalactite.

Bong!

'Press another button,' Lourds directed.

Bong!

The noise set off another brief pursuit that resulted in the discovery of another bone hammer operated by gold wire.

'The cavern,' Lourds said in disbelief as he directed his flashlight around, 'has been turned into a musical instrument.'

Natashya oversteered the pickup drastically in the darkness. The vehicle hurtled down the gradient. She watched the odometer and ticked off the tenths of a kilometre as they rolled around.

'Watch it!' Gary yelled hoarsely.

Too late, she saw the cave wall rush up at them out of the darkness. Natashya pulled hard to avoid it, but the pickup's tyres slid across the slick stone floor. The proximity of the Atlantic filled the air with humidity. In time, she knew, it would cause changes in the cave system and might even kill off some of the bacteria and fungus that grew there naturally.

The pickup slammed against the wall with bone-jarring force. For a moment Natashya thought she would be stuck for good. The rear tyres spun on the stone as they clawed for purchase.

The headlights of their pursuers got closer.

Then the tyres caught and they shot forward again.

Gary cursed and pushed broken glass out of the window. More of it had spilled across his lap.

'Thinking maybe you should have stayed behind now?' Natashya asked.

'Maybe a little more than I was,' Gary admitted. 'But I have to warn you, I was *really* not wanting to come to begin with. Starting with that attack back in Alexandria.'

Natashya smiled grimly at that. She pressed her foot harder on the accelerator. The pickup shot forward again.

Only a short distance farther on, the cave widened again. This time Natashya recognized the cave as the one that had been on television so much. It was the cave before the one where all the crypts had been found.

A quick glance ahead told her that they'd exhausted all their room to run. She hit the brakes and slewed

549

sideways as the rubber lost traction again. Before she could stop it, the pickup slammed into a parked earthmover. Her head hit the back of the cab and she almost blacked out.

The scent of petrol filled the cab.

Not all cars blow up, Natashya told herself, *that's only in American movies.*

But she also knew that enough of them blew up to warrant a hasty evacuation. She'd seen that happen in Moscow. Besides that, the men chasing them were almost on top of them.

She grabbed Gary's shoulder and shook him. 'Get out!'

Gary looked at her. Blood dripped from a cut over one eye. 'I thought we were dead.'

'Not yet.' Natashya threw her weight against the door and forced it open. She clambered out and filled her hands with pistols as the other vehicles bore down on her.

They're construction workers, she reminded herself. *They're just trying to do their job. They're not Gallardo or his men. They're not the ones who killed Yuliya.* She had to make herself remember that.

Gary couldn't get out on his side and had to climb out on hers. He swayed unsteadily as he took cover among the construction equipment.

Bullets tore into the pickup and drew Natashya's attention to three Swiss Guards standing sentry near a mobile building. The building and the guards stood out in the darkness of the cave due to the lighting strung around them.

She cursed mentally, grabbed Gary and shoved him under one of the earthmovers as they took cover. She and Chernovsky had been stuck in some tight places in Moscow over the years, but this wasn't looking good at all.

Then she noticed the steady drip of gasoline pooling beneath the pickup. With all the metal around them and the stone floor, it was a safe wager that a spark would be struck soon.

The construction workers managed to pull to a stop, but as soon as they did bullets from the Swiss Guard chopped some of them down and sent the others into hiding.

'Okay,' Gary said, 'they're bad guys.'

It was always about choices, Natashya thought. There was no reason to fire on the construction workers unless the stakes had been raised. The situation had clearly spiralled up to a new level of deadliness. She considered Lourds briefly and wondered how much trouble he was in.

Then one of the stray bullets scraped the ground nearby and the petrol caught fire. It blazed immediately.

'Move!' Natashya ordered. She butted Gary into motion with her head and rushed him toward the other side of the earthmover just as the flames under the pickup flared up and ignited the petrol tank. The explosion wasn't as big as the ones on television, but the concussive wave knocked her down and sent fiery debris in all directions. She scrabbled upright again and kept moving, reminding herself to use her peripheral vision and not to look at the Swiss Guards straight on. Too many hiding places had been given away by the gleam of an eye. She popped up on the other side of the earthmover and pointed her left pistol long enough to squeeze off three shots.

One of them hit a charging man in the face and knocked him from his feet. The two others took cover.

As she held her position, her nose and throat burning from the smoke pooling against the cave ceiling, Natashya saw one of the Guards break cover and throw a grenade against the mobile building. It turned out to be an incendiary one and went off with a *bamf* that carried to Natashya's ears. Immediately flames clawed up the side of the building.

'There are people in that building!' Gary yelled.

Natashya glanced at the windows and saw men's faces pressed against the glass.

'They're locked in,' Gary yelled.

'I know.'

'We can't let them burn.'

'I know. Let me think.'

But there wasn't time for thinking and Natashya knew it. Gary broke cover at once and ran for the building. One of the Swiss Guards stood up and shot him. Even as Gary fell, Natashya targeted the man in the darkness by marking his muzzle flashes. She fired several shots and didn't stop until he fell out of the darkness to the ground.

Shoe leather scraped on stone behind her. Knowing she'd been flanked by the other man, she ducked. A bullet caught her hip and sent her sprawling.

*

Lourds' subsequent exploration of the buttons revealed that each of them was connected to a bone hammer. He studied the stalactites and saw that each of them had been carefully shaped. The cave was no longer growing, so the stalactites hadn't changed in thousands of years.

'I've seen something like this,' Lourds said as he stood once more in front of the engraving showing the First Son. 'There's a cave system in Luray, Virginia. Luray Caverns. It has what's called the great stalacpipe organ, and it's based on one of the oldest musical instruments we've ever found: a lithophone. Normally lithophones are made up of stone bars of different lengths. Or wood.'

'Like a xylophone,' Murani said.

Lourds nodded. 'Exactly. However, the great stalacpipe organ was constructed using the same design. It uses electricity to power the clappers. They play the huge organ and actually sell records of songs they make.'

'But why is this here?'

Lourds shone his light at the symbols under the buttons. 'Believe it or not, I think it's an alarm code. If you trigger the right sequence, maybe the Book of Knowledge will be revealed.'

'What happens if you trigger the wrong sequence?' Gallardo asked.

'You mean, what if there's a trap?' Lourds asked. The possibility hadn't occurred to him. He'd been mesmerized by the whole set-up.

'Yes.'

'Then we're hosed,' Lourds said.

Gallardo didn't look happy.

'The trick is to not get hosed.' Lourds studied the wall and thought about everything he'd learned. 'The Keepers believed the instruments were the key to opening the Drowned Land. The inscriptions on the walls outside said the key was in five parts.'

'I thought that was just the clue to the hidden room,' Murani said.

'Maybe there's more,' Lourds suggested. 'Let's have another look at them.'

Murani sent Sbordoni to retrieve the instruments. When they were brought back, everyone examined them again. The susurration of the sea sounded outside the rock walls and echoed within the chambers.

Without warning, Father Sebastian ducked forward and evaded the Swiss Guards for a moment. He stamped on the drum and it shattered to pieces before the Guards got him under control again.

'Don't help him!' Father Sebastian shouted at Lourds and the Guards. 'He intends to use the Book of Knowledge! If he does, he'll bring God's wrath down on us again!'

Murani pointed his pistol at the priest. There was no doubt that he was going to kill the man. Lourds shifted his weight and caught Murani's wrist just in time to push the cardinal's arm up. When he fired, the bullet ricocheted from the ceiling above.

Gallardo hit Lourds hard enough to drive him to his knees. Pain exploded inside his head and the coppery taste of blood filled his mouth. He tried to get to his feet but he was rubbery-legged.

By the time Murani brought the pistol back down, three of the Guards were standing in front of Father Sebastian, creating a protective wall of living flesh.

'No,' one of the Guards said, the one with the scar on his face. 'There's not going to be a murder here in this place. We're here to do the work of the Society of Quirinus. If we find the Book of Knowledge, it needs to be locked away.'

Murani said nothing, but Lourds could see that he wasn't happy. The Swiss Guards were dividing among themselves. Two groups had started to form, one that stood with Father Sebastian, the other that aligned themselves with Murani. Lourds was stuck between them, and it was the wrong place to be. He looked down at the drum to see if it was salvageable. The instrument was a tangle of broken pottery and leather cords. Thankfully the shards had broken into big pieces. He thought he might be able to reassemble the fragments. Even better yet, the inscriptions looked intact.

Then he saw an inscription *inside* a shard, a series of lines with marks drawn on them.

'What is that?' Murani knelt down beside Lourds.

'I think,' Lourds said, fascinated, 'it's a musical score, maybe a diatonic scale. The ancient Greeks worked with music theory. They called it *genera* and developed three primary types. The diatonic was used for the major scales and church modes so it was also called the Gregorian mode.'

'Could it be the key the inscription was talking about?'

'I don't know. It's possible that –' Before Lourds could say anything more, Murani shattered the bell.

Lourds almost cried at the artefact's loss.

But the inscription inside was clear.

The shards had to be pieced together to reveal the musical score. Murani broke the cymbal, pipe and flute in quick succession. So much history, gone for ever. But inside each of them was a musical score.

'They go in order, right?' Murani asked. 'As they're shown on the engraving?'

'Who knows? Maybe.'

Murani arranged the score on the ground and ran through the buttons again. Then he began to play.

The cave came alive with the sound of music. Excitement filled Lourds. The beautiful notes took away some of his fear. Leslie joined him, standing beside him as the echoes of the music filled the space. She took his hand in hers and held on tightly.

For a moment after the last note was played, nothing happened. Then an explosion was followed by a rattle of gunfire. Everyone turned back in the direction of the caves they'd come through, looking to see where the sound originated.

In the next moment, the two factions of Swiss Guards separated even further. They had rifles pointing at each other It seemed each side was willing to kill – or die – for their cause.

In the centre of the cave the stones started to

move and jerked their attention back in that direction. The grumbling, rumbling noise filled the cavern as it echoed and re-echoed. As Lourds watched, the cavern floor irised open at the centre. Cunningly wrought stone teeth retracted and revealed a pit. A golden glow dawned inside the darkness.

Lourds started forward immediately. Leslie hung onto his hand and followed.

Murani hastened past Lourds, though, and reached the pit first. He aimed his flashlight, then the pistol, into it.

Surprising himself, Lourds hesitated a little as the thought of an Old Testament demon or some lurking evil hit him. *You don't believe in things like that*, he reminded himself. But here, with all the evil surrounding him, with all the impossibilities he'd uncovered so far, he suddenly found he could believe in anything. He took a tighter grip on Leslie's hand as he approached the opening.

Liquid fire burned Gary's side as he took a breath. For a moment there after the bullet had struck him, he'd forgotten how to breathe. That had scared him more than he'd ever been scared in his life. And that was saying something because there had been several close calls since he and Leslie had hooked up with Lourds and Natashya.

Get up, you great wanker! Them people are going to burn to death while you lie about!

Painfully, fearful of another bullet striking him because he could still hear gunfire echoing in the cavern, Gary forced himself to his feet. He felt light-headed, but he managed – and that surprised the hell out of him. He concentrated on breathing and walking. It turned out to be more of a lurch, actually, but he made it work for him. He felt the heat coming off the mobile building as he neared it.

The men inside had already broken the glass out of the windows, but there wasn't enough room to squeeze through to safety. They screamed at him in frustration.

Dizziness clawed at Gary's mind. He felt the darkness eating away at the edges and waiting to consume him.

The harsh, flat cracks of more gunshots sounded behind him.

Are we winning? he wondered. Even he couldn't see how they would prevail.

When he reached the building, he almost had to turn back from the heat. Instead, he made himself reach for the door. Someone had wedged a crowbar into it to block escape. He grabbed it. The heated metal scorched his hand, but he held on just long enough to yank it free then threw it to one side.

The men surged out. Two of them grabbed him under the arms and carried him away from the fire. All of them spoke Italian and Gary couldn't understand most of what they were saying. Somewhere in there, just as it was starting to dawn on him that he'd been a hero and been shot for his trouble, Gary fell into a black void.

*

Steps had been carved into the side of the pit and led down into darkness. Even though Lourds added his flashlight beam to Murani's the darkness didn't retreat enough to reveal what was below.

The golden glow seemed concentrated at the bottom.

Murani pointed his pistol at Lourds.

'You first,' the cardinal commanded.

Lourds thought about objecting and knew it wouldn't do any good. But that was only a small part of why he started down the steps. The other part, the larger part, was that he had to see what was there. If the Atlanteans, or whatever they'd called themselves, had taken the time and trouble to hide the Book of Knowledge in such an elaborate place as this, what else could be hidden there?

The smart thing to do was lower a light into the yawning abyss and see what pitfalls – literally – lay ahead. But Lourds knew that neither he nor Murani were willing to wait long enough for a cautious examination of the site.

Once of these days this curiosity of yours is going to get you killed, Lourds chided himself.

The pit was colder than the room above. The sound of the sea gurgling against the rock was louder as well. Lourds couldn't help thinking how far below the ocean's surface they were at the moment. It had to be 250 or 300 feet at least. And it was two miles back to the cave entrance.

The steps were narrow and shallow. There was barely enough room for Lourds to walk down. He hadn't seen any of the Atlantean corpses, but he was willing to bet they'd been small people.

Footsteps rasped behind him. When he stopped and looked up, he found Leslie behind him.

'It might not be safe down here,' he pointed out.

'It's not safe out there,' she replied.

'I suppose it isn't.'

'I couldn't let you go alone.'

Lourds gave her a small smile. She could have and they both knew it. He was willing to wager that her curiosity pushed at her as sure as his propelled him.

'Let's hope that coming down here was the intelligent thing to do.' He turned and headed down into the darkness.

A door lay at the end of the steps. It wasn't locked and opened inward easily at Lourds' touch. The air inside the room was stale and musty, but it carried odours that suddenly made the professor's heart beat faster and chase away the remaining fear in his head.

'Do you smell that?' he asked excitedly as he went forward with more confidence. He knew those scents immediately, and he'd know them till his dying day.

'What? The dust?'

'Parchment,' Lourds said. 'Ink. Lots of it.'

He shone the flashlight inside the room and was astounded to see rows of books. They stood neatly ranked on shelves on the walls as well as in freestanding shelves that occupied the floor space.

Lourds walked to the nearest shelf and plucked a book from the row. It was bound in a leather-like material, but it wasn't leather, at least not any leather that Lourds knew about. Leather wouldn't have held up for thousands of years without showing some kind of ageing. This book – *all* the books – looked as though they'd just been printed. He balanced the book, bound in bright blue, on his left forearm and opened it with his left hand. He held the flashlight in his right. It was hard doing that with his hands cuffed. Symbols like the ones he'd deciphered on the musical instruments filled the crisp white pages.

He shone the flashlight around the room again. There were hundreds – perhaps *thousands* – of books on the shelves. The titles hinted at histories, biographies, sciences and mathematics.

'My God,' Lourds said softly. 'It's a library.'

'Is that all you see?' Leslie sounded distracted. 'Look at this.'

Lourds followed the line of her flashlight beam as Murani, Gallardo and the others entered the room.

Drawn by the beauty before her, Leslie reached out her manacled hands to touch the amber figurine standing at the end of one of the shelves. Light glinted from the polished surface and fired the veins of its matrix with gold. The figurine stood almost four feet tall and displayed a man holding the model of a solar system in his hand. Six planets of different sizes orbited the sun.

'They had the solar system as sun-centric,' Lourds said. 'They were thousands of years ahead of everyone. And the size ratio looks right, too.' Wonder overcame him as he looked at the books.

'That's a big deal?' Leslie asked. 'I thought everyone knew the planets revolved around the sun.'

'No. In fact, the Church locked up Galileo for heresy for saying as much.'

'You're kidding!'

Lourds couldn't believe she didn't know that. 'No, I'm not kidding.'

'Astronomy's never been my thing,' Leslie admitted.

Like a child in a candy store, Lourds passed through the aisles and sought out titles he could decipher. 'Have you any idea of the knowledge that might have hidden here all these years? Do you know what kind of strides might have been possible in the world if other cultures had possessed this knowledge?'

'I'm assuming that all these old books are a big deal.'

'A very big deal,' Lourds said. His head was spinning with possibilities. It made him think of everything that had been lost in the library of Alexandria. A world of ancient knowledge here at his fingertips. He was overcome with wonder.

'Lourds,' Murani called out impatiently.

Lourds turned and was hit in the eyes with a bright flashlight beam. He raised his cuffed hands. 'What?'

'Where's the Book of Knowledge?' Murani demanded.

'I don't know. It must be here somewhere.'

'Here,' Leslie called.

Lourds followed her voice through the stacks. The others converged on her as well.

*

As soon as the construction workers fled the mobile building, Natashya knew the surviving Swiss Guard's game plan had altered from offence to defence. He'd also made the mistake of allowing her to get her hands on the second man she'd killed.

She put her pistols away and took up the dead man's rifle and ammo bandolier. She slung the bandolier across her shoulders and checked the magazine in the rifle. It was nearly full.

It was good having real weapons again.

Calmly, knowing her opponent had only two avenues open to him, Natashya hunkered down in the shadows by an earthmover and waited. She hated not being able to go to Gary. He was unconscious, unmoving on the cold stone of the cavern floor. A few of the men were bending over him. She hoped he was still alive. She hoped those he'd saved would save him.

The Guard broke cover and ran for the construction workers' vehicles. He'd opted for saving his own neck instead of trying to join his comrades in the caves further on.

Natashya shouldered her weapon, let the man go just a little, then squeezed the trigger. The round caught him in the neck just under the protective Kevlar helmet. The shot knocked him down. He didn't move again.

Satisfied that the cave was clear, Natashya ran to Gary's side. The construction men scattered away from her, obviously intimidated by the rifle she carried. Many of them headed for the vehicles and started to leave.

The rise and fall of Gary's chest let her know he was still alive.

Natashya looked up at one of the men. 'You,' she ordered in her cop voice.

'Me?' The man looked scared.

'My friend saved your life,' Natashya said. 'I want you to save his.'

'Of course.' The man called to another and together they lifted Gary from the ground.

'Carefully,' Natashya said.

The man nodded and headed toward one of the vehicles. He called out to the driver and the truck pulled over to them.

The men handed Gary up, then clambered aboard themselves.

Natashya watched them go. In less than a minute the cavern had been evacuated. She turned her attention back to the caves ahead just as World War Three seemed to start.

Leslie stood at the far end of the room next to a glass case in front of a mosaic of coloured pebbles. The mosaic showed the First Son standing on a meadow holding out His arms to call men and women from a dark forest filled with demons and ugly beasts.

Lourds read the symbols beneath the mosaic out loud. 'May we all be called back home again soon.'

A box of pure beaten gold sat on a small table. There was a note beside it. Lourds shone his flashlight on it and read it quietly.

'Can you translate that?' Murani demanded.

'Yes.'

'Then do it.'

The note was short and to the point. 'Here lies the Book of Knowledge. We took it from God's First Son, who came to the Garden to shepherd us. We pray that God forgives us of our sins.

'When the Tower fell after we built it to ascend into Heaven, hard times followed. We warred with ourselves because we no longer had a common language. Only a few of us were able to learn this tongue again. We swore that we would never teach it to anyone. But the book is God's, and there will always be those who assume they can be as powerful as God. They are wrong.

'After we sank into the sea, only a few of us remained within the caves. Already we are growing sick with a mysterious malady which has followed us into the depths.'

'Can a sickness survive this long?' Gallardo asked.

'No,' Murani said. 'Besides, you have other problems to worry about.'

'More than likely any bacteria or viruses succumbed to barotrauma,' Lourds said.

'What's that?' Gallardo asked suspiciously.

'Given that these chambers are dry, and that some of the people survived – at least for a time – the caves became a huge hyperbaric chamber. That is to say, the oxygen in the caves became more pressurized. Any time you dive below one hundred twenty feet for an extended length of time the same thing happens. That's why divers have to decompress and come up slowly. Or they have to use a decompression chamber, also called a hyperbaric chamber. Baro-trauma results from pressure changes inside the body that don't equalize during a dive.'

'I take it you knew a woman who was into diving,' Leslie said sourly.

Lourds couldn't for the life of him figure out how Leslie could even possibly imagine being jealous under the circumstances. But there was no doubt she was. He'd seen it – and dealt with it – far too often. And, actually, she was right. He'd dated a woman who had been a diving instructor. A very beautiful, articulate diving instructor in Greece.

'They got sick from being underwater,' Gallardo said.

'Yes. Men have attempted to live underwater in different places – such as Jacques Cousteau's Con-shelf habitats, Sealab and Aquarius. Dealing with saturation diving, and that's what the survivors were subjected to in a sense, can cause aseptic bone necrosis – the loss of blood to bones. Possibly the arms and legs became gangrenous.' Lourds was silent for a moment. 'It would have been a painful, hideous death.'

'Is there anything further in the note?' Murani asked.

Lourds resumed reading. 'I know that I won't live much longer, possibly only a few days, but I want to leave this warning for any who find this Book. God willing, the island will never rise again and our sins will remain buried in the ocean. But I have learned that God will do as He wishes.

'So if you have found this Book, if you can read my message, which is written in the old language that God took from us, heed my warning. Do not read the Book. Put it in a safe place until God returns for it and takes this burden from us once more.'

'It's signed, Ethan, the Historian,' Lourds finished.

'Back away from the Book.' Murani waved his pistol.

Reluctantly, Lourds gave ground.

Murani put the pistol in a pocket of his robe. He approached the box, removed the lid and reached inside. When he pulled out the Book, Lourds was surprised that the cardinal didn't burst into flame or vaporize on contact.

The Book of Knowledge was far smaller than Lourds would have guessed such a volume would be. Surely nothing that important would be – or *could* be – contained in such small dimensions. It might have been 12 inches wide by 20 inches tall, and no more than 3 inches thick.

How could all God's knowledge be contained in such a book?

Trembling, Murani opened it. At first, the page looked blank. Then it filled with symbols. They appeared so quickly that Lourds felt certain he just hadn't seen them at first.

Murani stared at the text. He looked angry, frustrated, and dumbfounded. He glanced up at Lourds and held the book out.

'Read this,' the cardinal commanded.

Lourds did, but the symbols played tricks on his eyes. They seemed to move and weave, and it was hard to hold them still.

'Know you that this is the Book of God, and that His word is holy and without –'

Murani snapped the Book closed. 'You're going to teach me this language, Professor Lourds. The fact that I can't read it myself is the only thing keeping you alive at this moment.'

Lourds couldn't think of anything to say to that.

'Gallardo, stay with him,' Murani ordered. 'Lieutenant Sbordoni, we need to see if we can get out of here.'

Lourds gave a last look at the books as he was forced up the steps. He hated leaving them. He wanted to look at more of them. But Gallardo put a hand in the middle of his back and shoved. Lourds barely prevented himself from falling.

Back in the Chamber of Chords, the détente between the two factions of Swiss Guards had reached critical mass. Lourds knew that at a glance from the way Father Sebastian stood protected within one of the groups.

'Cardinal Murani,' Sebastian said, 'you need to turn the Book of Knowledge over to me.'

Murani looked belligerent. 'And if I refuse?'

'Then we'll take it from you,' one of the Guards, the one with the cleft chin, said. 'I'd rather not do that.'

'Thank you, Martin,' Sebastian said. 'God knows His own.'

'You serve the Society of Quirinus,' Murani said to the Guard. 'You're supposed to help me.'

'To recover the Book for safekeeping, yes. But not so you can read it,' Martin said. 'That Book has done enough damage. It should be put away where it can't do any more harm.'

'This Book can strengthen the Church,' Murani said. 'It can bring us closer to God.'

'No. It will bring God's wrath down on us,' Sebastian said. He held his hand out. 'Give me the book, Cardinal Murani.' He paused. 'Please, Stefano, before your zealousness brings about the end of us all.'

For a moment Lourds thought Murani might honour the request. Then the cardinal took out his pistol and shot Sebastian before the Guards around him could close ranks.

That touched off the bloodbath that had been waiting to explode. When the bullets started flying, Lourds ducked away from Gallardo, who started firing as well. Staying as low as he could, Lourds ran for Leslie and grabbed her by the arm. He ran down the incline to the pit where the library was hidden. It was the safest place he could think of to wait out the gun battle. Guardsmen dropped all around him.

Murani opened the Book and his face, even amid the gunfire, was triumphant.

The cavern filled with noise, which swelled as the cacophony exploded in echoes that doubled and redoubled the auditory assault. Lourds felt the ground tremble beneath his feet and froze beside a tall stalagmite that offered some shelter from the storm of bullets.

'What is it?' Leslie asked. 'Earthquake?'

'Harmonic vibration. The cavern is an acoustic chamber designed to pick up and magnify sounds.'

The susurration of water grew louder.

A sinking feeling manifested itself in Lourds' stomach. 'No,' he whispered, 'I think when Murani opened the Book, he set off something even he can't control.'

Horrendous crackling filled the air and momentarily drowned out the gunfire. Then the walls fissured and split. The hungry sea lying outside the stone walls sprayed inside with enough force to knock men down. Water covered the cavern floor, then sluiced toward the waiting hole in the centre of the cave.

'No!' Lourds shouted hoarsely. He started to go toward the pit, but Leslie grabbed him and held him back.

'There's nothing you can do!' she screamed. 'We've got to get out of here!'

After everything he'd been through, after everything he'd survived, Lourds could only watch helplessly. Exhausted, he dropped to his knees as the water level swirled and became a whirlpool that drained directly into the library.

Leslie pulled at him. 'Come on! Get up! Get up or we're going to die down here!'

Lourds forced himself to his feet and staggered towards the cave entrance. Ahead, the survivors of the gun battle were in full flight as well, but several of them were still fighting.

Even as he ran, Lourds was grimly aware that the water level was rising too fast. With every step he took, he trod deeper and deeper in water. He leaped and vaulted dead bodies as he held onto Leslie's hand.

She screamed in terror.

'Save your breath,' Lourds told her. 'We can make it out of here, but not if you can't run.' He was lying. With the way the water was rising, he didn't think either of them would survive. They'd be drowned like rats.

Ahead of them, Murani stopped and pointed back at Lourds. Water swirled around the cardinal's waist. Although Lourds couldn't hear the man over the gurgling rush of water, he knew the cardinal was commanding his men to get him. Sbordoni and three of his men turned and ran back towards Lourds.

Lourds cursed and nearly fell as a tidal sweep of water slammed into his back and shoulders and toppled him from his feet. The salt water stung his eyes and nose. Panic filled him for a moment as his feet slid out from under him. Then he found solid footing again and forced himself forwards and above the water line.

Murani's men were there to receive him. They grabbed him roughly and yanked him into the next cave.

All of it, Lourds thought in shocked dismay. *It's all going to be lost.*

He barely noticed the pain of the handcuffs biting

into his flesh or the strain his captor put on his shoulder sockets by yanking on him.

Then he thought of Leslie.

Glancing over his shoulder, he was horrified to see that the men had left her behind. She was struggling in the water and was making almost no headway. The sea level crept up her body.

Lourds put his feet on the ground and tried to pull away from the man who was dragging him.

'Stop!' the man ordered.

'You can't just leave her!' Lourds bellowed. 'She needs help!'

'You're an idiot!' Sbordoni yelled. 'If you go back there, you're going to die!'

Lourds continued fighting. Then the officer slammed his rifle butt into Lourds' head and nearly knocked him out. Lourds' legs went limp and slid out from under him. The man continued dragging him through the water, his once jaunty goatee now limp in the general flood.

Lourds tried to concentrate but his thoughts swam inside his aching head. He finally got his legs working again and set his feet down once more. Sbordoni ground to a halt and spun around with his rifle butt raised again.

Lourds struggled to shield himself, certain that he'd be knocked unconscious this time. Instead the guardsman stiffened suddenly and sank down. Lourds only caught a glimpse of the hole in the back of the man's head before he disappeared under water.

'Lourds!'

Recognizing Natashya's voice, Lourds searched for her. He couldn't see her anywhere. There were too many hiding places amid the wall of rocks.

'Get him!' Murani screamed at the other two Swiss Guards.

The men started for Lourds, but both went down, neat bullet holes in their foreheads, before they reached him.

Murani, the Book of Knowledge tucked under his arm, drew his pistol and pointed it at Lourds. Before Lourds could move, a harsh crack sounded and Murani pirouetted and dropped into the water.

The Book! Lourds thought. Somehow he'd managed to hang onto the flashlight. He turned back to Leslie. She was barely staying above water as she swam amid the roiling sea.

'Hold your hands up!' Natashya cried out.

Lourds held his hands up without thinking. He concentrated on how he was supposed to save Leslie when it didn't look like he was even going to be able to save himself. He kept the flashlight trained on the young woman.

His hands jerked suddenly, then came apart when the chain between the cuffs shattered. The sound of a rifle shot echoed within the chamber.

'Go!' Natashya said. 'Save her!'

Lourds plunged into the water and swam against the inrushing water. It was hard to do that and keep the flashlight trained on Leslie. He hoped she would use it as a beacon to find him.

*

Gallardo moved quickly through the darkness. He knew he had to get to the surface, but he had one more mission to accomplish first, one last score to settle here. He'd managed to locate the Russian woman when she'd killed the Guards trying to get the professor. She was in between him and the exit. He could delay a few crucial seconds for killing such a tempting target. It would be a pleasure to end her. Wading through chest-high water, pistol clenched in one hand as he navigated toward the rock wall where he'd last seen her, Gallardo fought the water and surged forward.

He came up behind her. The other cave had lights and he used those to skyline her against the rock wall. He took deliberate aim at the back of her head.

The muzzle flash illuminated her features; Gallardo realized she hadn't been facing away from him. She'd been looking right at him. Indescribable pain tore through Gallardo's chest and heart. He tried to squeeze the trigger of his pistol but his hands no longer worked. His arms dropped to his sides as he fought to stagger away. His heart had stopped. He felt the dead silence inside his chest. Then the woman was on him. Her face was as hard as stone.

'You killed my sister, you bastard,' she snarled.

Gallardo saw one last muzzle flash, felt his head snap back, then he saw and felt nothing.

Lourds found Leslie in the raging waters and grabbed the chain of her handcuffs the way the Swiss Guard had held his. 'Hold on,' he spluttered through the water. His feet barely found purchase on the stone floor now, but he kept pushing them forward. He swam when he had to.

Slowly, his heart pounding frantically and his breath coming raggedly, he discovered that he was making headway against the rising water. Either the pressure was equalizing or the larger cavern was taking much longer to fill. He had no doubt that the library had already drowned. He tried not to think about that. Instead, he focused on the lighted mouth of the next cave. Water had already invaded there, too, but there were still a few vehicles the construction crew had left behind.

His throat, nose, and lungs burned as he finally reached solid ground. He pushed against the rock and hauled himself and Leslie from the water. It helped when she could reach bottom. Together they kept moving through waist-high water.

He began to believe that they might manage to make it out alive after all.

Then, like one of the undead in the old monster movies Lourds had loved as a child, Murani rose from the water in front of him. The priest's left shoulder was matted with blood, but he held a pistol steady in his right hand.

'Stop,' Murani ordered.

Lourds waited for Natashya to shoot the man, but no shot was forthcoming. Murani shifted the pistol toward Leslie and Lourds knew the cardinal was going to kill her, then take him prisoner.

A shot sounded from the carved images behind them.

Leaping forward, Lourds grabbed Murani's hand, then lowered his shoulder and drove the man back against the wall in a move that was highly illegal in soccer but one which Lourds had employed before when a game turned rough. Murani tried to knee him, but Lourds shifted and took the blow on the inside of his thigh.

The Book of Knowledge tumbled free of Murani's robes. It splashed into the water and started to sink.

Before he could think, Lourds released his hold on Murani's gun hand and reached for the book. He seized it before it could disappear in the water.

'No!' Leslie shouted. 'Thomas, look out!' She ran towards them, barely making headway through the water.

Half-turning, Lourds saw the pistol aimed at his head and Murani's face a mask of rage just behind and above it. There was no way the cardinal could miss at such close range. On instinct, Lourds lifted the Book of Knowledge as a shield. The muzzle flash lit up the cave for a moment and he felt the impact of the bullet against the Book. Lourds expected the bullet to tear through it easily and strike him.

But it didn't.

Holding onto the Book with his left hand, Lourds reached for Murani with his right. Instead of fighting, though, the cardinal slumped down bonelessly into the water. A bullet hole was drilled neatly between his eyes.

Not believing what had just happened, Lourds watched Murani's corpse float away. When he turned the Book of Knowledge over, he didn't even find so much as a scuff mark.

'Did you see that?' Lourds asked Leslie as she reached him. 'The bullet ricocheted.'

'We've got to get out of here.' Leslie pulled at him gently. 'Come on.'

Lourds ran his hand over the Book's cover. There wasn't a blemish or a divot to mark where the bullet had struck it, but he knew it had.

Natashya joined them. Blood spotted her face, but Lourds knew it wasn't hers.

'Gallardo is dead,' Natashya declared. 'My sister has been avenged.'

Lourds nodded, but his attention was on the Book. If the bullet hadn't harmed it, was it waterproof as well? He opened the Book and found pages wet but unharmed. The symbols floated across the page and he started to translate automatically.

'No.' Leslie closed the Book of Knowledge. 'Not this one. Read a million other books. A *billion* other books. But not this one.'

Slowly, reluctantly, Lourds accepted that. Together, they turned and ran into the next cave as the water continued to rise.

Epilogue

Atlantis Dig Site
Cadiz, Spain
16 September 2009

Lourds stood sweating in the humidity that rolled in off the Atlantic Ocean. Before him, the work continued to rescue what could be saved of the Atlantean civilization.

He'd only just been released from the custody of the local and state Spanish police who had descended on the dig. For the last two days he'd shared a small cell with some of Cadiz's worst criminals. He'd suspected that was meant to intimidate him. However, he had managed to ingratiate himself with his cellmates.

Harvard professor or not, Lourds had spent much of his life around the world with such men. Wherever artefacts beckoned with all their promise of riches, thugs like these congregated. Once he'd figured that out, Lourds had made it a point to learn to speak their language – whatever variant of the local vernacular it was. The thugs in his recent lodgings weren't exactly on his Christmas-card list, but they'd been sad to see him go. When the Spanish law enforcement teams hadn't been questioning him, he'd shared stories with the prisoners. He'd become something of a celebrity because CNN kept showing background information on him.

The United States State Department hadn't stepped in on his behalf too forcibly because they weren't sure exactly what Lourds had done. There were several international agencies waiting to speak with his little band. Natashya in particular had excited their interest.

In the end, Pope Innocent XIV had interceded and asked for mercy, citing their work for the Church. His captors listened. All of them had been released.

Gary was still recovering in the hospital. Natashya had gone to make phone calls. Despite the swathe of death she'd left behind her, the evidence to connect her with it was completely missing. It appeared she'd be able to clear up her 'indiscretions' with her country – the worst of which was apparently not filling out proper paperwork for her vacation time. And Leslie was making nice with the television studio that employed her because they'd discovered she had in her clutches many exclusives on the Atlantis story that CNN didn't yet have.

She, too, would come out of this relatively unscathed.

Several of the television people recognized Lourds and begged interviews. He turned them all down. He thought that would probably make Leslie happy, and he felt he owed her something.

It didn't take long for news of Lourds' presence

to reach Father Sebastian's ears. The old priest had gone to the hospital, had his shoulder taken care of, and had returned to the dig to take control.

'Professor Lourds,' Sebastian greeted him as he walked up. His left arm was in a sling and he looked pale, but he appeared hearty nonetheless.

Lourds returned the greeting. 'I trust the Pope got his package?'

Sebastian nodded. 'He was very happy to see it. It's been put away for safekeeping. It will not trouble you any further.'

The night they'd escaped from the caves, Lourds had discovered that Sebastian had survived being shot. Before the old priest had been medi-flighted out, Lourds had given him the Book of Knowledge. He hadn't been able to trust himself to keep it. He knew he'd never be able to resist reading it, whatever the cost.

Sebastian gestured to the security guards keeping the crowd back. They allowed Lourds to enter and Sebastian took him by the arm.

'I heard you'd been released a little while ago,' Sebastian said as they walked toward the golf cart Sebastian had driven over.

'Only just,' Lourds admitted. He pulled at his clothing. 'I should have found a hotel room and changed my clothes first, I'm afraid. I apologize. I've still got the stink of the jail on me.'

'But of course you are here. There was no other place for you, was there?' Sebastian smiled.

'No.' Lourds sat in the passenger seat as the priest

drove them back towards the cave. 'I keep thinking about that library down there. If the Book of Knowledge survived the bullet and the water . . .'

'Ah, but that Book is a very special Book. You can't expect the same of the others.'

'I can hope. Maybe the technology that went into making the paper and the ink was different than we have.' Lourds felt worn to the bone. 'Maybe it survived. I'm a trained diver. I've also done cave dives.'

Sebastian shook his head. 'Then you haven't heard the bad news.'

'What bad news?'

'It happened only this morning.'

Lourds waited and his gut wrenched in anticipation.

'The section of the caves where the library and the final hiding place of the Book of Knowledge were has been lost to us.'

'How?'

'How do I know?' Sebastian shrugged. 'I only know that nothing was there. Perhaps the sea took it away. Peeled it off the mainland and carried it off. All that remains is a huge hole that's allowed the Atlantic to fill most of the cave system.'

Lourds slumped back against his seat and felt defeated. For the last two days all he'd thought about was the possibility that the library might have survived.

Now it was gone.

'We might be able to save some of the wall sections, the crypt area and a few other things,'

Sebastian said. 'But now that the Church has what it came looking for . . .'

'The Pope doesn't want to keep emptying the coffers.'

'It would be foolish of us,' Sebastian agreed. He sighed. 'Still, I've been given permission to tidy up a few things before I leave. I can certainly bring in other interests – perhaps others can continue what we have started, eh?'

'That will also keep the media from wondering what you were really here after.'

'Unless someone tells them.'

Lourds shook his head. 'I won't. No one would believe me anyway.'

'What about the young reporter?'

'All Leslie's going to tell anyone is that we discovered clues to a library that had been hidden in the caves.'

'She's not going to mention the Book of Knowledge?'

'No. She's sticking to the standard Atlantis myth. It will play better in the ratings, she assures me. Besides, would anyone from the Vatican admit it existed, no matter what she said?'

Sebastian smiled. 'You'd be surprised at the number of things that don't exist. *Officially*.'

'I don't think so,' Lourds said. 'Not after this.'

The old priest stopped the cart at the cave mouth. 'Still, we may yet find a few surprises lurking in the caves before we go. If you'd like, you may join us in our search.'

'I would like,' Lourds said. 'There's no place I'd rather be than hunting for knowledge.'

'Maybe we'll find a few books that floated up out of the library.' Sebastian fished in a pocket. 'In the meantime, it appears that I'm not the only one who wasn't surprised to see you here. I have messages from your two female companions.' He handed over two folded pieces of paper. 'It appears they would like to have dinner with you. Both of them.'

'Ah,' Lourds said, smiling in spite of the disappointment he felt over the loss of that incredible library.

'I assume they're not going to be interested in dinner at the same time.'

'Probably not.'

'It appears that you have a scheduling problem.'

'No, it's lucky for me that I have a big appetite.' Lourds flashed the old priest a grin. 'After a couple days in jail, I can manage two dinners tonight.'

'If you eat sensibly and pace yourself. Of course, if you get caught eating two dinners that could be dangerous.'

'Perhaps.' Feeling somewhat better, Lourds shoved the papers into his pocket. 'This is the kind of danger I live for, Father. And I don't think either of those two women is looking for a permanent dinner companion.'

'What will you do after this?' Sebastian asked.

'The library of Alexandria is still lost,' Lourds said. 'I haven't given up hope of finding some of those books. History has too many missing pieces, too many possibilities buried in stories and languages over thousands of years. I'm going to keep poking around in those odd little nooks and crannies every chance I get and hope that I find something. That's the one true love I have.'

And Lourds knew it always would be.